India moved to the window and looked through the frosty panes at the fresh snow covering the lawn and at the Dunbar oak, standing regal and alone.

William, the first Dunbar to settle here, had planted the tree in 1280, and had made the pledge that had been handed down from generation to generation: While this oak tree stands, a Dunbar will always walk the land. India drew her eyes away sadly. If the property were sold, William's vow would be broken.

As she was about to leave, India caught sight of the small writing desk her mother had used for her private correspondence. An uncapped fountain pen lay on a sheet of half-written writing paper. She crossed the room and picked up what appeared to be an unfinished letter, realizing with a start that it was addressed to her.

My dearest India,

I am sending this ...
am most distress...
a dreadful dilemma and ...
to you urgently. Please come to Dunb...
as quickly as you can. I'd call, but I'm
afraid I will be overheard. You need to
be aware—

The letter was cut short, as though Lady Elspeth had been interrupted. India frowned, glancing at the date. The letter had been written on the day of her mother's death.

FIONA HOOD-STEWART

THE JOURNEY HOME

MIRA®

MIRA

ISBN 1-55166-606-5

THE JOURNEY HOME

Copyright © 2000 by Fiona Hood-Stewart.

Visit us at www.mirabooks.com

Printed in U.S.A.

*To
my darling boys,
Sergio and Diego,*

and

*in loving memory of Mummy,
my Lady Elspeth.
For all she was, and always will be to us all.*

The Tears of Scotland

Mourn, hapless Caledonia, mourn
Thy banished peace, thy laurels torn.
Thy sons, for valor long renowned,
Lie slaughtered on their native ground;
Thy hospitable roofs no more
Invite the stranger to the door;
In smoky ruins sunk they lie,
The monuments of cruelty.

The wretched owner sees, afar,
His all become the prey of war;
Bethinks him of his babes and wife,
Then smites his breast, and curses life.
Thy swains are famished on the rocks,
Where once they fed their wanton flocks:
Thy ravished virgins shriek in vain;
Thy infants perish on the plain.

What boots it, then, in every clime,
Through the wide spreading waste of time,
Thy martial glory, crowned with praise,
Still shone with undiminished blaze?
Thy towering spirit now is broke,
Thy neck is bended to the yoke:
What foreign arms could never quell,
By civil rage and rancor fell.

The rural pipe and merry lay
No more shall cheer the happy day:
No social scenes of gay delight
Beguile the dreary winter night:
No strains, but those of sorrow, flow,
And nought be heard but sounds of woe,
While the pale phantoms of the slain
Glide nightly o'er the silent plain.

O baneful cause, oh, fatal morn,
Accursed to ages yet unborn.
The sons against their fathers stood;
The parent shed his children's blood.

Yet, when the rage of battle ceased,
The victor's soul was not appeased:
The naked and forlorn must feel
Devouring flames, and murdering steel.

The pious mother doomed to death,
Forsaken, wanders o'er the heath,
The bleak wind whistles round her head,
Her helpless orphans cry for bread,
Bereft of shelter, food, and friend,
She views the shades of night descend,
And, stretched beneath the inclement skies,
Weeps o'er her tender babes, and dies.

Whilst the warm blood bedews my veins,
And unimpaired remembrance reigns,
Resentment of my country's fate
Within my filial breast shall beat;
And, spite of her insulting foe,
My sympathizing verse shall flow,

"Mourn, hapless Caledonia, mourn
Thy banished peace, thy laurels torn."

—Tobias Smollett, 1746

This poem was written by the poet and satirist
Tobias Smollett shortly after the Battle of Culloden,
and expresses Scottish rage at the treatment of the
vanquished Jacobites.

ACKNOWLEDGMENTS

Many thanks to all those wonderful friends who have been there all along the way. Emilio Lopez, for lending me my first laptop, David d'Albis, for his patience and long suffering teaching me about computers, and Simon di Rollo, for his Scottish legal expertise. Special thanks to Heather Graham Pozzessere, Sally Fairchild and Joan Johnston, whose encouragement and faith in me have been so precious. Thanks also to the lovely ladies at MIRA: Dianne Moggy, Amy Moore-Benson and Martha Keenan. Last but not least, my deepest thanks to Jean Marie Grimsley, for her tireless assistance, and Sondra Schneider for helping me see more clearly.

Prologue

The Lowlands, Scotland
1746

Rob Dunbar held his young bride, Mhairie, close. They huddled by the smoking peat fire, hungry and exhausted after their harrowing journey from the Highlands. The small band consisting of Rob, his gillie, Hamish, and Mhairie and her mother had made their way south, disguised as drovers driving their cattle to market in Falkirk. They had avoided the Redcoats, and the only stops taken were in smoky bothies of other loyal Jacobite supporters, or outside, in the clachans, where Rob had tenderly laid his plaid on the heather and bracken for them to lie upon.

He gazed longingly at his lovely young bride, his heart full. Words seemed pointless now that so little time remained, and he raged at destiny for tearing them so cruelly apart when all they wanted was each other. How fortunate that they had married despite their parents' opposition. Not that they had disapproved the match, but as Struan, her father, had remarked in his dour Highland manner, "What use is there te' take a wife ye'll nae have by yer side nor in yer bed, ma' boy? Better fer both of ye te' wait till all this warring is behind us.''

A sad smile touched Rob's lips and he straightened the dirk stuck firmly in the heavy leather belt that secured his twelve-foot kilt and plaid. Wistfully he realized that those nights of love among the heather would be their only comfort in the dark days of separation to come.

He gazed at the fire and thought of the Colonies. They seemed so very far. Rob sighed and covered Mhairie tenderly with her plaid, wondering if she would ever return. Enemy troops were everywhere. Edinburgh Castle was in the hands of the Hanoverians, and many Lowlanders had turned traitor and joined German Geordie's men. Even if Bonnie Prince Charlie won the battle that was brewing, hope of Mhairie's return was faint. And if he lost, their fate would be a dismal one. The Prince's followers would be vanquished men, stripped of their weapons, their estates forfeited to the English crown, and the whole uprising would have been for naught. Things had changed considerably since the uprising in 1715. Now Highland lairds were finding it hard to rally their men, and only the *crois tara,* the cross made of two charred sticks covered in blood which demanded on pain of death that a man follow his chieftain into battle, succeeded in persuading them.

Rob stroked his beloved Mhairie's locks. He'd faced the agonizing choice of going home to his lands in the south or rejoining the Prince. But even as he hugged his wife, he knew a man could not shirk his duties. His loyalty lay with his sovereign. Whatever the outcome, he must head back North and fight the last fight.

Still, the thought of Mhairie's departure in a few hours was devastating. He saw her shiver and held her closer. ''Are ye cold, ma' beloved?'' he asked tenderly.

'''Tis not the cold in ma' body but the chill in ma' heart that ails me, Rob,'' she whispered, shuddering.

He placed more peat on the fire before seating himself down beside her once more and cradling her head gently in his lap. He caressed the soft auburn curls that flowed, long and thick, about her heart-shaped face, wondering when, if ever, he would see them again.

Jamie, his dear and faithful friend, entered the low-beamed room, silently handing him a tumbler of pungent whiskey. They sat, Rob embracing Mhairie, Jamie brooding before the fire, the hours passing all too quickly. Rob's heart ached as dawn drew nigh and separation ever closer.

Soon they had mounted and were on their way to Leith where the ship lay at anchor, the seashore and brine sharp reminders of what little time remained. Rob whispered in Gaelic to his gillie, sending him ahead through the thick damp haar with the prearranged signals.

They stood, a silent group of ravished souls, listening with heavy hearts as the waves lapped the hull of the tiny craft, coming silently across the water to take them to the vessel, her sails rigged and ready to sail.

"That must be Captain MacPherson himsel'" Jamie whispered. "I'll gae' ahead and have a wee word wi' him." He disappeared into the early-dawn mist, leaving the young couple a few precious moments for their last farewell.

"Och, ma' Mhairie. Never forget how deeply I love ye."

"Nor ye, ma' beloved," she whispered, then gazed up at him, eyes pleading. "Come wi' us, Robby, there is still time fer ye te' come awa' wi' us. Dinna' return te' that godforsaken lot. Have ye not seen yersel' that 'tis a fruitless venture?" She grabbed his face between her hands, supplicating.

"Ye ken that a' canna' gae wi' ye, Mhairie. Ma' duty lies wi' the Prince. A' canna' let him doon. A' wouldna' be able te' face ma' ain sel' if a' did."

She sighed, resigned, knowing full well he would return, just as her father and brothers had done.

"I have something te' tell ye afore a' gae awa', Robby."

"Speak te' me, ma' Mhairie, open yer heart while there is still time," he begged, holding her close, his heart ready to break.

Tears filled her eyes and she clung to him, burying her head into the front of his vest. "A'm wi' child, Rob. A'm carrying yer bairn."

Wonder and joy overwhelmed him and he drew back, gazing down at her in awe, his hand moving to her belly, happiness piercing his misery like a shaft of bright light. But this was quickly replaced by the realization of his double loss.

"Och, ma' darling, ma' very ain Mhairie. When all this is fore' by and better days come, ye'll return to me and take up yer place as ma' lady, and our bairn as ma' rightful heir. But Mhairie—" His voice took on a sudden urgency as he glanced through the rising mist at the tiny boat reaching the shore and saw Captain MacPherson alight. With a sigh he faced bleak reality and opened his sporran, taking out a folded letter. "If a' canna' reach ye… If when ye return a' should be in hiding, or worse. Ye must gae te' Jamie and read what's in this letter. A've told him what te' do, and ye can trust him as ye would yer ain brother. And, ma' beloved wife, tell our bairn—" The words caught in his throat. "Tell the bairn how close a' hold ye both within ma' heart. Keep the marriage papers and this letter safe and close te' ye. They are the proof that ma' son is ma' rightful heir." He handed her the letter carefully.

"Yer son?" She took it, slipping it silently into her bosom, then gazed up at him, a tremulous smile on her tearstained face.

"Aye, ye'll see. 'Twill be a boy, as old Granny Bissett

predicted our first born would be. And a fine one at that." He held her close, his lips lingering on hers, his hand caressing her belly as he etched her in his heart forever.

Then it was time. He kissed her, bidding his love a last long farewell, tears welling in his eyes as she climbed weeping into the small rowing boat that slipped silently away from the shore, the captain anxious to set sail before the day broke.

Rob gazed out to sea, anger and rage battling as his eyes locked with hers for as far as they could reach. As the ship set sail, he watched the vessel head into the wind, carrying aboard his heart and soul, following her trajectory to the open sea, until she was nothing but a dot bobbing on the frothy swell on the horizon.

"'Tis time te' gang awa', Rob." It was only then he realized Jamie was standing next to him, silently sharing his grief. He cast one last look at the choppy gray waters, his soul desolate as he turned on his heel, kilt swinging in the wind, and walked with Jamie to where the horses neighed restlessly, their nostrils flaring. Hamish handed him the bridle.

"Awa' wi' ye, Rob, afore German Geordie's lads awake. 'Tis a lazy lot they are but, nevertheless, 'tis wiser to be on the safe side."

"Aye, 'twould be foolish te' die at the end of a rope instead of meeting ma' maker at the point of a sword," he answered, hoisting himself into the saddle.

"Och, I've nae fear fer ye, Rob. Ye'll be back anon. Yer time's not sae nigh as ye think. Are ye sure of what yer doing?" Jamie asked doubtfully.

Rob donned his blue bonnet, the eagle feather placed at a cocky angle, and straightened his shoulders proudly. "As sure as any man can be when his duty and his sovereign are calling," he replied with a smile.

"Then sae be it. God speed te' ye both."

* * *

On Tuesday the fifteenth of April, they crossed the Spey River and headed toward Culloden where Murray had set up his camp. Rob arrived with a sinking heart, for all he'd seen for the last few miles were exhausted Highlanders lying strewn by the wayside, their eyes hollow with hunger and despair.

As he stood at the entrance of Murray's quarters, the war pipes ringing in his ears, and saw the drawn faces of the earl and his men seated glum around the table, his heart sank.

He stopped before entering, filled with sudden foreboding, and gazed up at the heavy clouds of defeat bearing down upon them.

Then, with a heavy heart, he stepped inside and took his seat, the bleak countenances around the table telling their own tragic tales. Each man knew what destiny lay before him. Savage anguish pierced Rob's heart as the harrowing truth sank in and the hope he'd harbored of one day being reunited with his beloved wife and child withered.

A never-ending death knell would ring throughout the Highlands. Blood would pour as never before in all of Highland history, and Scotland, his beloved homeland, would be changed forever.

1

Midlothian, Scotland
1999

By the time he'd missed his third pheasant, Jack Buchanan was in a foul mood. It did not improve when, instead of falling to the ground with a satisfying thud, the last bird fluttered into the gray Scottish sky, unscathed.

He lowered the shotgun, irritated. Pheasants did not fly away. They fell obediently, just as junior executives and the other members of his entourage jumped into action when they were supposed to.

He entered the glen briskly, realizing he was having a bad day. He knew to expect it, for this particular day was always bad. Each year he thought he'd get the better of the pain that still rose to the surface, as boldly now as it had then, and every year it got the better of him. He cocked the gun in preparation, willing his mind to concentrate fully on the task at hand. The next bird would not escape him.

He didn't have long to wait before catching sight of his prey, and he aimed carefully before slowly squeezing the trigger.

A split second later he stood frozen to the spot, his gut clenched, cold sweat breaking out under the heavy shooting jacket. He'd just missed a figure who'd walked straight into his line of fire.

Missed, by an inch of fate.

Thank God for the reactions he'd learned years ago that enabled him to deviate the shot, sending it ripping into a tree trunk a few degrees to the right.

"Are you okay?" he shouted anxiously, trying to make out who it was. There was a moment's silence followed by the echo of his own voice. Horrified, he slung the shotgun through his arm, the dogs following close to heel. Bracken crackled noisily under his boots as he strode quickly toward a tall slender woman standing motionless among the trees, her ashen face surrounded by long chestnut hair.

"Are you all right?" he asked, eyeing her anxiously. Slowly tension gave vent to annoyance as he realized she was unhurt. "Don't you know it's not safe to walk in the woods in the middle of the shooting season?" he asked accusingly.

"Hey! Wait just one minute. You nearly killed me," she exclaimed, suddenly coming to life with a shudder. "Plus, if anyone has no business being here it's you. This is private land."

"I'm well aware of that, but I have the owner's permission to shoot every darn grouse or pheasant that happens to cross my path," he answered sarcastically, irked by her sudden self-assurance. "I'm sorry I scared you, but you're to blame for this incident, you know. You should keep your eyes on the ground, not up in the clouds, and be aware of where you're walking. Sit!" he snapped curtly, for the pointers were still scuffling in the undergrowth, trying to pick up the scent of the bird their master had missed.

"What nerve!" she exclaimed. "This land belongs to the Dunbar estate, and you're trespassing." She glared at him, steadying herself against the tree as she spoke. Jack looked at her properly now, suddenly struck by the strange color of her eyes, a grayish-green that reminded him of the North Sea on a windy summer's day. They also held a very determined look, and he was in no mood to argue.

"See that tree over there?" He pointed to his left. "That is where this property, namely Dalkirk—" he began patiently.

"Rot and rubbish. You're on *my* land, and if you don't leave immediately, I'll call the authorities," she said, cutting him short.

"And just how do you plan to do that?" he demanded, his tone as challenging as hers.

"None of your business. If you don't know how to use a gun properly, you shouldn't be carrying one. You're careless."

He bristled. No one called Jack Buchanan careless. "Look, miss. I'm a houseguest of Sir Peter and Lady Kinnaird. As I've already told you, I have their permission to shoot on their property."

She straightened, drawing her tall, slim figure to its full height, and cast him a withering look.

"Maybe in America being a houseguest gives you the right to invade other people's property, but let me assure you that in Scotland it doesn't. Now, I'd like to get past, please." She took a step forward, then halted. "By the way, for future reference, that fence over there is the boundary between the two estates."

Jack's eyes followed her gloved finger over the dogs' heads to a dilapidated fence, barely visible among the foliage and bracken.

Seeing it only made him more exasperated. He bowed in mock surrender as she strode past him, her head held

high, and watched as she started down the incline, her
shoulders ramrod straight in an old green jacket worn over
a pair of faded jeans.

Feisty, he remarked to himself with a spark of grim
amusement, then whistled to the dogs. The incident had
unsettled him. He knew he was at fault. Not entirely perhaps, but he should have been paying more attention instead of brooding over the past, as he had done on this
day each November for the last twelve years.

He was about to leave when something on the ground
caught his eye. He stooped. It was a solitary diamond pendant glistening on the bed of dead leaves and broken twigs.
Scooping it up, he called after the woman as she reached
the clearing.

"Hold it, I think you dropped something."

He watched her stop, sway for an instant as though trying to maintain her balance, then crumple silently to the
ground, like a limp marionette. Dropping the pendant into
the depths of his pocket, he raced down the incline to
where she lay, prostrate on the dank earth.

Habit made him prop the gun against a tree trunk, sheer
discipline keeping him from allowing emotion to cloud his
mind. He banished all feelings of remorse and self-
recrimination to the nether regions of his brain, and assessed the situation.

The raw November afternoon was fading fast, the sky
heavy with clouds, and a chill in the air announced snow.
Gently lifting her limp body, he gazed at her lifeless face.
All at once, past images sprung before his eyes, a shaft of
uncontrollable anguish tearing through him like a bullet,
ripping his heart and piercing his gut as another face, a
face so beloved and yearned after, replaced the one of the
woman lying still and pale in his arms.

That this should have happened today of all days was

the cruelest twist of fate. For a brief moment pain slashed into him, as rampant now as it had been then.

He forced himself to breathe deeply before heaving the woman carefully into a sitting position against his chest, her head propped against his shoulder. He sent up a silent prayer when she moved ever so slightly. Thank God she was going to be okay. When she finally stirred, he caught the fleeting whiff of her perfume. It lingered in the sea breeze that blew inland from the Firth of Forth and could still be felt, even here, in the heart of Midlothian. Her eyes twitched and he leaned closer, trying to catch the gist of her whispered words as she drifted back to consciousness. Then he set himself to the task of seriously reviving her.

India Moncrieff came to with a splutter. Something strong and pungent was burning in her throat. She struggled to sit up farther, but was restrained by a powerful hold.

"Drink some more," a firm, masculine voice ordered.

Before she could answer, more liquid was tilted down her throat. Finally she found her voice.

"Please stop," she begged, choking, her disjointed thoughts slowly taking shape. All at once she remembered. She'd been shot at. She hadn't been hit, but the shock and fear of the moment must have caused her to faint. She felt suddenly ridiculous. She'd never fainted in her life. Then she realized, to her dismay, that the arm behind her head must belong to the obnoxious American, the one responsible for this whole mess.

"Just do as you're told and stop arguing," the deep voice continued. "The alcohol will get your blood moving. I'm going to move you over there." Before she could protest, India was scooped up by a pair of strong arms, lifted as though she were a featherweight and deposited gently on a large tree stump.

"Where do you live?" he demanded, his hands still securing her arms in a firm grip.

"It's really none of your business," she muttered, wishing he would shut up. Perhaps then her head would stop spinning.

"You've made it my business. Whether I like it or not, you're my responsibility." He loosened his grip and stood up.

"Responsibility? I'd hardly call leveling rifles at people responsible. I'll be fine on my own, thank you very much." She passed a hand over her eyes and sat up straighter. Then, pulling herself together with an effort, she eyed the stranger, taking in the thick dark eyebrows that loomed ominously over a pair of piercing blue eyes. Eyes that held concern and, to her irritation, a touch of amusement.

"Do you think you can walk?" he asked doubtfully.

"Of course I can," she lied, attempting to rise. "I'll be perfectly all right. You can go now."

"I won't leave you here."

"Oh, please just go. You've caused enough trouble already. I'll be fine." But he stood his ground, looming over her, tall, dark and scowling, as confident as though he owned the place.

"All you've done from the moment I've met you is complain," he exclaimed, his mouth breaking into a smile that lit up his handsome face. "Now please. Stop arguing and be reasonable. If we don't get moving we'll be stuck out here in the dark, and I don't have a flashlight."

India eyed him with suspicion. "Who are you anyway?" she asked.

"My name's Buchanan. Jack Buchanan. Like I told you, I'm staying at Dalkirk with the Kinnairds. Are you their neighbor?"

"I suppose so."

"What's does that mean?" he asked, puzzled. "Either you are or you aren't."

"Yes, I am the neighbor—in a way. Though I fail to see what that has to do with you," she added, noticing the shadows flitting eerily to and fro in the failing afternoon light. She found the idea of being stuck by herself, with no light and little notion of how to get back to the house, rather daunting. She reluctantly swallowed her pride and rose.

"Since you're determined to come along, we'd better go, though I'm sure I could manage. Thank you all the same," she added as a grudging afterthought.

"Okay. Let's get moving. By the way, what's your name?"

"India Moncrieff," she replied, cross that she couldn't just walk off and dump him.

"Nice to meet you, too," he replied, making no effort to conceal the cynical glint in his eyes.

India straightened her jacket. If he was a friend of Peter and Diana's, there couldn't be much harm in letting him take her back to the house. Except for the damage it was doing to her pride, she realized ruefully, watching him pick up his shotgun and whistle to the dogs, his dark hair tousled by the wind.

They emerged from the glen and headed toward the burn. At the first blast of biting wind whipping her face, India's mood changed, as suddenly, all her reasons for being here today came to mind. She trudged on, thinking bleakly of what awaited her back at the house. She'd gone to the glen to flee reality, to try to find some peace, if only for a little while. But it had been a short-lived reprieve.

They crossed the rickety wooden bridge, the dogs splashing through the ice-cold water of the shallow burn, then shaking themselves vigorously on the other side.

As they began the short trek up the steep hill that led

to the gardens and the lawn, India thought of the future, and what it would hold for her now that she was alone. Serena, her half sister, was her only close family now; she barely knew her cousins. A stab of loneliness made her catch her breath, but she pushed the thought aside, and directed her focus to the man beside her. His presence was rather forbidding, despite his rakish American good looks and determination to escort her home.

She quickened her pace and reached the top of the hill ahead of him, exhaling small white wisps into the cold wind. She leaned against the huge trunk of the ancient oak tree that stood tall and alone and gazed over at Dunbar. To her astonishment the sight filled her with an unexpected feeling of expectation rather than gloom.

All was not lost, some unknown voice seemed to say.

A sudden surge of new strength coursed through her, followed by a mantle of peace that descended strangely upon her from out of the mist. The tight knot that had been in her stomach ever since she'd arrived at Dunbar slowly began to unwind, and for an instant she could have sworn someone was next to her.

But the moment passed, disappearing into the penumbra so fast she wondered if she'd been dreaming. It was all too easy to be entranced by the mysticism of the place. Too easy to sigh, too easy to hope, too easy to dream dreams that could never, would never, come true.

Scotland had a soothing effect on Jack. Ever since his first visit four years earlier he'd loved it. The rough natural beauty, the unspoiled landscape and heather-covered hills bathed in soft shades of white and purple had enchanted him, and he'd felt an immediate connection. Now the auburn tones of autumn were fading into winter, as the trees bared their branches, and frost sparkled, a fairylike blanket covering the fields. Damp leaves were being burned nearby and the smell brought back childhood memories of Tennessee, of his parents, both dead long since, and Chad, his little brother, running, kicking leaves up in the air to the sound of their mother's laughter.

He reached the top of the incline shortly after India and stopped, lowering his shotgun, drinking in the magnificence of the sight before him.

Across a vast stretch of manicured lawn stood Dunbar House, stately and majestic, its clean architectural lines softened by the gentle pink hue of the local stone, still visible among the fading shadows. A herd of Highland cattle, barely discernible through the mist, grazed peacefully in a field to the right of the east wing. Not a sound disturbed the magic tranquillity that reigned, serene and timeless.

It was an awesome sight, one that sent shivers running through him. "Does this place belong to your family?" he asked at last.

"Yes." Her eyes, like his, were fixed on the house. "There have been Dunbars here forever. At least since the late 1200s. They were baron raiders then, roaming the countryside in hordes, stealing their neighbors' sheep."

"The house is amazing. When was it built?"

"The mid-1700s. William started it, building on to a previous smaller structure, but it was finished by Fergus Dunbar, a cousin who inherited when William's son Rob was killed at the Battle of Culloden."

"What was the old house like?" he asked, suddenly curious.

"I think it was a small hunting lodge, but I'm not quite sure." She seemed anxious to go, but Jack stood still, entranced.

"It would make a fabulous hotel," he remarked thoughtfully.

"Hotel?" Her head shot round, her expression horrified.

"What a dreadful idea. I can't think of anything worse. Dunbar has always been a home."

"It was just a thought," he countered apologetically. "Tell me more about Fergus."

"Fergus did rather well for himself," India said, moving toward the lawn. "During the uprising in 1745 he supported the English, and made lots of money. Since the rightful heir, Robert Dunbar, was conveniently dead, Fergus inherited and added on to the house. There's a picture of him in the portrait gallery. I can't say I like the looks of him, though. He's always given me the creeps."

"Why?" Jack asked, amused. "What did he do that was so bad?"

"I don't know." She shrugged as they walked. "Some say he was a traitor. Lots of people around here were Jacobites, although they couldn't admit to it. But even though they didn't fight for Bonnie Prince Charlie, they never would have done anything to aid and abet the English."

"Is that what Fergus did?"

"According to legend." Again she shrugged and smiled. "I suppose stories get enhanced as the years go by. But he certainly made enough money to hire Adam to complete the house."

"One of the Adam brothers?"

"Yes, the most renowned architect of that period."

"He did a fine job."

India glanced at him, her eyes softening. "I think so, too. It's so serene, so...I can't quite explain it."

"I know exactly what you mean."

Their earlier antagonism seemed to have dissipated mysteriously in the cloak of gray mist surrounding them. By the time they reached the house and headed for a small door in the east wing, it was nearly dark.

Jack shuddered again for no reason and turned, glancing back across the lawn at the huge oak tree etched majestically on the dim horizon. Then his gaze moved to India, who was twisting the stiff brass doorknob on the heavy oak door.

"I guess you'll be okay now." He hesitated, catching a sudden glimpse of welcoming light that gleamed from behind the half-open door. "I think I owe you an apology," he added reluctantly. "I didn't think there would be anyone else out there today. My mistake." He hadn't meant it to sound so stiff, but he couldn't remember the last time he'd felt obliged to apologize to anyone. "I guess I'll be on my way. Would you mind if I call a cab? I don't know if I'll find my way back through the glen now that it's dark."

He glanced up at the sky. Evening was closing in fast, and all of a sudden he wanted to stay. He saw a flash of irritation cross her face followed by distant politeness. It increased his desire to remain and he was now determined to go inside and see the house.

Usually, when Jack decided he wanted something, he made sure he got it. Now, for some perverse reason, he wanted to stay at Dunbar. This woman, this amazing house and the aura of peaceful mystery he instinctively sensed here intrigued him. She'd walked into his life on what, for the last twelve years, had been its worst day, and in some inexplicable fashion she'd marked it.

"Come on in. The telephone's in the library."

As India waited expectantly in the doorway, shrouded in a halo of pale light, her thick mane of chestnut hair glinting softy, Jack found himself thinking of mythical knights and princesses and of Gaelic lore.

Then she stepped aside and he entered the cluttered cloakroom filled with old mackintoshes and Wellington boots. The dogs scampered inside. India sent them scuttling down a passage, then closed the door quietly behind them.

He laid his gun down on a wooden bench and slipped off his jacket, hanging it next to hers. Then he followed her up the worn carpeted staircase and along a wide passage lined with ancient volumes. He glanced up, fascinated by the carved bookcases. The coat of arms seemed vaguely familiar, but he couldn't place it. Nor could he explain his sudden sense of anticipation. He'd felt it before on two previous occasions in his life, both of which had been momentous. But perhaps it was just the mist and the enchantment of the place that were juggling his senses. This *was* Scotland, after all.

He smiled to himself as they reached the end of the corridor, realizing that, whatever the feeling was, it felt good. He stepped forward and opened the door for India, allowing her to pass through into the library, and was immediately struck by the room's warm, inviting atmosphere. The fire burned nicely amid seventeenth-century blue-and-white Delft tiles surrounding the grate, and, as in the passage, ancient volumes covered the walls from floor to ceiling. It was another example of that delightful shabby chic—as Diana Kinnaird referred to it—that enchanted him in Scotland and at which the British excelled.

"You Brits have a wonderful way of making everything feel as though it's been around forever," he remarked with a smile as they moved into the room, glancing at the tea tray strategically placed on a huge ottoman that stood between two sofas upholstered in bottle-green velvet. Some fringed paisley cushions and a cashmere throw were strewn on one, and a huge English sheepdog snoozed peacefully in the corner of the other.

"It's in our genes." Her eyes sparkled with sudden amusement. "Good quality, well-worn, not necessarily expensive but always comfortable. The phone's over there by the way," she added, pointing to a partner's desk that dominated the wall on the opposite side of the room. It stood alone between two high windows framed by sagging drapes whose faded pattern melted lazily into the shadows. All of the pieces blended congenially. The faded chair covers, the books, the mahogany furniture and even the threadbare Kurdistan rug before the fireplace appeared undisturbed by the passage of time.

"The number should be on that blue pad next to the phone," she remarked, moving toward the fireplace and rubbing her arms. "It was really getting freezing out there."

"Lying on damp ground in mid-November isn't going to warm you up," he remarked, picking up a somewhat wilted pad with numbers scribbled all over it. He narrowed his eyes, trying to decipher the writing. Some of the figures had been crossed out, others written over. The whole thing was so indistinct he wondered how on earth the inhabitants of this place knew where they were calling.

"Can't you find it?" India asked.

He looked up and grinned. "Sorry, but this writing is pretty hard to make out. Maybe you know which number it is."

"It should be about the third one down."

"That says old MacFee, I think," he said doubtfully.

"That's right. He's the local taxi driver. There is only one in the village."

"I see." Jack picked up the old-fashioned black telephone and dialed the rotary numbers, his fingers unused to the holes. There were several double rings, but no answer. He watched India, perched on the arm of one of the sofas, her long slim legs extending from below an oversize Aran sweater. He let the phone go on ringing, enjoying the sight. There was something composed and graceful about her, yet coupled with it was a restrained energy, rather like a thoroughbred ready to shoot out of the gate. To his utter discomfort he suddenly imagined what her eyes would look like when filled with deep emotions, such as pleasure.

He gave himself a good mental shake and hung up abruptly.

"It seems old MacFee isn't home. If you don't mind, perhaps I could try again in a few minutes."

"Of course. In the meantime, would you like some tea?" The invitation lacked enthusiasm.

"Thanks. That'd be great." Truthfully, he didn't like tea, but perversely he accepted.

"Mummy's writing is awful," India remarked, reaching for the pad, a sad little smile curving her lips as she sat down on the sofa near the blazing fire. "Shove over, Angus, you take up far too much room. There's a perfectly good rug for you to lie on." She gave the dog a gentle nudge and Angus slid reluctantly to the floor, where he stretched out lazily before the fire.

India scrutinized the phone pad. "I'm afraid the other taxi service from Pennickuik isn't on here. Anyway, I can't remember the man's name." She looked up and raised her shoulders in a shrug. "If worse comes to worst I'll drive you back. It can't be far."

"Thanks. I'd appreciate that." He settled back comfortably into the sofa and laid one leg casually across the other knee, in no hurry to leave, determined to discover more about this fascinating house and it's beautiful inhabitant.

India poured carefully from the large silver teapot and cast a surreptitious glance at the man sitting opposite, wondering how long she'd have to entertain him when there was so much she needed to deal with before tomorrow. He looked far too at ease, as though he planned to stay for a while. She tried to think who he reminded her of. Perhaps a taller, broader, American version of Pierce Brosnan. She laid down the pot, conscious that the pale yellow cashmere sweater and olive cord pants suited him rather well, and wondered how old he was. Mid-thirties, she reckoned, handing him a cup and looking at him full face.

Maybe it wasn't Pierce Brosnan after all, she decided, reaching for the milk, but his face seemed somewhat familiar.

"How long are you staying at Dalkirk?" she asked, wishing she'd rung for the taxi herself. Maybe he'd dialed the wrong number.

"A few more days. I come here from time to time. Peter Kinnaird and I are partners and friends."

"I suppose you must be in the hotel business, then?"

"Yes, I am. Say, I'll take some more of that tea, it's very good." His fingers touched hers lightly as he handed her back the cup. "Peter and I merged some of our interests a few years ago. Asia and South America mainly. Instead of competing we've joined forces."

"How productive."

"Yes, it is. I also happen to like Peter quite a bit, so we have a good time doing business. What do you do?"

"I'm an interior designer."

"Really? Private or commercial?" Jack asked, giving her his undivided attention, the force of his gaze making her shift her eyes quickly to the tray.

"Both, but mainly hotels. I did one of Peter's, actually. The Jeremy in London. Perhaps you know it?"

"I sure do. I was at the opening, but I don't recall *you* being there." His eyebrows came together in a thick dark line over the ridge of his nose, giving him a severe look, and India got the feeling he'd be a difficult client.

"Unfortunately I couldn't go. One of my closest friends chose that same weekend to get married."

"Most unfortunate." He shot her a quick smile. "You did a great job on the hotel. That statue in the hall, so linear and sleek in such a traditional setting, created an amazing effect. I like that look of understated luxury. You salvaged all the original architectural quirks, too, yet behind the scenes you created a modern hotel running like clockwork. That's a hell of a challenge.''

India blushed under his gaze, aware that, for some strange reason, his praise meant something to her. Carefully she stirred her tea before answering. ''I enjoy it. I could get lost in it if I'm not careful. There's always a new challenge, and the fine line that has to be maintained when placing modern elements in classical surroundings is half the fun.''

''Peter told me the design company was out of Switzerland. Do you work for them?''

''No, I live in Switzerland. La Dolce Vita is mine.''

''I thought you lived here.'' He raised a surprised eyebrow.

She hesitated a moment, then decided to tell him. ''Dunbar belongs—rather, belonged to my mother.'' For the last couple of hours she'd managed to put the strain and sorrow of the past few days aside. Now it returned in a torrential rush, reality pounding her once more.

''How come you say belonged? Has she sold it?''

''No.'' India looked away. ''She died, four days ago.''

In the silence that followed she folded the small linen napkin deliberately, determined to wink away the tears that pricked her eyes.

''I'm sorry,'' he said quietly, his expression dramatically altered, ''I shouldn't have asked—'' The nonchalance was gone, replaced by deep consternation and compassion.

''It all happened very suddenly. She had a heart attack. Mercifully she didn't suffer or have a long illness, and I'm awfully thankful for that,'' she added, trying not to think how much she would miss Lady Elspeth.

"I'm sorry," he repeated again softly.

For a short while they sat, the silence broken only by the crackling of a log shifting in the fire and Angus snoring faintly before the hearth.

Then India rose, her face shielded by her hair as she kneeled down next to the fire and removed the fireguard. She reached blindly for a log, trying desperately to hide the tears she could no longer hold back.

Jack moved swiftly to her side. "Let me do that." He reached out, placed his hand over hers and took the log gently from her.

"It's fine, don't worry," she mumbled, her voice quivering, tears trickling slowly down her cheeks.

After placing the log down on the hearth, Jack reached out his thumb and gently brushed away the tears. "You've had a rough day. I'm sorry I bothered you. I'll leave and let you rest." For an instant their eyes met and sorrow gripped him at the intense pain he saw written in hers. "It's hard to lose someone you really love. It takes time," he said quietly.

She nodded. "Thank you. I'm so sorry, I just…"

"You don't need to explain, I understand." He slipped a hand over hers, squeezing it before getting up. Then he took a crisp white handkerchief from his pocket and handed it to her silently before leaning forward and placing the log on the fire. He picked up the poker and prodded the fire, the flames picking up again. "It took me a very, very long while to recover," he murmured, as though speaking to himself.

India rose and stood next to him, her face pale. "Was it one of your parents, too?"

"My wife." He gave a vicious jab with the poker. A log fell at an odd angle and the flames rose higher once more. "She died twelve years ago today." He placed the instrument carefully back on its stand, and for a while they stood next to each other, staring into the flames, each lost in their own world, but bonded by their grief.

The magic of the moment receded into the shadows when she turned away and sat down. He sighed, understanding her inner battle to come to grips with her feelings. He wished there was something he could do to help, but knew only she could come to terms with her own grief.

Then she looked up and gave him a small determined smile. "Would you like to see some of the house since you're here?"

"Certainly. It'd be a pleasure," he answered, returning the smile, relieved. Then he followed her out of the library into the large and drafty stucco hall.

He was agreeably surprised when an hour later it seemed as though only moments had passed. He was more than a little enchanted by India's company, intrigued by her knowledge and what appeared to be her complete unawareness of the effect she had on a man. They'd wandered through endless rooms, turning lamps on as they went, while she told him stories, some amusing, others sad, about the ancestors who stared down at them from the Raeburn and Gainsborough portraits on the walls. With each tale her expression changed and watching her had become a fascinating diversion in and of itself.

They talked of hotels they knew, places they enjoyed and books they'd both read, and by the time they returned to the library, Jack was perplexed. He could not recall having established such an easy intimacy, in such a short time, with anyone.

"Gosh, it's seven already," India exclaimed as the hall clock chimed in the distance. "Would you like a drink before you go?"

"Sounds great," Jack replied, old MacFee and the taxi forgotten.

"Go ahead," she said, pointing to a silver tray laden

with decanters that stood on an eighteenth-century Boule desk in the far corner of the room.

"Beautiful desk," he remarked, pouring himself a whiskey. "What can I get you?"

"It is lovely, isn't it? It's said to have been bought at auction during the French Revolution. I'll have a glass of sherry, please."

Jack brought the drinks over to the fire and handed her a glass. "What are you working on now?" he asked.

"I have to be in Rio for the opening of La Perla, a hotel I finished a couple of months ago. There are still some last-minute touches to go over before the grand opening." She leaned forward and stroked Angus's head between the ears.

"That's the Cardoso Group's new place in Ipanema, isn't it? Nelson Cardoso's a friend of mine. That's a big job," he added, impressed.

"Yes, it was. I'm glad it's over, though I enjoyed it. Nelson's easy to work for, but the going back and forth got a bit trying by the end."

"How long will you be in Rio?"

"Actually, I'm going to Argentina first. I promised Gabby O'Halloran—she's an old friend from boarding school—that I'd redecorate the *casco* on her family's *estancia*. It's about an hour and a half out of Buenos Aires. I'll probably stay there for Christmas."

"You be careful in Rio. Last time I was there all the safes in the hotel were burgled. It's incredible the things that happen in that city. They have to be seen to be believed. Funny you should mention Buenos Aires. Astra's just bought into a partnership in a hotel down there."

India sat up and looked at him. "Astra?"

"Yeah, my company."

"You *own* the Astra Group?"

"Uh…yes. Is that good or bad?"

"Neither, it was just a comment." She seemed embarrassed at having shown surprise.

"We've gone into partnership with the owners of the Palacio de Grès. Are you familiar with it? It was a private residence that had already been partially restored. They'd begun building the hotel behind it. Then the funding went dry and they realized they'd need experienced management as well, so they came to us. We liked the deal, and what do you know? Off on another venture." He laughed, hoping to distract her.

"As a matter of fact, I visited the house once as a little girl," India remarked. "The owners, Señor and Señora Carvajal y Queiroz, were friends of my parents. They must be very old now if they're even still alive. I remember being fascinated by its beauty. It's a unique example of its kind in South America."

"Hernan Carvajal is the present owner. He told me he was left the property by his grandparents. I guess they must have been your parent's friends."

"What a treat to have the opportunity of working with such a wonderful setting. Are you going to preserve the house as the common area?"

"Exactly."

"But tell me, how has the new hotel been conceived?" She leaned forward, eyes alive with sudden interest.

"As I said, we're building vertically behind the house." He put down his glass and leaned forward, pushing the tea tray aside. Then he began drawing with his forefinger on the velvet surface of the ottoman. "Let's say this is the main house, okay?" She nodded. "When you go in, you have the black-and-white marble hall—"

"Which will be your perfect reception area!" she exclaimed, finishing the sentence for him. "You know, the old salon overlooking the gardens would make a perfect setting for tea. Even a bar," she added thoughtfully.

"Something in the style of what they have at the Alvear but—"

Her sentence remained in midair as the library door flew open, followed by a draft of cold air. Jack watched in astonishment as Lady Serena Hamilton marched into the room. What on earth would *she* of all people be doing here? he wondered, watching as she threw her suede jacket carelessly over a chair and walked toward the fire.

"I'm exhausted," she exclaimed, rubbing her hands. "The weather's simply foul and that wretched man at the funeral home is utterly incompetent. Ah, tea. Just what I need." Jack saw India stiffen. Then, glancing at Serena, who'd turned abruptly toward him, he rose reluctantly from the sofa.

"Jack!" she exclaimed, smiling archly. "What on earth are you doing here?"

"Hello, Serena," he countered. "I was about to ask you the same thing."

Her arrival couldn't have been more unfortunate. As had been their one-night stand, he reflected grimly, wondering how she was going to play out the scene.

India watched, intrigued, as Jack and her half sister sized each other up, like two opponents, waiting to see who would strike first. She noticed that under the urbane surface Jack's eyes had turned hard and unyielding. Like chips of blue ice, she realized with a shock. The relaxed individual of moments before had become a formidable adversary.

"You two know each other?" she asked, looking from one to the other, disconcerted by the underlying tension.

"In a manner of speaking." Jack glanced at her. "I made Lady Serena's acquaintance at a cocktail party the Kinnairds gave a while back."

"Acquaintance?" Serena lifted a shapely eyebrow and

threw him an arch smile before flopping onto the sofa next to where Jack had been seated. He remained standing and moved close to the fire. "You still haven't told me what brought you here today." She made a moue with her well-defined crimson lips.

"He brought me home from the glen," India interjected, wishing at once that she hadn't.

"The glen? What were you doing there?"

"I went for a walk," she answered curtly, annoyed that she had to explain. She watched Serena stretch out her long legs, encased in black leather pants and boots, toward the fire. Angus stirred and turned over before the hearth.

"I took a potshot at her." Jack smiled ruefully and glanced at India. "Since I nearly killed her, the least I could do was walk her home." He leaned back against the mantelpiece and assessed Serena as he might a potentially dangerous situation. "Now you tell me. What are *you* doing here?"

"I live here," she answered smugly.

This, India reflected, wasn't strictly true. Serena lived— or was supposed to be living—at her flat in Edinburgh, though, according to their mother, she and her dreadful boyfriend, Maxi von Lowendorf, had been frequent visitors of late. It was strange, for Serena and her mother had never got on too well. India sighed, wishing she herself could have been here more often. Her mother had sounded troubled the last time they'd spoken on the phone, and India wished Lady Elspeth had told her more of what was preying on her mind. Now it was too late.

"Oh, now, about that tea…" Serena reached forward, then gave a tight, disappointed smile. "Oh, it's cold and there's no cup, of course. Never mind, I'll just do without," she said with a long-suffering sigh.

"I'll get another pot," India replied, glad of an excuse to escape. "And I'll grab an extra cup, too."

"Would you, darling? That's awfully kind," Serena murmured with a condescending smile.

India left the library and walked smartly along the corridor to the pantry. One never knew if Serena meant what she said or if she was being sarcastic. She grimaced, wishing she could like her half sister more.

In the pantry she removed a cup and saucer from the cupboard and then passed by the kitchen, drawn by the delicious smells of fresh baking that had reached into the corridor.

"Mmm," India exclaimed. "That smells wonderful, Mrs. ." Laying the cup down on the counter, she went over to the kitchen table where the housekeeper was wielding a wooden spoon in a large enamel bowl with zealous determination. "What are you making?" she asked, switching on the kettle.

"Preparing fer tomorrow," Mrs. Walker answered with a sad shake of her gray head, her hazel eyes bright in a face creased with kindly wrinkles. "I wouldna' want yer poor dear mother te' feel ashamed, bless her soul." She cast her eyes heavenward. "It'll be quite a gathering. Lady Kathleen called earlier te' see if we needed anything from the village before she comes back. Always thinks she has te' be doing something, ye know. She's awf'y upset about yer dear mother, but so are we all." She laid the bowl down on the gnarled wooden table, and scraped the remains of the sponge cake batter off the sides of the spoon with a spatula. "Waste not, want not. That's my motto and I've always lived by it." She gave a satisfied last scour. "Well, as I was saying, Miss India, I said to Lady Kathleen, dinna' you worry. Thirty years I've served the Dunbar family, first yer uncle, Sir Thomas, and the Lord knows he was no easy man, and then yer dear mother, may she rest in peace. It'd be a fine thing, I told her, if I wasna' able te' see te' our ain guests.'' There was an audible sniff.

"I'm sure she meant well. Kathleen's always so thoughtful,'' India said tactfully before leaning over the table and surreptitiously passing a finger around the edge of the bowl.

"Och, Miss India! Away with those fingers now!'' Mrs. Walker swiped at India's hand with a dishcloth.

"Scrumptious, Mrs. Walker, you haven't lost your touch,'' she answered mischievously, licking the tips of her fingers.

"Dearie me, when will ye ever grow up.'' Mrs. Walker shook her head, smiling fondly. "I dinna' like te' think what yer poor mother would say.''

India grinned, picked up the cup and the steaming teapot and headed for the door. "I have to get back with Serena's tea. We have an American guest in the library. By the way, he ate four of your scones, plus jam and clotted cream.''

"Would that be Sir Peter's American? I've heard there's one staying over at Dalkirk.''

"One and the same.''

"Aye, I thought so.'' She nodded knowingly. "There's nae too many of them about these parts. Mr. Hunter, the butcher, told me personally that Miss MacGregor had heard from Mrs. MacC.—the housekeeper from Dalkirk, ye know—that the American gentleman's an awf'y nice-mannered young man. He brought her a special bottle of perfume all the way from America, and he never forgets te' leave a wee something for the staff.'' She gave another firm nod. "There was a lot of talk in the village when Sir Peter went into business with him, but it seems it's all worked out fer the best.'' Mrs. Walker began piling dirty dishes, and a plate slid dangerously from her arthritic grip.

India stopped herself from rushing to the rescue and pretended not to notice, knowing Mrs. Walker's pride would be sorely hurt.

She left the kitchen with a bright smile and heavy heart, dreading what the morrow might bring. She hoped desperately that the estate could afford to keep Mrs. Walker and the others on. There was old Tompson, and Mackay, the gardener. And the tenants. What would happen to them if— She pulled herself up short. There was no use worrying, she reflected, reaching the library. She heard voices just beyond the door and realized she'd completely forgotten about Jack and Serena, her mind so taken up with other things. She hesitated before entering and felt a pang of inexplicable disappointment. Somehow Jack hadn't struck her as Serena's type. She paused to gather her composure and heard Serena's smug voice.

"I suppose India was terrified. She probably didn't realize she was getting in the way. She's not used to our way of life, poor thing."

"The whole incident was entirely my fault," Jack replied in his pleasant American drawl. "It was my careless behavior, not hers, that caused the incident. I should have been paying more attention." His was a voice used to giving orders and not being thwarted, she noted, amused despite her anger at Serena's snide comment.

She entered the library and lay the cup on the tray, surprised that he'd admitted the blame so frankly, and feeling a glimmer of satisfaction at his deft handling of Serena.

"Thanks, darling." Serena smiled benignly. At thirty-six she looked good, the slim figure from her modeling days in London still intact, and though her clothes were too flamboyant for India's taste, she could carry them.

India wondered suddenly just how "acquainted" they

actually were. Serena's arched eyebrow and Jack's discomfort, though quickly disguised, had not escaped her.

And what did it matter anyway? She sat down heavily, suddenly exhausted, the emotional stress of the last few days finally catching up with her.

Serena was telling a long, drawn-out story about the Kinnairds, herself and some of her aristocratic connections. India listened with half an ear to the monotonous monologue, and tried to take a polite interest. But when she caught Jack looking surreptitiously at his watch, she realized it was time to intervene.

When Serena paused for breath, India grabbed her chance. "It's getting quite late. Please tell me when you feel we should get going."

"Get going? Where?" Serena demanded, her voice imperious. "Have another drink, Jack, there's really no hurry."

"No thanks. I've had quite enough."

The most unobservant person would have picked up the dryness of his tone. But not Serena. India was embarrassed despite herself. "I'm taking Mr. Buchanan back to Dalkirk," she said formally. "There's no cab available."

"You have to be joking. You? You wouldn't know your way to the end of the drive, let alone to Dalkirk." Serena gave her a smile that didn't reach her eyes.

"Why not? I'm perfectly capable of getting in the car and following some directions. I'm sure you can tell me the easiest way to get there."

"No, no. I can't possibly allow it." Serena turned to Jack. "She's so kindhearted, poor thing, always doing things for others, but I can't possibly let her go out on a night like this when she barely knows the way."

"Stop being ridiculous, Serena," India retorted, trying to mask her anger, writhing inwardly when Serena smiled patronizingly, as though she were explaining something to a very small child.

"I'll just call the cab again. Maybe old MacFee will be home by now." Jack stepped toward the desk.

"Good heavens, you won't find him in at this time," Serena interjected. "Old MacFee will be on his third round at the Hog and Hound by now. Don't worry, Jack darling. I'll take you. I know my way about like the back of my hand. I'm not likely to get lost."

Jack hesitated, obviously not too pleased. Suddenly India gave up the fight, realizing it was pointless to have a quarrel, and decided to let Serena take him if she so wanted to. Not having to go out in the dark, on a road she didn't know, and in what looked as though it might develop into a nasty snowstorm, would be a welcome relief. Her head was throbbing, her feet were killing her and all she wanted now was to get some rest. For a fleeting moment she wondered what Serena's motive was for wanting to go. Maybe they knew each other far better than she suspected. If so, it was none of her business, and the sooner they left her in peace, the better.

Jack opened the door to allow them passage into the hall. Serena grabbed her jacket and barged through, heading straight for the porch, and down the stone steps to the heavy oak front door.

"See you later, India. I'll lock up when I get back," she threw over her shoulder.

Jack turned. Serena's footsteps still echoed between them as they stood face-to-face under the high dome of the dimly lit stucco hall. There was a sudden lull, each waiting for the other to speak.

"You take care," he said finally, taking her hand, and, to her surprise, raising it to his lips.

She blushed despite herself, thankful for the shadows.

"Thanks for bringing me back." She wanted to say, "And for being so understanding," but instead she hastily retrieved her hand and tucked it in her pocket. "That's Serena hooting in the car. The weather seems to be worsening by the minute. You'd better go."

"Right." He paused, lingering. "When are you leaving?"

"After the funeral. I have to get back home to Switzerland and work."

"I guess that's it then. Who knows, perhaps our paths will cross one day. Thanks for the tea and the tour of the house. I really enjoyed it. Goodbye for now, and good luck." He seemed to hesitate, then smiled. India wasn't sure if it was the light or her imagination, but all at once his eyes seemed alight once more with depth and understanding. As though he cared. She told herself to stop imagining things, and watched him head down the stone steps.

Halfway down he turned back, his eyes finding hers through the darkness. "And by the way, just to set the record straight, my name's Jack, not Mr. Buchanan."

Her mouth broke into an involuntary smile. "I'll remember—Jack. By the way, don't forget your gun and the dogs—and your jacket. Tell Serena to stop at the side door. It's open."

"Thanks, I will."

He disappeared, leaving her to the haunting emptiness of the night and the echo of the front door closing loudly behind him. India shivered, pulled the cashmere cardigan closer about her shoulders, and wandered over the ancient Persian rug, its hues mellowed by the passage of generations of Dunbars. She stopped at the drum table standing alone in the middle of the vast hall and looked down at the vase of roses set there. Once more her heart filled with grief.

They were the flowers her mother had been arranging at the time of her death.

They remained, just as Lady Elspeth had left them. She had placed the last delicate rose in the Waterford vase, then been struck by a massive heart attack, dying as gracefully as she'd lived. India decided to take the roses and dry them. They would be a tiny part of her mother that would remain with her always.

Wandering over to the grand piano, she smoothed the surface of the instrument and sat down, gazing through the shadows at the keys. Slowly her fingers reached out to the keyboard and she began playing, the strains of Chopin enveloping her as she drifted into her mother's favorite nocturne. India played in the dark, paying a last, solitary tribute to her mother, a woman she loved, yet who'd been somewhat removed from the realities of life.

The notes lingered, reaching up toward the high-ceilinged dome. Outside, snow fell, heavy and silent. The sitting-room lamps flickered, and shadows danced eerily on the stucco walls as India poured her feelings into the music. Love, vexation and anger mingled with a deep, abiding sense of loneliness. Finally her tears flowed unimpeded.

As nocturne came to a close, and the last resounding chords echoed, she lifted her hands from the piano and her tears flowed unimpeded. It was a precious moment she would always remember.

India rubbed her eyes thinking now of the problems ahead—debts, tax issues and God only knew what else. Lady Elspeth had always skimmed over the subject, uneager to dwell on anything disagreeable, and India had no clue how the estate had been left. It was another subject non grata. In a way it might be easier if Serena inherited the lot. As for her mother's house in Switzerland, India had learned only the other day that it was mortgaged to the hilt. Poor Mummy. If it hadn't been for the Marchese, her old and faithful admirer who'd helped her take charge of her affairs during these last few years, she would have ended up penniless.

But there was no point in dwelling on the negative.

India closed the lid of the Steinway, then trod wearily up the stairs, the strain of the last few days finally taking its toll.

On reaching the bedroom she flopped onto the faded counterpane of the four-poster bed, but the room was chilly, so she crawled under the covers, relieved that it would soon be all over.

The more she thought about it, the more sense it made that Mummy would have left Dunbar to Serena. After all, she herself hardly knew the place. Tomorrow, by this time, the funeral and the reading of the will would be over. Then she could leave, back to Chantemerle, her house by Lake Geneva, and to sanity.

She huddled sleepily under the quilt, wishing she'd brought a hot-water bottle. Turning on her pillow, she remembered her conversation with Jack. He'd struck her more as a big-business sort of man, yet he'd seemed genuinely enthusiastic and knowledgeable about his new project, the Palacio de Grès.

For a while she lay there, half-asleep, too tired to undress. She listened to the still night, broken only by the lonely hoot of an owl, thinking of all she had to do in Switzerland before leaving for Buenos Aires. But her mind kept returning to the look in Jack's eyes when she'd told him about her mother. There had been true concern there. Something had occurred in that serene moment, as they stood, side by side, before the crackling flames. Something she couldn't explain.

Strange, she reflected as sleep finally came, that the only true moment of peace she'd achieved since her arrival at Dunbar had been found in the company of a stranger.

2

The Range Rover progressed at a snail's pace, as snow-flakes pelted the windshield relentlessly

"What a dreadful night," Serena remarked, eyes narrowed. "I hope it clears for the funeral tomorrow, or it'll be damn difficult for the hearse to get up to the house."

"I was sorry to hear about your mother," Jack said, remembering India's sad expression.

"Oh, that," she replied vaguely. "Mmm, it's rather a nuisance really. Such a tiresome time of year to be plodding outside in this dreadful weather. What's going to be even more of a bore is getting everything ready for the sale."

"What sale?"

"Dunbar."

"You're selling Dunbar?" Jack asked, surprised. When he'd commented to India that Dunbar would be an ideal setting for a hotel, her eyes had darkened, and she'd replied in such withering tones he'd felt like a jerk for allowing the thought to cross his mind.

"Yes, I've pretty well decided," Serena continued. "I've no desire to keep it. It's far too big. The heating bill alone is outrageous, and quite frankly, I'd rather have the money." She slowed as they slid on a patch of ice. "Whew! That was close," she remarked. "Awfully slippery out here."

"When is your mother's funeral?" he asked casually.

"Tomorrow at two. The burial will be afterward at Cockpen. We'll probably all freeze to death while the minister blabbers on. He's such a long-winded old bore."

Jack tried to conceal his rising disgust. During his life, he'd crossed men and met with situations he'd rather not remember, but rarely had he come across a more self-centered, callous woman. Serena showed none of the sadness India obviously felt at her mother's passing. Apparently all that concerned Serena was her own well-being, and how she could profit. He glanced sideways at her. The fact that he'd actually slept with this woman—brief, inebriated fling though it had been—filled him with abhorrence.

He tried to forget Serena, and considered the idea that had been taking shape hazily ever since he'd set eyes on the property, and that her words had reignited. He couldn't help it. He was always picturing places as hotels. *His* hotels. If Dunbar could be acquired, it would be the perfect addition to the small group of upscale establishments he and Peter were investing in.

"Is your sister interested in selling the property, too?" he asked, casting Serena another sidelong glance. His eyes had gotten used to the dark now, and he tried to distinguish her expression. Something didn't fly in all this for the two sisters to have such different views on the subject.

"It's none of her business."

"What do you mean?"

"I mean, Mummy's surely left the estate to me. India couldn't possibly have any interest in it. She's never spent time there. She already had the property in Switzerland, of course, which is actually worth more and is probably a damn sight easier to sell. It would have been out of the question for her to live at Dunbar.''

"Really, why's that?'' he asked, surprised, remembering India's rapt expression as she'd shown him the house. She'd seemed enchanted with it, as though it was an important part of her existence.

"You weren't brought up here so you probably wouldn't understand. It's rather difficult to be accepted in these parts if you're not born into the right milieu. Of course, a foreigner's very different,'' she added, casting him a suggestive smile, "especially a wealthy, eligible one. In America you're far more understanding of these things, aren't you? Too understanding if you ask me. That's why you have all sorts of riffraff mixing with their betters.''

Jack didn't respond, still wondering what could possibly have induced him to end up with this woman in the Kinnairds' second guest bedroom a few months back. That'd teach him not to mix his drinks, he reflected somberly. She'd been conveniently there, sexy, in a slinky black dress that did wonders for her figure, and before he'd known it they were on the carpet, Serena pulling off his clothes. And, he had to admit, doing a pretty damn good job. Lady Serena was a pro.

India's face flashed to mind, and he experienced a sudden burst of discomfort. Two more different women would have been hard to find. On the one hand, India, poised, natural and beautiful—with something more Jack couldn't put his finger on, but which further acquaintance might reveal. On the other, this obtrusive female who, although she was attractive and sexy, clearly lacked her sister's quality.

"Are you going to list the property with a broker?'' he asked, his mind jumping back to the possibility of acquiring Dunbar.

"Why? Would you be interested?" she asked archly.

"I could be…if the numbers were right."

Serena glanced at him. "Why don't you come over one day before you leave and take a look around."

"Okay. Sounds like a good idea. If you could have some specs on hand—you know, information about the property, plans and so on, it'd be helpful."

"Of course, I'll see to it. When are you leaving?"

"I'll be away for a couple of days, but I'll be back on Saturday."

"Fine. I'll give you a ring or you can call me. Do you have the number?"

"I'll find it."

"When did you say Peter and Di are getting back from Perthshire?" she inquired, the wheels of the Range Rover crunching the freshly fallen snow as they rolled slowly up the drive.

"The day after tomorrow."

"Good. Give them my love and tell Di I'll be giving her a buzz." They stopped at the front door. "You know, we should get together for dinner one night. I make a jolly decent soufflé, and we could think up something *terribly* exotic for dessert," she purred, looking him over greedily.

Jack gave an inner shudder and opened the door of the vehicle. "Good night, Serena. Thanks for the ride. How do I get the dogs out?"

"It's unlocked, just press the button," she said, revving up the engine crossly.

Jack went to the back of the car, opened the hatch, letting the dogs loose, and picked up his gun. The snow was falling so thick that by the time he reached the front door he was covered.

Jack realized he was hungry after his day in the fresh air, even after the scones at tea. He cleaned his gun, then changed into more comfortable garb, all the while pondering the possibilities of Dunbar. He had a strange feeling about the place. Deep down, he just knew it could work. If the numbers were right and the specs were what he imagined they might be, this could be the gem he'd been searching for.

He slipped on a pair of loafers and wandered down the passage to the kitchen in search of Mrs. MacClean, the Kinnaird family's housekeeper for over twenty-five years. Dunbar could wait; dinner, on the other hand, could not.

He opened the door and watched as Mrs. MacClean bustled happily about her business, unperturbed by the old-fashioned kitchen, not bothered by drawbacks that, by American standards, would be considered archaic. Jack guessed she'd probably protest vehemently if any changes were suggested.

She glanced up from the oven with a broad smile. "Och, here ye are, Mr. Jack. I was about to call ye fer yer dinner. It'll be ready in just a wee while. I'll get the table set."

Jack stopped her. "If you don't mind, Mrs. MacC., I'll just eat in here tonight. Will you keep me company?" he asked with a winning smile.

"Lonely are ye, dearie? Well, all right. I'll set the table in here fer ye. I won't be half a tick." She laid her oven gloves on the counter and extracted a table mat with a faded hunting scene and heavy silver cutlery from the cumbersome drawer below the kitchen table.

Jack leaned against the counter, savoring the delicious smell of roast lamb that filtered from the large Aga oven, and relaxed, enjoying the scene. He usually ate in restaurants or in one of the hotels. And when he was home at the penthouse in Miami—which was rarely—he ordered takeout. He recalled a time when he'd enjoyed eating in, way back in the days when Lucy was alive and they were two kids, playing at keeping house. She'd loved French cooking. It was ironic that, at the present stage of his existence, he'd eaten enough fancy French food to last him a lifetime.

He sighed. The memories and the what-might-have-beens were so present today. Time had not faded her image or blotted out the sweet moments of his early youth. He rarely allowed himself to unlock the safe within his soul, because when he did, the thoughts of Lucy were still so vivid they hurt. He could almost reach out and touch her soft golden hair, and lose himself in those blue eyes he'd loved so well.

Sometimes, but not often, he let himself think about their life together, how they'd fought to get married when everyone had told them they were too young, and how glad he was that they had. There had been so much young love, so many hopes and expectations. Ironically he had fulfilled most of them. Alone. Now he owned all the material things they'd dreamed of possessing, had traveled to all the places they'd conjured up as they cuddled under the covers in the little frame house that Jack had proudly put the down payment on with money he'd earned working nights and summers while his friends were goofing around or dating girls. But for him it had always been different. Ever since fifth grade he'd known he wanted to marry Lucy, just as she had him.

Then in one horrifying instant everything had changed. Lucy never saw the truck speeding toward her on the icy snow-covered road. And from then on his life had become an empty place. At twenty-two he had stood by her grave, a devastated young widower bereft of his child bride and the baby she was carrying. Overnight the boy became a man, bearing pain that only years of determination and discipline would teach him to handle.

"There ye go. We're just about ready. Sit yersel' doon, Mr. Jack, while I get the roast out of the oven fer ye."

Jack snapped back to his present surroundings, startled by Mrs. MacC.'s voice.

He sat down at the table and thought of India, with her exotic name, her high-bred British accent and her green eyes that changed constantly, like a kaleidoscope. She'd seemed so vulnerable perched on that tree stump, with her knees tucked under her chin, staring at him warily and wrinkling her nose at the whiskey. She'd made him think of a woodland elf, yet that same instant, he'd envisioned her draped on a sofa in a black evening dress, diamonds around her throat and a glass of champagne in her hand.

The differences between India and Serena were really quite striking. But Serena's oblique references to her half sister's background had left him curious, and he wondered if Mrs. MacClean could be induced to shed some light on the matter.

He knew Dunbar was very special. His intuition never failed him when it came to choosing sites for hotels. In his history as a hotelier he'd made only one mistake, and that was ten years ago, when he was twenty-four and just beginning. Even then he'd salvaged his money.

The possibility of perhaps acquiring Dunbar was increasingly enticing, and he looked forward to getting his hands on the specs and an in-depth look at the property. Of course, the place would need a tremendous overhaul if anything did materialize, but the advantages far outweighed any drawbacks of that nature. Being so near the airport, a half hour's drive at most, made it easy to include in luxury packages to London.

He wondered if Peter, who was involved in local politics, might think it was too close to home. The locals might be sticky about a hotel. Worst-case scenario, he could go it alone. But it seemed a great fit with everything they already had going, including the Buenos Aires project.

"Here ye go, Mr. Jack," Mrs. MacClean said, whisking

the roast onto the table. "Have yer supper afore it chills. There's nothing worse than half-cold food. I brought ye the bottle of Burgundy Sir Peter opened. He says it does the wine good te' be open fer a wee while."

Jack snapped out of his reverie, picking up the white linen napkin from the old pine table, its patina softened by years of elbows and beeswax. "Sir Peter's right," he said, picking up the bottle, reading the label, impressed. "Good red wines usually do benefit from being uncorked for a few hours before they're consumed."

"Well, that's what Sir Peter always says." Mrs. MacClean looked pleased as she padded back and forth with different items. "Now, are ye all set?" Her small eyes scanned the table critically from above ruddy, weather-beaten cheeks.

"Yeah, thanks, this looks great." Jack carved a large portion of lamb and poured himself a glass of the Chambertin '61, raising it reverently to his nostrils, appreciating the strong body yet delicate bouquet. "Sir Peter sure chose a fine bottle, Mrs. MacClean."

"Och aye, just like his father afore him. Old Sir Peter was one fer knowing the wines."

Jack toyed with his glass appreciatively. He'd acquired a taste for good wines, and his wine cellar in Miami held some interesting acquisitions, mostly bottles and lots picked up at auction. He hoped when the time came to consume them they would still be drinkable. The bottles were supposed to have been recorked at the château of origin before maturing to twenty-five, but you could never really be certain.

Remembering his objective, he cut to the chase. "Mrs. MacC., tell me about the lady who died over at Dunbar House. The Dunbars sound like an interesting family."

She held a dishcloth in midair and looked thoughtful. "Aye, I suppose they are, in their ain way. Poor Lady

Elspeth, they say she had a lovely death.'' She sighed dreamily, folding the cloth and laying it down. ''She was arranging the roses in a vase—och, she was a beautiful flower arranger, Lady Elspeth was—when Mrs. Walker, she's the housekeeper at Dunbar, came to bring her the secateurs. And what did she find but poor Lady Elspeth lying dead on the floor next to the table.''

''She must have had a massive heart attack.''

''Aye, that's what Dr. MacDuff said when he came from the village. Gone before she knew it, he said. It was a terrible shock for poor Mrs. Walker, her wi' her heart an' all,'' she added, shaking her head.

''Was Lady Elspeth married?''

''Twice widowed, poor soul. Her first husband, Lord Henry Hamilton died, oh…over thirty years ago. Then she married a Mr. Duncan Moncrieff.'' She lowered her voice and pursed her lips. ''The family was most upset, him not being of the same *ilk,* if ye know what I mean.''

Jack pricked up his ears. ''No, actually I don't. What was wrong with the guy?''

''It wasna' anything *wrong* exactly, he just wasna' from their world. He was a wealthy shipbuilder from Glasgow—not at all what the family was used to,'' she added with a conclusive shake of her head. ''He and old Sir Thomas had words, and Mr. Moncrieff wouldna' set foot at Dunbar after the quarrel. Old Sir Thomas told him he wasna' good enough for the likes of his sister, and Mr. Moncrieff left very angry. 'Twas a good thing they went te' live abroad. People were talking, and it would have been awf'y tricky. When old Sir Thomas died a bachelor and Lady Elspeth inherited Dunbar, she was already widowed for the second time. My, how time flies.'' She sighed, pouring some thick, butter-colored cream for Jack's apple pie into a jug. ''It seems as if it were only yesterday.''

''Yes, it does fly,'' he agreed wistfully, thinking how

the years had flown. If Lucy and the baby had lived— He banished the thought, having learned long ago to discipline his mind.

"Did they have children?"

"Aye, a wee girl. Miss India."

"India. That's a strange name."

"Aye, but ye see, that's where Lady Elspeth was born. Old Sir William, her father, was in India wi' the Scots Guards, ye know. She must be twenty-five or -six by now."

Jack reflected on this as he savored the succulent lamb, beginning to better understand the roots of Serena's contemptuous attitude toward her half sister. So this was why the Dunbar inheritance had been left the way it had. No wonder those boys back in 1776 had taken the reins into their own hands—and a damn good thing, too.

To him, an American, earning money and rising from poverty to riches was commendable. It seemed absurd that India's father had been ostracized merely because he wasn't born into the same social class as her mother.

Surely things couldn't be as old-fashioned as that. This was the '90s after all. He wondered if this was the general attitude, or if perhaps Mrs. MacC. was part of a dying breed. Diana and Peter certainly didn't come across as being in the least bit snobbish or narrow-minded. Maybe they would be, though, if one of their daughters wanted to marry out of the mold.

"Tell me more about the Dunbars. They've lived there forever, haven't they?"

"Och aye. The Dunbars have been in these parts fer as long as anybody can remember. So have the Kinnairds, mind ye. Now they say that Sir Jamie Kinnaird—"

"But haven't the Dunbars been here even longer?" He interrupted, regretting it the minute he'd spoken.

Mrs. MacClean drew herself up to her full four foot nine

and looked him straight in the eye. "The Kinnairds, Mr. Jack, are the *oldest* family in these parts. It's a known fact that Sir Peter's ancestor fought wi' Robert the Bruce himsel', and they were here long, long afore that," she said, waving the dishcloth and making the Battle of Falkirk sound like a recent event.

"Of course. I remember Peter telling me that," Jack lied.

"As for Lady Diana's family," she continued, warming to the theme, "it goes sae far back they canna' even tell nae more. The Dunbars have been here *almost* as long, but the Kinnairds were *definitely* here first." Her tone left no room for contradiction. "There's the legend of Rob Dunbar, of course—that was back in the rebellion in '45. He went to fight fer Bonnie Prince Charlie, although most of the Dunbars were loyal te' Wee German Geordie."

"Most interesting, Mrs. MacClean. You know, this pie is fit for Bonnie Prince Charlie himself!" He grinned at her in a shameless bid to return to her good graces.

"Och, yer a flatterer, Mr. Jack. I'm sure ye've eaten much finer dishes in those fancy hotels ye and Sir Peter are forever running around in. It seems to me neither of ye ever sit doon te' breathe."

"Fancier perhaps, Mrs. MacC., but certainly not finer."

She shook with laughter and then stood still, listening. "Is that a car I hear? Who the de'il could be coming here at this hour?"

The dogs were barking near the door. "I'd better gae and see. You get on wi' yer pudding."

"I'll come with you. I've just about finished anyway," he said, laying the napkin aside, not liking the idea of her going alone.

Mrs. MacClean laughed. "Och, dinna' worry, I'll be fine. There's nae criminals in these parts, Mr. Jack. This isna' America."

A knock sounded at the side door. Whisking off her apron, she hurried to answer.

"I'll be off, then. Good night, Mrs. MacC., and thanks. That was one great dinner."

Jack headed down the corridor to Peter's study. He pushed aside some papers and brochures on the desk, making space for himself. His eyes wandered around the busy room filled with old relics, faded photographs and ancient weapons that lay strewn amongst the paraphernalia and stacks of books. Peter was a hoarder, he remarked, smiling to himself as he watched Felix, the older of the three retrievers, scratching the threadbare hem of the drapes. "Hey, don't do that, Felix, that's destruction of property," he chided. Felix paid no attention.

He suddenly remembered that evening five years ago, in Hong Kong, when he'd sat with Peter at the bar of the Penn, celebrating their partnership. The two men had liked each other from the start. There was something frank and straightforward in Peter's ruddy face. The man stood straight as a ramrod when he was on the job, his military days in the Black Watch not forgotten. Jack's instinct had told him he was dealing with a straight shooter, and time had proved him right. Both their business and friendship had prospered.

Jack rose and poured himself a brandy from the decanter before selecting a Cohiba from the humidor. He gently rolled the tip in the amber liquid, Cuban style, before lighting it. The smoke spiraled up, climbing slowly on its narrow path toward the ceiling as he recalled their dinner at Gaddi's and the strange atmosphere of the evening. Both men had been subdued rather than elated, as though aware they were stepping into a new era. Suddenly Peter had turned to him and said, "Why don't you visit us at Dalkirk, Jack. I think you'd enjoy Scotland. We've some fairly de-

'cent shooting and fishing, and I'd like you to meet my wife, Diana, and the girls.''

Jack's thoughts were brusquely interrupted when the door burst open and Chloë entered, wrapped, like a snow queen, in a three-quarter-length sable coat and hat.

"Hello, Yank. I didn't know you were here." Diana's lovely young sister threw her Vuitton tote on the leather armchair, and removed her coat, then came over and gave him a hug.

"What brings you here out of the blue?" he asked, watching, amused, as she slowly wound down. Chloë was like a fashionable pixie, short and dark-haired, with bright blue eyes that sparkled mischievously in a pert face. It always surprised him how someone so small could have so much energy. "Would you like a drink?" he asked.

"Oh lovely! G and T please, I'm exhausted. I'm here on an emergency," she added, her expression suddenly sad. "Where are Peter and Di?"

"At your mother's for the girls' half-term break."

"That's right, I forgot. Why didn't you go?" She eyed him curiously.

"I didn't feel like it."

"Sorry, I just asked. I had a rotten journey by the way. There were no taxis at Turnhouse, so finally I rented a car, which I'll have to leave at the airport on the way back. But I had to come." She gave a heavy sigh.

"I've gathered that, but you still haven't told me why," Jack said patiently, handing her the drink before retreating once more behind the voluminous desk.

"Funeral." She grimaced, looking distressed. "My best friend's mother died. We've always been there for each other since boarding school. I popped up on the shuttle, and I'll leave tomorrow night or early the next day."

"Do you mean India's mom?"

"Yes...but how do you know that?" Chloë asked in astonishment.

"We've met."

"You didn't!" She laid the glass of gin and tonic down and leaned forward, herself once more. "You must tell me all about it."

"Nothing much to tell. I met her in the glen. She almost got herself shot. Should have been paying more attention."

"Are you telling me someone almost shot India?"

"I'm telling you I almost shot India."

"What on earth would you want to do that for?" She frowned blankly.

"Jeez, Chlo, it was a mistake, dammit." It irritated him even to think about it.

"Golly. What on earth did you do? What did she do?" Her bright blue eyes sparkled, rampant with curiosity, her romantic streak clearly at work.

"Threw her on the ground and raped her," he replied sarcastically.

"Don't be so rotten-tempered. Tell me the truth. I'll bet she was livid."

"She was—told me to get lost, said I was trespassing."

"That's India for you. Very much the grande dame when she sets her mind to it. Go on," she egged, her sadness momentarily swept aside.

"You're too darn nosy."

"No I'm not, I'm a journalist," Chloë replied with dignity. "It's my business to acquire information and relay it truthfully to the public."

"Chlo, you're a society gossip columnist, for goodness' sake. Next, you'll even have me believing you."

She ignored him and frowned. "So India left in a huff, I suppose, and then what?"

"And then she fainted, and I took her back home. How's that?"

"India, fainting?" Chloë shook her head in amazement, then said sadly, "It's probably due to all the strain she's going through, poor darling. But isn't she gorgeous?"

Of course she was, Jack acknowledged privately, but he was darned if he was about to admit it. "She's okay," he replied casually. "Not my type though, so don't start scheming. I don't need complications in my life now—or ever, for that matter. I'm fine the way I am," he said, pushing back his chair with a shove. For some reason, he didn't want to talk about the moments he'd spent with India—he was still trying to figure them out for himself.

"Poor, darling Indy. I can't believe you don't think Indy's gorgeous, all men do. She keeps them at arm's length, though."

"What's she doing with a best friend like you then?" he asked, taunting.

Chloë eyed him darkly and shook a finger at him. "Now I know why you're not married. Nobody could stand that obnoxious streak of yours. I'm getting myself another drink."

Jack grinned in response and gazed into the fire while Chloë poured herself a generous gin and tonic. He felt good at Dalkirk. It was perhaps less perfect in style than Dunbar, the house having been added to over the years with more attention paid to comfort than aesthetics, but it was very homey. There were lots of nooks and crannies where the little Kinnaird girls loved to play hide-and-seek. Diana's presence and good taste could be felt throughout in the small details, like the bowls of heather-scented pot-pourri or a small vase of flowers on a Chippendale table.

The house was just untidy enough to feel truly at ease in. Not like the penthouse, he realized gloomily, where everything stood dusted to perfection on the gleaming marble floors and glass shelves. He'd bought it for its spectacular view, its proximity to his office and because it was a great real estate opportunity. But a house was a house, he reflected, feeling suddenly nostalgic.

Scotland seemed to have carved a special niche in his heart, and ever since that first spontaneous visit, he'd become a regular guest here. Dalkirk was the closest thing to a home he'd known in years, for the Kinnairds had adopted him as part of the family, with Chloë teasing in a sisterly fashion and Diana hovering, her maternal instincts aroused.

As he watched Chloë climb back into the large leather sofa, curling her small legs beneath her, he realized how much he'd truly come to care for them all.

"A penny for 'em," Chloë said, watching him closely from under her thick dark lashes.

"Just thinking about you Kinnairds. You've been real friends to me," he said, pulling on the cigar.

"Jack, darling, we adore you. The old place wouldn't be the same without you!" She lifted her glass, smiling at him affectionately. "And I have someone to tease whenever I come home. Anyway, why wouldn't we be real friends?"

"You'd be surprised." He gave a harsh laugh. "Most people only invite me to their homes when they want something. They can't cut straight to the chase, so they go through the BS of having me to their home, wining and dining me, before getting to the point. But the first time Peter invited me here, he genuinely wanted me to come, and I felt it. You guys have made me feel at home ever since."

"Well, you are rather a decent chap. If you weren't so odiously overbearing, I'd have a go at you myself," she said teasingly.

"Forget it. I'm a rolling stone."

"You pretend to be but I don't believe you are at heart.

You can be quite sweet at times, when you want,'' she added perceptively.

"Chloë, give me a break. I've had a long day. I only got back from Dunbar a couple of hours ago. Serena drove me.''

"What, that horrible creature?''

"No shit!''

"Swear away, don't worry about me!'' Chloë said blithely. "Though I agree with you about Serena. Behind all that elegance and class, India's a very lovely, sensitive person. And a lot of fun, too, when she wants,'' she continued as though the subject hadn't changed.

"She seems to know her business back to front.''

"We *have* been observant, haven't we?'' she teased. "What was Serena doing there anyway? Getting ready for the spoils, no doubt.''

"Looks like it. Apparently she's inherited Dunbar.''

"That's very possible. Lady El may have left it to her. Maybe she thought Serena might as well have Dunbar. After all, Indy's never really been attached to the place. I'll go over early tomorrow to give her moral support. She'll need it with Serena around. By the way, that brings something to mind,'' she said, a mischievous grin replacing the sad look of seconds earlier. "What happened that night at the party in September? I saw the two of you slipping upstairs.''

"That's none of your business. I will only say that it was a regrettable incident that I'm not proud of. Anyway, a nice girl like you shouldn't be talking these things over with guys.''

"It's not guys, it's only you,'' she said disdainfully.

"Thanks a lot. Just don't you start opening your big mouth to Peter and Di.''

"Promise.'' She crossed her heart, looking pensive all

of a sudden. Jack watched as her eyes turned misty, and she gazed into the flames.

"New man in your life, Chlo?"

"How did you know?" she exclaimed, almost spilling her drink.

"It's written all over you."

"Jack," she said, eyeing him seriously, "I think this time it's the real thing."

"Shoot."

"He's...different, you know, not like the other chaps I meet."

Jack rolled his eyes. "That's what you said about the last three."

"There! You see? I knew I shouldn't have said anything, now you'll be horrid," Chloë exclaimed crossly.

"He's bought the magazine. He's diversifying his interests," she added grandly.

"And what are those?"

"He's in oil and all sorts of things. He's from Texas."

"What does he want with a gossip magazine?" Jack asked, curious.

"He wants to expand it. In fact, he's offered me the job of chief editor in New York," she said casually, knotting the fringe of the cushion. "I don't know, though. I love London, but everything is happening over there. Lots of Brits in the business on Madison Ave., you know."

"Do you come in the package with the paper?"

"What a horrid thing to say," she exclaimed, aiming the cushion at him. He dodged it. She brooded for a second then asked, "Did Indy look miserable? I talked to her yesterday, and she sounded pretty down in the dumps. Not her usual self at all. Lady El was so super, we'll all miss her."

"I don't know." He replied, his tone noncommittal, "I learned about her mother's death by pure fluke. If I hadn't put my foot in it, she probably wouldn't have mentioned it. She was the perfect hostess.''

"Typical!" Chloë exploded. "I wish she'd loosen up. It was that marriage to that prick, Christian, that made her clam up like that."

"She's married?'' He felt an inexplicable stab of disappointment.

"Not anymore, thank God," she added darkly, taking a long, thoughtful sip of her drink.

"How long were they married?''

"A couple of years.''

"What happened?''

"Now who's being nosy?''

"Mere curiosity.''

Chloë frowned. "He dropped her like a hot potato for a German heiress, a Princess von something-or-other, when he found out that Lady El had pretty well got through Indy's father's fortune. Hopeless with money, poor Lady El. I can't think why India's father didn't leave it in trust for them, but anyway, he didn't. So that was that as far as the dashing Comte de Monfort was concerned.'' She looked up, her eyes full of anger. "The coward didn't have the guts to tell her outright. He wrote her a long rambling letter—he even had the bloody nerve to say he owed it to his family to preserve the family fortunes and the purity of their lineage. Can you believe it?''

"What a jerk," he said, feeling unaccountably angry on India's behalf.

"Yes, and now all she ever does is work. I could murder Christian for what he did. It was the last straw. It affected her more than she'll admit. That's why she's thrown herself into La Dolce Vita so intensely. That and the fact she needed to make money or she would have lost Chantemerle.''

Jack listened intently, dying to ask more, but knowing it would only excite Chloë's curiosity.

She yawned. "I'd better go and phone Indy, poor darling, then I'm off to bed. I'm exhausted."

"Good night, brat." Jack rose and handed her the fur coat.

"Brat indeed," Chloë sniffed as she picked up her bag.

"You need a guy who can keep you in line, young lady."

Chloë stuck her tongue out at him and left.

Jack turned back into the room, smiling. He picked up a book left open on the table next to the sofa and glanced at it. It was the latest Grisham. That should keep him busy for the evening.

Making sure the fire was out, he turned off the lights. Then he walked into the hall and slowly up the main staircase, his mind straying back to India. By the time he reached his room, he'd persuaded himself there was nothing unusual about his interest. It was just an interesting set of circumstances and frankly, he'd feel sorry for anyone in her situation—it was only natural.

He glanced at the book wryly. It was a long time since he'd needed anything to keep his mind from straying to a woman. *Don't get involved, Jack. It'll only mean trouble,* a little voice inside him warned. But his gut told him otherwise, and Jack always followed his gut.

3

The visceral attachment to Dunbar that India was experiencing had caught her wholly by surprise. Considering she'd never lived or spent any long periods of time here, she was unable to fathom why everything felt so strangely familiar. She hadn't been back much since her childhood, yet she felt at home, as though part of her being had remained fettered here all these many years. It was like a colorful tapestry and she a silken thread, woven into the intricate pattern that reached deep into Dunbar's soul.

She wandered through the picture gallery and gazed up at the portrait of Lady Helen, her great-grandmother. Something in the soft hazel eyes spoke of wisdom and understanding, as though Lady Helen were telling her not to worry, to go on her way in peace. India found herself smiling back.

Moving silently in the early-morning hush, she went from room to room, etching each detail to memory. This was a special moment, possibly one of the last she would ever spend here.

The thought of the estate being sold made her cringe. Walking through the house with Jack yesterday had brought home just how much Dunbar really meant to her, and she wondered for the umpteenth time what its final destiny would be. Even if Serena inherited, would she be prepared to keep up the property, to put in the time and work it would take? She considered her half sister for a moment and sighed. Probably not. If the past was anything to go by, Serena would sell and be out of there before she could say Jack Robinson.

She reached her mother's bedroom, gently twisting the handle of the large oak door. The tranquillity within the lavender-scented room remained intact, as though Lady Elspeth were merely out for a while. The bottle of Yardley's scent she'd perfumed her handkerchiefs with stood on the skirted dressing table. Beside it stood the Charles of the Ritz face creams, next to the crystal container of cotton wool.

India trailed her fingers nostalgically over the chintz counterpane, stopping to gaze around the room, reliving for a heartfelt moment the ever-present images of her mother. Then she looked through the frosty panes at the fresh snow covering the lawn. The white blanket shimmered under the silver rays of winter sunshine, playing a silent game of hide-and-seek with the ponderous clouds traveling south toward the hills beyond. It was a peaceful sight and she stood for a while gazing at the Dunbar oak, standing regal and alone.

William, the first Dunbar to settle here, had planted the tree in 1280. Suddenly she remembered her mother repeating his pledge, which had been handed down from generation to generation: While the oak tree stands, a Dunbar will always walk this land.

India drew her eyes away sadly. If the property were sold, William's vow would be broken. The scene reminded her of the Constables and other paintings hanging on the drawing-room walls. One in particular came to mind, and she wondered how many of them would have to be sold to cover the taxes and death duties she knew would be crippling.

As she was about to leave, India caught sight of the small writing desk Lady Elspeth had used for her private correspondence. An uncapped fountain pen lay on a sheet of half-written writing paper. She crossed the room and picked up what appeared to be an unfinished letter, realizing with a start that it was addressed to her.

My dearest India,
I am sending this off to you today, for I am most distressed. I am suffering from a dreadful dilemma and need to speak to you urgently. Please come to Dunbar as quickly as you can. I'd call, but I'm afraid I will be overheard. You need to be aware—

The letter was cut short, as though Lady Elspeth had been interrupted. India frowned, glancing at the date. The letter had been written on the day of her mother's death. What could possibly have been troubling Lady Elspeth so deeply? What was this fear of being overheard? India took the note and, folding it carefully, slipped it into her jacket pocket, frowning. She couldn't allow herself to think about this now. Later, after the funeral, she'd try to piece things together.

The house was still quiet as she descended the main staircase and headed to the breakfast room, trying to shake off the troubling sensation the note had left.

Reaching the door, she took a deep breath and straightened the skirt of her black Chanel suit, hoping Serena was still in bed, and that she might have the place to herself before the onslaught later that morning.

But no such luck awaited her. Serena lounged at the table, one leg flung carelessly over the arm of the next chair. She looked up as India entered.

"Good morning." She waved languidly to a chair at the table and lit a cigarette. "Have some breakfast, God knows we'll need it. Kathleen was in here a few minutes ago bumbling on about Ian and that lawyer Ramsey being here at ten. You know, I don't know how Mummy stood Kathleen around her the whole time. She can be such a bore. The way she goes on, you'd think she owned the place," she added resentfully.

India murmured good morning, then sat down, listening to Serena with half an ear. She wasn't hungry, but the last thing she needed was her tummy rumbling throughout the reading of the will.

She opted for toast and went to the sideboard, placing two pieces of bread in the toaster. Serena seemed preoccupied, but over the years India had become used to her sudden changes of mood. One minute Serena could be effusive, the next sarcastic. Now she seemed far away.

India watched the toast pop up, thinking how odd it was to have the same parent, yet feel so distant. It made her suddenly sad, especially now that only they remained.

"Toast," Serena exclaimed suddenly, making India jump. "Not a bad idea. Pop in a piece for me, will you?" She stubbed out the last of her cigarette in an empty glass of orange juice, and reached down her leg. "I tripped on that wretched carpet in the hall. It's all ragged at the edge. Almost broke my leg. In fact, I think I've twisted my ankle." She grimaced and rubbed her shin gingerly. "Funny finding Jack Buchanan here," she continued as though the subject were one and the same. "Do you know he hardly even thanked me when I dropped him off at Dalkirk? I thought it was damn nice of me to go out on such a filthy night. Some people are thoroughly bad-mannered—but I suppose they've never been taught otherwise. By the way, what did you think of him?" She glanced at India. "He's

Peter Kinnaird's partner, you know. Stinking rich, of course. I'm surprised someone hasn't nabbed him yet.''

"Perhaps he's involved," India remarked, returning to the table and handing Serena the silver toast rack.

"Not him! He's very much the ladies' man. *That* I can assure you," she said with a sly smirk. "Not your style though, I shouldn't think. He's more the *let's get straight to it* type, which I'm sure you'd disapprove of."

"It's nothing to me what or who he is," India replied indifferently.

"Just don't get your fingers burned, darling. I saw the way he was eyeing you. He's tough as nails, you know, but between you and me, he's a damn good fuck."

India set her teacup back in the saucer with a snap. "Serena, I don't care if he's God's gift to women. All that concerns me right now is Mummy's funeral and what's happening later on this morning. I think you might show a little more respect."

"Oh, la-di-da. Excuse me for offending your sensibilities." Serena cast her a sarcastic look. "Anyway, what matters now is getting the will business dealt with," she exclaimed in a very different tone.

"Do you have any idea how things stand?"

"No. Ramsey keeps harking on. He says we mustn't mention the difficult straits the estate's in. As if I would. I'm the last person to want a rumpus. I'd be out on the street if it weren't for the bank loaning me money because I stand to inherit Dunbar." She lit another cigarette and mused. "I'm going to have enough to do here as it is without a bunch of panicked tenants and staff on my hands." Serena flicked back a strand of her long blond hair with a disdainful sniff.

India said nothing. She knew very little about the intricacies of running an estate, but imagined they must not be easy. Serena spoke as though she already owned the place, and India wondered with a pang if she'd be a good caretaker. It would make sense if Serena inherited. After all, she was a part of this closed little social enclave, where she herself was—or at least had been made to feel—an outcast.

"The home farm has to be dealt with. As for the shoot— But I shouldn't be boring you with things that you know nothing about. I'll just have to get on with it, I suppose— unless I decide to sell," she added casually.

"Sell?" India asked, dismayed despite herself. "But there have been Dunbars here for over seven hundred years, Serena. I gather things aren't in great shape financially, but surely everything should be done to try and hold on to the property. I think that's what Mummy would have expected."

"I don't know if I'm prepared to go to all the trouble and expense of keeping the place. Plus, think of the money I'd make. *You* don't have to worry about that sort of thing, do you?" Serena raised a haughty eyebrow.

Up until that morning India hadn't thought seriously about the will, her mind too consumed with the shock of her mother's death, but her hackles rose at Serena's blithe disregard for the estate she apparently already assumed was hers. "If you mean, can I get by with what I make? Yes, I can. It's taken me a few years but things are running pretty smoothly at La Dolce Vita, and this last job in Brazil finally got rid of the mortgage on Chantemerle. But that has nothing to do with this. I don't know that *I* want to sell Dunbar."

Serena looked astonished. "Who says you'll have anything to do with it? You don't really think Mummy would expect me to share Dunbar with *you?*"

"I see no reason why not," India answered levelly. "You seem to forget that I have as much of her blood as you."

"Yes, unfortunately. Mummy was a traitor to me and to her class. She had no business marrying your father, and much less having you. She *owes* me Dunbar."

India controlled her temper with an effort, finally understanding Serena's veiled sarcastic comments over the past years. She stood up and went to the fireplace.

"It must be lovely to waltz through life so completely convinced of one's innate superiority, Serena, but forgive me if I don't curtsy and kiss your ring. You have no right to speak to me like that," she said, her voice controlled.

"I'll tell you exactly what gives me the right. I was born before you and my father was a nobleman. You are nothing but a bad mistake, one that Mummy regretted but was too proud to do anything about. I suppose you think that if you inherit Dunbar you'll become one of us. But you won't, you know. You'll always be an outcast." She gave a short, harsh laugh.

"Surely you don't think I care what society thinks of me?" India gave an astonished laugh. "I stopped worrying about fitting in years ago. What I'm worried about is Dunbar, about the land and the people, like Mrs. Walker and old Tompson, who've worked here for thirty-some years and now have nowhere to go. Surely that must mean *something* to you, Serena?" India struggled to master her fury, swallowing the bile that rose bitterly in her throat and clenching her fists till her knuckles turned white. "And as for rights, I am as much a part of this family as you, whether you like it or not. This is the home of my ancestors, too, and there is no reason why I shouldn't have exactly as much say when it comes to Dunbar's future."

"You're either nuts, India, or you simply don't understand these things." Serena shook her head pityingly and reached for more coffee.

"Good morning, ladies." The sound of a guttural male voice made India spin on her heel. Maxi, Serena's German boyfriend, stood in the doorway, pasty and stiff with his formal bow and immaculate dress. His blond hair was cut short, with geometrical precision, and slicked back from his forehead. He'd obviously had his ear glued to the door, she realized angrily.

She looked him over, studying the supercilious twist of his lips, the watery blue eyes void of expression, wondering, not for the first time, what Serena could possibly see in him. And she refused to discuss their family affairs in front of strangers.

"I'm going upstairs," she announced, not bothering to conceal her dislike.

"Temper, temper," Serena murmured as India prepared to leave. She turned to Maxi, laughing. "India actually thinks Mummy might have left her Dunbar," she exclaimed with an amused smirk as he moved over to the table and sat down.

At least he had the grace to appear uncomfortable, India noted. But she didn't like the ease with which he settled at the table, looking for all the world as though he owned the place.

"Don't be late for the reading of the will," Serena threw at her. "A mere formality I'm sure, but one that has to be gone through. Then we'll know *exactly* how things stand, won't we, India dear?"

"Yes, we shall," India replied curtly, staring Serena straight in the eye. "But let me make one thing perfectly clear. He's not to be here for the reading of the will. This is a family affair."

"How dare you speak like that to poor Maxi, when he was so kind to Mummy." Serena's voice rose angrily.

"Hmm. Tell me, Serena, why was Mummy so anxious for me to come here? Why did she write to me, requesting I come in person?"

"I have no idea what you're talking about, India. But I'll have whoever I want in this house."

"Not until we know whose house it is." She turned and faced Maxi, who stared at her with undisguised disdain. "I think you've both been trying to pressure Mummy to sell Dunbar, and that's why she was so upset."

Serena rose abruptly, and the two women faced each other. "Don't you dare speak to me or any of my friends like that. Pressuring Mummy indeed." Serena leaned forward, blond strands falling wildly about her face. "You say one more word and—"

"I've taken about as much rudeness from you as I'm prepared to stand, Serena," India replied, knowing she was losing her temper, but beyond caring. "I won't have you insulting Mummy's memory on the day of her funeral with your abominable behavior. At least you could *pretend* you care."

"How dare you? How dare you speak to me in that tone?" Serena's voice rose to an even higher pitch.

"I should have spoken to you like this years ago, but I never did because I didn't want to upset Mummy, and I had the misbegotten idea that someday we might actually get on together."

Serena cast India an angry look and returned to her seat at the head of the table.

"Serena, darling, calm down, my dear." Maxi walked over and placed a hand on her shoulder.

"I'm sure you understand that this is a family affair and that you have no business here. It's nothing personal," India said, addressing him as calmly as she could.

"He's not leaving. I have every right to have him here. We're getting married, after all. At least *I* can hold on to a man."

"You're wasting your time, Serena. I refuse to rise to your bait." India turned on her heel and walked from the room, closing the door loudly behind her.

She sighed with relief, unclenching her fists, and headed

quickly up the stairs and along the passage to her bedroom. There she lay down on the bed, determined to calm down before the reading of the will, careful not to wrinkle her clothes. The Chanel suit was special, a gift from Lady Elspeth a few years back when money had been no object. India smiled. Her mother had always been so chic, she'd want her to look her best today.

She thought suddenly of Jack and what Serena had said, wondering if he had slept with her. And what did it matter if he had? It was really none of her business. Today she had vital issues to deal with, issues which could change her life, and the lives of those who had served her family so faithfully. She closed her eyes and breathed deeply, conscious that all she could do was wait and prepare to deal with the worst.

Mr. Ramsey, the gray-suited family solicitor, put on his tortoiseshell glasses and addressed the room at large.

India sat on the sofa next to her cousin Kathleen, who, over the past few years, had been Lady Elspeth's faithful companion. At forty-seven, Kathleen was plump and cheerful, her rosy cheeks wide and round below a pair of twinkling hazel eyes. Her hair was short, nondescript and graying, and the faded tweed skirt and jacket she wore were as threadbare as the sofa they were sitting on. Mrs. Walker sat on India's left, sniffing now and then into a large handkerchief. Ian, India's second cousin, sat opposite, his thin frame stiff, his dim blue eyes glancing disapprovingly at Serena, who sat next to him looking bored with the whole proceeding. She obviously considered this a triviality in the bigger scheme of her taking possession of Dunbar. Thankfully, there was no sign of Maxi.

When the family arrived, Kathleen had assumed the role of hostess, warmly welcoming Mr. Ramsey and suggesting suitable seating arrangements. She'd asked Mrs. Walker to bring out some of her famous scones, and then busily set about pouring tea for everyone. Serena had sulked in the corner of the sofa, pretending India didn't exist. Not that it mattered, she reflected impatiently. After the morning's scene, she hardly wanted to acknowledge the relationship herself.

After the tea and scones had been consumed, a hush fell over the room as the solicitor cleared his throat.

"We are assembled here today for the reading of the last will and testament of Lady Elspeth Caroline Moncrieff, formerly Hamilton, nee Dunbar." Mr. Ramsey's voice droned on for several minutes as he read through the legal formalities.

Some special bequests were made to Kathleen and Ian, and also to the old family retainers, Mrs. Walker and old Tompson.

India wondered if Mrs. Walker would want to stay on now that her mother was gone. She'd been very fond of Lady Elspeth. India glanced down at the gnarled hands clutching the hankie and her heart sank. It would kill Mrs. Walker not to be fussing around the kitchen, scolding, making scones and worrying about what was happening in the village.

When the main section of the will had been reached, Mr. Ramsey peered at India and Serena over the rim of his glasses.

"To my daughters, Serena Helen Hamilton and India Dunbar Moncrieff, I bequeath my entire estate, to be divided equally between them. Dunbar House, and the property pertaining to it, shall be owned and operated by them both. In the event one of my daughters wishes to retain ownership of the aforesaid property, she will acquire the other's share at fair market value."

Serena sat up with a jerk. Rising abruptly, she interrupted Mr. Ramsey. "What do you mean *both?* You've read that wrong. Here, give it to me!'' She rushed forward, grabbing the will from the astonished Mr. Ramsey's hand.

"Serena!'' Ian jumped up. "Control yourself, for goodness' sake!''

"My, this is quite an unexpected turn of events,'' Kathleen said distractedly, her face very pale. She stared shrewdly at Serena and then laid a hand on India's knee. "I've always thought she had a loose screw, but this…''

India sat perfectly still, oblivious to Serena's ranting, letting the information sink in. She owned Dunbar—albeit in co-ownership with Serena—but it was hers. Elation ran through her as the full meaning of Mr. Ramsey's words registered. She did belong here after all.

"I'll contest it, I tell you! I'll get it revoked, do you hear?'' Serena waved the sheaf of papers wildly. "Mummy would never have left Dunbar to *her!*''

Mr. Ramsey spoke up. "Lady Serena, this is a legal proceeding, I must ask you to be seated so that we may continue in an orderly fashion. These matters can be discussed at another—''

"Oh, shut up! You connived this with her. You're to blame, you—''

"Serena, that's quite enough. Control yourself.'' Ian took a firm grip of her arm. "If you can't get a hold on yourself, I think you'd better leave. Your behavior's deplorable,'' he added in a low voice as he conducted her back to the sofa. "I'm sorry about this, Ramsey. But I think we may proceed without further fear of interruption.'' He cast a meaningful look at Serena as she sat down, disgruntled.

The reading of the will continued with the disposition of special items of jewelry Lady Elspeth had been particularly fond of.

India's eyes watered as her mother's final bequests were made. "To my dearest daughter India, I leave my Van

Cleef & Arpels diamond necklace and bow brooch, the sapphire and diamond Chaumet ring given to me by her father on the occasion of our engagement..." Everything had been very fairly divided between the two girls. India wondered how her mother had been able to hold on to such expensive jewelry. The Marchese probably, she realized fondly. Giordano, Lady El's longtime friend and admirer, would have died twice rather than allow Mummy to part with her jewelry.

The forbidding look on Mr. Ramsey's face told her there was bad news to come. Maybe the necklace and the brooch would have to be sold, however much it would hurt her to part with them. She knew Mummy would understand. Dunbar and its retainers were more important than anything now.

Kathleen was talking rapidly, her face somewhat strained. "Serena's livid at the way things have been left," she commented in a loud whisper. "Silly girl, to think she deserves Dunbar all for herself. Now she's joint owner with you and doesn't have the money to buy you out. Serves her jolly well right. Are you in a position to buy her portion?" she inquired casually.

India shook her head. "No. We'll have to make do as best we can."

"You can count on me for any help you may need, my dear. As you well know, I was very fond of your dear mama. I feel dreadful that I wasn't here when she died. Of all the silly times to have been visiting Great-Aunt Moira." She shook her head sadly. India noticed that she seemed even paler than before. What a shock her mother's death must have been for Kathleen.

"Thanks." India turned and smiled, genuinely grateful for the kind offer. "Of course, you will stay on here, won't you, Kathleen?"

"That's so sweet and generous of you, India." Kathleen

squeezed her hand fondly, her eyes bright with unshed tears. "I hope I'm not being too proud when I say I know the place better than anyone. I believe I may be of some help to you. Of course, it's no easy task to run an estate. God only knows what I would have done if my father had lived and I'd inherited," she said with a sigh.

Mr. Ramsey finished speaking and Serena began grumbling again. "She had no right to leave things this way. I mean, let's face it, we all know India isn't one of us. She can't possibly want Dunbar. She wouldn't have the slightest clue how to manage it. She shouldn't even be here in the first place!"

"Stop making a bloody fool of yourself, Serena," Ian exclaimed, his face white with anger. "Aunt El had every right to leave things however she pleased, as Ramsey here will tell you. Whether you agree or not is irrelevant."

"That's correct, Sir Ian. By Scottish law Lady Elspeth could leave her property to whomever she pleased, for there is no entail on the property any longer. That ended when the late Sir Thomas died, and there were no more male heirs alive to inherit. Now, if Lady Kathleen's father had outlived Sir Thomas, then things would have been different and the entail would have ended with her." Mr. Ramsey shook his head. "To think he died only three days before his poor brother. A terrible thing it was." He hesitated an instant, then continued. "This will was rewritten only a few days before Lady Elspeth's death. I came here myself to make the changes."

"I knew you were responsible for this," Serena said, turning on him again angrily. This time Ian grabbed her by the arm and marched her from the room.

A general sigh of relief followed Serena's departure.

"Well! That gets her out of the way. So much for the theatrics. Pay no attention to her, India. The will is perfectly legal, as Mr. Ramsey has said. She's just jealous,"

Kathleen said decisively. "All the Hamiltons are mad as hatters. Serena's no exception, believe me." She pressed India's hand again in a kindly fashion and smiled bravely.

Kathleen's forthright remarks helped alleviate the tension in the room, and India was thankful for her cousin's support. It was true that Kathleen knew as much as anybody about Dunbar, and her assistance would be invaluable in the months to follow.

Ian came back, and the screeching of wheels on gravel confirmed his next words. "She's gone to Edinburgh to consult a solicitor. Shocking behavior, I'm afraid. The poor girl's lost it," he said, shaking his head. "I'm so sorry, Ramsey, I don't know what's come over her. The way she spoke to you was scandalous. I shall see to it she apologizes."

"Och, don't worry, Sir Ian, I've seen this kind of thing before. It's very sad really. People create expectations they never should have had in the first place, and are upset when faced with the truth."

"Very true, Ramsey. I think Serena already considered herself Lady of Dunbar. A dashed nerve, really, when you think of it," Kathleen commented dryly.

"I agree. And don't you let yourself be jostled around by her, young lady," Ian continued, pointing at India. "You have every right to be here and she knows it."

India smiled at him, appreciating the kindness and solidarity that her cousins were showing. She realized, with a touch of regret, that perhaps her father's prejudice had kept her from developing some wonderful family relationships.

But she was an outsider in their world, and realistic enough to know that finding the true roots and home she'd always longed for was an illusion. It was a society that would not easily accept her. She might not like Serena's words, but there was a disturbing ring of truth to them that made her doubly appreciative for Kathleen's and Ian's offers of support.

"Thanks, Ian, and you, too, Kathleen, you've both been wonderful. But, in a way, Serena's right. Maybe Mummy should have left Dunbar to her. She probably is far more able to deal with matters than I am."

"Hogwash! All she wants is to be able to say she owns the place or to sell it. She doesn't give a damn about the estate or the people on it. Serena is only interested in one person and that," Ian said flatly, "is Serena."

"I'm afraid you're right," Kathleen agreed. "For as long as I've known her she's been a selfish, egocentric *you know what.* I think the whole thing goes deeper. The Hamiltons are an ancient family, but they're poor as church mice. Serena lived off her father's trust and Lady El's generosity, and hasn't done a day's work since she stopped modeling. I think she planned to sell Dunbar. Now that India's involved, that won't be the case, will it?"

"You may be right," Ian agreed thoughtfully. "If that fellow she runs about with had any say, she'd be up and selling like a shot. The von Lowendorf family never got back on their feet financially after the war, and Maxi seems to have a taste for wealthy, single women. Kath, you remember that rich widow from Manchester he was chasing before he hooked up with Serena?" He gave a mirthless laugh. "Well, if you do decide to sell, India, she'll have to content herself with half the proceeds."

"I hope that won't be necessary. I feel we should do our utmost to keep Dunbar," India murmured.

"I don't understand how she ever got this insane notion that Dunbar belonged to her in the first place," Kathleen exclaimed.

"Wishful thinking," Ian replied grimly.

The party got up and headed to the drawing room, where a cold luncheon was being served. The meeting with Mr.

Ramsey concerning practical matters would have to wait till after the funeral, which was to be conducted later in the hall. Afterward, they would drive Lady Elspeth to her final resting place in the little graveyard on the hill, and India would be left to deal with the future as best she could.

"I won't have it," Serena exploded, steering her old Volvo along George Street at a spanking pace.

"Calm down, Serena. This isn't a time for nerves. It is a time for thinking," Maxi replied soberly. Things were not going as planned.

"What do you mean, calm down? Something has to be done about this, dammit."

"We'll find a solution, my dear," he said in an even tone. "There is always a solution. Remember, revenge is a meal best eaten cold. And so it shall be." He gave a crack of cheerless laughter.

Serena took her eyes off the road and glanced at him crossly. "Well, I hope you've got some bright ideas, because except for contesting the will outright—and from all I've gathered it's legal—there's not much I *can* do."

"You'd be surprised. Let things take their course. It's still early. Things need to fall into place. In the meantime, we'll be thinking, watching, observing. The secret to success lies in the details, not in the obvious."

His quiet voice calmed her, and she began to think that perhaps he was right. "Stupid creature. It's not fair—"

"Hush. Be very careful what you say. Even moving cars can have ears." Maxi took a surreptitious glance around, as though some device might be hidden in the ancient upholstery of the Volvo.

"Oh, come on, Maxi, do stop being ridiculous. This is Scotland, not a spy movie." She veered down Frederick Street, annoyed with the traffic. "I suppose I'll have to get back for the funeral. And *you're* jolly well coming," she added. "I'm damned if I'll have her dictating who comes and goes from Dunbar. Who the hell does she think she is anyway?"

Maxi stayed silent for a few moments as they drove along Prince's Street and past the Scots monument, where Serena was obliged to come to an abrupt halt for a group of tourists in bright anoraks, waiting to cross the road.

"I think it would be wiser to placate her for the moment," Maxi said thoughtfully.

"What do you mean?" Serena almost rear-ended the car in front as they passed Marks & Spencer. "I'll have whomever I choose in my own house. I—"

"I know, I understand," Maxi soothed, "but you can't antagonize her. Let her think you're playing her game. Make up the quarrel with her. Remember, you need her agreement if you're going to sell. Don't overdo it, though, or she'll suspect something," he added. "Just enough to let her relax. She will, you'll see. She's that type, stupid and unsuspecting. It's often so among the bourgeois class. If you're intelligent about this, *meine liebe,* you can wrap her up nicely."

"What about Buchanan? What if he makes an offer? We'll need her to agree." Serena ground her teeth audibly, furious at the situation. "I can't believe Mummy did this behind my back."

"A mere contretemps," he said with a disdainful flick of his long smooth fingers. "Nothing that can't be dealt with, my dear. I think you should go to the funeral and play the game. Be indifferent but not unpleasant. After that, we'll see."

"Are you sure?" Serena queried doubtfully, casting him a resentful glance. "You said everything was going to work out fine and look what a pickle that's left me in," she finished bitterly.

"You've lost a small battle. What matters is who wins the war. As long as she believes she has the upper hand you're fine. As for the American, you've already set things in motion by suggesting he come and visit the house. Just make sure you have all the information he requested on hand. Americans like to work fast and efficiently, which could be to our advantage if you play your cards right. He won't suspect anything since you made it clear you'd inherited the property. By the time any concrete offer is made—if he makes one—the solution will have presented itself, believe me." He squeezed her hand with a reassuring smile.

"It goes against the grain but so be it." Serena shrugged and shifted gears without pressing her foot down properly on the clutch. Maxi grimaced. "I'll drop you off at the hotel, and go back to Dunbar." She glanced at her watch. "I haven't much time if I'm going to make the funeral."

"Excellent. Don't worry about me, I'll be waiting—and thinking."

"Yes, well, you'd better do a lot of *that*. The whole thing's most unsatisfactory, and damn inconvenient."

"Serena, again, I have to warn you. You can never be too careful," Maxi urged her anxiously. "The less said, the better."

"Oh, all right," Serena mumbled irritably. Everything was getting on her nerves today, including Maxi. She waited impatiently as he got out of the car, not bothering to wave goodbye as she weaved her way back into the midday traffic, her mind set on her plans. He was probably right. It would be unwise to make decisions in the heat of the moment.

The image of India, all natural grace and determination, made her swear under her breath. The girl's very existence was an insult, and she hated her mother for it.

* * *

India sat at the dressing table, pulling the hairbrush through her hair, a wan face staring back at her from the oval mirror.

Dunbar. She'd never actually thought of owning it, yet now the remote piece of her mother's world had become an integral part of her existence, one whose future would have to be decided.

Only when she'd met with Mr. Ramsey after the funeral would she know the truth of how things stood.

"Indy?" Chloë peeked round the door, and then rushed across the room. The two girls embraced, holding each other tight.

"Thanks for coming, Chlo." India smiled at her through eyes filled with unshed tears.

"You didn't think I'd stay away, did you? I'm so sorry, Indy. We'll all miss Lady El," Chloë said, a quiver in her voice. "Here, take this." She handed India one of the glasses that she was balancing precariously.

"Oh, thanks. I can use this."

"I don't think Lady El would mind, do you?" Chloë asked wistfully.

"Not in the least. She'd be the first to recommend it," India said with a sad smile, taking a long sip of the gin and tonic before sitting down again on the stool. "God, Chlo, what a mess this whole thing is."

Chloë sat down on the bed and threw off her shoes. "Tell me what's been happening. Have they read the will yet?"

"Yes. Serena and I have inherited everything fifty-fifty. She's livid, of course. Thinks she should get the lot. She seems to believe that her noble origins give her special rights."

"I thought she—" Chloë stopped abruptly and frowned.

"You thought what?" India swiveled on the padded chintz stool and looked questioningly at her friend.

"No, nothing. I just thought perhaps Lady El might leave Dunbar to Serena and you all the Swiss stuff. You've never been very connected here."

"You're right, but it's the oddest thing, Chlo. Ever since I've been back, I've had this feeling. I can't quite explain it, but I feel as though I'm a part of the place." She shook her head and glanced at her dear friend. "It's uncanny."

"What about Switzerland?" Chloë asked, her expression serious.

"Pretty well gone as far as I can gather. Mummy's house is mortgaged to the hilt—apparently to pay for debts here. I think all that's left is her jewelry." India shrugged sadly. "And that'll probably have to go, too, if we're going to keep this place up."

"Are you seriously thinking of keeping Dunbar?" Chloë asked, looking at India curiously.

"I don't know yet." India frowned thoughtfully. "I haven't a clue how things stand. After the funeral we'll have a talk with the solicitor to find out the true state of affairs, but I don't think they're good. By the way, keep that to yourself. We don't want a panic."

Chloë nodded soberly. "Indy, you'd better think this one over very carefully. It's a huge responsibility to take on, you know. I see Peter and Di. God knows what things would be like if Peter weren't so successful. Any money that comes out of the estate seems to go straight back in, and more." She sighed, meeting her friend's eyes, her own filled with sympathy. "It's rotten for you, darling. I just wish there was something I could do to help."

"You being here today is enough, Chlo. You've no idea how alone I've felt the last few days, though Ian and Kathleen have been absolutely super."

"That's something at least," Chloë answered gloomily. "I can't believe you're thinking of keeping Dunbar though. I don't think it's very realistic."

"Probably not, but I'm sick of always being realistic, Chlo. My life seems to consist of being practical, always doing what has to be done. Anyway, this is more a gut thing. When Ramsey read the will and told me I had inherited half the place, I felt all warm inside." She smiled sheepishly at her friend. "You'll probably think I'm crazy, and maybe it's wishful thinking, but I have the feeling that I'm meant to be here."

"That doesn't surprise me. You've always had a mystical side to you, Indy. And I wish you good luck if it's what you think you should do. By the way, I saw Jack last night. He told me he'd met you."

India met her gaze and smiled. "We had a bit of a run-in, did he tell you?"

"Sounded quite exciting to me. He's rather good-looking, don't you think?"

"I suppose so. A bit full of himself though. Acts as though he's the bee's knees."

"Oh, come on, Indy, it's me you're talking to, remember?" Chloë looked at India and made a face.

"Okay. On a scale of one to ten, I suppose you could say he's an eight. Satisfied?"

"Eight? You must be balmy. The man's an Adonis, as rich as Croesus, plus dreadfully sexy."

"If he's so great, why don't you have a go at him yourself then?" India inquired.

"I love him dearly, but like a brother. We've become very fond of him over at Dalkirk. A bit like that stray Diana picked up in the village…"

"Really, Chlo, how can you compare the man to a stray dog?" India laughed weakly and shook her head.

"Well, he is, in a way. Alone, if you know what I mean. He lost his wife twelve years ago. It must have been awfully sad, though he never talks about it."

"Actually, he told me about his wife."

"He did?" Chloë raised a quizzical eyebrow and climbed off the bed. "He's usually pretty closed about that." She glanced at her watch. "I suppose I'd better go back downstairs. Don't be long, Indy, will you? After all, you're the hostess now." She put her shoes back on and went over to give India a kiss. "You're not alone, you know. We're all worried about you."

The two girls hugged again. "Thanks for being here. You've no idea how much it means to me. Better take this glass with you, Chlo. I don't know if Mrs. Walker would approve of us imbibing under the circumstances. And tell Kathleen to hold the fort, I'll be down in a couple of minutes."

"Right." Chloë gave her a peck on the cheek, picked up the glasses and left the room.

For a while she stared dreamily into the long mirror, seeing much farther than her own reflection, thinking of Dunbar, her life and her future. Then all at once a picture formed of the lawn on a fresh summer's day, children running across it and— She turned abruptly away, for the image of Jack, hoisting a child on his hip, had suddenly appeared in the vision. She must be delusional to be thinking of a man she'd met only yesterday and whom, in all likelihood, she would never see again. But the daydream lingered.

She grabbed the long mink coat she would wear to the burial, then left the room and made her way slowly down the main staircase, wondering if the ancestors who gazed down at her so severely from the heavily framed portraits were reading her mind. Perhaps they were already expressing their disapproval at the possibility of the property being sold. Yet keeping Dunbar was not something she could easily work into her life. It was not a house you merely moved into. With it came a world of responsibility and deep personal commitment to all those who were inextricably part of the house and the land.

As she glanced up at the wall, a pair of twinkling blue eyes seemed to peer down at her from one of the paintings on the stair. They belonged to a little boy of about seven or eight, with thick dark hair and a mischievous curve to his mouth. He stood in a satin outfit—resembling the Blue Boy—next to a fair, rather pudgy child, who appeared older. There was something oddly familiar about him.

For a moment India stood perfectly still, experiencing the same electrifying sensation she had felt yesterday by the oak tree. She tried to identify it, to capture it in some shape or form. She glanced at the lower right-hand corner of the canvas. The date read 1730. Once again she could have sworn that she wasn't alone, and that she knew that face.

For an instant she listened intently, but the only sounds were the muted voices of the guests mingling in the oak room. Deciding it must just be her imagination, she continued down the stairs, bracing herself for the hours ahead. But the feeling lingered, warm and reassuring, and she reached the hall strangely comforted.

The funeral service began at two o'clock sharp. The guests stood silently round Lady Elspeth's coffin, which was lying, covered in wreaths, in the center of the vast stucco hall.

India listened to the ceremony in a daze, soothed by the beauty of the flowers Lady Elspeth had loved so dearly. She felt her mother's presence, as though Lady Elspeth had come to say her final goodbyes, her spirit hovering above, giving India a feeling of peace.

Serena had returned and made an effort to be polite during lunch, although she seemed uninterested in the proceedings.

"It's an awf'y sad day, Miss India, but the flowers do her proud. That one in the middle came from Edinburgh this morning," Mrs. Walker said, pointing to a particularly lovely wreath standing before the coffin.

Chloë, who was standing next to her, stepped forward. White lilies intertwined with baby's breath were set delicately within the foliage, but the gold lettering on the white satin ribbon was hard to distinguish.

"India, look," she said in a hushed whisper. India stepped forward and read the inscription.

Thinking of you. Jack Buchanan.

She felt her heart quicken. He'd remembered. She looked around, as though expecting to see him, but of course he wasn't there. It was a private service. Perhaps the wreath wasn't even meant for her, but for Serena's benefit. She took a surreptitious glance at her sister, wondering if she'd seen it.

"He didn't say anything to me last night or this morning," Chloë whispered.

India's eyes wandered back to the wreath, and she was reminded suddenly of her father's funeral, and of how lonely she'd felt. But today was different. Here people lived and died watched over by their ancestors, each generation assuming the responsibility of preserving and bettering that which was bequeathed them, and which they, in turn, would pass down to their heirs.

Yet if Dunbar fell into the hands of strangers, almost eight hundred years of history would end. She remembered Jack's words—*It would make a fabulous hotel*—and shuddered inwardly. The mere thought of Dunbar becoming some sort of hotel or institution was unbearable.

She took a last glance at the wreath. There was definitely something appealing about Jack. Perhaps it was his air of self-assurance, or his devil-may-care look, as though he was accustomed to wielding power without abusing it.

Whether or not it was meant for her, the wreath had been a thoughtful gesture and his kindness touched her.

The mourners stepped back to allow the pallbearers through. They raised the coffin to their shoulders and carried it reverently down the wide stone steps, following the piper who had begun his lonely Highland lament.

Chloë took India's arm and together they followed in silence to where the family and other friends were getting into their cars. The funeral cortege made its way sedately down the drive. They would accompany Lady El on her last journey, through the Midlothian countryside, past the hills and meadows she had loved so well, to the small graveyard on the hill where she would finally be put to rest.

The day was sunny but cold. A wintry nip could already be felt in the air, and the trees were fast losing the last of their wilting foliage. Small gusts of wind scattered the dead leaves across the patched remains of last night's snowfall.

Then they were walking, the piper leading them down the narrow cemetery path, his tartan plaid blowing in the blustery wind, the mournful lament bringing hot tears to the mourners' eyes. Then, with Kathleen, Ian and Serena, India lowered the coffin into the ground in a medieval act of ritualistic finality.

Ashes to ashes, dust to dust. From this earth they had come and to it they would return. And sudden loneliness gripped her as the rope went limp in her hand.

After a while they made their way back among the ancient moss-covered tombstones, India grateful for Chloë's support, knowing it would have been so much worse without her.

It was then she saw him. A tall dark figure in a black cashmere coat standing at the cemetery gates.

India hesitated, thinking perhaps he'd come for Serena.

But as she approached and he walked toward her, she knew why he was there.

He was there for her.

As Chloë and she passed through the wrought-iron gates, he reached silently for her hands.

"Are you okay?" His voice was low and concerned, his thick dark hair ruffled by the wind, his tan incongruous among the pale British faces surrounding them.

"I'm fine. Thanks for coming," she whispered, keeping a grip on herself.

"I wanted to."

She realized that Ian and his wife, Francesca, were watching, uncertain whether to approach. But Chloë smiled at them.

"Let me introduce you to Jack Buchanan, Peter's partner."

"Nice to meet you. Sorry it's on such a sad occasion." Ian shook hands with Jack. "I hope we'll have the chance to meet again. India, are you coming with us or are you—"

"Yes, I'm coming with you," she replied, glancing at Jack.

"I'll walk you to the car." He drew her arm into his. India was bewildered, her thoughts as muddled as her feelings. Here she was, at her mother's burial, her pulse racing because of a man she barely knew. It was almost sacrilegious.

The others had moved away but Jack's eyes never left hers.

"I'm on my way to the airport, but I wanted to make sure you were okay."

"Thanks, it was awfully kind of you."

"Take care of yourself," he said, leading her to the car where Ian, Chloë and Francesca were waiting. He opened the door and for a moment they faced each other, eyes locked.

Then India felt her throat constricting. "Thanks for coming, Jack, I— Thanks." She tried to smile, not knowing what else to say, and got quickly inside.

Slowly the cars began the return journey, followed by the haunting strain of the pipes. India could still feel the warmth of Jack's comforting grasp. Suddenly the tears she'd been holding back fell silently down her cheeks, loss and loneliness overwhelming her as she gazed blindly through the window. The vehicles moved gently down the country lane, off toward Dunbar.

Jack watched the rain streaming down against the plane's windows, drenching the tarmac as the Gulfstream readied for takeoff. He'd removed his coat and taken out the papers he'd be working on. As usual, Jonathan, his steward, had brought him a Glenfiddich on the rocks.

He stretched his legs as the plane picked up speed, reflecting upon what could have prompted him to go there this afternoon. Why had he gone to a cemetery—a place he avoided on principle—to see a woman he barely knew, and whom he might never see again? He smiled to himself. It was rare that he acted out of sheer impulse. Would they ever meet again? Possibly. There were a number of places their paths could cross. He might even be in Buenos Aires at the same time she was. But that didn't necessarily mean anything. She'd looked so sad, he'd felt like taking her in his arms and holding her close. The thought made him jerk his head up.

The plane took off, rising swiftly into the leaden sky, the rain beating harder as they gained height.

Soon they were traveling south. Jack looked down at the countryside below, peering closely, trying to distinguish through the blur what he was sure must be Dunbar, standing like a dollhouse below. Excitement stirred in his veins. Dunbar was quite distinct now, even through the rain. It was magnificent. He could hardly wait to get hold of the specs Serena had promised him.

Taking a sip of whiskey, he began making some ball-park estimates of what the renovation might cost. By the time he reached London he was in a fair way to having a game plan together, and his determination to acquire Dunbar increased. Something deep inside told him he couldn't let it go. And all at once Jack knew he'd go every inch of the way to making it his own.

4

Jack spent Christmas as he usually did—on a plane. Chad, his younger brother, and Marilyn, his sister-in-law, had invited him to spend the holiday with them at their cabin in Aspen. As usual, he'd found an excuse not to go. Though he adored his niece and goddaughter, Molly, it was easier to avoid situations that reminded him of the past.

In the early new year Peter flew to Bangkok and began a month's tour of all their Asian establishments. Jack headed down to Buenos Aires to meet with his partner, Hernan Carvajal, whom he'd met only briefly during their negotiations in London some months earlier.

After four days he was familiar with the Palacio de Grès project, and discovered Hernan to be both a smart businessman and an excellent host. By the fifth afternoon they'd gone through a long list of remodeling issues, building costs, future projections, and had finally—after various interruptions from engineers and foremen—reached some final decisions.

Jack stretched, ready to go back to the Alvear Palace. It had been a sweltering afternoon, and he was ready for a long cold shower. The old-fashioned air-conditioning unit in the improvised offices of the Palacio de Grès still hadn't been replaced, and had finally given up its battle with the torrid sun.

He leaned back in the old leather chair and looked over at Hernan. The other man stood gazing at some blueprints, his elbows propped on the huge trestle table that stood perched in the middle of the room, a strange contrast to the ornate chandeliers and gold-leaf wall sconces.

"I guess we're pretty well set." Jack gave a final glance at the notes he'd been scribbling. "Of course, there's still the issue of the interior design to be resolved." He left the question in the air.

"Mmm—" Hernan was still absorbed by the plans before him. "You know, I'm worried about this garage entrance. I'm just not sure the way it's been designed is going to be the most functional. Perhaps if we moved the plants a couple of feet over to the left—" He sighed and looked up with a smile. "Oh well, there's not much point in worrying about it now. You were saying?"

"The interior design. We still haven't decided who we're going to hire." Jack laid down his notes, twiddling his pen thoughtfully.

"You're right, it should have been done months ago. We're already running behind schedule. There are various possibilities but none of them quite fill the slot. You see?" He raised his hands. "Another problem. I tell you, it's never-ending. Of course, it'll require someone with a deep understanding of art history and a good knowledge of period furniture." He frowned, blond hair falling over a bronzed forehead. "I wish we could spirit in David Hicks," he added, grinning, and opened the refrigerator door.

Jack sat up abruptly. He'd been tossing an idea around for some time and sensed that now was the right moment to broach it. India kept popping into his thoughts at unexpected moments, and a few days ago he'd realized why. She was the ideal person to do the interior of the Palacio de Grès. He had already made some discreet inquiries, and discovered that she was here. It was as though fate had placed her in his path.

"Have you heard of the company La Dolce Vita?" he asked.

"The name rings a bell."

"They did Peter Kinnaird's hotel in London, the Jeremy."

"Of course, the one in Belgravia. It was a fabulous job."

"I was pretty impressed by it, too," Jack said, casually twiddling the pen between his fingers. "I met the owner when I was last in Scotland, a gal called India Moncrieff. Her family owns the neighboring estate to the Kinnairds'."

"Really? I thought Peter said something about a Swiss company, but I must have been mistaken." Hernan took a bottle of chilled Quilmes beer out of the refrigerator. "Want one?"

"Sure." Jack raised a hand and caught the bottle tossed his way, wiping the frost off on his worn jeans. "She's here."

"Who is?" Hernan asked, his eyebrows coming together.

"India Moncrieff, the owner of La Dolce Vita," Jack replied patiently. "She's staying with an old school friend of hers, Gabriella O'Halloran." As he pronounced India's name, Jack realized how good the words felt. Too good. But he was relieved to know why she'd been on his mind lately. He must have known subconsciously that she was the perfect person for the job. He took a long satisfying draft of beer, thinking it would be nice to see her again. And if she accepted the job, being with her every day in a work setting would help dispel any misguided fantasies he might have inadvertently conjured. The more he thought about it, the more the idea appealed to him. He watched Hernan carefully, gauging his reaction.

"Gabby O'Halloran?" he exclaimed. "She's my second cousin, once removed—or something like that. We're such a large family it gets hard to remember what the exact relationship is. I think my mother's father and her grandmother are—"

"Spare me the details. I'd never remember anyway." Jack laughed.

"I know." Hernan grinned back at him. "But now I also understand why my great-aunt Dolores has been so insistent I come for a visit to the *estancia*. Tell me, is this India tall, beautiful, talented, and wealthy to boot?"

Jack felt a stab of irritation. "As a matter of fact, now that you mention it, she is. Beautiful, I mean. I don't know about wealthy though. From what I've heard, her dad's fortune has pretty well dwindled. I'd guess she makes a good living with her business." He resumed his study of the pen. "She's a very talented professional."

Hernan was still laughing. "You don't understand. My aunt's and my mother's primary objective in life is to marry me off to someone they consider suitable. Apparently they feel your friend more than fills the spot." He shook his head, then sat down on the table and watched Jack attentively. "But tell me where your mind's at, Jack."

"Well…" Jack drank some more beer, measuring his words. "I figured that, since she's here and is certainly one of the best designers we could hire, it might be worth contacting her, to see if she'd be interested. What do you think?"

Hernan nodded, swinging himself down from the table with an enthusiastic smile. "It makes a lot of sense. Let's get in touch with her immediately. I'll call my aunt. She usually has a *parilla* at the Estancia Tres Jinetes on Saturdays. Or perhaps I should ask Gabby to arrange…'' He paused, met Jack's eyes across the room, and seemed to change his mind. ''Or maybe you should just call your friend? I can give you the number of the *estancia*.''

''Thanks, maybe I'll just do that.'' Jack tossed the beer bottle in the trash and hoisted his legs off the desk. ''If she's interested, it might be easier to have her come into town.''

''True. I think I'll go and take a dip at home, then, if you like, I can pick you up at the hotel and we can grab some dinner. By the way,'' Hernan said, grinning like a mischievous schoolboy, ''I have two models—great-looking girls, one's twenty-one and Swedish, the other twenty-two—both dying to meet you.''

Jack grinned. ''Thanks, but I'll take a rain check. I'm beat. I need an early night.''

''As you wish. If you change your mind call me on my cell.''

''Sure thing.''

They left the construction site, Hernan roaring off in his Testarossa, Jack wandering down Alvear, enjoying the languid laziness of the late afternoon. He smiled to himself. Although they were close in age, Hernan often made him feel old and worldly-wise. They'd had very different lives. While Hernan had been leading a privileged existence, playing polo in Palm Beach, studying in Europe and skiing in Gstaad, he'd been on those crazy missions into El Salvador and Nicaragua. Hernan was good for him though, his youthful enthusiasm refreshing. But the scene he still found fun had grown old for Jack. Lately he'd begun to realize just how old.

But the thought of seeing India again put a spring in his step. He crossed the mezzanine to the gift shop to buy the *Herald Tribune,* pleased that everything was falling into place. He glanced at his watch, wondering if he'd still catch Quince, his attorney, or his brother, Chad, at the office in Miami. He needed to be brought up-to-date on the dealings with Dunbar since his visit there with Serena. She'd done her homework well and had had the information he'd asked for on hand. Yet once again he'd felt that same strange sensation as on his first visit, and he'd left the property even more convinced that he would meet Serena's asking price and get the deal moving. It was a pity he hadn't had time to consult with Peter, but he'd decided to acquire the property in any case. He let himself into the suite, laid down the paper and headed immediately for the phone.

Mr. Ramsey cleared his throat while Serena waited impatiently for him to speak. It was imperative she keep calm. If the man had the slightest suspicion of what she was up to, the whole plan would fall through.

"I sent Miss India all the latest figures," he said, shaking his head sadly. "But I haven't heard back from her yet."

"That's because she's in South America," Serena answered brightly. "We've talked several times on the phone," she added casually.

"Really?" Mr. Ramsey looked surprised. "South America. That would explain her silence. I would imagine the telecommunications are not too reliable over there." He gave a stiff smile and Serena immediately responded, realizing it was his idea of a joke. She sat eyeing him across the large mahogany desk. He reminded her of an owl, peering from behind those odd tortoiseshell glasses, his thin hair combed carefully over the balding patch on his head. She stifled a sudden desire to giggle and concentrated.

"In fact, that's one of the reasons I'm here," she continued. "India and I have— Well we've made up our differences, if you know what I mean." She did her best to look modest and embarrassed. "Based on your fax, she has agreed we must sell the property and has promised to send you a full-fledged power of attorney as soon as she returns to Switzerland. There seemed to be some difficulty about having it done in English over in Buenos Aires. But she definitely wants us to get on with the negotiations. As you know, the American buyers are anxious to set things in motion. They will require complete confidentiality as to their identity as they are buying the property through an offshore company." She was pleased at how professional she sounded.

"This is quite surprising." Mr. Ramsey took off his glasses and wiped the lenses with his handkerchief. "Quite surprising indeed, in view of...er...the last encounter."

"Oh, that!" Serena gave a high-pitched laugh. "That was just me being silly. But that's all behind us now. I realized myself how important it was for us to work together on this matter. I suspect my behavior was due to delayed shock over Mummy's sudden death," she said demurely, looking down.

"Well, well, I'm very pleased to hear you tell me this, Lady Serena. A spirit of cooperation will make matters much simpler to deal with. Much simpler indeed."

"My sentiments exactly." Serena flashed him another bright smile. "So you can be expecting news from the American attorneys any day now."

"Very well. I must say it's a most generous offer, and one that will not likely be repeated. Under the circumstances, I can only advise you to take it. You're sure Miss India is in agreement?" He seemed suddenly doubtful.

"Absolutely. She says she's tried to get through to you, but as you so rightly pointed out, these remote places are not well connected. I could barely hear her at one point during this morning's conversation. I don't know how people actually live in those places.''

"I don't know if it's quite as bad as that, Lady Serena, but I would imagine the efficiency which we're used to here at home is probably sadly lacking there.''

"Exactly. So no need to worry about India, she's in agreement with everything. And by the time the closing comes through she'll be back anyway.''

"Quite true. Then I will wait for the lawyers to get in touch, and take it from there.''

"Perfect. Well, I think we've covered everything. I'd better be going, as I've already taken up far too much of your time.'' She smiled graciously as she got up.

"I'll see you out, Lady Serena.''

When they reached the front door, Serena thrust out her hand and smiled with what she hoped was a beguiling expression. "Thank you again, Mr. Ramsey. I don't know what we'd do without you.''

"No, no.'' Mr. Ramsey gave an embarrassed cough. "May I just say, Lady Serena, that I am delighted you and your sister have made up the...er, rift. A family should stand united.'' He shook her hand.

"That's exactly how we feel. Goodbye, Mr. Ramsey.''
"Goodbye.''

Serena stepped out into Charlotte Square and put up her umbrella. As she headed for George Street, a blast of wind nearly blew it inside out, but she was so elated the meeting had gone so well, she didn't care. Maxi would be pleased, too.

With business out of the way she headed toward Jenners. A little shopping was exactly what she needed, especially now that she would have unlimited funds to spend. She might as well get into the habit right away.

* * *

India stretched out lazily on a chaise longue at the *estancia,* idly daydreaming, as the hot afternoon shifted gently into evening. The subtle scent of the gardenias surrounding the veranda was intensifying with the approach of dusk, and the bougainvillea, so colorful during the day, had taken on a softer hue. A soft breeze blew in gently from the pampas, and the tall eucalyptus trees bordering the earth track that led to the corrals and the stables swayed gently to and fro. Only the occasional croak from the frogs in the pond, the chant of the crickets commencing their evensong and the distant shouts of gauchos bringing home the cattle disturbed the tranquillity.

India had arrived in Buenos Aires in time to spend a somewhat nostalgic Christmas with the O'Hallorans. But soon afterward she and Gabby had thrown themselves wholeheartedly into the task of redecorating the *casco,* choosing fabrics and new sofas, and refurbishing some of the present furniture. It had been fun and distracting, but her mind often wandered to Dunbar. She knew that as soon as she returned home a decision had to be made. Mr. Ramsey had sent her a fax only a few days ago. The news was not encouraging. Slowly, but sadly, she was getting used to the idea that keeping Dunbar was a virtual impossibility. At least if it was bought by a family, or someone who would appreciate it, she would not feel quite so bad.

But what if it was transformed into some dreadful tourist trap? Or turned into a hotel? This last thought turned her mind to Jack Buchanan. She'd thought quite a bit about Jack over the last few weeks. In fact, he'd been making constant appearances in her subconscious ever since he'd stood at the cemetery gates on that gray Scottish afternoon.

She wondered suddenly what he was up to, and how his hotel project was going. She must go by there one day. Apparently Jack's partner was some relation of Gabby's whom the family wanted to introduce her to.

"Señorita India." Her thoughts were interrupted by the appearance of Severina, the maid.

"*Sí, Severina, qué pasa?*" She twisted her head around. The wizened little woman approached. "*Teléfono para usted, señorita.*"

"*Quién es?*" she asked, wondering who could be calling her at this time.

"*Señor Djabugan,*" Severina answered.

India rose and went inside, mystified, for few people knew she was here. She picked up the receiver.

"*Aló, India hablando.*"

"India?"

Her stomach lurched. Immediately she recognized the deep American voice coming down the line.

"It's Jack Buchanan, how are you doing?"

"Uh…fine." She faltered nervously. It was uncanny. Only moments ago she'd been daydreaming about him.

"I got your number from Hernan Carvajal, my partner. He seems to be related to your friend Gabriella. So, how are things?" There was a moment's hesitation, neither knowing where to go next.

"Fine, thanks. I wasn't expecting to hear from you," India replied, her heart racing. "How is your project going—the Palacio de Grès, wasn't it?"

"It's going fine. In fact, that's one of the reasons I'm calling you. Hernan and I are ready to plan the interior renovations, and the decor of the new building, and I was wondering if perhaps you might be interested in taking a look." He sounded casual yet professional.

India swallowed, disappointed. It was merely a job proposal, and one she might even consider. She hadn't taken any projects on since her mother's death, wanting to give herself some time, but the Palacio de Grès was tempting.

"I wasn't planning to take on anything new for a while, but it certainly sounds interesting."

"Why don't you come into town and take a look? I think it's right up your alley. I mentioned to Hernan that you'd been to the place as a little girl. He says it hasn't changed much."

The idea was growing on India by the minute, but what about Jack? Was he staying or leaving?

The answer came soon enough. "I'll need you to come this week if you're interested. I have to be back in Miami in a few days. I wondered, if you're not too busy, if you might be able to come in, say, Friday? Would that suit you?" He sounded businesslike, as though he was flipping through his agenda.

India decided it couldn't do any harm to look at the place. After all, it was a fabulous opportunity, and she had time on her hands before heading to Rio for the opening of the La Perla hotel.

"Is there somewhere I can call you back?"

"Sure. I'm staying at the Alvear Palace. If you want I'll give you the office number, too."

She grabbed a pen from the desk next to the phone. Her hand shook as she wrote down the numbers, and she chided herself for being absurd. "I'll call you back tomorrow once I know what my plans are."

"Okay. I guess that's it then. I'll expect your call." There was a moment of pregnant silence, as though he wanted to say more.

"Fine. I'll be in touch. Goodbye, and thanks for calling." She laid down the receiver, then leaned against the cold, whitewashed wall. What was it about the man that made her tingle from top to toe? The mere sound of his voice had a disturbing effect on her. She wandered back to the veranda, watching in the distance as the shorthorn cattle made their way slowly home, across the red and dusty darkening horizon.

Her mind drifted back to Christian, her ex-husband. Had

she felt anything like this for him? she asked herself. The answer came loud and clear. No. Everything between them had been so measured and well behaved. When they'd made love, he'd directed, and she'd followed obediently, accepting that he knew how it was supposed to be. At the time she'd believed it was love. That's why it had hurt so much when he'd left. And what had she gotten for her pain, for trusting him?

She sat down on the edge of the balustrade, remembering Chloë's assertion that India would have been miserable if she'd continued being married to Christian, that she was damn lucky he'd backed out. And, India realized ruefully, Chloë was undoubtedly right.

But she'd vowed to herself that never again would another man make her feel so vulnerable, or hurt and humiliate her again. The sudden awareness that Jack might have that power sent a streak of fear through her.

Perhaps it would be better to refuse the offer and not court trouble. On the other hand, his tone had been professional and he had said he was leaving for Miami in a few days. Anyway, before she could even consider the job, she needed to take a good look at the state of the building.

A flutter of ivory silk accompanied by a whiff of Shalimar interrupted her thoughts as Gabby's grandmother, Dolores, wafted gracefully through the French doors out on to the terrace.

"Ah, there you are, dear girl." Dolores O'Halloran smiled brightly. "I was wondering where you and Gabby were."

"She's out riding with Santiago. They went to take a look at the newborn foals."

"Ah, yes, and you?" Dolores asked, approaching India and lifting up India's chin, her expression concerned. "What are these misty eyes I see? I hope you are not still mourning your dear mama too deeply, my love. I am certain Lady Elspeth is at rest," she added quietly.

"I know she is. It's not that."

"Tell me." Dolores glided to a large rattan armchair where she arrayed herself among the white cushions, a picture of serene elegance and breeding.

India smiled, embarrassed, not quite knowing what to say. "It's a chap I met in Scotland. A long story really. Well, actually it isn't. What I mean is, I met him when Mummy died, and he almost shot me by mistake, then he came home for tea and—" She stopped, flushing, realizing she was making a complete hash of it. She looked up and met Dolores's amused but understanding eyes.

"Do go on, my dear, he sounds delightful."

"Well, to cut a long story short, he's bought into a hotel in Buenos Aires—you know the old Palacio de Grès that belongs to one of your relations."

"Of course I know it. Hernan inherited it. He's my great-nephew, a charming boy. I think I've already mentioned that you should meet him," she added with a conspiratorial smile. "He's single, handsome and very good company."

India laughed, "Don't matchmake, Dolores."

"Well, darling—" Dolores made a moue with her well-defined lips "—there's no harm in bringing two nice young people together is there? But tell me more about…?"

"Jack Buchanan."

"British?" she asked casually.

"No, American."

"Ah," Dolores said, "American. Is he a handsome American? I've always had a *faible* for American men ever since I saw Gary Cooper in *High Noon*—there's something so very masculine about them." She lifted a perfect eyebrow and leaned forward. "You know what I mean, don't

you? That air of *A man has to do what a man has to do,*
as though they'd conquer the world *sans problème.*" She
waived an elegant bejeweled hand.

"Well, there's also something very annoying about this
one." India plucked a gardenia viciously from its stalk and
twiddled it between her fingers. "He almost shot me in
the glen, then made out it was my fault. He even made me
faint," she finished crossly, blocking out the image of Jack
reaching for her hands at the cemetery gates.

"Do go on, darling, he sounds fascinating."

Dolores curled up among the cushions, her eyes sparkling and expectant. India realized there would be no escape until Dolores had been fully regaled with all the details, so she summarized them briefly. "He's seen the work
I did on the Jeremy, in London, and now he wants me to
take a look at the Palacio de Grès."

"It sounds an excellent idea to me, dear," Dolores replied thoughtfully. "After all, you're here, and it would
do you good to get involved in something nice. I'm sure
you'd enjoy working with Hernan, too. You did say this
Jack is leaving for the States again?"

"That's what he said."

"It can't do any harm to look," she said encouragingly.
"Why not go to Buenos Aires and see the Palacio? You
can stay in the apartment if you like, it's empty during the
summer."

"Thanks. I suppose I should go and see it at least."
India mulled over the idea, lifting the wilted gardenia to
her nose. "Professionally it would be a great opportunity."

"Go," Dolores said firmly. "Don't be afraid of taking
chances. If you don't, you'll grow into a regretful old lady.
Believe me, I know too many of them. But then look at
me," she said, smiling, her eyes mischievous yet nostalgic.
"I've had my ups and downs, buried three husbands, and
had my *aventures* along the way. But if I could go back,

I wouldn't change a thing. Life is to be lived, not looked at from a distance. I only wish there was more of it. Time seems to fly by so quickly. Before you know it, *you'll* be sitting on some veranda, proffering excellent advice to a lovely young person like yourself.'' She gave a tinkling laugh, the laugh of a young girl. ''Stop being afraid, India,'' she chided. ''Why not bring the boys over sometime? We can have a big *asado,* and your American friend will enjoy seeing a real *estancia.*''

''Perhaps.''

''Don't worry, I'll tell Gabby to arrange it with Hernan. Now run along, dear, and get ready for dinner. I'm making my special soufflé tonight and I refuse to have it flop because of you all being late. Everyone must come to dinner on time.''

When Jack received the message saying that Miss Moncrieff would be in Buenos Aires on Friday morning and wished to make arrangements to see the property, he felt a spark of masculine triumph. *So she was coming after all.*

He spent the next two days upbeat, satisfied that everything was falling nicely into place. At times he found it difficult to focus and cut himself a couple of times shaving.

On Friday morning he arrived late at the meeting, having spent almost an hour on the phone with Quince, discussing the structuring of the Dunbar deal. He entered the Palacio, nodded a friendly good-morning to two passing workmen and, stepping over some wires and plaques of plaster, headed straight for the office in the old drawing room. The door was ajar and he pushed it silently open.

India was by the window, her back to him, gazing out across the gardens. The sun poured through the engraved glass, lighting up her hair that cascaded onto her glistening tanned shoulders and her short white linen dress. Jack's eyes drifted down the long, never-ending bronzed legs.

Then, as though sensing his presence, she turned. He hastily entered the room.

"Good morning," he said briskly, giving her a quick professional smile. "I'm glad you were able to make it. Sorry I'm late. Has anyone taken care of you?"

"Yes, thank you. Hernan Carvajal was here, but the foreman called him away—something to do with a drain problem," she answered with a small reserved smile. "He told me to have a look through the blueprints."

Jack took his time arranging some papers, buying the extra moments he needed. He'd never guessed he would have such a violent reaction on seeing her again. After all, she was just one more lovely woman, wasn't she?

For the first time he began to wonder if the Palacio de Grès was the only reason he'd called her. Seeing her here—bronzed and beautiful, the scent of her perfume so intoxicatingly fresh and hauntingly familiar—obliged him to take a more serious look at his motives.

Thankfully Hernan returned at that moment, and the three began to review the renovation plans. But although India was charming, she treated Jack with casual interest, addressing him only when something related to the project and needed to be clarified. Finally she asked if they would mind her taking a look at the Palacio by herself. He was almost glad to see her go, unsettled by the effect she'd had on him.

"You look put out." Hernan gave him a curious glance. "I thought you liked her, that you were friends." They had wandered out to the terrace to wait for India.

"She is my friend. I mean— Heck, I don't know." Jack cleared his throat and threw up his hands, irritated. "To tell you the truth, I hardly know the woman."

Hernan studied him skeptically for a moment, then shrugged and went in search of Eduardo, the architect. Jack gazed impatiently at the perfectly tended Italian gardens, but he didn't see the well-trimmed hedges, the immaculate *parterres* or the neatly raked gravel paths. All he saw was her.

On entering the Palacio de Grès, India fell in love.

It was everything she'd anticipated and more. Her distant childhood memories in no way did justice to the beauty and perfection of the mansion, and she wandered from room to room, drinking in the details, reveling in the atmosphere and history of the place.

By the end of her tour she was convinced that only some of the original furnishings should remain, eliminating those too valuable to bear the wear and tear that all hotels suffered. However appreciative guests might be of art, they had a funny way of not taking care of what wasn't theirs.

She wandered outside and down the shallow stone steps to the sedate gardens below, admiring the clipped hedges and perfectly plotted stretches of grass. Small gravel paths led to a central fountain that stood in a small flagstoned courtyard bordered by classical stone columns. A quaint bird fountain with an appealing bronze frog playing the flute made her smile as she headed through a trellised archway of rambling clematis and wisteria to a stone alcove. It was delightful, and a temptation too great to resist.

She was honest enough to admit that she'd known she'd take the job the moment she'd walked in. Her mind made up, she raised her eyes toward the mansion. It was then she saw Jack, his rolled-up white shirtsleeves contrasting with his dark tan above faded jeans. He leaned on the balustrade. Evidently he hadn't seen her, for there was no sign of recognition. He'd been somewhat distant, and she watched him for a moment, wondering at his cool professional attitude. She made her way back to the steps leading up to the terrace reflecting that a purely professional re-

lationship was probably safer. But a twinge of regret nig-
gled in the back of her mind as she walked up the steps.

Jack turned and took his foot off the balustrade.

"Well? What's the verdict?" he asked, smiling, the
same person she remembered from Scotland. Her pulse
beat faster.

"It's wonderful. Simply wonderful."

"Are you ready to take on the job?"

She took a breath. "Yes. It's irresistible. I don't think
I'd ever forgive myself if I didn't."

"Great. Let's shake on it." He held out his hand and
she took it, very conscious of the strong pressure of his
fingers as they wrapped around hers for a moment longer
than necessary. "We'll find Hernan and have lunch. This
requires a bottle of champagne."

He guided her by the elbow, helping her over some elec-
trical wire, and India wondered if she'd imagined his earlier coldness, suddenly happy with her decision. Here was
a fabulous opportunity to do what she truly loved: preserve
the old, create the new and guide the Palacio de Grès
gracefully into the new millennium.

A week later India was not so sure. She and Jack were
into their seventh discussion as to what should and should
not be done about the air-conditioning ducts.

"Tear out the ceiling."

"Are you utterly mad?" India gazed at him, horrified.
"How can you even think of it?"

"It's the quickest solution."

India looked from Jack to Hernan in shocked anger.
"Do you realize this is one of the most unique buildings
in South America, and you want to tear down parts of it
simply because they're a nuisance?"

"India, this is a hotel, not a museum. We're on a budget.

We can't waste time while you work out solutions to keep a few pillars in place,'' Jack replied tersely.

"I'm well aware of that." She raised her chin haughtily. "What I fail to understand is why you bothered to hire me at all. If you wanted to build a generic hotel, I'm sure you could acquire one of their—what is it you Americans like to call them?—*cookie-cutter* plans? But," she continued, her tone brooking no argument, "if you want to preserve the Palacio de Grès—which is what I was led to believe—you've got to work with what's already here. I wouldn't be a decent professional if I didn't give you the right advice, and believe me, it's not gutting the place."

Jack's expression was closed. "You just don't want to understand, do you?" She turned to Hernan in exasperation. "Well, don't just stand there, see what *you* can do. Perhaps you can talk some sense into him." India sat down on the bottom steps of the marble staircase and eyed Jack. Why couldn't he just get on a plane, go home, and leave Hernan and her to do what had to be done.

Ever since she'd agreed to take on the job, he'd been putting spokes in her wheel, arguing about every last detail. If the Palacio weren't such a wonderful place she'd regret having signed the contract. All he seemed to care about was his damn hotel and what it was going to make. She watched him now, leaning against the Ionic pilaster, in his usual outfit of faded jeans and white shirt. He looked to be intensely concentrating, just the way she'd seen him that first day on the terrace. She swallowed, remembering how good it had felt when he'd smiled and his fingers had touched hers. And earlier this morning, when they had looked over the blueprints for the restaurant. They'd been so close she could feel his body heat.

She wondered where his mind was. Calculating, most likely. Behind his handsome face and casual demeanor lurked an incredibly astute yet obtuse mind. She glanced at Hernan and smiled, remembering the lovely bouquet of flowers he'd gallantly presented to her that morning while Jack had raised an amused eyebrow. Hernan held the difficult position of partner and owner, wanting to please them both. But the numbers stuck out like a sore thumb. Either they got cracking and took drastic measures to open by late autumn, or things could get tricky.

"Stop sulking, India," Jack taunted. "You know as well as I do we can't waste time. If we're not ready to open on schedule, we'll screw up our budget."

India jumped up, facing him. "Of course I realize that, and I'm not suggesting we should waste time. I'm merely working on a solution that will get us there, on target, and preserve the building. I can assure you it isn't complicated. I can explain it to you if you like." She saw Hernan shifting uneasily from one foot to the other. Changing tactics, she looked up at Jack through her lashes and ventured a smile. "Please?"

He studied her for a moment, eyes inscrutable as she waited anxiously. Then he grinned. "Okay. But don't explain anything to me. Just bring me a practical solution in twenty-four hours, not a minute more. Is that clear?" He glanced at his watch.

She bit back the answer that was on the tip of her tongue and instead challenged him with a bright smile. "I promise you won't be disappointed."

She went to the stairs and grabbed her hemp tote, knowing exactly what had to be done.

"I hope you find an answer, India," Hernan said. "Like you, I feel we must preserve as much of the original structure as possible."

"Don't worry, Hernan. It's a done deal."

"Twenty-four hours, remember. And I think you're wasting your time," Jack murmured as she passed him.

"You've told me that already," she said sweetly. "I'm

not deaf and I can tell the time. By the way, count me out for dinner.''

"You just said you'd found the answer. Plus, you have to eat.''

"I do, but I also have to work, and unlike others I could name, I find art more interesting than *asado*. You, on the other hand, have no appreciation for anything but the stock of that company of yours.''

"Believe me, neither do the shareholders,'' he murmured.

She pretended not to hear. She knew exactly what she had to do, and found it amazing that no one had come up with what was an obvious and simple solution to solve the problem of the air-conditioning ducts. If he'd allowed her, she could very well have pointed it out to him and saved herself the trouble of drawing the changes into the plans. But she wanted it done perfectly, and it was well worth the effort just to make him eat his words.

Jack looked at the clock for the umpteenth time. It had not been a good night. He'd missed her at dinner, then tossed and turned most of the night, unable to sleep. At three-thirty he'd called India's room but there was no answer.

He showered and dressed, then dialed her room again. But there was still no reply. Could she have stayed at the Palacio all night? Stubborn creature that she was, she probably had. And he had to admit that she'd been right about several things they'd butted heads over during the last week. He smiled, thinking how sexy she looked when she worked. Usually she sat on a high stool, her hair caught up with a ballpoint pen, biting her lower lip in a way that was surprisingly distracting. Perhaps working together wasn't such a good idea after all, he reflected, making his way through the lobby and out onto the street.

It was early, barely seven o'clock on a Sunday morning. The avenue was quiet without the usual bustle and flow of traffic. Only a few stray cars, the odd pedestrian and a dog walker holding six animals on leashes of various lengths could be seen. Jack sauntered along the pavement, enjoying the quiet. Sunday mornings were very much the same everywhere. He nodded to the cigarette vendor on the corner and crossed the street, quickening his step, trying not to feel anxious.

He still couldn't figure out what it was about India that attracted him so. She treated him as one professional would another, with camaraderie and a certain distance. But there had been moments…

He'd had fun, too, during the week, more fun than he remembered having in years. He'd watched her—the way she moved, how she talked, her changing expressions—wanting her as he'd rarely wanted a woman before. Was it just because she didn't even look his way? Perhaps that was part of it, but he was honest enough to admit to himself that he hadn't felt such a deep attraction in a long while.

Well, he reasoned as he turned the corner, there was only one way to deal with *that*. If he couldn't get her out of his mind, he'd have to get her into his bed. Plus there was his schedule. He couldn't stay here indefinitely. Quince had already made several veiled remarks concerning his prolonged absence, and Chad was teasing him, saying there must be a woman responsible for him staying away this long from the office. And there was, he realized ruefully. More than he liked to admit.

As he strode towards the Palacio, he found that the iron gate leading into the side entrance was open. He set out to look for her, anxious to assure himself that she was okay, knowing he would never forgive himself if she wasn't.

* * *

India was stiff after having deliberated over plans most of the night and then fallen asleep on an old couch with two broken springs. She grimaced, amazed that she'd slept all night. She left the architect's improvised office and sat down on a stone bench in the garden, soaking in the rays of the early-morning sun.

The day was fresh and serene, the whirr of the sprinklers irrigating the garden soothing. Only the faraway sound of the traffic in the Recoleta reminded her of her whereabouts. She leaned back, eyes closed, and relished the moment, satisfied that the work was well-done and ready for the architect. The actual implementing of her plans had to be precise. The exact measurements and detailing of the moldings she would add to hide the air-conditioning ducts needed to be perfectly clear so that, when viewed from the ground, the correct proportions would be sure to be maintained.

She yawned, tired but content, and wondered sleepily what Jack would say when he realized how obvious the answer was. It would serve him right for being so pigheaded. At times during the past week she thought she'd seen glimpses of the man with whom she'd shared that special moment before the fire in the library at Dunbar, but they'd disappeared all too quickly. On the rare occasions when they'd retrieved a little of that friendly intimacy, something had inevitably come up to place them at odds again.

She stretched and rested her head on the back of the bench. Maybe Tía Dolores was right, life was meant to be lived. All she'd done since the divorce was work, dedicating herself, heart and soul, to building up La Dolce Vita. It had been a conscious decision, she reminded herself, and well worth it. In five years she'd accomplished what would normally have taken ten. She now had name recognition, and could pretty much pick and choose the work she took on. But all of a sudden, not having anyone to share things with was bothering her.

She sat up abruptly and put her sketch pad and pencils into her tote. She slipped around the side of the building and, stepping over some rubble, reached the front of the Palacio. Slowly she retreated a few steps, back to the gates, admiring the layout as she had done several times since her first visit.

The original building was attached to the modern glass and metal structure rising behind it by a huge atrium. India looked up to the top of the building critically, where a metal pediment, identical to the one on the front of the Palacio, had been erected, tying the whole structure creatively together. It was a work of art, where old and new, ancient and modern, blended in perfect harmony. The architects had walked a fine line with this daring scheme, but the result was spectacular.

She studied it, oblivious to everything but the building, imagining the final touches in her mind's eye. Then she stifled a yawn, ready for a shower and some sleep in a comfortable bed.

"Up bright and early I see," a voice drawled behind her.

She jumped and turned swiftly, almost falling on top of Jack. He grabbed her arms, steadying her.

"Hey, not so fast."

"You gave me such a fright. I wasn't expecting anyone to be here," she replied, retrieving her balance. His dark hair was slicked back and still wet from the shower, his beige chinos pressed, his white polo shirt crisp. She became suddenly conscious of her own rumpled state, her tired face and unbrushed hair, realizing she must look a mess.

"Did you stay here all night?"

"Yes. I ended up falling asleep."

India found his scent intoxicating, a blend of Hermès soap, cologne and morning breeze. His face was so close and his lips so near that, for a split second, she wondered what it would be like if he kissed her. She caught her breath unsteadily and turned away.

"It's not my fault you're always pulling surprises on me," she said reproachfully. "What are you doing here at this hour, anyway?"

"Checking on you. There was no answer in your room, and the front desk said you hadn't been back all night. What happened?"

"I told you. I decided to take a short rest on the sofa, and the next thing I knew it was daylight."

He shook his head disapprovingly. "Darn dangerous to be hanging around all night on your own in a place like this. Thank God it isn't Rio. By the way, did you come up with anything?" A doubtful smile hovered at the corners of his mouth.

India took her time to answer, allowing him his thirty seconds in the sun. "The solution was obvious from the start, Jack. If you'd allowed me the time to explain yesterday I could have shown you exactly what I planned to do. It was merely a question of drawing some details into the plans."

"What do you mean?" His expression changed to one of deep interest, his eyes bluer, as something caught his attention.

"Faux moldings, of course. It's a simple solution but one that works, especially with ceilings this height. I was worried they might look too heavy when viewed from the ground. What took me time was figuring out the correct proportions. The conduits will simply pass through the back. Why nobody thought of this in the first place beats me." She gave a shrug. "I've left the plans for Eduardo to give the engineer tomorrow. I'm pretty beat or I'd show you.''

''Let me get this straight. You're telling me that all it takes is adding some moldings and the problem's solved?'' He spoke deliberately.

''Exactly. It's as plain as pikestaff.''

''So I've been paying a team of people thousands of dollars to solve problems, and all they've done is waste my time and my money?''

''Pretty much. But don't worry—'' she smiled cheerfully ''—you're not alone. It happens all the time. I don't suppose you feel like breakfast?'' she added hopefully.

''Sure. But just tell me this, what made it so obvious to you?''

''Well, I try to look at the so-called problem, and think how I can make use of it, rather than eliminate it. I never try to hide elements. Rather, I make them look as though they were there intentionally. After all, they aren't going to disappear. They have a necessary function within the structure as a whole.'' She paused, then saw he was listening carefully. ''I just try to use them to my advantage, that's all.''

''It makes sense.'' He nodded in agreement.

''Actually, all we're going to do is embellish the existing moldings. Nothing will look out of place, just slightly more ornate. But we have the height and the volume to carry it.'' She knew she'd floored him, and was unable to suppress a thrill of satisfaction.

After a moment he spoke, his voice harsh. ''There'll be heads rolling tomorrow morning. What a bunch of incompetent idiots. Do you realize just how much we've been paying these people to come up with solutions?''

''Uh…as a matter of fact, I do,'' she said, unable to suppress a grin.

He looked at her, and slowly he grinned back, his eyes

filled with laughter and admiration. "Great job. From now on you call the shots. I won't say another word."

It was India's turn to be floored. "Do you really mean that?"

"Cross my heart," he said, the playful laughter in his eyes mixed with something undefinable. She looked down, all of a sudden embarrassed, and began walking toward the gates. "I'll do my best not to disappoint you."

"Believe me, India, you'll never disappoint me."

As they reached the entrance of the hotel, India glanced down at her creased clothes. "I'll need to take a quick shower, then perhaps we could head to San Telmo for breakfast and see what they've got at the antiques market. Have you been there yet?"

"Nope."

"It's great fun, a sort of cross between Portobello Road and the Marché aux puces. Do you mind waiting?" she asked, smiling tentatively.

"Sure, go on. I promise I'll wait patiently for as long as you need."

"Give me fifteen minutes."

India disappeared into the elevator. She reached her room and pulled her clothes off with a chuckle. Stepping into the shower she felt extraordinarily elated at the thought of spending the day with him. It sent an unprecedented thrill up her spine. Ridiculous, of course, she told herself as she frothed the soap.

But in truth, she was enjoying every minute of it.

5

Jack leaned against the bar counter and ordered another espresso, keeping an eye discreetly on the elevator. His mind overflowed with tantalizing images of India, lying naked and beautiful on his bed upstairs in the suite. It wasn't much use knowing that he should pack up and forget the whole thing when he could think of little else. He sipped the strong coffee thoughtfully. Today he'd feel his way, test the terrain.

Five minutes later, he watched her get out of the elevator, enjoying the fluidity of her movements and the natural refinement she exuded. He wasn't usually conscious of what women wore, but the way India carried herself, how she wore the simple short white skirt and top with a navy sweater thrown casually over her shoulders made him swallow.

"Sorry I took so long. Shall we go?" she asked, smiling.

"Sounds great," he replied, signing the check. "I'm starving. This coffee hit me on an empty stomach. Still, it's better than Cuban coffee."

"Is it terribly strong?" she asked, laughing as they walked through the lobby and out to the waiting car.

"It's a shot of adrenaline straight in the vein. If nothing else'll wake you up, that sure will." He opened the door for her and gave the driver directions.

His eyes glided down her bronzed legs and he shifted positions. Legs like that were meant for more than merely being admired. They should be curled around him, intertwined with his. Before his imagination could run away with the image, India drew his attention to the window, and he leaned over to take a look at a landmark she was pointing out. He casually rested his hand on her knee, noting that she didn't pull away. That was a good sign, he reflected with some measure of satisfaction. A very good sign, indeed.

Tucked into the inner recesses of the city, San Telmo was already busy. Some strolling dancers were setting up for a tango show, women chatted and men sat at small tables on café terraces discussing a soccer match that would take place later in the day.

They selected a café bordering the square and ordered breakfast, while enjoying the easygoing tempo of the plaza. Neither said much, both content to enjoy their cappuccinos and watch the tourists and locals amble among the booths, and in and out of the small antique shops.

Their attention was diverted by a large English lady, in an extravagant straw hat, bustling by, harrying her thin, cowed husband. "For goodness' sake, hurry up, Nigel, you're always straggling behind and holding up the whole bus party." Jack's eyebrows rose in exaggerated horror, and they exchanged a silent smile.

It was as though an invisible barrier had dropped, and the road between them opened. India raised the coffee cup to her lips and flinched as the heat stung the skin on her hand where she'd accidentally cut herself.

"What's wrong?" Apparently he missed very little.

"Nothing, just a small cut. There was some broken glass in the office and stupidly I cut myself," she said, minimizing the incident.

He leaned over and took her hand in his, peering at the cut. "Have you cleaned this? Looks like it could use some peroxide, and a bandage. It could get infected." He looked up. "Let's ask the waiter where there's a pharmacy." He signaled with his free hand, still not loosening his grasp.

"Don't worry, Jack, it'll be fine."

But he insisted. They followed the waiter's directions and walked down a little side street to the nearest pharmacy. Once they'd bought the peroxide, cotton balls and bandages, Jack made her sit still while he cleaned the cut.

"It's not a big deal," India said, embarrassed.

"No, but it's deep. Just stay still while I pour some peroxide over it. It may sting." He glanced up before lifting her hand gently. "Ready?"

She nodded. He seemed concerned as he poured the peroxide slowly over the cut, then dabbed it with cotton wool. It felt good to be cared for, and all at once she wished the moment would prolong itself. Even the liquid didn't hurt, and when he carefully placed the Band-Aid on, it felt like a caress.

"Okay, you're all set."

They wandered back to the square, Jack resting his arm lightly on her shoulders. India remembered how Christian had often done the same thing, but his gesture had been more proprietary than pleasant, as though he owned her. Jack's arm felt light and reassuring.

They sauntered among the booths, picking out items of interest and exchanging pleasantries. She saw a pair of attractive Georgian candlesticks in the window of a little antique store on the corner of the plaza and made a mental note to pop in there on their way back. Out of the corner of her eye she caught sight of a tent filled with bric-a-brac and antique books. Dusty volumes of all age and size were piled on a large rickety table. Behind the table sat an old bearded and bespectacled gentleman absorbed by his book, apparently oblivious to the goings-on around him.

"Look, Jack." India picked up a worn leather-bound book from the pile, so old the title was barely legible, and carefully turned the yellowed pages. "I think this must be a first edition of Tobias Smollett's *The Tears of Scotland*."

"Very observant young lady," the old gentleman remarked in perfect Oxford English, lowering his book. "It is a first edition of Smollett's work, and very unique. I was going to keep it, but I seem to accumulate so much. Are you interested in Scottish poets? I have an excellent edition of *The Child's Garden of Verse*, and *Young Lochinvar* if I'm not mistaken." He rose, moving unhurriedly to the back of the stall.

India gazed down at the volume, traveling back in time to the drawing room in Switzerland where, as a little girl, she'd sat before the fire drawing while her mother read aloud. She could hear Lady Elspeth's melodious voice reciting these very words, and then explaining the sad history behind them.

Tears stung her eyes and she closed the book gently, laying it aside. It was time to move on, not to look back. For although the memories were happy ones, the knowledge that they were gone forever left a void in her heart. All at once she thought of Dunbar and its destiny, of the future with no more roots in her life. Then she glanced up, ready to leave. "Let's come back later, after we've looked at the rest," she suggested. But he'd turned and was picking up the book.

Jack lifted the volume, noting how quiet she'd become, and opened it. "Why don't you read to me. I'd like to hear it."

"I don't think I—"

He heard the tremor in her voice and continued gently. "Yes, you can. Please, for me."

Her misty eyes told him how raw her feelings still were, and suddenly he felt real anger at the way things had been left. Dunbar meant a lot more to her than others seemed to realize. His meeting with Serena suddenly flashed to mind, her anxiety to sell badly disguised. He felt a pang of regret for India, who evidently loved the place so dearly. She'd never once referred to it. All of a sudden he wondered if he should mention it. But for some reason this didn't seem to be the right moment. Perhaps once she understood what he had in mind she'd be more accepting. He watched her carefully, vowing to himself that, once Dunbar was his, he'd find a way of making it up to her.

He pressed the book back into her hands, determined not to let her bury her memories as he'd done. It was better to face the pain. He knew. He'd learned the hard way.

She hesitated, then took the small volume and flitted through the pages, stopping when she found the right passage. Softly she began reading and something stirred in him. Whether it was the sound of her voice, or the words, he couldn't tell, but from somewhere deep within came a response and an inexplicable yearning.

"Mourn, hapless Caledonia, mourn,
Thy banished peace, thy laurels torn.
Thy sons, for valor long renowned,
Lie slaughtered on their native ground.

"Then there's a less interesting bit...oh, I like this part, though it's so sad," she continued.

"Thy martial glory, crowned with praise,
Still shone with undiminished blaze;
The towering spirit **now** is broke,

Thy neck is bended to the yoke:
What foreign arms could never quell,
By civil rage and rancor fell.''

She ended quietly, raising her eyes from the book. ''Smollett wrote this particular poem in 1746, just after the Battle of Culloden. Scotland was never the same again.''

''You really care about Scotland, don't you?'' he remarked, gauging her reaction.

She nodded, then hesitated, as though about to say something more. But she remained silent.

''Dunbar is a wonderful place. Will you mind very much if it's sold?''

''Yes, I will, but I'm afraid I don't have a choice.'' She gave a quick smile. ''But don't let's spoil this lovely day with sad thoughts.''

''You're right. Will you read me some more? I like it, I guess it must be my Scottish ancestry coming out.''

''That's right, your background is Scottish, isn't it?''

''Yeah, way back.''

''Funny, how one's roots can be important, even though one's spent very little time in a place. I only learned that recently,'' she remarked with a little smile.

He nodded, knowing exactly what she meant. He'd felt the same thing the first time he'd visited the Kinnairds. It had felt like coming home.

''I never thought much about it till my mother died,'' she continued, ''but now it seems far more important than before. Perhaps it's just fear of breaking with the past.'' She looked down at the page once more, saying hurriedly, ''Here's another passage I like.

''The rural pipe and merry lay
No more shall cheer the happy day,
No social scenes of gay delight

Beguile the dreary winter night:
No strains but those of sorrow, flow,
And naught be heard but sounds of woe,
While the pale phantoms of the slain
Glide nightly o'er the silent plain.''

Jack stood quiet, listening to the melodious sound of her voice, the plaza replaced by the tranquil image of Dunbar as he'd seen it that first day, standing beside India in the misty afternoon shadows. An uncanny shiver passed over him, the same sensation he'd felt, when, on arriving at the door of Dunbar, he'd turned and gazed back at the huge oak tree, stately and alone in the falling dusk.

He realized she'd stopped reading. For a fleeting instant their eyes locked, and he knew that she'd been there, too.

"Let's go," he said, feeling a sudden urge to move on and shake off the lingering sensation.

"You go. I'll catch you up," she replied, fingering the volume of *Young Lochinvar* the book vendor had brought her.

"Okay, I'll take a look at those weapons over there," he said, indicating the booth next door filled with ancient guns and swords. He made his way over and browsed through, handling the First World War Mausers and an old Remington 12-gauge. Then he stopped in front of a pair of pearl-handled dueling pistols lying in a silk-lined leather box. He picked one up, feeling its weight, wondering what it would have been like to challenge another man to a meeting at dawn on some misty heath. Not so different from some of the situations he'd known himself in the past, he reflected wryly, replacing the pistol on its silken bed.

"Here I am." India appeared at his side.

"Take a look at these." He pointed to the dueling pistols.

"Gosh, they're beautiful. I wonder how old they are."

"Early nineteenth-century English, I would think."

She glanced at him curiously. "You seem to know a lot about weapons. Are you interested in collecting?"

"I could be. Lately I've come across some interesting pieces. Particularly in the East."

"Do you have any hobbies?"

"Work," he said with a laugh. "Skiing and tennis when I have time, but mostly work."

"All work and no play makes Jack a dull boy," she remarked playfully.

"That's why, young lady, when I play, the stakes are high." His eyes pinned hers suggestively.

"Point taken. I'll consider myself warned. Do you mind if we go back to the shop on the corner? There was something I wanted to take a look at." She hesitated, then thrust out her hand. "This is for you."

Jack looked down at the small paper package she was handing him.

"For me?" he asked, embarrassed.

"Open it."

Jack began unwrapping, knowing instinctively what lay within. The paper fell to the ground and he stared at the volume of poems. Opening the cover he read the inscription she'd written.

To Jack,
For loving Scotland the way you do.

India

It was followed by the place and date. He was unexpectedly touched by her gesture and read it a second time.

"Thank you, this is— It's a wonderful gift, thanks."

"You're welcome. I can carry it in my bag if you like." She smiled, and he handed her back the book carefully. "Shall we go to the shop I mentioned?"

He took her arm and guided her through the melee of tourists and amateur collectors, treading the narrow cobbled pavement thoughtfully. He'd been given everything from Dunhill lighters to diamond cuff links, but the book meant more to him than he would have believed possible. She had captured a special moment in time that was theirs alone, and whose presence would be felt at the turning of each page.

India pointed to the store. "That's the one. I thought I saw an interesting pair of candlesticks in there."

A bell chimed as they entered the poky shop filled with antique furniture, paintings and silver. "Are those the ones you like?" he asked, pointing to a pair of three-branched silver candelabra on a mahogany lowboy in the window.

"Yes." Stepping past an ornate gold-leaf and pink velvet Recamier chaise, India picked them up to study them more closely.

She was strong but gentle, Jack noted, watching as she examined the candlesticks critically. It was then that an idea struck him. Once the Dunbar deal was closed, he'd offer her the restoration of the place. He smiled, the idea increasingly appealing. For a moment there in the square he'd almost told her he was making an offer for the place, but something had stopped him. Now he was glad. He would surprise her. Planning Dunbar's future would link her to her heritage.

"Are they what you're looking for?" he asked, seeing her set the candlesticks back carefully on the mahogany surface.

"It depends what they're asking for them," she replied, casting a professional eye over the pieces and turning to the owner who stood waiting expectantly behind an elaborate Louis XV desk.

"*Cuanto valen, señora?*" she asked, pointing out the pieces.

The woman quickly quoted her a price.

"That's outrageous," India whispered to Jack. "They're not worth half that. By the hallmarks I can tell they're not rare. Very decorative, but highly overpriced. I can pick up similar ones in London anytime."

"Just take them."

"No," she answered firmly, shaking her head and laughing, "I refuse to be taken for a ride."

"But you like them, don't you?"

"Yes, but that's not the point." She moved toward the door and nodded goodbye to the lady.

Jack stood still, trying to understand women. "India, if you like the darn things just take 'em. I know you've already imagined them someplace. See?" He smiled at her look of surprise. "I'm beginning to know you." He turned to the owner of the store.

"Jack, you don't understand. Of course I would like them, but I'd feel a perfect idiot if I overpaid, and I'm not in the mood to bargain, which is what she expects. And it's too hot in here," she added, heading purposefully toward the door. "Let's just go."

"No. Wait a minute."

The shop owner watched carefully, gauging whether the *Americano* was going to buy. He quoted her a price.

"*Señor...no se...*" she replied, shaking her head doubtfully, prepared to enter into a long discussion.

"It's that or *nada*," Jack stated firmly, looking her straight in the eye. She shrugged, then smiled, and picked up the pieces to wrap.

"Jack, please, you mustn't..." India stood by the door, fidgeting uncomfortably as he removed a credit card from his wallet. He signed the slip, pocketed his copy of the receipt and picked up the bag. "I'll carry it, it's heavy."

"Jack, I never meant for *you* to buy them." Her face was flushed, her eyes troubled.

"Why not? You gave me the book. How would you feel if I said I didn't want it?" he asked, opening the door for her.

"That's different, it's a book. It was a spur-of-the-moment thing, you know—"

"No, I don't. You gave me something that each time I look at will remind me of today, of this place, of this moment and you. I'd like you to be able to do the same."

They stepped out onto the pavement and India smiled reluctantly. "Put like that, there's very little I can say except thank you."

He glanced at his watch and smiled. "You're welcome. Tell you what—" he slipped his arm firmly through hers, guiding her along the sidewalk "—why don't we go back to the hotel, you take a long nap and we'll go out for an early dinner later on. If that suits you, of course," he added, in case his invitation sounded arbitrary.

"All right. But please, no more shopping or we won't get back to the hotel. An American tourist with more money than sense is every merchant's dream."

Jack gave a low laugh as they turned the corner, aware this was the first time any woman had tried to *stop* him from buying her something. Usually they made certain he was on the right side of the sidewalk to pass by Cartier.

India studied herself critically in the long mirror. The beige silk pants and shirt looked good, but there was still something not quite to her satisfaction. She donned her diamond studs and Lady Elspeth's pearl necklace, then took a last glimpse at herself before spraying on some Joy, the perfume she always wore.

On returning to the hotel she'd fallen fast asleep, as Jack had predicted, and woken only an hour ago. She looked fondly over at the bag containing the famous candlesticks. Jack had glossed over the gesture so smoothly, making it

seem natural. Yet it didn't seem quite comme il faut to be
accepting expensive gifts from a man. Lady Elspeth would
definitely not have approved.

But if the truth be told, and her behavior that morning
were anything to go by, she was the one with ideas. If
anyone had told her a month ago that she would feel weak
at the knees every time a man she barely knew walked
into the room, or that the scent of his skin mixed with
cologne would make her heart beat faster, she'd have told
them they were mad.

Yet she'd caught herself daydreaming a number of times
during the last week, when her mind should have been
focused on important tasks. It was ridiculous, childish
even, when all week they'd been at odds.

Yet this morning something had changed. He'd conceded immediately when he'd realized she was right about
the design problem, accepting defeat gracefully. Then
later, at San Telmo, she'd caught him looking at her in a
way that made her skin tingle and her mouth go dry. Sometimes she had the uncomfortable feeling Jack knew exactly
what was going on in her mind. She'd definitely have to
do a better job at disguising her feelings, she realized ruefully, picking up her silk jersey and throwing it lightly over
her shoulders.

At 8:05 sharp she crossed the mezzanine. Jack was sitting at the bar, relaxed and handsome in a white-and-
burgundy striped shirt and navy blazer. He rose to greet
her, taking both her hands in his and smiling at her.

"Did you sleep okay?"

"Yes, very well, thanks," she replied, disengaging herself.

"Champagne," he requested, signaling the waiter. "Oh!
And add a strawberry on the side."

"How did you know I like strawberries with champagne?" she asked, intrigued.

"I notice these things," he replied, grinning. "Where shall we go for dinner? Puerto Madero or shall we just walk over to the Recoleta?"

They decided on the Recoleta. Since the evening was pleasantly cool for the time of year, they strolled along the Avenida Alvear, then down some side streets until they reached the lively stretch of café tables and umbrellas on the promenade bordering the park of the cemetery. The city was refreshingly quiet, most people out of town on summer vacation in Punta del Este, or toasting themselves under the torrid Brazilian sun.

Jack seemed more at ease tonight than he had all week. She hoped it would last.

"I love Buenos Aires. It's like a mixture of London and Paris, with a touch of tango," she remarked.

"Good description. It's rather unique, more like Europe than South America."

"Sometimes I think it's a place I could actually live."

"Do you?" Jack gave her a sidelong glance. "The only places I think I could handle outside the U.S. are London and Scotland."

"Scotland?" India raised her eyebrows, surprised. "I'd have thought you were more a fun-in-the-sun sort of person. After all, you live in Miami."

"That's because it's convenient for me, not necessarily by choice."

"The same way I feel about Switzerland," she remarked as they crossed the road and wandered onto the sidewalk. "I love Chantemerle, but somehow it doesn't have that feeling of permanence, of— I don't quite know how to explain it. Roots, I suppose."

"I know. Like you're not really a part of it. You're only passing through."

She nodded. "That's it exactly." And why giving up Dunbar was going to be so awfully hard, she reflected, her heart sinking again. As she'd admitted to Jack earlier to-day, she virtually had no choice. Only a miracle could save it from being sold, and there were none in sight on the horizon. She sighed inwardly and put the thought aside, determined not to cloud the evening.

Jack stopped at one of the restaurants. "Do you feel like pasta? This place has great fettucine. Hernan and I have been here a couple of times. Not very adventurous to keep coming to the same spot, I know. On the other hand, it's better to be safe than sorry. What do you think?" he asked good-naturedly.

"I think it sounds delicious. I'm quite hungry after that long rest you made me take. What did you do all day?"

"Got some work done," he replied, pulling out a chair for her. They sat down to enjoy the twilight conversation and laughter surrounding them. Jack signaled the waiter and ordered her another glass of champagne, with a straw-berry and a wicked smile.

"Jack, I don't always have to have a strawberry, you know," she said with an exasperated laugh.

"Maybe you don't," he replied, leaning back, eyes glinting in the candlelight. "But seeing you nibble it is utterly delectable, believe me."

India eyed him warily, aware of the sudden intimacy that had sprung up between them. When the waiter ap-peared with the drinks, she instinctively put the strawberry to the side, sensing it had become potentially dangerous. Jack eyed the discarded fruit. He didn't comment, but there was something she hadn't seen in his look before, some-thing that left her feeling beautiful and pliable. She choked suddenly and began coughing. Jack leaned over and patted her on the back.

"Are you okay?"

"I'm fine. Something went down the wrong way," she answered lamely.

"Perhaps if you'd eaten the strawberry…" he began in a low, taunting voice.

"If I hear one more word about that wretched strawberry—"

"Okay, okay, I didn't say a word," Jack retreated, raising his hands and laughing. "Let's see what there is to eat," he added, picking up the menu.

In the park adjacent to the restaurants, couples lay on the grass, chatting and kissing in the evening shadows, listening to the melancholy strains of a tango coming from a portable radio. Suddenly the volume was turned up and a young couple rose and began to dance, their slim bronzed bodies locked in tandem. They paced out the steps with haughty grace, their severe expression etched in the glimmer of the votive candles shining unsteadily on the nearby tables. India watched entranced as they glided over the grass as if it were the parquet floor of a ballroom, admiring the fluidity of their steps and the languorous yet intense sensuality. She turned, suddenly aware of Jack's riveting gaze fixed on her. All at once she felt her skin glowing wherever it touched. It took a moment before she was able to drag her own eyes away.

Jack listened to the words of the tango, wondering what they meant, intrigued by the mysterious flow of the dancers. They moved with all the sensuality and grace of two leopards courting in the wild. But what fascinated him more was India, her eyes filled with an expression very sensual in its intensity.

For a fleeting moment as the tango reached its crescendo, he found himself yearning for something more than another fling. But he stopped himself immediately. Years ago he'd vowed not to allow deeper feelings, complications or commitments to affect his life. Up until now he'd been successful.

"Aren't they graceful." India sighed as the couple twirled into a dramatic finale and the music died.

Like the tango itself—so mannered and yet so erotic—India hid passion beneath a thin sheath of reserve. He just knew it. And the fact that she herself seemed totally unaware of it made it all the more enticing. He contemplated her for a moment, objectively, imagining that beautiful lithe body lying in his bed, rising to his touch, those huge green eyes dilating with all the unadulterated anticipation and pleasure he felt certain lay hibernating, waiting to be awakened.

"By the way, I nearly forgot…" India exclaimed matter-of-factly, bringing him crashing back to earth with a thud. "Dolores has invited you to come to the *estancia* for an *asado.*"

"Excuse me?"

"Dolores, Gabby's grandmother and Hernan's great-aunt," she explained patiently. "She's invited you on Saturday. Hernan's mother and sisters are going to be there, too. I believe Mama Carvajal thinks you might make an excellent husband for one of her daughters," she murmured demurely.

"Good Lord!" he exclaimed, horrified. "Where'd she get that notion?"

"I've no idea. But I think she feels that any bachelor of your standing and reputation should not be allowed to slip through her fingers without at least a fair try."

"What do I do?" Jack asked, looking both comically horrified and surprised.

"I suppose you could say you are married," she suggested, "or tell them you have a *novia.* You know, a fiancée. That might work."

"Great. We'll just tell 'em you're my *novia* and end of problem. You don't mind helping out an old pal, do you?"

"Don't even think about it. I refuse to do your dirty

work, Jack. I was hired to do the Palacio, not pose as the fiancée of the C.E.O. of the company.''

"It's just a small favor," he cajoled, his eyes intimate. ''Would it really feel *that* bad to pretend you cared for me a little?''

"That's not the point," she said, taking a sip of champagne and nibbling unconsciously at the strawberry.

"Then why don't we just pretend." He watched her take a tiny bite, and had to take a deep breath to keep his mind on the subject at hand. "We could carry it off."

"Don't be silly, Jack." She gave an embarrassed laugh. "Anyhow, once you meet Hernan's sisters you might regret it. One of them's simply gorgeous, tall and slim, with long black hair and flashing black eyes. She dresses beautifully, too." India tilted her head. "Although, now that I come to think of it, Angeles might be more your style," she added, warming to the theme. "She's more docile, very lovely, too, and about nineteen. Easier to manage perhaps—''

"There's only one problem—" he interrupted.

"And what's that?"

"I have not the slightest intention of marrying anyone, least of all some child almost half my age. And what gave you the idea I'd want to be with a woman who's docile?" he challenged.

"I don't know. Just an impression, I suppose. You do quite like running the show. But I could be wrong, of course. What a good thing you've told me that you're out of the running. Now I can discreetly dissuade Mama Carvajal from pushing the girls your way." She peered at him mischievously through the shadows.

"Thanks a ton," he replied sarcastically.

"Oh, you're most welcome."

Jack wondered if she had any idea how sexy she looked. He shifted in his chair, thankful that, for a bright gal, she could be mighty unobservant, and for the waiter's timely appearance with their order.

"*Fettucine al tuco para la señorita,*" he said, placing the large plate in front of India with a flourish. "And for you, *señor,* the fettucine carbonara, *correcto?*"

"Yes, and bring me a bottle of Malbec."

"Of course, *señor.* Immediately." The waiter moved away, circulating with ease between the small round tables.

"I hope you'll like the wine."

"I'm sure I will," she said doubtfully, realizing she'd already had quite a bit of champagne. She eyed the plate before her. "This looks wonderful. I hope I can do justice to it."

"You're slim enough." Jack looked her over, noting the swell of her small breasts under the silk, and her face, which even in the dark he knew was flushed. "You don't pick at your food. I hate women who push their fork around their plate and leave two-thirds of what they've ordered."

"I suppose it's thought to be ladylike. I suspect I'm just greedy."

"Sweetheart, you're the epitome of what a lady should be. For one thing, you're yourself. The only other person—" He stopped, realizing he was about to talk about Lucy.

India's eyes questioned, quietly waiting for him to continue.

"Good stuff this fettucine," he said gruffly, plunging his fork into the pasta.

India laid her fork down, expecting him to go on. But what was the point? The evening was going along just fine. Why spoil it with the past?

He glanced toward the park, where another couple had risen, and the melancholy strains of the tango had resumed.

"Is that the same tango over again. Can you translate the words?"

India listened, then peered at him over the flickering flame. "'If I had a heart, the heart that I once gave, and if I could love as I once did yesterday, if only I could forget how it was destroyed and could love you, I would...'"

Jack bit into the pasta, his mind in a frenzy, wishing he'd kept his mouth shut. He knew instinctively that India was waiting for him to reveal something of himself.

But he never talked about Lucy, not to anyone. She was a sacred part of himself that he kept hidden deep inside. At twenty-two he'd stood by her grave weeping silently. Lucy's casket was not the only thing buried that day in the small graveyard back in Tennessee. Jack's feelings had gone six feet under with each shovelful of earth.

For a while he'd tried to survive, but the scent of the flowers she'd planted in the yard had driven him crazy, so he'd left and joined the military, training for Special Ops, then been selected for missions simply because he was prepared to take risks others wouldn't. For one terrifying instant India, the candles and the chatter were blotted out by the haunting smell of death and the damp, cholera-infested heat of the jungle.

India's soft gaze searching tenderly through the shadows suddenly came into focus. Hesitantly she stretched her hand across the table. "Don't talk about it if you don't want to, Jack, but sometimes it can help to face the past. You taught me that this morning."

The knot in his throat tightened as her fingers caressed his hand. Then, to his utter surprise, he realized that he did want to talk about the past, about what he'd lost, about what he would never recover. But it was hard, and he began haltingly.

"It was so long ago, but for some reason it's always

here, always. Lucy—that was my wife—she was…'' He raised his shoulders, finding it hard to explain. "She was my girl and I loved her," he said finally. "We'd grown up together. I guess we always knew we were made for one another. It was a heck of a rumpus when we decided to get married. Our parents were against it, so we waited till her eighteenth birthday, then announced it to our folks." He smiled, reminiscing. "We had two perfect years. We never quarreled, always seemed to laugh. Of course, we were just two kids and maybe it wouldn't have lasted. She was expecting a baby when she died. We'd had the first sonogram done the day before she died. I've kept it all these years. Sometimes I look at it and wonder what my son would have grown up to be like." He looked up. "You think you'll never pick yourself up, and then in the end you do. You have to. But part of the pain and anger stays around."

She sighed, nodding sadly. "It must have been terrible. I can't begin to imagine. Nobody who hasn't been through it could." She squeezed his fingers and he drew them away abruptly, suddenly aware that he didn't want sympathy. But seeing the hurt surprise that swept over her face, he reached out again, realizing he'd been brusque when she was only trying to help. He turned her fingers over, playing with them, his mind racing.

"How did you deal with it? How did you manage to move on and stay alive inside?" she asked quietly, her eyes fixed on the candle.

"I joined the military and did some crazy things for a couple of years. When I came back I felt better. Not entirely, but some of the anger was gone and I was able to see more clearly and get on with my life. That's when I started in the hotel business." He realized she knew nothing of the world of military operations, the scent of danger, of escaping death just when all seemed lost and being responsible for other men's lives. "Like I told you, the day we met was the anniversary of Lucy's death. That's why I wasn't concentrating. You walking into my life made me feel a darn sight better though. It's a tough day every year."

He lifted her hand again, studying her long tapering fingers. Beautiful fingers. Fingers he could teach to touch. Again he quelled the sudden urge to stop talking, to push her away from him. It was his fault for having opened up, and not fair to rebuff her. "Like I said, you learn to move on and make a new life for yourself. Mine's been made up of a lot of hard work. I guess things have been tough for you, too. Losing your mom and dad can't have been easy."

"I don't think what I'm feeling can compare with what you've been through. My mother's death was natural, and I feel blessed that she died without ever being ill. I just miss her, that's all." She sipped her wine carefully. "It's also knowing that part of one's life has come to an abrupt end, and that from now on I'm on my own."

"What about your sister?"

"We don't get along too well. I suppose Serena has her own set of problems. I think she's very mixed-up, but I wish she didn't resent me so much."

"She'll get over it," he replied dryly, thinking of the huge sum of money that was about to exchange hands. Serena would become a very wealthy woman. "And you're not necessarily alone," he added, picking up his fork and pushing the fettucine around his plate in geometric patterns. "Life has a funny way of replacing in other ways what it's taken."

"That sounds very philosophical. Did it for you?"

"No," he said slowly. "Not really."

"Why do you believe it then? It doesn't make sense."

"I guess not, but I like to think it could."

"But for something good to happen you'd have to let it."

"What do you mean?" Jack watched her warily. The conversation was moving onto dangerous footing again. He signaled to the waiter and asked for some water, creating a break, then he smiled and changed the subject. "You did eat that strawberry after all."

"You're right, I hadn't noticed. Just habit, I suppose," she answered lightly, discreetly withdrawing her fingers, picking up on his obvious desire to change the conversation. "By the way, the people from the municipality office called. I wrote the message down and left it for Hernan."

"Good, he'll deal with it," he answered, grateful she'd taken his cue.

They chatted easily, sipped the rest of the wine and lingered for a while over their espressos. Jack glanced at his watch. "Shall we go?" he suggested. "It's getting late."

"Yes. Thanks for a lovely dinner."

Jack picked up her silk sweater and laid it over her shoulders, then tucked her arm in his. They sauntered slowly back toward the hotel.

"It's been a wonderful day, Jack, and great being able to chat with you by myself for once. We always seem to be surrounded by other people."

Jack shifted gears, the blood pumping faster in his veins. But his hopes were dashed by her next words.

"It's always nice when you're working in close quarters with someone to get to know them on a personal level, don't you think? I find the outcome of a good project often depends on that."

"Do you mean you consider our relationship purely professional?"

"Well, no, not entirely, but—"

Jack stopped, gripped her arms firmly and turned her gently toward him.

"I think, maybe, I don't know—"

"Stop thinking, Indy, and be honest with yourself. We both want the same thing." Then, before he could stop himself, he pulled her to him and lowered his mouth on hers. She stiffened but he didn't let go. Her lips were soft, her mouth a surprised mixture of resistance and compliance. He probed further, demanding a response. It came. Hesitant at first, then slowly he felt her fingers relax, course up his throat to touch his cheek, then glide to the back of his neck, caressing, sending a shaft of desire blazing through him.

Now all he wanted was the feel of her skin against his, to kiss every inch of her until she lay quivering in his arms, helpless. What was it about this woman that bewitched him so? He hadn't reacted like this in years. It was both frightening and exhilarating. She was perfect. He molded her to him, pressing his hand into the small of her back, ready to plunder. When she pulled away abruptly, he drew her back.

"What's wrong?" he whispered, looking down at her face, exquisitely outlined in the glimmer of an old-fashioned streetlamp. He read doubt, wonder and raw desire in her eyes, but there was something else, too. Something he couldn't identify.

"I'd better get back to the hotel," she murmured, looking away.

"Why? Don't spoil this, Indy. You know we've both been waiting for this."

"I don't think it's suitable for us to be— Our working relationship— I don't want to get involved, Jack."

"Stop kidding yourself, Indy," he cajoled. "We've been aware of one another all day, have been all week. Heck, have been since the first time we met. And anyway, who's saying anything about being involved?"

"What are you suggesting?" she asked, stiffening. "An enjoyable bout of sex?"

"Why not? We're two consenting adults. What's wrong with wanting to enjoy more than just eating and talking together? Mutually satisfying sex can be a lot of fun, you know."

"Really? Well, thanks for explaining. We obviously have very different views on the matter. Just because you're a charming, handsome American, used to getting what you want at the snap of your fingers doesn't mean I'm ready to jump into bed with you. *Or* that you're irresistible. I'm sorry if this comes as a surprise, but I can think of a number of ways of relaxing that don't entail jumping on the first mattress with the nearest available male escort." There was an angry catch in her voice, and she finally wrenched her arm away.

"Why are you so angry? You're acting like a fourteen year old."

"Well, good for me." She turned and began walking down the street.

"That husband of yours can't have known what he was doing," Jack threw after her as she began walking. "If I had a woman like you in my bed for the taking, I'd make damn sure she was well taken care of."

"I won't put you to that trouble," she threw back, her tone arctic. "If you want to get laid, Jack, go find someone else. I'm not interested."

He rammed his fists into his pockets, wondering where he'd gone wrong, and then followed her down the street, uncomfortably aware of his blunder. Why couldn't he just accept that she wasn't like the other women he was used to, that things weren't going to be the same with her, however much he might want to believe they were.

Because that would mean he cared for her.

The thought hit him like an inside curveball. She wasn't

just another meaningless fling like all the others. He strode quickly after her, ignoring the voice that warned him he was getting in over his head. Of course India was different—deliciously, tantalizingly, adorably different, and he was a fool for not recognizing it. The knowledge that he'd hurt her, acted in a way so foreign to his nature, was killing him.

He came alongside her, but she marched straight ahead, her expression stony.

"I'll take you back to the hotel," he said, matching his stride to hers.

"I'm not going back to the Alvear. I'll go to Dolores's apartment, I have the keys."

"But all your stuff's at the hotel."

She didn't answer, and they continued in tense silence until they reached the curb. "I'm sorry, Indy. I didn't mean to hurt your feelings. Please, come back to the hotel."

She hesitated, then glanced at him. "All right," she said coldly.

All Jack could think of was how entrancingly beautiful she was, and how sloppy and immature he'd been. She had a dignity all her own, yet under it he sensed a dormant volcano, a bed of lava ready to erupt. As he pushed the revolving door of the Alvear and they entered the lobby, Jack wished he could turn back the clock.

"I owe you an apology," he said quietly as they rode the elevator. This was the second time he'd found himself obliged to apologize to her. "I'm sorry."

"That's quite all right." She gave him a regal nod, leaving him empty, annoyed and at a loss.

"No, it's not."

She glanced up, and he shamelessly took advantage of her split second of surprise. Before she could react he had her in his arms, tightly held to his chest. His fingers entwined in her hair, pulling her head slowly back, forcing her gaze to his, his senses intoxicated by her subtle fragrance. "Tell me you don't want me as much as I want you," he whispered, "and I swear I'll let you go. But don't play games, Indy. Be honest with yourself."

"Jack, please—" She stood rigid in his arms.

"I won't hurt you. I didn't mean to push you or— God, you're so damn beautiful, Indy. So desirable it hurts. And you want me, too. Admit it. Don't lie to me or to yourself." Her expression went stonier still, her eyes turning from emerald spears to icy jade. "Okay, have it your way," he said, loosening his hold as fast as he'd taken it, anger and pride getting the upper hand. "Go on pretending to yourself if that's what'll keep you happy."

She stood, hair tumbling about her face, eyes alight with every mixed feeling he could name.

The elevator doors opened and they stepped out into the corridor. "Good night." He gave her a curt nod. "I'll see you tomorrow. And don't worry," he added with a short, harsh laugh, "you won't be bothered again."

Then feeling a complete fool, he turned on his heel and walked away.

India watched Jack's retreating figure, then turned down the corridor to her room. Oh, but the man was odious. Proud, arrogant and so damn sure of himself. He'd talked as if sex were some sort of therapy, like shiatsu massage. He might have been offering her an after-dinner drink for all the importance he gave it.

She let herself into the room and flopped down on the bed in the dark, remembering his hand leaning on her knee and the playful way he'd toyed with her fingers. She rolled over on her side and propped her elbow on the eiderdown, leaning her head pensively on her palm. If she was honest about it, she'd have to admit he'd been touching her off and on all day—and she'd loved it.

She sat up abruptly. Perhaps he'd taken the small gestures—that she liked to believe were merely friendly—as something more. It wasn't surprising he'd treated her the way he had, probably thinking she was like Serena, an easy lay, that it ran in the family.

She slammed a fist down on the silk counterpane and closed her eyes tight. Why did the man have to be so impossible? So desirable? So sexy?

She blushed in the dark despite herself. Why she'd ever consented to stay at the Alvear in the first place was ridiculous when she could perfectly well have gone to Dolores's apartment.

To her dismay, she realized she'd done it to be near him, unconsciously setting the scene. Never in her life had she behaved this way, allowing baser instincts to dictate her behavior, and she wasn't about to begin. She'd finish what she had to do at the Palacio, then leave for the *estancia* as soon as she could. Hopefully when she got back he'd have packed up and left for Miami.

She stormed into the bathroom to change then brushed her teeth vigorously. She'd had just about enough of Jack Buchanan, with his mercurial chops and changes, and regretted having signed that wretched contract. Of course, now it was too late to back out. An agreement was an agreement and she wasn't about to let her emotions interfere with her professional reputation.

But as she lay in bed, she remembered the look in his eyes when he'd asked her to face the truth. Was she lying to herself? And what if she was? He had no business asking her to go to bed with him, as if it meant nothing more to him than a particularly good cigar.

And *that*, she realized ruefully, was what truly hurt.

Burying her head in the covers, India gave a muffled groan. Why couldn't the wretched man just disappear, leave, get out of her life and let things go on as before?

After tossing and turning for several minutes she threw an offending pillow across the room and closed her eyes tightly, determined to go to sleep, damned if she was going to let him disturb her rest, even if he did haunt her dreams.

6

~~~ooo⊙oo~~~

The next few days were spent in stiff, silent awareness. India was polite. Jack was polite.

When by accident they knocked into one another as they turned the same corner, they excused themselves profusely, each continuing their separate ways.

The atmosphere was intolerable, and India could hardly wait for the week to end. She worked late, finishing all that was required of her, and by Thursday afternoon was ready to leave Buenos Aires and return to the *estancia*.

She'd tried desperately to relegate Jack and his callous behavior to the back of her mind, one minute rejecting it in horrified indignation, the next chiding herself, wondering if perhaps she *was* trying to fool herself. The truth was, she'd never experienced anything like this before. Day and night, she was haunted by thoughts of his strong, firm body molded against hers in the elevator, making it almost impossible to concentrate. Seeing him every day, while trying to maintain a dignified front, was no easy task either. But she was determined not to let down her guard. He would never have the satisfaction of knowing that he was right, that she did want him with a desire both shocking and exhilarating.

That particular realization hit as she was preparing to leave on Thursday afternoon. Jack stood in the office talking to the architect. As though sensing her presence, he turned. Their eyes locked for a fleeting instant and ignited all the latent feelings she'd been so determined to quell. She closed her eyes as a wave of uncontrollable images flashed before her. Turning hastily to the refrigerator, she poured herself a large glass of water, wondering how she could have such an intense response to a man who'd made it abundantly clear all he wanted was a satisfying adult liaison. There'd been no talk of affection, let alone love. Only an open declaration that what drove him was pure desire, nothing more.

Infuriated and humiliated, she downed the water and hastily picked up her things, ready to leave. The office wasn't large enough to contain both his presence and her feelings.

India drove fast, speeding through the countryside, venting her pent-up anger on the steering wheel. If he was categorizing her with Serena he had another think coming, she reflected savagely, whipping round the next bend on two wheels. She kept up the fast pace until she reached the small road that turned off to the *estancia*.

She cruised through the sagging wrought-iron gates hanging painfully on their ancient hinges, thankful that this weekend would give her some time for quiet reflection. Just driving up the alley of eucalyptus trees, breathing in their strong fragrance as the slim branches swung gently to and fro in the pleasant evening breeze, soothed her flustered nerves. She could understand why the Jesuit monks who'd first settled here had chosen this site for their monastery; the spot was the ideal setting for a sanctuary, an oasis of inner peace.

She pulled the car up to the front door, and Juan, the elderly manservant, came out to assist her.

"Señorita, permítame," he said, his voice tremulous with age. "Allow me to carry the bag."

"Gracias, Juan." India smiled. She felt awful letting him take the suitcase. His stooped back and thin arthritic body should not be subjected to the effort. But it would have been useless to protest. After thirty years of service, Juan would rather have handed in his notice than allow one of Doña Dolores's guests to carry their own luggage. India followed him slowly up the steps, asking after Severina, his wife, and his daughter, Lucia, who had just had a fifth baby. By the time they reached her room, India had learned all about the rigors of the birth and the thriving state of the mother and newborn child.

On entering the cool bedroom, with its four-poster bed, crocheted eiderdown and lace curtains framing the open window and the reddening sky beyond, she made a firm decision: no more thinking about Jack. She hung her clothes in the massive eighteenth-century armoire, convinced the secret lay in exercising self-control. But his image kept popping up no matter how hard she tried.

"Stop it!" she exclaimed, grimacing angrily at her own reflection. "Stop making a fool of yourself!" She wished there was something she could smash—preferably over Jack's head. Taking a deep breath, she decided the best solution was to go for a long swim before dinner and pretend the man had never existed.

She changed into a swimsuit and left for the pool, convinced she could take charge of the situation. Of course she could. There was nothing a little perseverance and self-discipline couldn't take care of. Plus, she had other things such as Dunbar to think about.

"Oh, dear, that wretched telephone again," Kathleen exclaimed, hurrying into the library. "Dunbar House," she announced grandly. "The lady of the house speaking."

"Kathleen? Is that you?" India's voice came down the line and Kathleen swallowed nervously.

"Yes, dear, it's me. I've taken to announcing myself because we've had a number of odd callers lately asking all sorts of questions. I put them off by letting them know that they're dealing with someone in authority."

"Oh, I see. Yes, of course. How are things getting along, Kath?"

"Very nicely, dear. We had the tenants in for the yearly party—that went very well, of course—but otherwise things have been very quiet. Serena came for tea on Sunday with that dreadful man, but mercifully they didn't stay long. He's a very odd fish!" she exclaimed, glancing out of the window as a car pulled up on the gravel.

"I may be away for a bit longer than I'd originally planned," India said. "I've taken on a job here and I may need to stick around for a while. But as soon as I get back I'll contact Mr. Ramsey."

"There's no rush, dear. The last time he phoned he said everything was under control."

The door opened abruptly and Serena entered the library. Kathleen put a finger to her lips, then covered the speaker. "It's India," she said in a loud whisper.

"Hope she gets gobbled up by a bloody croc," Serena hissed in a loud whisper, throwing herself onto the sofa.

"Shh. For goodness' sake, Serena." Kathleen covered the mouthpiece apprehensively. "The line's excellent."

"Hello? Are you there?"

"Yes, of course, that was just Mrs. Walker passing through. She sends her love."

"Send her mine. And thanks for all you're doing, Kath. Just knowing you're there gives me peace of mind. If there was anything urgent you'd tell me, wouldn't you? You have my numbers."

"Of course, dearest. Don't worry about a thing. I explained to Mr. Ramsey you were in South America, so he won't be expecting to hear from you until your return."

"Oh, thanks, that was most thoughtful of you."

"Not a bit. Take care of yourself, dear. Don't pick up any odd bugs or anything. I've heard those places can be most insalubrious."

"I'll survive. Bye for now, Kath, and thanks again for all your support. I don't know where I'd be without it."

"Goodbye, dear. *À bientôt.*"

Kathleen hung up and turned to where Serena sat eyeing her with a smirk. "What did she have to say for herself?"

"That she needs to spend some more time in South America. I told Mr. Ramsey when he last called."

"Good. Now she won't bother to correspond with him," Serena murmured thoughtfully.

"Excuse me?"

"No, nothing. Just mumbling to myself," Serena answered dismissively. "By the way, do you know if Peter Kinnaird is back?"

"No, he isn't. I met Diana yesterday at the baker's and she told me he'll be away in Asia for at least a month. Did you need to see him about something?" Kathleen casually picked up a copy of the *Edinburgh Tatler.*

"Nothing that can't wait till he gets back."

"There's a lovely picture of India in the *Tatler,* page ten." Kathleen opened the magazine. "Have you seen it?"

"India? What on earth would the *Tatler* want to put *her* picture in for?" Serena grabbed the magazine and stared down at India's lovely face. "What a bloody nerve. Listen to this. They say *she's* inherited Dunbar with her half sister! I'll phone the editor and complain. Don't they know who's who anymore?"

"Apparently not," Kathleen murmured, tongue-in-cheek.

Serena threw herself back crossly on the sofa, casting

her eyes about the room disdainfully. "I can't wait to get rid of this pile of rubble," she remarked.

"I'm sure," Kathleen answered blandly, pensively folding the throw that had fallen to the floor. "In your position perhaps I'd feel the same." Then she picked up a dirty coffee cup and smiled to herself before slipping discreetly from the room, leaving Serena to enjoy her daydreams alone.

Jack sat next to Hernan, gazing out over the pampas, enjoying the hot morning breeze and the smell of the land as the Testarossa sped toward Lujan.

"This whole region around Buenos Aires is great for raising cattle and breeding horses," Hernan commented. "You'll see the Aberdeen Angus and the shorthorn cattle at the *estancia*. Tío Candido, my mother's cousin, has cattle and breeds polo ponies."

"How long have they had the place?" Jack asked.

"It's been in their family for several generations. The first O'Halloran arrived in 1852, and it's been handed down from father to son ever since. They've been very astute, never getting involved in the various political uprisings that have taken place over the years, and the *estancia* has prospered."

"What exactly is an *estancia?* A cattle ranch?" Jack inquired.

"To be an *estancia* a property must be over four hundred hectares in size. The first *estancias* were given to the settlers by the Spanish crown as land for their cattle to roam on, and ownership was identified through the branding of the animals. By the time the O'Hallorans came things were different, and people were settling down."

"O'Halloran? That's Irish." Jack was surprised. He'd imagined most people here would be of Spanish descent.

"There are various well-known *estancias* in the region,

many of them owned or built by Scots and Irish families. The Gibsons, the Maguires, and many more.''

Jack leaned back and let his mind wander. He hadn't caught a glimpse of India since Thursday afternoon. She must know he was coming today, for she'd told him about the invitation to the *asado*. But what would her reaction be? Anger? Or worst of all, indifference?

"Say, what's going on between you and India," Hernan asked, giving him a sidelong glance as though he'd read his thoughts. "Don't take this the wrong way, but there's been such an atmosphere in the office, I couldn't help noticing. She's not been around the last couple of days either. Did you guys have a fight?"

"We don't see eye to eye, that's all."

"About the Palacio?" Hernan cast him an amused look from under raised eyebrows. "You have to be kidding. I may look dumb, but I'm not blind. It's nothing to do with work, it's man-woman stuff."

"I don't need involvement in my life, Hernan. Fooling around with a woman like India is an open invitation for trouble. And believe me, I don't need that," he answered flatly.

Hernan gave him another sidelong glance but said nothing, and they drove on in silence for a while. Soon they passed through a hamlet, then Hernan turned off to the left and drove down a small, potholed road for about a mile.

"Here we are," he said, stopping before two large stone gateposts covered in ivy that supported a large wrought-iron gate. "Can you open up?"

"Sure." Jack got out and pushed open the creaking gate for the Ferrari to pass through, immediately struck by the tranquillity and the rich scent of eucalyptus coming from the trees bordering the driveway. When the house came into view, he was agreeably impressed by the arched stone porch and faded terra-cotta facade where creeping ivy and hibiscus wove their way up the walls. The house reminded him of a convent, but was topped by an extraordinary tower, completely out of character with the rest, like that of a small castle. He remarked on it as they got out of the car and walked up the flagstone steps to the huge paneled front door.

"An ancestor with extravagant tastes," Hernan commented, laughing. "Looks really strange, doesn't it?"

He tugged a thick, well-worn bellpull, the ring echoing deep into the nether regions of the house. Soon steps could be heard and the door opened, revealing a small maid in a black uniform and white starched apron. She poked out her gray head, eyes bright with anticipation.

"*Señor Hernan!*" she exclaimed, throwing up her arms and giving him a broad, near-toothless grin. "*Que bueno verlo che!* When Doña Dolores told us you were coming, I said to Juan it must be at least seven months since we've seen Señor Hernan. Come in, come in," she urged, grasping Hernan's hands, her tiny brown face withered as a dried olive, and her bright smile revealing an interesting array of gold teeth and empty spaces where the replacements should have been.

"*Donde está mi tía?*" Hernan asked, smiling at Jack. "This is Severina. She knows of all my escapades from the time I was two. There's no hiding anything from her." Apparently she was also somewhat deaf, for he bent close to her while he spoke. "This is my American partner, *el* Señor Jack."

She nodded and smiled at Jack approvingly, then led them through a black-and-white marble-tiled hall and down a whitewashed passage. The walls were decked with stag heads and weapons of various eras interspersed with dark paintings and portraits. Then, reaching a wide archway, they descended two shallow steps to the main living area.

Jack stopped for a moment. The room was amazing. The gleaming hardwood floor was strewn with Oriental rugs, and a huge stone fireplace reached almost to the ceiling, while fine pieces of period furniture stood against the walls and were dotted about. Jack looked up at the ceiling, interested in the heavy dark beams he figured were *pau d'arco* and must have been brought from Brazil during the last century.

A regal woman he assumed was Hernan's aunt sat in the corner of a huge sofa. "Tía Dolores," Hernan exclaimed, going over to kiss her. "It's wonderful to see you looking younger and more lovely every day." He turned to Jack. "Tía, may I introduce Jack Buchanan, my partner in the Palacio de Grès."

"Mr. Buchanan," she said in very British English, extending long, graceful fingers to him. "What a pleasure to receive you here at the Estancia Tres Jinetes." Jack automatically raised her hand to his lips, amused that he was being thoroughly scrutinized.

"Thank you, ma'am. It's a pleasure to be here."

"I've heard so much about you," she said, smiling elusively like the Mona Lisa. "Do sit down and we'll have some coffee." She waved a bejeweled hand in the direction of the sofa, then signaled discreetly to old Severina. Jack glanced around, still struck by the room. The sofa looked new, and oddly out of place among the stiff, formal furniture.

"As you can see, Mr. Buchanan, we are redecorating. My granddaughter, Gabby, and her friend, India, whom I believe you're acquainted with, say the place looks like a mausoleum," she explained with a languid sigh, the diamonds on her rings sparkling as she raised a hand to her throat. "India insisted I buy this sofa to replace what she fondly called the *monstrosity* that previously stood in its place. So you see we have this odd mélange of furnishings.

But they're probably right. One needs to throw out the old and let in the new. Just as in life, don't you think?'' She smiled, arching a perfectly shaped eyebrow.

''I guess so,'' Jack murmured, fascinated by this amazing character.

''How long do you plan to stay in Buenos Aires?'' Dolores asked, crossing one slim bronzed leg over the other and draping an arm gracefully over the back of the sofa.

''I don't know exactly, it depends on Hernan and the project. Things seem to be running pretty smoothly, so I guess I won't have to stick around too long.'' Jack realized that, despite her age, he had rarely beheld a more elegant woman. She was a true grande dame. Well, perhaps one other, he thought ruefully, his mind returning to India, wondering when she would make an appearance.

''I would imagine you have a life fraught with fascinating experiences, Mr. Buchanan. From what I hear, you are a man of...many responsibilities,'' she said with another discreet smile, her almond-shaped hazel eyes bright and attentive. He suspected she already knew everything there was to know about him.

''Well, I get to see some interesting places,'' he replied blandly. ''Unfortunately, most of my time is spent in offices working, though I find time for some other activities, too,'' he added with a smile.

''Ah, how exciting. A man of action!'' she exclaimed, nodding to Severina, who set the coffee tray down on the table among the art books and ashtrays. ''You are very charming, and probably thoroughly wicked.'' She smiled knowingly as she poured the coffee, then handed him a dainty china cup. ''If I were a few years younger, I would flirt with you myself. But alas, I must leave that to the younger generation.'' She laughed. ''Have you introduced him to anyone, Hernan? Perhaps Alejandra Fierro de Lima. She's a lovely girl, very well brought up. And naturally my granddaughter Gabriella will be delighted to meet you."

"*Tía,*" Hernan warned, laughing and wagging his finger. "No matchmaking. Jack is well able to fend for himself. Anyway, he's not looking for a wife. Or are you?" Hernan asked, his expression suddenly comical.

"Of course not, *querido,*" Dolores murmured placatingly. "I wasn't suggesting anything of the sort. I was merely thinking that some pleasant feminine companionship can never do any harm. We can't have a handsome man like you wandering around Buenos Aires without a suitable escort."

"Don't worry about me, ma'am, I'm doing just fine," Jack replied, sipping the strong coffee.

"Ha!" Hernan laughed. "Believe me, *Tía,* he doesn't lack *feminine companionship,* as you put it. I'm not sure you'd approve of some of the candidates, though they—"

"Silly boy, drink your coffee and don't be rude," Dolores interrupted, rapping him lightly over the knuckles with her ivory fan. "*That* wasn't what I was referring to." She returned her gaze to Jack's, allowing the fan to slide gracefully open. "Ah, this dreadful heat," she began, fanning herself languorously. "Gabriella and India are by the pool. After coffee you might like to join them, Mr. Buchanan."

"Please, call me Jack."

"In that case, you must call me Dolores. It's so much easier to dispense with formalities, isn't it? In the old days people were so prim and proper. Now things are much more *décontracté.*" The woman clearly had everything running to her liking, and Jack couldn't help but admire the neat way she handled everyone.

She waved the fan once more, her fingers poised, her expression suddenly pensive. "You know, your name reminds me of an uncle of my husband's—Jack O'Halloran.

Such a handsome, remarkable man, and wicked like you."
She gave him another mischievous smile, full of worldly
wisdom. "Unfortunately the poor man was eaten by a
crocodile in the Amazon. Such a shame, it was a great
loss."

She got up suddenly, snapping the fan shut. "I'll leave
you children now, for I have to get back to my painting.
I'm trying something modern. Your uncle says it's quite
ghastly, Hernan, but I'm sick of impressionist flowers,"
she confided with an amused shrug. "The girls will entertain you, and I'll see you later at the *asado*. Hernan, dearest, remind Severina to get the Malbec Centenario from
the cellar, will you?"

"Of course, *Tía*." The two men rose as she glided from
the room.

"That's one great lady," Jack observed. "She must
have been something in her heyday. And this place is
amazing." He gazed around the room again, then wandered to the French window and looked out across the
garden to the pampas that stretched interminably on the
hazy horizon.

"She was. She and Evita Perón were great rivals. You
should see the pictures of her. She was very cunning, too.
She had all her jewelry copied, keeping the real stuff in
her safe at the bank. Evita had a predilection for other
women's jewels, and expected them to be handed over
immediately if she so much as admired them."

"Ha! Good for Dolores. But is she really the same generation as Evita?"

"We're absolutely prohibited from asking her age, but
I assure you she's much older than she looks. Come on,
let's go see what the girls are doing. Actually, you go
ahead and I'll join you. I'd better see to my aunt's wine
or there'll be hell to pay later if it hasn't been opened
right." Hernan eyed Jack speculatively. "I presume that

since you're not interested in India, you won't mind if I..." He paused, cocking an amused eyebrow. For the first time in many years, Jack found himself at a loss.

"Where's the pool?" he asked gruffly, leaving Hernan's question unanswered.

"Just go through that arched veranda over there, and you'll come into a courtyard. It's there."

"Okay, see you in a while."

"You bet!" Hernan winked and left in the opposite direction.

Jack found the pool, set serenely among white wooden pergolas covered by a riotous explosion of hibiscus and bougainvillea.

He stared across the water at the figure lying facedown on a wrought-iron chaise longue. There was no one else in sight.

He walked around the pool, certain it was India, wondering how to approach her. Should he be casual, as though nothing had occurred? He was damned if he was going to apologize again. As he got closer he noticed she'd opened the back of her bikini top and was covered only by a tiny white bikini bottom; the rest was a beautiful expanse of golden tanned skin. Her hair, thrown up from her neck, was fanned voluptuously over a plush white towel.

Jack approached quietly, realizing she was asleep. My God, she was splendid. He let his gaze wander, traveling slowly from her heels, up the long shapely bronzed legs to the perfect derriere, then on up her smooth back to the chestnut mass beyond. For an instant he hesitated; she seemed so peaceful. A surge of tender desire rushed through him. Then, catching sight of a bottle of suntan lotion lying next to her bare shoulder, he shoved away the tenderness and stuck with the desire.

He picked the lotion up and squeezed some into his

hand, faltering for only a moment. Should he? he wondered, his hand filled with white cream. Things couldn't get much worse than they already were. And it probably wasn't good for her to be lying like this without enough protection.

Satisfied with his motives, he crouched next to her and began gently massaging the cream into her bare back. Lord, she felt good, her skin silky and warm as his hands wandered, gliding softly down to the edge of the bikini, then back up to her neck. He gently kneaded her muscles, feeling the sun penetrate his back.

She moved very slightly, making a little sound of pleasure that left him dizzy with longing. His mouth went dry, and he wondered if it had been a good idea to come at all. He knew he should leave, just get up and go before it was too late. But how could he when the urge to take her in his arms was so intense? He closed his eyes for a moment, loving the sensation of her body under his touch, realizing that only God knew what might happen if he stayed.

India could feel herself growing languid, succumbing to the pressure of someone's hands, incredible hands that she hoped would investigate farther.

Then slowly she opened her eyes, remembering where she was. This was no dream. Someone *was* stroking her back. Horrified, she whirled swiftly around, forgetting her unclasped bikini.

"What on earth— Oh my God!" she exclaimed, one hand flying to cover her breasts as the other fumbled behind her for the bikini top.

"I was just putting some cream on you," Jack replied reproachfully. "You shouldn't be lying in the sun like that without enough protection. You could get burned. Here, let me help you." He reached down and handed her the bikini top, then stood behind her to help fasten it.

India helplessly allowed him, knowing she'd never manage it herself, wondering why, instead of being furious, her pulse was beating ten to the dozen. He finished the task matter-of-factly, then sat down beside her without being asked. He was tanned and very handsome in off-white pants and a faded jean shirt, his eyes even bluer than she remembered them. That same unmanageable desire that had overcome her in the office returned with an overpowering rush, and she felt dizzy, trying desperately to remember all she'd told herself about self-discipline and quiet composure. Where on earth had they gone?

"What are you doing here?" she asked nonchalantly, forgetting she had told him of the invitation.

"I came with Hernan for the *asado,* remember?"

"Well, nobody mentioned you were actually coming, that's all. I suppose this was her doing," she said crossly, realizing Dolores had been up to her tricks again.

"Yeah, well, you're probably right," he said soothingly.

India got up abruptly. "Well, don't just sit there. Say something, for goodness' sake. Why did you come? I don't think it was very tactful under the circumstances." She tried to infuse distance into her words, but succeeded only in sounding petty. Frankly she was fed up with him popping into her life, upsetting her equilibrium, and cross with herself for conveniently forgetting it was Saturday.

"Calm down, Indy," he said, picking up her basket filled with suntan lotion and magazines. "Don't get mad at me. I'm here on a peace mission. Look, I messed up and I'm sorry. I should never have spoken to you the way I did, or said the things I did. It was despicable, and I'm sorry." He sounded contrite. "I know it's a lot to ask, but would you consider starting all over again? Wipe the slate and pretend none of this ever happened? I swear I'll do better this time." Then he gave her a smile so beguiling her heart did a double somersault, and she leaned down and busied herself with the towel, trying to mask her confusion.

"Please, Indy?" he pleaded.

"Jack, I—"

"Come on. Give me a break, a chance at redemption?"

She turned and, seeing the beseeching look in his eyes, couldn't help herself from smiling. His eyes held that special look she'd seen only fleetingly. Perhaps she hadn't been wrong—and the Jack from Scotland did exist after all, hidden somewhere below the surface. She eyed him skeptically, disarmed by his penitent expression, then stretched out her hand. Part of her wanted to savor the moment—to see him pleading was surprisingly satisfying—but as he took her fingers, a breathtaking current ran sharply through her.

"Thanks," he said, raising her hand to his lips and brushing the inside of her wrist. "I promise you won't regret it. I'm sorry I've behaved like a jerk."

"You're forgiven." She returned his smile, letting him hold on to her hand. Their eyes met, electricity sparking between them once more. He drew her to him and gently folded her in his arms. It felt so right, India realized, allowing her head to rest on his shoulder. Then she raised her face and he deposited a soft chaste kiss on her lips before gently drawing back.

"We'd better go," he murmured regretfully. "Looks like they're preparing some good stuff out there and I have a feeling Hernan's going to be here in a couple of minutes." He flashed her a grin, his old self once more.

They picked up her stuff and sauntered slowly back through the cloistered arches to the house. She knew that by allowing him to stay she'd surrendered. She'd finally admitted the truth and recognized what she wanted.

* * *

It was a magnificent day, and Dolores proved herself to be a skilled and entertaining hostess. Jack took care to stay close to India as they sat around the huge brick barbecue, where an immense piece of meat lay covered in rock salt, cooking slowly. He hadn't talked much to the other twenty people, except for Hernan's great-uncle who had taken them to see the polo ponies in the stables. Otherwise his undivided attention was given to India.

"Why don't we go back to town tonight and have dinner," he suggested once he'd managed to drag her away from the crowd.

"Yes, I suppose I could. I have to be in the office early tomorrow anyway. Eduardo's made those changes on the bathroom layout I asked him for, and I want to see it before anyone gets in to work."

"Fine, then ride back with Hernan and me. Are you staying at Dolores's place?"

"Not tonight. Her cousins from Montevideo are there, so I'll take a room at the Alvear."

"At the company's expense," he said firmly.

"There's really no—"

"Shh, no arguing. That's the way I want it. Let me find Hernan and see what time he wants to leave." Jack was anxious to get back to town, to be alone with her away from all these people. *Cool it,* the small voice inside his head commanded. *Just cool it.* They rose and strolled back along the dirt road, past the corral and through the gate into the garden.

He found Hernan and soon they were taking their leave.

He noticed Dolores whisper something in her ear, and saw India blush as she kissed her goodbye. Then Dolores cast him that elusive smile of hers.

They had a pleasant drive back to town, squeezed in the Testarossa, joking and talking, enjoying the fresh air and the sunset.

"What about tonight?" Hernan asked. "Would you like to go out?"

"I think I'll pass. Tomorrow's gonna be a long day," Jack replied, nudging India's shoulder.

She lowered her head, hiding a smile. "Thanks, Hernan, but I should turn in early, too. Plus, we ate such a huge lunch, I don't think I could manage anything else."

Jack hid a flash of triumph. After this it would be clear sailing—and this time he'd make sure he got it right.

They sat beside one another in the smoky half-lit atmosphere of the Africa, the nightclub next to the Alvear Palace, his arm thrown casually around her shoulders. India glanced sideways at him. He was so damnably handsome. But there was more to it. She couldn't remember ever thinking about another man like this. And since her only lover had been Christian, she didn't have any basis for comparison.

That, she realized, amused despite her professed intention to take things slowly, was a status Jack would be only to happy to alter. She drank him in, loving everything about him. She let herself lean just a little closer, enjoying the feel of his fingers brushing her shoulder, caressing her bare skin. Dinner had been delightful, Jack attentive and charming, and when he'd suggested they go to the nightclub for a drink, she hadn't hesitated.

"I like this," he remarked when the music changed from salsa to a slow romantic bolero. "Let's dance." He drew her up and led her on to the dance floor. India held her breath when his arms closed firmly around her. They swayed to the rhythm of the music, Jack's hand sliding up her back, drawing her head into the crook of his shoulder, his body molding hers just as she'd dreamed so many times since that first disastrous evening in the Recoleta. She wished the dance would go on forever, for being in his arms felt so right. Too right, she reflected ruefully, his fingers lacing through her hair, sending tiny shivers down her spine. She was tempted to throw caution to the winds, but realized she wanted far more from this man than he was prepared to offer. And the thought of being hurt once more loomed before her.

Since that first morning in the drawing room of the Palacio, she'd gone through a plethora of emotions. Attraction, desire, followed by anger and self-recrimination, then longing. She'd never had to deal with this side of herself before, hadn't known it existed. And she wasn't sure she liked it either, not when it left her feeling out of control and vulnerable.

He stroked the small of her back tenderly, guiding her into a dark corner. She lifted her face from his shoulder and his mouth covered hers, gentle but demanding, teasing responses from her she didn't know she had. They danced on, neither wanting to break the magic, his kiss and caresses a torment of sensual emotion.

When the music ended they moved slowly apart, India dizzy and elated. She'd never imagined it could feel so good simply to be in a man's arms and be kissed. She looked into his eyes, feeling a sudden rush of tenderness, then caught herself up in time, remembering that all he wanted was fun.

"Is something wrong?" he asked as they sat down. His voice was husky, making it hard for her to think straight.

"I'm fine," she replied, determined she would be.

Jack's fingers caressed her. "Just relax," he whispered.

Suddenly, fear of suffering the pain and humiliation she'd lived through after Christian swept over her, and she tensed.

"What's wrong, Indy?"

"Nothing, I'm fine," she lied.

"That jerk husband of yours hurt you badly, didn't he?"

He slipped his fingers under her chin and turned her face toward him, his eyes scrutinizing her face intensely.

"It's past history and not worth talking about," she whispered, tears unaccountably stinging her eyes.

"Don't talk. Just let it go." He drew her to him and cradled her, resting her head on his shoulder, stroking her hair.

"What are you so afraid of?" he asked at last.

She shrugged, drawing away and taking a quick sip of her drink. "Nothing and everything, I suppose. It's silly, I know. Chloë's always telling me to let my hair down and enjoy life. And I try. But sex isn't everything, after all, is it?" She glanced briefly at him, gauging his expression.

"No, of course not." He lit a cigar, rolling it slowly in his fingers, his eyes never leaving hers. "But it sure makes up an important part of a relationship. And it can be very pleasurable, though apparently you don't seem to think so." He said the last with a tender smile.

"What do you mean?" she asked, embarrassed. "I'm not a nun, you know. Of course I realize sex can be fun."

He puffed on the cigar and grinned wickedly. "Maybe we should try, just to make sure."

"Jack, you're impossible." She laughed. "You never take anything I say seriously, because you're arrogant enough to think you can change my mind. Just accept that we don't see eye to eye on the subject. For you sex is an amusing pastime, for me— Well, I equate it with deeper feelings."

"Do you really think that if we made love, I would consider it simply as a relaxing way to pass the time?" He leaned closer, slipping his arm back to its former position, his eyes penetrating.

"That's basically what you implied the other night," she replied doubtfully.

"Forget the other night. That was a bad mistake which I've regretted ever since. I try to deny things to myself. I have a habit of not allowing my emotions to get involved." He looked straight at her. "What would it mean to you?"

"Maybe we should go," she said, suddenly flustered, not knowing what to answer.

"What would it mean to you, Indy?"

"I haven't the faintest idea," she answered, irritated. "I've never had casual sex. I know you'll think it dreadfully provincial of me, but I still think it involves a commitment, and neither of us wants that. So you see? There's no way the twain can meet."

"I want you, Indy. I've wanted you since the first time we met. It's not just sex, it's something more, but right now I can't define it." He pulled away abruptly and asked a passing waiter for the bill. Then he leaned over and kissed her again. "No need to rush anything. There's a right time for everything. You'll see."

They left the club and headed back to the hotel, chatting pleasantly, the tension dissipating as they rode the elevator and headed down the corridor to her room.

When they reached her door, India had a split second of doubt. It must have shown, for he looked down at her, smiling the crooked smile that made his eyes crinkle at the corners. Then he drew her close.

"I'd better leave," he murmured huskily into her hair.

She nodded into the lapel of his blazer, wishing she could take the plunge.

"Lock that door behind you," he admonished. "I might be tempted to come back. Let's meet downstairs for breakfast at eight."

"Yes, boss."

"Don't get sassy with me, young lady. Just open that

door before I change my mind.'' He dropped a kiss on her mouth and saw her in.

India let the door close gently behind her, feeling strangely empty. She moved to the dressing table and removed her jewelry, surprised when she looked into the mirror how bright her eyes were. Jack Buchanan was altogether too tempting, too sexy and far too near for safety. At least now she had a good idea what the expression ''walking on a cloud'' meant. And in a strange way she was beginning to trust him.

Soon she was undressed and in bed. Turning off the lamp, she lay staring at the shadows that fluttered over the ceiling, reflecting on the strangeness of her situation. Here she was, a twenty-eight-year-old woman, lying in bed alone, dreaming about a man a few rooms down the corridor. How absurd could one get? Maybe it was time to make the dream come true, to finally go after it instead of always shying away, wondering what the consequences would be. She remembered Dolores's words, spoken in her ear on the steps as they'd departed from the *estancia*. *''Give yourself a chance, darling, he's worth any and every future regret, believe me.''* Typical of Dolores, of course, but perhaps not wrong.

She wished Chloë weren't in Sydney, wondering what time it was in Australia. Perhaps she could reach her.

Suddenly the phone rang, and India picked up, surprised.

''Hello?''

''Hi, it's me. I just wanted to say good-night, make sure you were okay.''

''I'm fine, Jack. Thanks,'' she replied softly.

''Good. Sleep tight and wake up bright-eyed and bushy-tailed as we say in the South. There's lots of work to be done!''

"I know, and I just remembered I have to be in Rio by the end of the week. I'd completely forgotten about the hotel opening."

There was a moment's silence. "Why don't I come along? It's not a place you want to go on your own. It's darn dangerous."

"Don't be silly. I've been there often enough and nothing's ever happened to me. You just have to know the ropes."

"Still, we could fly up in my plane. That way I could see Cardoso's hotel. I have an invitation somewhere," he said, laughing. "And on a practical note, much of what you described there could probably be applied to our project here."

"There is that, but—" She was suddenly hesitant. The whole thing was moving too fast, memories of the other evening's fiasco not entirely forgotten. Of course, it *would* be a good idea for him to see the hotel firsthand, and there were a number of interesting aspects of La Perla that could be adapted to the Palacio de Grès.

"What do you say? Shall we do it?"

She took the plunge. "All right. Why not? I think it would be a great idea. The hotel does have some interesting features."

"Okay then, that's settled. Sleep tight, princess," he said softly and hung up.

India had never been called princess before, and it sounded oddly pleasant. She was touched he'd taken the trouble to call, and excited at the idea of him joining her for the trip. Perhaps for once she'd allow things to take their course.

She fell asleep almost at once, feeling strangely happy, and the dreams she dreamed would have left Jack breathless, had he been privy to them.

* * *

When was the last time he'd dropped a woman off at her door and not gone inside? Jack asked himself. Longer than he liked to remember, he reflected, smiling as he switched on the bedside lamp. Then he went to the window and gazed down at the lights on Alvear.

India. This whole episode was an exercise in self-control. Maybe if she hadn't looked up at him, her eyes so full of trust. If she hadn't tensed in a way that told him better than words she'd been badly hurt. Why hadn't that worried him a few nights ago? After all, he'd known then about the husband who'd obviously caused her more damage than he'd at first believed.

Tonight he'd sensed her deep-rooted terror of being hurt once again. He clenched his fist and turned back into the room, angry. It was obvious her broken marriage had left a deep scar. He suddenly wished he could smash his fist into the face of the son of a bitch who'd caused her that pain.

He'd go with her to Rio and then head straight home to Miami. There was no use prolonging the torture. After all, if he did make love with her and left her, he'd be a bigger jerk than her ex-husband.

He opened the windows, allowing in the buzz of the late-night city traffic, then flung himself in an armchair. He didn't feel like going to bed, not his bed anyway. He groaned and lit a cigar, but he didn't feel like smoking.

He got up, stubbed out the offending cigar and took out his laptop. If he couldn't sleep, at least he could check his e-mail and get some work done. He logged in and retrieved his messages. There was one from Quince concerning Dunbar. He leaned forward, glad to learn their offer had been accepted. Then he moved on to Chad's. *Ancient family documents I think you'll be fascinated to read...* Chad was always digging up old bits and pieces from their family history. He should have been a genealogist or a historian instead of a businessman, Jack reflected, pondering a while on his younger brother's interests.

Then he focused on tomorrow's memos, India thankfully forgotten—for a little while at least.

Serena eyed Kathleen suspiciously, wondering why she'd been so insistent they come to tea *again*. She was nothing but a poor relation Mummy had kept on out of a misguided sense of duty. Serena sniffed, disgusted, having little patience with sentimental nonsense.

Thank God for the sale to Jack Buchanan. The offer was excellent and she'd signed her agreement happily, already dreaming of the money in her account, proud of the way she'd managed old Ramsey. To think she'd convinced him she and India had made up their differences. He must be getting doddery. It was natural, he'd said, with the pride of an old retainer, that a property of Dunbar's standing should attract the interest of important buyers before it appeared on the market. He hadn't even questioned India allowing her to deal with the Dunbar affairs while she was away. Silly old fool. He didn't seem to realize that Buenos Aires was one of the most modern cities in the world and India only a phone call away.

But the less he thought, the better. Now that she'd put Ramsey in touch with Jack's company lawyers she couldn't afford any slipups. The whole deal had to be sewed up tight before India found out the true state of affairs. By then things would be too far gone for her to do anything about it.

"More tea, Serena dear?" Kathleen inquired.

God, how she loathed that stupid motherly tone Kathleen adopted. As though the woman had any rights at Dunbar. Thank God all this would soon be over. But Ramsey had been clear. No one at Dunbar must be told about the sale at present. Things had to be done properly. As if she wanted to let the cat out of the bag! "No thanks, Kath, but I will have another piece of this delicious shortbread. Is it your recipe?"

"Actually, I got it from Aunt Honoria shortly before she died. An odd old fish, wasn't she? Do you remember her?"

"Vaguely. She was always crotchety and smelled of mothballs."

Maxi laughed. "I had an aunt like that. Every summer we were obliged to visit her in Hamburg. A dreadful old battle-ax. An infliction on all old, aristocratic families, I suppose," he said with a supercilious twitch of the upper lip. "Mercifully, she died of a stomach ailment."

Kathleen tittered and passed the shortbread. "Have you any news of Buchanan, Serena? He seemed so interested in the house the day he came over, I thought perhaps he might be inquiring about buying it."

"Unfortunately not." She shrugged. "A pity, but there we are."

"Perhaps it wasn't meant to be, dear. Things happen for a reason." Kathleen smiled benignly.

Serena stuck her tongue in her cheek, glad she'd put Kathleen off track. She didn't trust her, and the last thing she needed was for Kathleen to blabber to India and upset the applecart.

"India sent me a lovely postcard from Buenos Aires. She hasn't been in touch again though."

"It's probably difficult to get through." Serena forced herself to exercise patience she never knew she possessed, frankly impressed at her own willpower.

Her eyes wandered around the room, feeling no compunction when they alighted on her mother's portrait or any of the other treasures that would soon be gone, transformed into a wonderful wad of cash to be tucked away in high-yielding shares in some offshore haven.

She gave Kathleen a sweet smile. "This is simply delicious, Kathleen dearest. We must come more often. You've made such a home out of Dunbar. I don't know what we'd do without you. You run it so much better than anyone else."

She watched Kathleen's pink-powdered cheeks glow, and caught Maxi's eye. All it took was some buttering up. Stupid creature. As if she was going to confide her plans to Kathleen. It had been a pity Kathleen was around when Jack had visited, but it was unavoidable. Never mind. Perhaps it had been worth wasting an afternoon after all, if only to quell any doubts the old bag might have.

Serena forced down the last of the sickly shortbread and dreamed of cocktails at sundown in the Caribbean, on the Camper & Nicholson yacht she planned to lease when all this was over.

It wouldn't be long now.

7

India spent the next few days preparing for the trip to Rio, and Jack left for Uruguay and Bolivia on business. They barely saw each other until Friday afternoon, when they met in the lobby of the Alvear to go to the airport.

The flight to Rio was relaxing, Jack doing everything to put her at ease, knowing how tense he himself got before an opening. Once they arrived, he made himself scarce, allowing her to get on with any last-minute commitments.

Now he wandered through the crowded reception room, genuinely impressed by what he saw. Few things impressed him anymore, but this was state-of-the-art. He doubted the hotel could be acquired. The investment had been tremendous, and as always, Jack knew exactly what money lay behind it.

He was not a connoisseur of style or antiques, but he knew quality and class when he saw them. This place had a subtle elegance and sophistication that was all the more singular because beneath the beauty lay a crisp, functional and flexible design.

He'd learned that often the very lovely hotels were mere veneer—like an overripe orange, beautiful on the outside and rotten within, lacking the necessary efficiencies to make them profitable operations. They didn't sell easily, the rehab costing more than the actual acquisition. Jack shied from anything of this nature, knowing that it spelled trouble from the day it was bought until the day it sold. *If it sold.*

He lifted another glass of whiskey off the silver tray of a roaming white-gloved waiter, and headed toward the far corner of the lobby. A woman glided sinuously past him, smiling seductively and exuding a sensual aura. At another time he would have responded to the overt invitation, but lately, he'd developed a taste for demure beauties who had no qualms about sending him about his business. He watched, amused, as she sidled off, a moue of disappointment on her lips as she merged with the other guests. Then he focused on the guests. They were a good-looking bunch, the jet-setters.

But Jack didn't waste much time on idle small talk. His life had been composed of hard work for as long as he could remember, and he liked it that way. He finished his whiskey and was about to rise, when he noticed Nelson Cardoso—his host and owner of the hotel—making a bee-line toward him.

"Jack, my friend, such a long time! *Que saudades!*" he exclaimed. "I've been wanting to have a word with you all evening, but you know how it is. Crazy, totally crazy." He laughed, smoothing the few strands of hair remaining on his bald head into a ducktail above his collar, an eye on his guests.

"Hell of a setup you've put together, Nelson. I'm particularly impressed by the way you've integrated the operational aspects with the decor. It'll cut the operating costs tremendously."

"Coming from you, I take that as a great compliment. I know how exacting you are." Nelson beamed.

"I pay too high a price if I'm not," Jack replied dryly, eliciting a knowing smile.

"That's why I took the time to do things right. Frankly, I owe most of it to India. Some of the ideas she came up with to resolve what might otherwise have become potential nightmares were impressive. But where is she? The last I saw her she was talking to Senador Antonio Carlos Magalhães." He leaned forward, lowering his voice. "Apparently he came especially to see her and compliment her on the hotel. Quite a triumph to have one of the most powerful men in South America making an appearance here tonight, don't you think? But then, everyone's been flooding her with compliments all evening."

"I know. That's why I'm letting her deal with business for a while. You know, networking and so on."

Nelson gave him a wry smile. "Come on, let's go find her. By the way, *meu amigo*, you be careful," he warned, wagging a finger. "Rio has a funny effect on people. It has magic in the air!"

"Okay, let's go look for her. She must be around," Jack replied, avoiding Nelson's laughing eyes, all the while searching the glittering and bejeweled crowd for India. He hadn't realized his interest in her was so obvious. Nelson forged a passage among the chattering guests, and they wove their way through, holding their glasses high to avoid collision.

The crowd's dazzling reflection shimmered subtly in the eighteenth-century French mirrors. Crystal sparkled, jewels gleamed and laughter mingled with expressive gestures, accompanied by multilingual accolades of admiration as the guests cooed and exclaimed *bellissimo, fabuleux* and *fablehaft*. There was no doubt that La Perla was a success, and Jack felt secretly proud that most of the triumph was India's. Her fine work was the talk of the evening. Guests had flown in from all over the world for several days of partying, climaxed by this brilliant evening of glitz and glamour that the *cariocas*—the inhabitants of Rio—were such masters at. Nobody knew how to throw a party better.

Shining hair, from black to blond, swung over slim bronzed shoulders, framing an array of exotic faces. The lean, fit bodies made perfect mannequins for the expensive but simple designer gowns floating among the tuxedos under the twinkling chandeliers, as the crowd swayed gently to the strains of *Girl from Ipanema,* drifting out from the piano bar to the lobby and reception rooms.

''There she is.''

Jack followed Nelson's gaze, his eyes narrowing. He'd know that pair of shoulders anywhere, he realized, heading to where India stood by the French windows across the room. His gaze traveled appreciatively down the scooped back of the white silk gown that ended dramatically at the crook of her waist. But the stiffness of her stance made him move quicker. Instinctively he knew something wasn't right.

He left Nelson, who'd been accosted by some guests, and came up behind her, following her gaze to the terrace beyond. But all he could see were the immense buffet tables, swathed in white linen and lace, overflowing with a splendid array of dishes and the exquisite flower arrangements surrounding the champagne fountain in the center. It was as decorative as it was appetizing.

He slipped an arm over her shoulder, wondering what was bothering her. ''Everything okay?'' he asked, noticing the furrow between her eyebrows.

''Uh-huh,'' she replied, preoccupied.

Then he caught a slight movement from among the tropical foliage behind the buffet. Like fleeting shadows, four crouching figures edged their way around the table. Jack's hand went immediately to his hip, but of course he wasn't carrying a weapon. An oversight in a place like Rio, he reflected, annoyed at his own lack of foresight. He stepped forward but India held him back.

"Shh—don't, they're just children. I've been watching," she said in a low voice. "They're trying to get at the food. Imagine how awful it must be for them to see this abundance when they barely have enough to eat," she exclaimed in a distressed whisper.

"India, you can't allow people to come in here and steal," he replied, keeping his voice low.

"They're not stealing, they're just eating, poor little things. Wouldn't you do the same if you were in their place?"

"Maybe. But that's hardly the point. Stealing's stealing, no two ways about it. I'll call security and have them deal with it."

"No, you will not." She grabbed his arm. "I'll talk to them. Please, Jack, don't. You'll get them into trouble. You've no idea how hard things are for people here," she whispered, biting her lip. "I was talking today to the maid who does my suite. She has five children all under fourteen, her husband has left her—just disappeared—and she has to care for the family. One child works at a supermarket. He brings home about seventy dollars a month. Can you believe it? I don't know how she does it— Well, actually I do," she continued, her tone angry now. "She's worked three shifts for the last two months, trying to earn enough money to hold on to the shack she has in the Morro— That's up there in the slums, what they call the *favelas*." She pointed to the flickering lights of the tiny dwellings, huddled one on top of the other above the city.

"Indy, I know it's terrible," Jack answered patiently, "but we still can't allow these kids to come in here and rob from the party. They might be dangerous. Next they'll be robbing us. You have to keep some order, otherwise you'll have utter chaos on your hands."

Nelson walked out to join them, his face beaming. Jack tightened his grip around India's shoulders, feeling her stiffen.

"Nelson, I think there are intruders over there." He pointed to the lavish buffet and the floodlit plants beyond.

Nelson's eyes narrowed. Immediately he took out a cell phone and spoke in rapid Portuguese.

"Now you've really done it," India exclaimed angrily as two burly security guards appeared from nowhere, dragging the children by the scruff of their necks into the open. "Nelson, they're only hungry children," she pleaded. "Don't let these people be rough with them."

"The security guards will call the police," he said, flustered and apologetic. "I'm dreadfully sorry for this intrusion, but don't worry any more about it. It'll be taken care of."

"No." India laid a hand on his arm. "Wait a minute, you can't do that. Imagine what the police will do to them. Nelson, I don't think you understand, these children are hungry. They're not out to steal from you or hurt anybody, they're merely trying to fill their stomachs."

Jack met Nelson's gaze across India's head, both men realizing this was not going to be easy.

"I know it's a problem, *querida*," Nelson replied, embarrassed, "but I can't have thieves in the hotel. What will my guests do? Offer them their food? India, people come to Rio for fun, not to deal with social problems. The government must take care of them."

"But it can't, can it? The population problem's just too overwhelming," she said, looking him straight in the eye while the children squirmed, still in the hold of the guards who awaited instructions.

"As you so rightly say, it's an overwhelming problem. One hundred and forty million people in our country—and most of them poor." He gave a philosophical shrug and raised his hands. "The government can't be expected to cope."

"Exactly," she retorted, smiling brightly. "Which is why *we* in the private sector should do more. I know we can't save the world, but at least we can help these children."

"They're mostly beyond rehabilitation," Jack murmured, wishing the episode were over.

India spun around like an avenging goddess. "How dare you make that judgment? Have you looked at them? That little one can't be more than five or six. Do you really believe that such small children couldn't change if they were helped and given a chance?"

"I don't know. Statistically—"

"Statistics are a very convenient way of hiding what's under our noses." She moved forward before he could stop her, smiling at the security guard. "Do you mind?" She crouched in front of the two smallest boys, while the others stood scowling, knowing what awaited them. She held out her hand, signaling for the guard to let the two go. Jack glanced at Nelson, who threw up his hands in an exasperated gesture of agreement. Then she began speaking softly to the children, who answered hesitantly in Portuguese.

"Probably pitching her a pack of lies," Nelson muttered. "Women, *meu Deus*. Sentimental craziness, that's what it is."

"Right." Jack nodded, but he couldn't help feeling impressed by the way India was dealing with the kids. They looked different already. No longer dangerous varmints, but children, their eyes smiling from their little old faces. Faces, he realized with a stab, that had seen too much, too soon. He knew that look. He'd seen it before, in the East, but over time, habit and business had blinded him to it, he admitted with a hint of shame.

"Nelson," India said, holding two children by the hand, "these are Marilene's sons."

"And who is Marilene?" Nelson replied, exasperated.

"She's the maid who does my room. You see, she's been working so hard to make money during the opening that the children have been left alone. They came looking for their mother because they're hungry. They haven't eaten because yesterday she didn't get paid, and the grocer won't extend them any more credit until *he's* paid."

Nelson shifted uncomfortably from one foot to the other. "Your mom didn't get paid?" he asked, addressing the children. They shook their heads in unison, eyes wary, while Nelson swore under his breath. "Goddamn head of housekeeping's probably pocketing the money and holding up the payments," he said angrily. "That's what makes this country go to hell. You try to run things right and all you get is corruption the whole way down the line."

"Perhaps they could be taken to the kitchen so they can eat," Jack suggested.

"If they're properly treated I have no objection." India glanced at the children, then crouched down again and explained the offer while stroking their dirty faces. They shook their heads vigorously. But Nelson was talking to the security guards, who nodded.

"You're sure they'll be all right?" she asked cautiously.

"They'll be taken care of, don't worry," Nelson promised.

She pushed the children gently forward, and they left with the guards, who were smiling broadly. In an instant the whole atmosphere had changed. Now the men were joking playfully, rubbing the children's heads, happy to help. They had merely been doing their duty.

Nelson was pacing the terrace, agitated. "You know what, Jack? India's absolutely right. I'm afraid I'm just going to have to be more vigilant in the future."

India smiled. "I'm sure you will be. It's so difficult to keep an eye on everything. Thanks for what you did, that was nice. But, Nelson, do you think there's something more we could do to help? You know, the children seem to spend so much time alone. Perhaps if there was somewhere for them to play and be fed while their mothers are working— You know, like a small day-care center."

"In theory everything seems easy, but in practice it's a tremendous expense. We're not a charitable organization, I'm afraid."

"He's right, Indy, this is business," Jack interjected. "Charity has to be dealt with at a corporate level. That way it can be used as a write-off."

He regretted the words as soon as they were spoken.

"Is that how you view charity? As a write-off? Don't you think that perhaps you're missing the point?" she asked icily. "Your mentality is precisely what's wrong. We don't hear, we don't see, because it's much easier to say I gave X number of dollars to charity last year, and go to sleep feeling good with yourself. I'm not saying that doesn't help in its way," she conceded, turning to Nelson now, "but what I've learned here, and perhaps hadn't understood before, is just how truly ravaging these problems can be in people's lives. I think charity should be more personal."

"I really don't see how," Nelson replied with a sympathetic shrug and a glance at Jack.

"By starting a place for the children of the employees. Don't you see," she said, her eyes pleading, appealing to Nelson's sense of justice, "you could do so much to help these people."

"But it would cost a fortune!" he exclaimed. "The hotel hasn't broken even yet and won't for at least a year and a half. Then we'll have to start showing profit and—"

"I know." India looked at them both with a sparkle in

her eye. "But there's always fund-raising," she said, smoothing the top of her evening purse.

"That takes more money, what with charity balls and I know not what else. But I'll think about it," he replied in a conciliatory tone. "Now, shall we return inside?"

"Just a second." India's eyes narrowed thoughtfully. "If I could get you the money, would you promise to go ahead and make a day-care center?" She cast Nelson a questioning little smile.

"Sure. If I had the money, of course. We would all like to help if we could, *querida*. The trouble is we haven't got it," Nelson replied matter-of-factly.

Jack watched, intrigued. He knew her well enough now to know she was up to something.

"Is that a promise?"

"Yes, my dear, if it pleases you. How could I possibly say no to such a beautiful woman?" he replied gallantly. "You find me the money and I will see to it the shelter gets created."

"Good. Then you can get started right away. Here." She handed him a slip of paper she'd removed from her purse. "Take this to begin the shelter for the children."

"India, don't be ridiculous. That's the check I gave you earlier this evening, the remaining balance for all the wonderful work you've done to make this place what it is. Don't be silly."

"I insist," she replied firmly. "I'm sorry it's not more, but I'm afraid at the moment I have certain obligations to meet."

"Indy, I can't accept. *Ay meu Deus do céu.* My God, what a situation," Nelson moaned, waving the check. "This is absurd." He turned to Jack, pleading for some male support. "Surely you must understand that it would be impossible for me to accept."

India spun round, and he read the appeal in her eyes.

She expected something of him, and to his utter surprise he realized it felt good to know she needed him.

"What's the amount of the check?"

"Twenty thousand dollars," Nelson wailed.

"I'll add a zero to mine if you'll grant the lady her wish," he said quietly, standing behind India and laying a firm hand on her shoulder. If she was ready to put down hard-earned money to back up what she believed in, then the least he could do was follow suit. The yacht rehab would just have to wait.

"*Nossa, Santa Maē,*" Nelson exclaimed. "This is absurd. Jack, she doesn't understand, there are thousands— And now you, too." Nelson passed a worried hand across his forehead.

"I'll have the check in your office by tomorrow morning." Jack's eyes met the other man's, unflinching.

"Here, don't forget this." India picked up the check that had fluttered to the floor.

"I can't accept." Nelson shook his head vigorously. "This is the money you've earned from your work, India. You have your own problems to solve. What about that mortgage you mentioned?"

"Don't worry, it's been taken care of. What you paid me before more than settled it." She stretched out her hand, smiling disarmingly. "Please, Nelson, if we can't do something to help those who need it so badly, then what's the purpose of life?"

Slowly Nelson looked from one to the other, finally accepting the check from her, his eyes bright with emotion. "I will accept, my friends. And I want you to know that I take this project very seriously. I, too, will put up the same amount. Thank you. Thank you for reminding me of my duty to my own." His voice cracked as he folded the check and slipped it into his pocket.

India rushed forward and hugged him. "Nel, I knew I

wasn't wrong about you. Thank you for understanding.
And thank you, too.'' She turned to Jack with a shy smile.
''That was incredibly generous of you.''

''My pleasure, princess,'' he replied, watching her intensely, marveling that in a matter of seconds she could
transform from Amazon back to decorous young lady.
''How about a drink?'' he suggested, slipping his arm
through hers.

''I have to be off.'' Nelson smiled at them. ''Jack, you
take care of her, and please, no more social dilemmas!
That was enough for one evening.'' He raised his arms in
mock despair and disappeared, leaving Jack and India
standing silently close to one another. Slowly, she raised
her eyes to his. Then, to his amazement, she reached up
and placed a kiss on his lips. A gentle kiss of appreciation,
for understanding, for sharing this moment and for accom-
plishing something worthwhile together.

His eyes traveled over her exquisite features, past the
delicate diamond necklace and down the graceful outline
of her body. She was sensational, elusive, sensual. And, at
least for now, she was his. Jack felt suddenly possessive
and his arm snaked around her waist. ''Come on, let's have
that drink,'' he said, his throat suddenly dry. All the emotions of the last hour had made him thirsty.

''I hope you don't mind what happened.'' India glanced
at him, uncertain.

''Mind? I thought you were great. And right, too.
You're a force to be dealt with, Miss Moncrieff,'' he said,
guiding her through into the reception room. ''And as for
the hotel, you've done a great job. It's a winner.''

Tonight Jack had seen yet another side of India—talent
and twenty grand's worth of compassion. He also realized
that if she'd had ten times the amount, she would have
handed it over without a thought. Would she never cease
to surprise him? She was gradually getting under his well-

honed defenses, and he had half a mind to throw caution
to the winds, open the gates and let her in. Her genuine
concern had touched a dormant chord, one he'd forgotten
existed. Maybe with her he'd relearn that there was more
to life than making another buck.

Her eyes brightened with unshed tears and he put his
arms around her, wishing he could sweep her off somewhere and have her all to himself. It pleased him that she
wasn't another social parasite, thinking only of her personal comforts and petty desires.

But enough good deeds for one night, he reflected, passing his fingers through her long hair. "You can't save the
world, India. At least the hotel's creating jobs. There's no
use gettin' maudlin over it all," he said with a lazy South-
ern drawl, making her smile.

"Doesn't it suit you to feel bad?" she challenged, turning her face up to his.

"No. And it doesn't suit me to spend the rest of the
evening sparring with you either. We've done what we had
to do. There's no point in pursuing the subject." Jack
stepped back but kept one arm firmly round her shoulders
as they penetrated farther into the crowded reception room.

"You wait right here and I'll get us some drinks," he
ordered.

"What am I supposed to do? Salute?" she murmured,
laughing as he guided her to a spot next to one of the
columns.

"Don't move. I'll be right back." He dropped a kiss on
her forehead.

"Gosh you're bossy," India complained.

"Indy—" His laughing eyes narrowed.

"Run along and get the drinks, Jack. If you're quick I
might just be here when you get back," she replied flir-
tatiously.

Finally he caught the barman's attention and ordered

their drinks. Then he leaned sideways on the counter and watched her, their eyes bonding across the room, hers alive with everything he'd been hoping for. The thought that tonight he might break down that reserve and fear, remove those layers of decorum and ignite the fire he was sure lay beneath sent a shaft of heat coursing through his body, making him catch his breath.

He picked up the glasses, ready to return, when a scream wrenched the air.

Sudden panic let loose. Jack stopped dead in his tracks, all his senses alert, smelling the danger. Another scream followed and he searched desperately for the cause of the hysteria that was breaking out around him. A woman almost fell on top of him, and he cursed as he lost sight of India. He helped the woman regain her balance, and continued to search the crowd, still trying to identify the cause.

Then he saw them. Three gunmen in tuxedos, their faces covered with stocking masks, were pushing the crowd back with machine guns. They must have sneaked in as guests, he realized, absorbing every detail.

Reactions that years ago had been second nature to him and he'd believed forgotten were suddenly present once more.

One of the gunmen was shouting and Jack swore in frustration, not understanding a word.

"Ninguém meche, tudo mundo calado."

"What's he saying?" Jack whispered to the man next to him.

"For no one to move and to shut up," he whispered back.

Jack took stock of the situation, evaluating positions, distances, the layout of the terrain. There were three gunmen in sight, and probably a couple more guarding the entrances. They were clearly nervous, looking constantly from the French windows to the main door. Again he searched for India, his heart tightening when he caught a glimpse of her squeezed against the column between frantic bodies. She was turning this way and that, looking for him. He felt desperate that he couldn't go to her.

The gunman was shouting again.

"What's he saying now?" Jack whispered.

"That everyone must take their wallets and jewelry and put them in the bag that will be passed around," the man replied in a thin voice.

Once more Jack studied the room, chiding himself once more for having come here unarmed. The two gunmen had the exits covered, and the third was passing around a large brown paper bag, into which the agitated guests hastily dropped their valuables. Women were weeping and the tension was rampant.

Jack glanced once more at India, realizing there was nothing he could do. *Never allow emotion to cloud your thinking.* He could hear the sergeant at training camp repeating the words over and over. And they'd served him well. In the next few seconds he went back into a mode he'd thought he'd left behind in the jungles of Central America ten years earlier. He knew where his duty lay and immediately he began evaluating his chances of escape. Nelson had brought in a top security team, that he knew, and by now they would have called in the SWAT team equivalents as well. But they would need a break to take control of the situation. Slowly he began searching for an opportunity.

He reconnoitered the terrain with military expertise, conscious of how easily this could turn into a bloodbath.

For one agonizing second, images of heavy rain beating down relentlessly, blood and the stench of death flashed before him. Then the truck and the car crushed beneath it, the cops pulling Lucy's lifeless body out from beneath the mangled mess.

One middle-aged woman in a sapphire gown was having difficulty with the clasp of her necklace. The gunman snatched it from her throat, kicking her to the ground as the crowd looked on in horror.

Jack focused his attention on the task at hand. One of the French windows to his right stood ajar. If he could reach it and jump the other gunman on the terrace, he might give the SWAT team the break they needed. It was worth the risk. His instincts told him things were getting out of hand.

Again he searched the crowd, desperately hoping that India would look his way, willing her to turn in his direction before he began his mission. At last his eyes met hers and held. He read the fear hidden under the outer sheath of calm, but all he could do was silently transmit all he felt for her. Then he dragged his eyes away.

Total concentration and cold calculation were needed to achieve any degree of success. He steeled himself, realizing he was dependent on the robbers' movements, his own instincts and the guy beside him for guidance.

Tugging the man's sleeve, he signaled to the window with his eyes and received a slight nod. Very slowly they edged their way back against the wall toward the half-open door, unobserved amidst the general confusion. The gunman with the bag still had quite a ways to go before reaching them. His companions were shouting at him, and one sent a spray of gunfire into the ceiling, causing more panic among the petrified crowd.

Only a few more steps and he'd reach the French doors, opened just wide enough to slip through without being noticed.

He readied himself, but as he was about to take the final step, a movement—so slight he might have imagined it—reflected in one of the gilded mirrors. Only Jack's total awareness warned him it was real. He slammed his arm against his companion as the glass door trembled and another robber burst in, dressed in the uniform of a security guard.

"Estão chegando!" the man shouted.

"What?" Jack whispered to the man beside him, frustrated.

"He says they're coming."

Then shots were fired outside. In one swift movement Jack fell to the floor, pulling his companion down with him. Crawling on his belly, he dragged himself inch by inch toward the bar, unconscious of the trampling feet and the pandemonium, determined to reach his final objective—the bar counter.

When he finally reached it, he threw himself underneath, barely escaping a shot that whistled dangerously close to his ear. He listened, pulse throbbing, every nerve a live wire. The robbers were shooting wildly, desperate to maintain control of the crowd, their escape frustrated by the squads of SWAT teams gathering outside. It would be a miracle if no one got hurt.

This panic was precisely what he'd been dreading. The robbers could lose it in a heartbeat and shoot the place to bits. He shut his eyes tight for a split second, and for the first time in many years he prayed—that India was okay. Then he banished her from his mind, forcing himself to pace his breathing and regain complete control of his movements.

Sweat dripped into his eyes as he crouched below the counter, carefully picking up the direction of the shots. The bartender was cringing fearfully under the counter in the far corner, and Jack signaled to him, indicating a pistol. The man motioned with his head toward the corner of the bar above Jack's head.

Raising his hand cautiously, he edged his fingers carefully over the cold marble ledge. It must have been only seconds but it seemed endless. His skin burned hot against the cold stone slab, and when the familiar touch of metal met his fingertips he tensed, deftly retrieving the object— but it was only a spoon. Again beads of sweat formed on his forehead, the room increasingly stuffy, as if body heat and apprehension had conspired to defy the powerful air-conditioning units, leaving it an airless vacuum.

He continued the search, his hand roving over the sink, past some slices of lime and a cutting board. He glanced at the barman once more and received a hopeful nod.

Then all at once he felt it, and a sigh of relief escaped him as he made contact, the familiar curve of the Beretta molding into his palm. He eased the gun gently into a firm grip and lowered it.

He assessed the weapon—high precision, full clip. Releasing the safety, he raised his head cautiously above the ridge of the counter, just enough to gauge the situation.

The gunmen were scattered among the frantic mass of guests, and seemed out of control. People were sweating, eyes glazed, surprise and horror written on their faces.

Then, just as he was about to calculate his shot, the unthinkable happened. He watched, helpless, as one of the gunmen appeared out of nowhere, grabbed India in a vise-like grip and stuck a revolver to her temple. Two of his cohorts shouted at him, but he shook them off and tightened his hold. Jack forced himself to duck again and reassess before he did something foolish. He steadied his ragged breathing. Keep calm, he told himself over and over. But why her? Oh, not her, please, God, not again.

To his horror he realized her life was in his hands.

Gripping the gun firmly, he peered over the counter once more. The gunman's body language told him all he needed to know.

Suddenly the man jerked India's head up. In a split second Jack moved swiftly into position and focused on his target, oblivious to all the shouting, tension and madness. And when he saw his chance he took it. In one swift movement he rose, took direct aim at the gunman holding her and pulled the trigger.

The sonic boom of the reverberation echoed through the enclosed reception room as the bullet pierced the target's forehead. His body lurched, then crumpled to the ground, bringing India down under him, blood splattering her gown and forming a dazzling red puddle on the white marble floor.

Shots from outside followed hard on his. Doors burst open and shouts of triumph mingled with tears of relief as the other gunmen were pinned to the floor and the SWAT teams took over.

Jack vaulted the bar. The few feet that separated him from India seemed endless as he forged a passage among the astonished guests to where she lay, frozen under the prostrate corpse.

The crowd stepped back in awe as Jack pushed the limp body aside, hands trembling. "It's okay, baby," he whispered hoarsely. "It's all right, darling." He took her into his arms, gazing down at her pale face, assuring himself that she was unharmed. He brushed the strands of damp hair from her face, laughing from relief as he rocked her, the knot in his throat loosening as her eyelids fluttered. He didn't like her pallor but it was probably just shock. He closed his eyes, feeling suddenly light-headed, unaware of the crowd, conscious only of the relief, the sheer and utter relief of knowing he hadn't lost her.

The guests began to applaud as the barman, hands waving and talking excitedly, gave a vivid description of Jack's actions to an enthusiastic throng of onlookers.

Then Nelson was there, kneeling next to him, his face creased with concern. "My God! Jack, is she okay?"

He nodded. "She'll be fine. It's just shock."

"Should I call an ambulance? We must get her out of here. Somewhere quiet, where she can rest."

Jack nodded and rose, lifting India carefully in his arms, cradling her head against his shoulder.

The band began playing again, and an almost frenzied atmosphere of excitement followed in the aftermath of all the panic. Couples began dancing wildly to the rapid beat of the samba. Champagne corks popped, one woman nearly pouring some over him as she laughed hysterically. But Jack moved ahead, holding India close to the torn front of his tux as Nelson cleared a path for them. The crowd fell back respectfully.

Jack barely noticed the tears of admiration and thanks from the women, the grateful pats on the shoulder from the men. He just wanted her out of there, somewhere he knew she'd be safe and where no one would disturb them for a long time.

India awoke, hazily conscious of cool, scented linen and her throbbing throat. Then little by little she remembered. Voices shouting and screaming, others calling for champagne and music, cold metal at her temple and an iron grip straining at her throat. Suddenly she sat up screaming, bathed in cold sweat.

Jack rushed to her side, his arms encircling her. "It's all over, darling. You're just in shock, nothing happened to you."

"I don't remember— I— Where were you? I was sure you would do something—then I saw you aim. I thought I was going to die," she whispered, confused.

Jack lifted her head and placed another pillow carefully behind her. "It's all over now. Nothing's going to happen to you." He reached down and kissed her softly on the lips. "You know I'd never let anything happen to you."

She leaned back, bewildered, her eyes wandering round

the dimly lit room, recognizing the heavy white curtains and the tropical palms etched in the lamplight. All at once she knew she was in her suite, lying in the king-size bed, naked. He must have undressed her, she realized, feeling sudden heat rising to her face as he came back with a glass of water. She shivered, remembering the blood, her dress, the body falling on top of her, aware that Jack had saved her life.

He sat down on the edge of the bed and she saw how disheveled he looked. His shirtfront was torn and grimy, and his bow tie was a piece of black satin ribbon strung haphazardly around his collar. When he lifted the glass to her lips, she saw the cut on his cheek and the look of deep concern in his eyes.

Raising her hand, she wiped the dirt from his tanned cheek, her fingers feathering the cut.

"You must take care of that," she whispered hoarsely.

"Don't worry about me, I'm fine. Drink some water, it'll help your throat." He held the glass to her parched lips and smiled a smile so tender that her heart leaped, making her choke on the water as she gazed into the eyes of the man she loved.

There was no use denying it to herself any longer. She leaned back against the soft pillows, watching him, fascinated.

"Jack?" she whispered as he carefully inspected the bruise that had formed on her wrist before raising it to his lips and kissing it. "When you were behind the bar, did it ever occur to you that you might shoot me instead of the gunman?"

"Excuse me?" He shot her an amused look.

"Couldn't you have missed?"

"At that distance with a 9 mm Beretta? It was a clean shot. There's no way I could've missed!"

"You seem awfully confident." She smiled tenderly, amused by his masculine pride.

"Of course I'm confident. You don't shoot in a situation like that unless you know exactly what you're doing, baby. Believe me, I'd never take a risk with anyone as precious as you."

He ran his forefinger over her lips. "You know, you're always complaining about my shooting, and frankly, on both occasions I don't think I've done too badly."

"That's true," she admitted, acutely aware of the change in his eyes, the sudden intimacy between them and her nakedness under the covers.

"I hope there won't be a third," he said huskily. "I don't know how long I can stand worrying about you." His eyes were alight with a new intensity as his hand caressed her throat, making her catch her breath. His touch left her limp and wanting, her body alive with newfound expectation. As his fingers slowly trailed down her throat, India loosened her grip on the sheet she'd been holding tightly to her chest, allowing him free passage to wherever he wanted to go.

His hand stopped abruptly and their eyes met.

"I want you so much, Indy," he whispered as his thumb tenderly grazed her cheek. "I want to take you places you've never been, places I think you're ready to go. There's no room between us for pretense. But you've just had a hell of a scare. I don't want you to do anything you might regret." His hand stopped again at the base of her throat, as though questioning the right to go farther.

"I promise I won't regret a thing," she whispered, closing her eyes and raising her lips to meet his in a long, passionate kiss, knowing that unconsciously she'd been waiting for this moment, wanting it as much as him. She would let Jack love her, let him take her wherever he wished to go—even if it changed her forever.

* * *

He couldn't remember a time when he'd felt so tentative, but he was determined to make this a memorable night for both of them. His eyes devoured her. She was all woman, lying naked below the sheets, her hair splayed out on the pillow as though by accident, highlighted by the distant twinkle of the lights from Ipanema that shone through the large glass doors. Yet her eyes were like those of a child on the brink of a new discovery. Under that cool outward loveliness, there was vulnerability coupled with fire. And she was smiling that soft, tentative little smile, inviting him to be her lover as her hands dropped from the front of the sheet. His heart quickened and he leaned closer, following the exquisite structure of her throat, caressing her collarbone, his thumb skimming the silken texture of her skin. Then gently he lowered the sheet and allowed his fingers to circle her small firm breasts, his thumb lightly grazing the tips, his body reacting at her quick intake of breath. He wanted to make passionate violent love to her, to penetrate the depths of her being until he reached that magic spot he knew instinctively was his and his alone. But he held back, gently lowering his mouth to hers, feeling the tremors of desire shuddering through her as his hands wandered farther, mastering himself, determined to give her all the pleasure he'd promised himself he would.

When his fingers finally reached their destination, she let out a soft gasp of delight, arching back, her eyes closed. Slowly he took his lips from her mouth and lowered them gently to her breast, laving it, taunting her with his tongue, until she writhed, helpless in his arms, reaching out for him.

He raised his head, watching her, wanting to experience each sensation to the fullest. He quickened his caresses, driving her to the teetering edge of a deep crevasse then slowly back, watching her eyes open and darken, her hair tumble wildly about her shoulders. When she finally fell over the edge, she arched back crying out his name, then lay shuddering in his arms.

He rose and ripped off the remains of his shirt, anxious now for the feel of her skin on his. He could tell instinctively by the surprised wonder in her eyes that she'd never experienced anything like this before, and the thought thrilled him.

"Jack," she murmured hoarsely.

"Shh—let yourself go. I'll do the rest," he said softly as he lay down next to her and began caressing her again, waiting until he knew she was more than ready for him.

Then, and only then, did he allow himself the ultimate pleasure of loving her, entering her slowly, his eyes fastened on hers, afraid of frightening her. But it was India who curled her legs around him, hips arching, demanding that he delve deep within her.

His resolve gave way.

Mouth to mouth, skin to skin, they devoured each other, Jack deep within her, assuaging the insatiable hunger that had been consuming him since the day they'd met. He held on long enough to hear her final moan of pleasure and fulfillment, then, when he couldn't bear it anymore, he lost himself within her, surrendering to the passion and feelings he'd tried to escape for so long. And for the first time in many many years, he knew what it was like to feel whole again.

India stroked a strand of his thick dark hair, amazed at how natural it felt for him to be lying next to her, one arm lightly touching her thigh, both of them drowsy yet happy after the eventful night and its final culmination.

She smiled, thoroughly spent, savoring the delicious new ache in her muscles. He'd promised her a journey and she'd traveled with him into the unknown, riding on the crest of his lovemaking and her newfound emotions.

Jack stretched and rolled onto his side, but she didn't want him to go. As though sensing her need, he reached out and drew her into the crook of his arm, nudging her leg over his until they lay entwined.

"Tired?" he whispered, placing his hand comfortably on her breast as though he'd been doing so for years.

"Mmm—deliciously tired," she responded, delighting in his familiar gesture and wondering, hoping, that it had been as breathtaking for him as it had been for her.

"You should get some sleep," he murmured drowsily, tenderly stroking her cheek with his free hand.

But she didn't want to sleep. It had taken twenty-eight long years for her to begin discovering the clues to this mystery. Sleep could wait while she continued the treasure hunt.

Gently she dragged her nails down his spine, thrilled to feel his immediate reaction.

"Indy, if you do that I'll—"

"Yes?" She was enjoying this strange new power, and something in her gut told her this was just the beginning. That if she wanted, she could make him slip over that same precipice she had. That they would free-fall together.

Oh, how she loved him. But she held back the words that rushed to her lips. Not yet, not now. And when Jack entered her again, more tenderly this time, she gave a delighted sigh and stopped thinking altogether. Tomorrow would take care of itself.

8

India leaned against Jack's shoulder as the jet soared upward. Rio receded quickly into a sprawling mass of ocean, concrete and tropical vegetation that stretched from the sugar loaf and the Cristo Redemtor—his arms outstretched over the city—to the *favelas* amassed far up on the steep slopes at the edges of the city.

It was a relief to leave the torrid, damp forty-degree heat. As the plane headed south, the dense vegetation lessened, giving way to the vast wheat fields of Parana stretching for miles and miles in neat squares and rectangles. Soon those would be replaced by endless expanses of sweeping green pasture, as they crossed the Rio Grande do Sul and entered Argentine territory.

India was content to sit back and enjoy the quiet camaraderie they had established over the last few days. And what wonderful days they had been. Days spent lying by the pool or in bed, talking constantly as though to make up for lost time, interspersed by endless hours of pleasure spent among tangled sheets, learning each other's secrets.

She watched as Jack studied some papers, deciding he looked incredibly attractive in his business mode.

She loved him. It was a simple truth. Not complicated

or remote, just something she knew deep inside. There had been no promises, no words of love, only tenderness and passion. Yet she felt happier and more fulfilled than ever before.

She gave a contented sigh, continuing to survey Jack, her heart full. She gazed at his hands, those strong yet gentle hands that were able to ignite such passion. She'd discovered a new being within herself over the past few days, and it was both thrilling and frightening.

"Sorry." Jack threw her an apologetic smile. "I'm almost done." He leaned over and dropped a kiss on her lips then continued to work on his notes. It felt so natural, so right, as though they'd been doing this forever. After a while he put the paperwork aside and took her hand. They said little. They didn't need to, for they basked in that blissful intimacy born of shared thoughts and moments, a secret plain that only lovers knew. Then slowly he raised her fingers to his lips and kissed them one by one, his eyes never leaving hers.

"Don't," she whispered halfheartedly.

"Why not? It's my plane. Where's the problem?"

"Jack," India exclaimed, embarrassed. "What about Jonathan and the crew?"

"What about them?" He continued to trail his lips over the inside of her wrist.

"They'll think it very odd. It's embarrassing. By the way, when are you going to Miami?" she asked in a brave attempt to change the subject.

"Do you want me to go?" he asked, his voice husky.

"No, of course not."

"I'm going to have to go real soon," he said regretfully. "I've been neglecting too much for too long. Chad and Quince are getting antsy. And it's all your fault," he added with a reproachful grin, letting his hands wander.

"Really?" she asked innocently, wanting to hear him say it.

"You know very well you've been taking my mind off my work."

"Do you mind?"

"Quite the opposite." His fingers snaked behind her neck, drawing her into his arms. "I just don't want to become completely addicted," he murmured, lowering his mouth to hers, tender at first then commanding as his fingers glided down her throat to her breast. She felt the familiar thrill when his thumb grazed her nipple through the thin cotton blouse and bra, her body melting as she surrendered to his touch. For a few moments she floated on air, but withdrew hastily when his hand shifted to her inner thigh, on a fast journey upward. She pulled away, trying to look composed, leaving him with a raised eyebrow.

"Jack, this is neither the time nor the place."

"The coast's clear, no problem." He pressed a button on the control panel, making India wonder woefully how many women he'd made love to on this wretched plane for the staff to be so well trained. It was embarrassing but, she had to admit, the most exciting experience she'd ever had. Then he swooped down on her, tongue flicking her throat, one hand slipping to the small of her back while the other embarked on its own adventures.

Sometime later Jack watched, tenderly amused, as India did her best to appear calm and collected, and not as though she'd just spent the best part of an hour making love.

"Are you hungry, princess?"

"A little."

"You should be ravenous after all that exercise," he said, laughing, leaning over to do up a button she'd forgotten. "There. May I call Jonathan now?"

She nodded and Jack rang for the steward, who materialized out of nowhere.

Soon they were eating, Jack attacking a large steak and India nibbling some smoked salmon and toast with a glass of dry champagne.

"This is delicious. By the way, the other day you promised to tell me about Chad and Quince," India said between nibbles.

Jack laid down his knife and fork and thought about the boy he considered more a son than a brother. "Chad's six years younger than me and really quite the opposite in nature. You couldn't find a steadier, more straightforward guy than him. He's been married to the same girl for eight years."

"Why do you say opposite?" she asked. "You seem pretty reliable to me. And if things had been different, you probably would still be married to the same girl, too."

"I guess. Maybe we are more alike than we seem. They have the cutest little girl called Molly. She's my goddaughter," he added proudly. "You'll meet them sometime when you come to Miami." He reached for the sour cream and added a dollop on his baked potato, realizing that he would truly like to take her to Miami. "Quince is an old friend who came back unexpectedly into my life. We grew up together back in Tennessee. I was looking for someone with a legal background specific to the hotel business to help in the everyday running of Astra. He applied for the job. I couldn't believe it when I finally realized who it was."

"You mean he didn't tell you beforehand?"

"Nope. Just sent his résumé like everyone else and waited. I'd already decided he was the best candidate by the time I realized."

"How incredible."

"It was. Quince comes from a poor background and has

made his own way. It wasn't easy being black in the South when he was growing up. Still isn't, though things are changing, thank God.''

''Is there still much discrimination?''

''Too much for my liking, but I believe the New South is on the move. It was rough for Quince because he had a widowed mother and a younger brother and sister to take care of. We lost touch after Lucy died. He put himself through college on a football scholarship and then went to hotel school. Once he was working, he studied law at night. The guy's incredible. He's put both his brother and sister through college. His brother's studying psychiatry at Harvard. I don't know how we'd manage without Quince.'' He glanced at his watch. ''We'll be landing in about fifteen minutes.''

''What about Chad? Does his family live near you in Miami?''

''Not far,'' he said affectionately. ''They live in a house in Coconut Grove. It's a kind of bohemian—you know, tropical vegetation, artsy and crafty. Marilyn's crazy about plants and flowers, so they have an incredible garden. They'll love you,'' he added, thinking how well India would fit in. Their home reminded him of the simple things in life that seemed to elude him. It would be the first time he'd ever introduced them to any of his female friends.

''They sound like a delightful family,'' she remarked as Jonathan cleared the table and they prepared for landing.

''They are,'' he concurred, noticing a new sparkle about her. It was as though she'd come alive, and he felt a possessive surge of pride.

''Tell me about you and Serena,'' he asked, wanting to hear her version of the story, wondering if she would mention Dunbar.

''There's not much to tell. She seems to resent the fact that our mother married my father. I suppose it must have been difficult for her. Imagine how you'd feel if your father's family were telling you how dreadful it was that your mother was marrying this—what did they call him?—*parvenu.*'' She gave him a wry smile. "Serena never bothered to get to know my father, never realized what a wonderful man he was.''

"Are you unhappy about how the estate was left?'' he asked quietly, taking her hand and squeezing it in his.

"In a way. But the debts are crippling and I know it will have to be sold. I suppose I'm still rather confused and upset about it all,'' she replied with a tight little smile that made Jack's heart go out to her. And knowing he might be able to ease some of her pain by bringing her on board the renovation project made him feel better. He thought about Dunbar for a moment, pleased that the reports he'd received showed things were moving smoothly. Again he was almost tempted to tell her, but resisted knowing it would spoil the surprise he had reserved for a special moment.

"Almost there,'' he commented, glancing out the window. "Boy, has this flight gone by fast.'' He flashed her a wolfish grin.

"Really?'' she replied casually, her cheeks flushed and her eyes alight.

Jack laughed and pulled her toward him. "Come here, beautiful temptress. Sit here,'' he said, placing her on his lap facing him and buckling the seat belt around them both. Then he brought his arms up around her, hugging her close, as the plane began its slow descent to Ezeiza airport.

"There's Hernan,'' India exclaimed as they exited the plane. "How sweet of him to come and pick us up.''

They descended the steps of the aircraft. Hernan walked slowly toward them, and Jack looked him over, amused.

"You look terrible, man, rough night?" he asked.

But there was no answering smile, and when Hernan came to a sudden halt a few feet away, his features drawn and an anguished look in his eyes, Jack's pulse missed a beat. A cold chill set in, for he recognized the shock and grief written in the other man's eyes. It was the same look the young cop who'd knocked on his door that fateful night twelve years ago had worn.

"What's wrong, Hernan?" he asked in a hollow voice.

"Jack—" Hernan seemed to find it difficult to continue. "I—I don't know how to tell you this. I—"

"What the hell's going on?" he demanded, panic-stricken. "Tell me, for Christ's sake!"

"It's your brother—"

"Chad? What about Chad? What's wrong with Chad?"

"He's had an accident," Hernan said.

"Oh my God," India exclaimed, her arm reaching for Jack's.

"When? Where? Is he okay?"

"This morning. He was flying back with Marilyn from Key West, they hit wind shear and—" Hernan lifted his hands in despair, his eyes bright with tears.

There was silence as Jack registered the enormity of it all. "Marilyn?" he asked, his voice breaking.

"Gone, too," Hernan replied, his eyes meeting Jack's. "I can't believe it. I even wondered if it was true, but Quince called. He's been trying to contact you all morning. Apparently he couldn't reach you on the plane."

"Give me the phone," Jack said dully, walking like an automaton to the car while India and Hernan followed in shattered silence.

"I don't think you'll reach him. I tried earlier but the circuits are all busy. Better to try from town."

"I'll leave for Miami right now."

"Jack, let's go to the Alvear or my apartment. We can call from there."

"I have to leave now." Jack turned back abruptly, striding toward the plane where Jonathan stood at the top of the steps.

"We're leaving in half an hour," Jack ordered.

"In half an hour, sir?"

"Yes." Jack mounted the steps and went to the cockpit. "I need you to fuel up, Bob, I have to get back to Miami."

The pilot turned around and then frowned. "Are you okay, Jack?"

"Just get me home."

The gray-haired pilot eyed him, then rose from his seat. "It may take a little longer than half an hour, I don't know what the conditions for refueling are right now, but I'll find out right away."

Jack turned and saw India standing beside him, her eyes filled with grief. He'd forgotten everything in his shock. "You go back to town with Hernan, Indy. I'm sorry, but I have to leave right away."

"I'm so sorry," she whispered. He nodded absently.

Bob talked to the tower, then came out of the cockpit. "I'm sorry, Jack, but we can't leave before early evening. I have to do a full check on the engines. I left it for here rather than doing it in Rio," he said, his tone apologetic and his hazel eyes worried. "Is there something wrong?"

Jack nodded. Bob had been with him a while and they understood each other. "It's Chad. He caught wind shear leaving Key West," he said, his voice dull.

"Jesus—" Bob blanched, understanding the implications as only a pilot could.

Their eyes met for an instant, Bob asking the silent question, and Jack nodded sadly. "Just get me out of here as soon as you can."

"It'll be at least three hours."

"Okay. I'll go get my stuff," he said automatically, walking back down the steps, his mind in a daze.

They got in Hernan's car and sped toward Buenos Aires. Jack sat in silence, his face closed and pale under the tan. India sat quietly next to him, wishing there was some solace she could offer but knowing there was none. Nothing could replace a brother and a sister-in-law, who—from the little she'd learned—were an essential part of his existence.

India suppressed the tears welling in her eyes, blotting out the vision of the happy young couple, the horror of the accident and all it meant to Jack. She had to be strong for him, even if right now he was unable to recognize that he might need that strength. She stretched her hand out tentatively and laid it over his. He didn't stir, but she left it there all the same, willing him to let her in, desperately wanting him to let her share the burden of his grief.

Jack dialed from the cell phone once again. He had to find Quince. Why didn't the goddamn phone work? He swore under his breath, still hanging on to a last thread of hope that it might all just be a terrible mistake. Maybe they'd identified the wrong plane, and Chad and Marilyn were home by now. But deep down he knew there was no mistake. They were gone.

He pictured Marilyn, her eyes filled with fear, Chad desperately trying to control the plane, then reaching out to her in a last effort to help her. Jack closed his eyes for a moment, seeing the plane pitching headlong onto the reefs, sinking into the depths of the ocean, the tail bobbing up and down, a trail of smoke lingering until it, too, disappeared and the waters resumed their relentless flow. He passed his free hand over his eyes as the scene played out before him like a macabre movie. This could not be happening. Not again. Not to Chad, not to him.

Then memories followed in quick succession. Chad

stuck in the cherry tree trying to rescue the cat; Chad making his first home run; the times they'd gone hunting together and the times they'd quarreled. Visions of Marilyn, with her dreamy eyes and her lovely smile. He remembered standing as best man at their wedding, the moment she'd said yes in that husky little voice of hers. Then the hospital, Chad and him pacing the corridor half the night, Jack as worried as his brother waiting for the news about— Molly! He sat up with a jerk. In his overwhelmed state he'd forgotten her, thinking only of the couple, their young lives dashed onto the brine of the ocean bed. He flinched as the full horror of it all hit him in the gut.

When they reached the suite, he sat down automatically at the desk, his mind still trying to cope and understand.

"Darling?"

He looked up. India was standing beside him, grief-stricken.

"Molly," he said with an effort. "Either she's gone, too, or she's completely alone."

India's eyes met his. Tears and a world of compassion brightened her eyes. "Oh God. Poor little soul. It's horrific." She shook her head then knelt down. "Jack, I'll go with you if you want."

He heard her from a distance, then suddenly her words sank in. He'd done things on his own for so long he didn't know how to accept her offer. Yet he was so very tired, and all at once this woman with whom he'd shared a part of himself he hadn't realized still existed was ready to go with him, to share not only the good times but his pain also. He hesitated, realizing even in his grief that it was too much to ask of anyone. But the thought of having her with him brought a tiny measure of peace that he so desperately needed.

"Would you really come?"

"Of course," she answered, rising.

"Are you sure?"

"Of course I'm sure, darling. Wait here and I'll get my things." She squeezed his hands, then moved silently across the room to the door. He watched her go, knowing he'd be eternally grateful to her. Then he tried to focus on Molly. Was she alive? And if she was, did she know yet? Had somebody told her? Or was she still playing happily at a friend's house, thinking her mommy and daddy would be home soon?

He gave an anguished groan. How could they, of all people, have been taken? Anger gripped him and he slammed his fist against the arm of the chair then got up and paced the room. There was no justice, and the price for caring about others was always too high to pay.

The reverend's office at St. Mark's Episcopal School was peaceful and bright, but Jack sat tapping his foot nervously wondering over and over how you told a seven-year-old child that her parents were never coming home. He had faced bleak situations in his life, but nothing had prepared him for the devastating task before him. His eyes roamed about, seeking some guidance, and for the second time in many years he dropped his head in his hands and prayed.

Where would he take her? Home to the house Marilyn and Chad would never return to? To his apartment? Should he take her away for a few days with India to help her forget? But you never forgot, you merely learned to live with the pain.

Maybe he should have consulted a psychologist before coming, someone who knew about kids and how they reacted. What if he did it all wrong? Would his bumbling explanations traumatize Molly for life?

She was his now. His to love and care for. Chad's soul could go in peace, he vowed, for Jack would make sure

Molly made it through as unscathed as possible. He would care for her to the best of his ability. They would share their grief and he would see she remained whole.

The thought of India waiting at the Grand Bay Hotel soothed him, too. And although he'd barely seen her since their arrival, she was there, quietly present, a Rock of Gibraltar in this time of trouble.

He braced himself, delving deep within the recesses of his soul for the strength to get him through the next half hour, knowing he had to be there for Molly, strong and powerful.

And as he sat in the small office, looking out onto the rectory garden, Jack felt a strange sensation overtake him. He'd never believed in spiritual forces, but he could have sworn Chad and Marilyn were in that very room, telling him not to worry but to do what he did best, follow his gut. And when the knock finally came, followed by the entrance of Reverend Raymond, he was ready.

At last it was over, the harrowing ordeal of the last few days finally behind them. Jack sat down in the worn leather chair of his den, his mind and body drained. He looked across at India seated on the couch, aware not for the first time of how significant she'd become in his life. Rosa— the Nicaraguan maid who had been with the child since she was born—had packed Molly's things and brought them over to the apartment with Bart, Chad's Saint Bernard, and Jemima, the little black kitten Red Berry from the baseball camp had given Molly a few months before.

They'd tucked Molly into bed in the former guest room that India had managed to transform in record time into a warm, welcoming little nest. Molly's doll and teddy bear were safely squeezed next to her. India had read a story from the little girl's favorite book while Jack had gently stroked her golden hair until she'd fallen asleep, overcome by exhaustion.

He never could have gotten through the last few days without India's support, he realized. She'd been there every inch of the way, never obtrusive but always available, her quiet strength a true solace, not only to him but for Molly, too. He leaned back, unable to erase the nightmare of telling the child what had happened to her parents. He didn't think he'd forget it as long as he lived.

A damp nudge at his hand made Jack look down. Bart was swaying mournfully next to the chair.

"I think he misses his master," he said to India, patting Bart and kneading the flesh around the dog's neck. Huge soulful eyes watched him sorrowfully. "How are you doing, old buddy?" Jack hoisted his legs onto the ottoman and smiled across at India, too tired even to talk. Every bone in his body ached, as though he'd been running nonstop for a week. The last two nights Molly had woken up with nightmares, screaming, wanting her parents. He'd spent half the night next to her, soothing her fears, helping her through the valley of darkness into which they'd both been flung, but where he, at least, had more means of coping.

"You need to rest, Jack." India's voice was quietly soothing. "I'll get you a drink." She came over behind him and massaged the taut muscles in his shoulders.

"That feels wonderful." He sighed.

"What a courageous little thing Molly is. She held up so bravely at the funeral."

"She is brave, isn't she? God, Indy, how's this all going to work out?" He closed his eyes, her hands on his neck a release. "I don't know if I can be everything she needs."

"Yes, you will, Jack. You're much more capable than you believe," she said with quiet confidence. "I think you'll be a wonderful father to her. You are already. Look how she clings to you, how she already turns to you for advice and comfort."

"I don't know." He shook his head doubtfully. "It seems to me it's you she looks to. You have such a way with her. It's a tremendous responsibility to raise a small child on one's own. Heck, I've no experience. Especially with a girl."

"Stop worrying about it. Last night you managed to get her back to sleep even after the nightmares, and already she talks about you with complete trust."

"She does?" He felt a twinge of gratification. Perhaps he could get it right. India gave him a final rub, then dropped a kiss on his head. It had become so natural to have her by his side he almost forgot it was soon coming to an end. He rose wearily and put his arm around her. It felt as though years had flown by in the last few days, and he wondered what it would be like to be without her. Lonely, that was for sure.

"Come on, let's get a sandwich."

"Good idea. You get us a drink and I'll make the sandwiches. Will tuna do?"

Jack gave her a squeeze. "Anything you like, princess."

Like anxious parents, they peeked in at Molly on the way to the kitchen. India pulled the covers gently over the young girl, and allowed Jemima to jump up on the end of the bed where she purred protectively. Jack looked down on his niece, his heart full. Then they tiptoed out and went to the kitchen. Jack turned on an Enya CD, the soft Celtic music appeasing, and sat at the bar pouring them a drink while India busied herself making the sandwiches.

"I love that music, it's so relaxing." India peered at him anxiously as she moved about the kitchen.

He took a long sip of whiskey. The apartment felt different since she'd arrived. Lived in, he realized with a tired yawn.

His mind kept jumping back to the events of the last few days, unable to control the thoughts. And his heart ached once more as he recalled Molly's small hand gripping his, her eyes uncomprehending as the caskets were carried down the aisle of the packed church. The moment was surreal, as though he and Molly, with India discreetly in the background, were in a world of their own, sharing a secret pain only they could fathom.

When the time came for them to walk out of the church, he'd felt her little legs trembling beneath her, and had swept her up in his arms. He'd carried her, head buried in his shoulder, as they followed Chad and Marilyn to their final resting place.

He forced himself to stay within reality and glanced at the clock, flexing his arms. His muscles were stiff from stress and lack of sleep.

"Here you are." India placed the plate before him and sat down on the opposite bar stool. "You have to eat, darling, you can't get weak," she said tenderly. "For her sake, as well as yours."

"You're right," he answered, reaching for her hand across the marble counter. "I know I haven't told you how grateful I am, Indy. I'm sorry you've been landed with all this." They'd barely talked in the last few days but her presence had been essential. "Thank you for everything."

"You don't have to thank me, Jack. I'm here by choice. It's where I want to be. I'd be very upset if it was any other way."

"You're a wonderful woman, India." He leaned over and stroked her cheek fondly. "I never believed I could care for anyone like this again until I met you. I know I haven't paid you any attention but—"

"Stop worrying about me, that's not what I'm here for," she interrupted, planting a kiss on his mouth. "I'm fine.

Now eat your sandwich and then I'll take a cab back to the hotel.''

"No way, I'll drive you.''

He watched India nibbling her sandwich, seeing the strain around her eyes. She'd been quietly beavering away, making sure Molly's move was done quickly and quietly, sharing long moments of play with her, ironing out any glitches and ensuring that their new life ran as smoothly as possible. For the first time in memory, he had someone to share the sorrow and the rage with, someone who understood.

"Don't you think you should stay with Molly? I can just take a cab.'' she asked, picking up the plates and putting them in the sink.

"No, I'll drive you. Rosa's here, so even if she wakes up she'll be fine.''

Before leaving, they looked in on the child one last time. There was a soft glow from the night-light on the commode, and they peered at her from the door, relieved she was peaceful, careful not to disturb her all-too-fragile sleep.

India slipped on her nightgown, then opened the glass doors and stepped out onto the terrace. The lights of Dinner Key Marina illuminated the bay, and a few cars circulated along Bayshore Drive, heading toward Coconut Grove.

She was too wired to sleep. Too tense. For the last few days she'd put her own worries to the side, throwing her heart and soul into the tasks that needed to be done to help Jack and Molly through their dreadful ordeal.

But now, in the quiet of night, she thought once more about Dunbar, aware the time had come to go home and take care of her own obligations. Perhaps it was selfish to worry about a piece of property when poor Molly and Jack were suffering so much, but nevertheless it was her responsibility, and one she couldn't shirk.

Her thoughts turned fondly to Jack. How cruel fate had been to him, yet how close they'd become in this last week. Right now he was raw and hurting, but even in his pain he'd told her how much he cared. Those words he'd said tonight meant so much to her. He'd opened the door to her and shared his pain, overcoming his fear of loving and losing at a time when he might have feared it most.

Her heart ached for him and she wished she could stay. In the few days they'd been together she'd become so attached to Molly it was going to be a double loss. But the longer she remained, the harder the separation would be, and the truth was, they each had to deal with the reality of their lives.

Perhaps the future would be different, she reflected, turning her back on the terrace and reentering the room, but for now this was the way it had to be.

9

On entering Chantemerle India was immediately struck by the familiar scent of dried lavender and pine. She loved traveling and working away, but returning to her enclave by Lake Geneva was an essential part of the enjoyment.

It was barely light as she entered the living room, so she pulled back the Indian-silk curtains and gazed out over the garden to the far end of the lake. The sun was peeking tentatively from behind the Alps, their white caps etched by the early-morning rays that shimmered like specks of gold dust over the still waters. It was an exquisite sight, one she knew she would never tire of. Silently she sent up a little prayer of thanks—thanks for this tranquillity amid the hiatus her life had become, and thanks also for finally feeling truly alive. She sighed and leaned against the French door, remembering the goodbyes.

Jack had held her close for a long silent moment, as though he were losing a part of himself.

"I can't believe you're leaving," he'd said softly, his mouth caressing her hair. "It'll be damn lonely without you, princess. It's as though you've always been here." Then he'd stood her slightly away from him, his gaze impaling her. "You'll come back, won't you?" he asked, demanding confirmation.

"I'll only be gone a little while," she'd whispered, loving him, wanting to kiss away all the lines which had appeared so suddenly in the last few days.

"Why do I feel as if I shouldn't be letting you go, as though—" He seemed troubled, then shook his head. "I'm sorry everything's been so crazy, I guess I feel something will happen to you, too."

"It won't, darling. What could possibly happen?"

"I don't know, I just wish I was going with you." There was an uneasy look in his eyes.

"Don't worry about me, nothing's going to happen to me, or to us."

"Indy, I couldn't stand losing you, I—"

She'd willed him to say it, to voice what she was feeling, to say those three little words that were on the tip of her tongue. But she held back, needing to hear them from him first.

"Princess, we need to talk. Not now, not here, but soon. Will you go away with me for a few days? Just the two of us?"

She'd caught sight of Molly running toward them with Rosa and Bart in tow. "Of course I will, darling. And promise you'll take care of yourself, won't you?"

"I'll call you tomorrow and we'll talk."

Then Molly had reached them, and India was down on her knees, hugging Bart, kissing Molly, giving last-minute recommendations to Rosa about the medicine the child took for her sinus allergy. India's last image was of Molly, straddling Jack's shoulders, waving with all her might under a riot of golden curls, and Bart, his tail swaying languorously and his ears flopping wistfully, as though he, too, were feeling her departure.

The truth was, a vital part of her being had remained

there with them. It had taken only a few days for two beings, a cat and a dog she hardly knew, to become an essential part of her life. All at once she breathed, worried, cared and laughed—because of them.

India's thoughts now wandered to Dunbar, and her heart sank. There was no more room for delay; the sooner she got on with it the better. Why was it, she wondered, that she was able to achieve that sense of being at one with God and nature at Dunbar and not here?

But she knew why. At Chantemerle, she was merely one of many owners passing through, viewing this same scene with their respective eyes and feelings. But it wasn't the same. Here there was no sense of continuity, no heartfelt, ingrained attachment to the land. Dunbar was her heritage, a bond that only the passage of time, blood ties and the handing down of legends could convey.

But it had to go and there was no point in dillydallying any longer. It wasn't fair to any of them—Serena, the servants or the tenants, even herself—to let things drag on. The sooner it was sold and gone, the better. There was no use in prolonging the agony. And how thankful she was she'd finally cleared the mortgage on this house. That, at least, was one less thing to worry about.

The sun was rising fast from behind the jagged peaks, and India's eyes watered as she opened the glass door and stepped out into the biting cold. She shivered, pulling her jacket tightly about her, and wandered over the terrace, then onto the grass. She picked up some shriveled leaves, making a mental note to tell the gardener to plant some bougainvillea later in the spring.

Two swans flew low over the still waters of the lake, the flutter of their wings all but audible as they made their majestic flight. They landed, posing quietly on the large rocks at the water's edge, where ritual required that each year they build their nests.

Her thoughts were interrupted by the faint ring of the telephone, and she hastened back inside, leaving the doors ajar, allowing the room to air, wondering who could be calling her at this early hour. Maybe it was Jack. Her heart beat faster as she went to pick up the receiver.

"Hello." There was a short silence, then a female voice that at first she couldn't place spoke.

"India? Is that you?"

"Yes...oh, hello, Serena," she answered, doubly disappointed.

"India, I'm sorry to phone you so early, I—"

India tensed, irritated. All she needed after barely walking in the door—exhausted from a long trip and the strain of the last few weeks—was Serena.

"India, are you there? It's Serena," she said, sounding anxious. "I've been trying to reach you." She sounded warmer than usual.

India resigned herself, wondering what she wanted this time. "I've been away," she replied coldly.

"I know, your secretary told me." There was a moment's hesitation, then she continued. "Look, there's something I need to talk to you about."

"Could I get back to you later? I've literally just walked in the door."

"I'm dreadfully sorry, so thoughtless of me, but as we're on the line, it won't take a minute."

"All right," India answered somewhat ungraciously, but not caring. She flopped into an armchair next to the phone and waited.

"We've had an offer for Dunbar." Serena sounded short of breath.

India sat up and leaned her elbow on the wide arm of the chair. This was all rather too fast. She'd barely come to the realization that there was no alternative but to sell, and here was Serena coming with an offer.

"What sort of an offer?" she inquired skeptically. Knowing Serena, it could be anything as long as there was money involved.

"Perhaps I'd better explain," Serena said in a placating tone. "It's really quite a surprise."

India listened attentively, determined to pick up any giveaway signals on Serena's part. "Who wants to buy it?" she asked in a neutral tone.

"The person interested is the chairman of an international company."

"How on earth would someone like that know we might be intending to sell?" India countered cautiously.

"Apparently he heard it through the grapevine. Masses of people must be wondering what we're going to do. It's common knowledge that in all likelihood we'll sell."

"Mmm," India pondered, acknowledging the truth of the statement. By this time half of Edinburgh was probably speculating about the future of the property. But she still wasn't satisfied. "What's he offered?" she asked, loath to think of Dunbar being overrun by uncaring strangers.

"Ah! That's the best part, he's willing to pay a very substantial amount." Serena replied brightly, "He wants to live there with his family. Not the whole time, of course, but I think he's based in London and wants to come up on the weekends and holidays. Isn't that super? I remember you commenting that if we did have to sell, you'd like Dunbar to go to a family, rather than have it go commercial. You do realize there's really no alternative, don't you?" The rest was left in the air.

India's brain was working ten to the dozen. It was all so sudden.

"Well? What do you think?" Serena insisted.

"I'll think it over and get back to you in a couple of days. By the way, you haven't mentioned this to anyone, have you? Remember, Mr. Ramsey said we should be discreet about Dunbar's crushing debt. Apparently he told Mummy not to say anything either. I wouldn't mention it, particularly to Kathleen and the staff at Dunbar. I'd hate for them to panic.''

"Of course not, I wouldn't dream of it,'' Serena gushed. "But don't take too long making your mind up, will you, darling? We don't want to lose an opportunity like this, especially as we won't have to pay estate agent fees. They're willing to pay the price Mummy had the property valued at, which is really quite something. They didn't even quibble. Even Mr. Ramsey—and you know what an old bore he is—was enthusiastic about the offer,'' she added as the clincher.

"As I said, I'll think it over and call you back in a couple of days.''

There was a short hesitation. "Good, well, I'll be waiting to hear from you. How are you otherwise?''

"Fine, and you?'' she answered automatically, surprised Serena had even bothered to ask.

"Oh, I'm fine, too. I was thinking about you the other day. You know, its funny, now that Mummy's gone it seems rather lonely sometimes, doesn't it?'' There was a hint of nostalgia in Serena's tone.

India moved the phone to the other ear, surprised despite herself. She'd never heard her sister like this before. "I know what you mean,'' she replied awkwardly.

"Perhaps we should try and see more of each other. Oh well,'' Serena continued hurriedly, as though embarrassed at her sudden outburst. "Bye-bye for now, I'll speak to you in a couple of days.''

India hung up, shaking her head, mystified. In all the years she'd known Serena, she had never heard *one* solicitous word pass her lips.

Still puzzled, she went to the kitchen and opened the fridge. After scanning it, she poured herself some orange juice and sat on the bar stool, watching the sparrows assemble on the terrace, recalling some of her mother's words concerning Serena. *She's not really bad underneath; it's an inferiority complex; Serena's had a lot to cope with; she'll come around in time.* Could their mother's death in some way have made Serena conscious of their true relationship?

India opened the garden doors, still skeptical, and threw the birds some scraps of the dry bread that she kept in a bag by the sink. They immediately rushed forward, twittering. But before they could partake of the feast, a fat blackbird bore down purposefully on the crumbs, pushing the smaller fledglings away and grabbing the largest morsel swiftly with his beak. The other birds fluttered around in a futile attempt to recuperate some of the fare, but Fatso—as India immediately christened him—would not allow them to get near as he strutted around the terrace, swaggering, his breast thrust out like a pompous headwaiter. Even in the animal world there were bullies to challenge the weak, she reflected, drinking the last of her juice and shooing him away to give the others a chance. The quest for gain and survival was present at every level of life.

She thought again about Serena. If her half sister was sincere in wanting to heal the breach, it would be only right to meet her halfway. If only for Mummy's sake. She knew it had saddened Lady Elspeth to know the two girls didn't get along. If need be, she'd let bygones be bygones. But first she needed to talk to Mr. Ramsey and find out more about this offer Serena had described as so perfect. For all she knew, it could be a figment of her vivid imagination, or at the very least a deviation from the truth.

She picked up her things and trod up the steep staircase to her bedroom on the second floor, smiling as she walked through the diminutive sitting room overlooking the lake.

She stopped a minute, imagining Jack reclining lazily on the small plump sofa, his long legs swung up on the ottoman before the fireplace. What would he think of her setup? she wondered, entering the bedroom and hoisting her luggage onto the bed.

She unzipped the case and carefully unwrapped a photograph of Jack and Molly she'd taken the day at a baseball game and had framed. Then she looked around the room for the right spot to put it. She decided on the eighteenth-century Bauern chest of drawers she'd bought in Munich, because there she could see them as she lay in bed.

She placed the frame at an angle, then stepped back and gazed at their faces, reading all the pleasure and pain written in their eyes, remembering Molly and the home run. There were a couple of other smaller pictures—of Dolores, and of Gabby and her—that she placed on the coffee table piled high with copies of decorating magazines and among the well-stocked bookshelves.

India glanced at her watch. It was still too early to call Jack and Molly; they'd be fast asleep. She bit her lip, smiling at the thought of Molly curled up in her little four-poster with the white lace curtains, and Jack in his boxers and Miami Heat T-shirt, spread over the king-size monstrosity he called a bed, the covers falling off and the air-conditioning on too high.

If she was quick, she'd just have time for a walk before Michelle, her secretary, and Philippe, the architect, arrived. She slipped on a pair of black leggings, an oversize gray sweatshirt, tennis socks and sneakers. Then she left the house, crossed the garden and slipped through a hole in the hedge that gave on to a narrow towpath bordering the lake. She walked briskly, passing the villas—many with closed shutters that were only opened when the owners returned in the spring. Everything was wintry and quiet, the water still and the cold invigorating. At every step she saw Jack's face, missing every inch of him, longing for his presence and his touch. How had she lived before? she wondered, aiming a pebble into the water, alive with a new energy she never knew existed.

After a couple of miles she turned and walked briskly back to Chantemerle, dreaming of what it would be like if Jack were lying in her bed with the fire crackling in the background, his eyes piercing her soul as he penetrated her body.

She pulled herself together firmly before reentering the house, realizing she had to stop wandering about like a gooey-eyed teenager. She had a business to run, problems to deal with and a number of other issues that required her attention. Not to mention Dunbar and Serena's unexpected phone call.

The first thing was to find out about the offer, and if it was satisfactory. Climbing up the narrow wooden staircase, she reached the loft, stopping on the top step to take stock of her studio. She loved this vast stage of drawing easels, blueprints, sketches and Rotring pens, mingled with breadths of multicolored silks, chintzes and trims cluttering the floor. She caught sight of the drawing board and went over to take a look at Philippe's latest project, studying the fine points of the drawing, a design for a client's new living room in her chalet in Gstaad.

Then she crossed the studio to her large Directoire desk that stood stacked with papers, wondering where to begin. She sat down with a sigh and began the daunting task of plowing through five weeks of backed-up mail. After the first few letters she decided to let Michelle show her what had already been sorted and get on with calling Mr. Ramsey. She flipped through the Rolodex for the number then dialed, tucking the receiver between her ear and shoulder while she sifted through some invitations.

"Good morning, this is India Moncrieff. Could I speak to Mr. Ramsey, please." She ditched two of them summarily into the wastepaper basket.

"One moment, please," the pleasant Scottish voice responded and she was put on hold.

"Miss India. Ramsey here. It's a pleasure to hear you."

"Good morning, Mr. Ramsey, thank you for your fax."

"I hope you had a pleasant trip?"

"Yes, very pleasant. Thank you," she answered politely, then gloomily she continued. "There's no way out, Mr. Ramsey, we're going to have to sell."

"I'm afraid so." He tut-tutted down the line, and India could imagine him shaking his head.

"I suppose we'd better get on with it then. Serena seems to think there's an offer. Some chairman of an international company. Has she told you about it?"

"Yes, Miss India, she has, and to be honest with you it's the best solution. It's really an excellent offer. It's sad to say, but under the circumstances I feel obliged to recommend that you accept. I'm waiting to hear from the solicitors. They're in…let me see—"

"It doesn't matter," she said hurriedly, suddenly aware that if she was going to sell she wanted nothing more to do with it. The sooner she detached her emotions from Dunbar the better. "I'm sure you'll deal with the sale very efficiently, Mr. Ramsey. Serena said the buyer was willing to pay the full value, which I found pretty amazing. Who is he anyway?" she asked, suddenly curious.

"I don't have his name, Miss India." Mr. Ramsey sounded apologetic. "These tycoon types like to handle everything through offshore companies and keep a very low profile. We probably won't know until we're ready to close, if then."

"Probably not," she agreed, recognizing the truth of the matter. The buyer would be loath to appear for tax purposes. "But hasn't he been to see the place?" She frowned and tilted back her chair.

"Lady Serena had his representatives come and visit. It would seem that they pass on the information to their principal."

"How very odd. I would have thought anyone buying a property of that magnitude would want to see it for himself." She shrugged sadly. "But I suppose that's his problem, not ours, Mr. Ramsey. I will have to come over and deal with dividing the movable property with Serena. I'll work it into my schedule and keep you advised."

"Right-o. If there's any news in the meantime, I'll keep you abreast. Now that you're back we won't be needing the power of attorney."

India's eyebrows drew together. "What power of attorney?" she asked, mystified.

"Well, I presume that you'll be signing any papers relating to the sale yourself now you're back home, isn't that right?"

"Absolutely. Just courier them on through when the time comes and I'll return them to you immediately," she replied. Mr. Ramsey must be getting doddery. There had never been any talk of a power of attorney.

She said goodbye and hung up, surprised that for once Serena appeared to be telling the truth. Maybe it was destiny that Dunbar should go so quickly, and, as she'd hoped, to a family. Time to move on, she realized, firmly ignoring the nostalgia that was creeping up on her. She leaned back and glanced at her watch. She'd try to reach Chloë later on in the day—if she was in, which was rare these days. Chloë seemed to be flitting round the world from New York to Sydney, in a never-ending whirlwind of activity.

She reached again for the phone, unable to resist the temptation, and dialed, remembering Jack's parting words and wondering what they signified, aware that it was silly to foment false expectations.

A warm thrill raced through her when she heard his groggy voice on the line. Just hearing it obliterated everything—Serena, Dunbar, even the sadness she felt at the sale. Just knowing she had him in her life made it well worth living.

Later that afternoon Jack sat in his office, listening to the ring of India's telephone, imagining her curled up in the corner of a sofa, probably in a nightgown. He'd never seen her in a nightgown, he reflected, amused. Only dressed, or lying naked in his arms, her warmth and the silk of her skin—

"Hello."

"How are you doing since we last talked?" he asked, his train of thought abruptly interrupted.

"That was three hours ago," she replied, laughing softly. "I dread to think what our phone bills are going to be like."

"That's Astra's problem, not yours. You must see how important it is that I be in constant contact with the designer of one of my biggest projects. Something might go drastically wrong unless I keep on top of her."

"Well, that won't be easy from a distance, will it?" she replied, her laugh deliciously provocative.

"True. But you're only a plane ride away. Did you have a good day, princess?" he asked softly, swinging in the black leather chair while gazing out through the panoramic windows over Biscayne Bay, but seeing her instead.

"Not bad. I've been trying to catch up." He heard her hesitate.

"Something wrong?" he asked, suddenly concerned.

"No, not really. Just, I've had to make a rather difficult decision today. Oh well, never mind. I'll tell you about it another time. I've decided to put it out of my mind for now..." Her voice drifted off, as though she was thinking.

"As long as you feel okay with it. Does it feel right?"

"It didn't a few weeks ago, but now I'd say yes. Yes, it does," she said in a firmer voice.

"If there's anything I can help you with, you know I'm here, don't you, Indy?" There was another hesitation and he wondered if she was going to tell him. He didn't want to push her, he knew instinctively it was still too soon. Hopefully she'd open up at her own pace. Then he gave her the best advice he knew. "Follow your gut and you'll do just fine."

"I will. But don't let me bore you. How was your day?"

He wanted to say that she'd never bore him, but instead he gave her an amusing description of Molly's departure for school, relayed a phone call with Eduardo concerning the Palacio de Grès, and wished she were not miles away sitting by a lake in Switzerland, but right here with him, where he could feel her, smell her, touch her. It was frightening how quickly she'd become such an important part of his life. Waking up and knowing she was gone had left him emptier than he already was. And how he ever would have gotten through this difficult time without her, he'd thankfully never know. He just hoped one day he could do for her half of what she'd done for him.

Soon, at least, he'd be able to give her the surprise he'd been planning. He was dying to mention it, and had come real close a couple of times, biting his tongue at the last minute, realizing the surprise would be spoiled unless he remained silent. But just the thought of seeing her eyes light up with happiness, wonder and anticipation was well worth waiting for.

Five days later India was woken at 6:00 a.m. by the strident ring of the phone. She answered, still half asleep.

"Hello lazybones. It's me!"

"Good Lord, Chlo, what on earth's the time?"

"Oh, around six. Guess where I am?"

"Judging by the time I'd say Tokyo," India replied with a yawn and a smile.

"Wrong. Get up and get that espresso machine of yours working. I'm at the Geneva airport. I'll be there in under an hour. Bye."

The phone went dead. India stretched and pulled herself out of bed laughing. She should have been expecting one of Chloë's impromptu visits.

Forty-five minutes later the espresso was just perking as a car pulled up. Soon after Chloë was dumping her bags in the hall and heading for the kitchen.

"Gosh, it feels good to be here. It always smells so deliciously…you!" she exclaimed, giving India a quick hug.

"I'm so glad you came. I've got lots to tell you." India poured her some potent dark brew.

Chloë closed her eyes and inhaled. "Smells like heaven. I can't wait for you to tell all. By the way, I flew in from Bangkok. Where's Jack?"

"In bed I would imagine. It's the middle of the night in Miami, dear."

"You know what I mean, silly. Was it wonderful? Are you madly in love, darling? I told you he was gorgeous, didn't I?"

"Yes to all of the above." India laughed.

Chloë suddenly yawned. "I'm whacked. I think I'll have to hit the sack. Do you mind if we catch up later?"

"Of course not. I've put you in the room next to mine. Let's take your stuff upstairs and you can have a nap."

A few minutes later India smiled affectionately down at Chloë who had curled up in a ball and promptly gone to sleep. Typical of her, India reflected fondly. Chloë was such a free spirit, wafting in and out, here today and gone tomorrow, yet when it truly mattered she was always there. In fact, she became very protective and focused when her friends met with trouble. India laid a soft woolen throw over the sleeping girl, then pulled the curtains closed and left the room quietly, leaving her to rest.

Later that day Michelle, her secretary, put an express package on her desk. India gazed at it, knowing exactly what it contained—the papers from Scotland. Reluctantly she picked up the pearl-handled letter opener and slit open the envelope. After she'd signed, there would be no going back.

She pulled out the sheaf of papers and laid them in front of her on the desk, leafing through them, recognizing the standard contract language, not paying much attention to detail. Laying them aside she took a sip of coffee. Then all at once she set the mug down on the desk, nearly spilling the contents, and grabbed the documents once again. Quickly she flipped back to a paragraph that mentioned the buyer. It was an offshore company from Curaçao, *Tenn Holdings*. She frowned, knowing she'd seen the name before, trying desperately to place it.

For a time she sat thinking, drumming her fingers, knowing she'd seen it recently. Then Michelle walked in with a list of things they needed to discuss and she put the papers reluctantly to the side.

It was only later that morning as she was about to go downstairs and check on Chloë that she stopped dead in her tracks. A horrific doubt swept over her and she hesitated, staring at the file cabinet on the opposite wall. An icy chill ran down her spine and her hands went clammy. Shaking, she crossed the room, afraid of what she might discover. But the doubt that had sprung so vividly to mind had to be clarified. She swallowed, pulled open the metal drawer, and fingered nervously through the manila folders until she came to one labeled Argentina. Removing the file, she laid it on top of the cabinet, sifting through it until she found what she was looking for.

With trembling hands she withdrew the contract entitled Palacio de Grès. Turning to the window she began to read.

10

Heart pounding, India compared the Argentine contract to the one she'd just received from Scotland, glancing from one to the other, unbelieving. Yet there it was, Tenn Holdings, written in bold black in both contracts. She even remembered being amused by the name.

"Why Tenn?" she'd asked Jack.

"Short for Tennessee," he'd replied gruffly.

Surely there could be no relation between this Tenn and Jack's Tenn. Coincidences like this probably happened all the time, she reasoned, peering uneasily at the carriage clock on the desk.

"Look at this, Chloë. This is the weirdest coincidence." She glanced at Chloë who had woken up and was now lounging on the daybed, flipping through *Hello*. "The company that's buying Dunbar has the same name as Jack's offshore company. They're even both from Cura-çao." She gave a nervous laugh.

"But that's impossible. You can't have two offshore companies with the same name in the same jurisdiction. Even I know that. By the way, did you know that Fergie has her own show on telly now? She looks absolutely super. Met her the other day in New York. She seemed awfully nice.''

"Chlo, pay attention. This is important."

"Sorry." She lowered the magazine and their eyes met across the room. "What's wrong Indy? You look like death."

India jumped up, drumming the papers against the smooth surface of the desk, her head on fire, a thousand thoughts battling in her mind.

"Indy, you're white as a sheet. Oh my God!" Chloë's mouth dropped open, horrified. "You don't think that Jack—?" The question hung in the air. Then she shook her head firmly. "No, Indy. It's too far-fetched. Forget it. I know where you're coming from, but no. Jack's not like that. According to Peter he's the straightest chap he's ever dealt with. There has to be a mistake."

"But as you just pointed out, two offshore companies can't have the same name. And what about Serena? I told you she'd phoned and told me about this offer. I think— no, I *know* because she made a point of telling me—that she and Jack had a fling. He's very cagey and refuses to talk about it." She sat down again, her legs weak, and gazed blindly at Chloë. "You don't think he just wanted Dunbar all along and that was the reason he— Oh God, Chlo, I don't think I could bear it if—" She buried her head in her hands. Chloë rushed over and hugged her.

"Stop it, Indy. We mustn't jump to conclusions. It might just be a silly mistake and you'd be torturing yourself for nothing. Come on." She shook India's limp arm gently. "Go phone him and clear the whole thing up."

But India was miles away, remembering Serena and Jack in the library, how before her departure from Scotland Serena had been friendlier than usual, and then the phone call with the offer on her return. It was all too coincidental. Perhaps Jack's presence in Buenos Aires, and getting her involved in the Palacio de Grès was simply part of a master plan to acquire Dunbar. Perhaps all they had shared over the past few weeks was nothing but a well-staged farce.

She remained slumped in the chair, Chloë crouching silently next to her.

Finally she raised her head. "Please, Chlo, find out for me, will you?" she whispered hoarsely. Chloë nodded.

"I'll get Michelle to make some inquiries."

A few minutes later India watched Michelle speaking on the phone as though she were watching a scene from someone else's life. Then Michelle set the receiver down and swung her chair around. One look at her eyes and India knew the answer before the words were spoken.

"It's the same company, isn't it?" Chloë blurted out.

Michelle nodded silently. There was nothing to say. "*Mon Dieu,* that's the doorbell," she exclaimed. "I'll get it, India. Are you expecting anyone?"

"I don't think so. Oh, Christ." She closed her eyes, remembering. "I forgot. Giordano's coming by this morning. Can't one of you two go? I can't talk to him in this state," she pleaded, suddenly desperate.

"No," Chloë replied firmly. "You go down and deal with the Marchese. In the meantime, Michelle and I will see what else we can find out. There is nothing you can do right away. We need time to think this whole thing out." Her down to earth manner helped India regain some control.

"You're right," India conceded, doing her best to pull herself together.

"*Ça va?*" Michelle asked, worried, securing her arm. "Can you make it downstairs on your own?"

"I'm fine. You and Chloë find out all you can." India descended the steep staircase, feeling dizzy. When she reached the front door she opened it up quickly, embarrassed at the delay.

The Marchese Ambrognelli stood erect, the black velvet collar of his cashmere coat a stark contrast to the thinning white hair that framed his lined, aristocratic countenance. Even in her distraught condition, India's heart jolted when she saw how much he'd aged. Poor Giordano, he still hadn't gotten over Lady Elspeth's death. He probably never would. For a long silent moment they held hands, sharing their common loss.

Giordano Ambrognelli had courted Lady Elspeth from a suitable distance since her father's death, and was a close friend of the family. It was he who'd christened India's company La Dolce Vita, urging her to ignore Christian's disapproval and follow her own ambitions regardless. Without his support she might never have found the courage to launch her own business.

She pulled on his hand gently. "What are we doing standing here in the cold? Come in and let's go to the salon."

"Very well. Tino—" He turned and addressed the chauffeur, who waited patiently next to the car.

"Sì, Signor Marchese?"

"I will sit with Signorina India for a little while. You go up to the village and buy me the *Financial Times*, please, and be back here, oh—let's say in an hour or so. *Va bene?"*

"Sì, Signor Marchese, con piacere," the young man replied with a slight inclination of the head.

"I tell him to buy the newspaper, that way he can have a cappuccino at the tearoom next door." Giordano gave her a conspiratorial smile. "It must be very boring to drive an old man like me around."

She smiled and helped him remove his overcoat. As always, he was perfectly turned out in an immaculate Saville Row suit. He glanced in the mirror and straightened his somber tie.

Then arm in arm they made their way together to the drawing room, India acutely conscious of how slow his steps had become. What a kind old man he was, she reflected, always so considerate of other's needs, never taking anything for granted, the perfect gentleman. He stopped for a moment as they passed the dining room, peering amused through the archway at the amalgam of wares covering the George IV dining table.

"La Dolce Vita," India said with an apologetic shrug. "It's awfully untidy."

"*Cara mia,* I am an old man, I am not worried about such things as tidy or untidy anymore." Turning slightly, he studied her closely. "I worry only when I see you looking so sad, so—what would your dear mother have said? *Come se dice?*" He searched for the word. "Disheveled?"

"I know I look awful."

"Not quite *that* bad, my dear." He squeezed her arm and gave her a wise, gentle smile. "Such a beautiful woman could never be referred to in those terms, only worried perhaps?" His bushy white eyebrows drew together.

"I'm fine, Giordano," India lied brightly, determined not to allow her mood to spoil the visit. She installed the Marchese in a comfortable Regency chair near the fire, knowing he liked the high back, and watched as his pale gray eyes stared out at the choppy waters of the lake. India curled up on the large sofa, remembering the many times they had spent together. For a while only the occasional shriek of the gulls and the tinkling masts of the sailboats in the Port de Pully broke the silence.

Then the Marchese scanned the room appreciatively. "You know, India, my mother was a wealthy heiress who spent a large portion of her existence and fortune refurbishing my father's impoverished, but beautiful, *palazzi.* Seeing your home reminds me of her. She had the same refined taste as you. That is an exquisite painting," he said, leaning forward, removing a pair of gold-rimmed glasses from his breast pocket and peering through them to get a better view. "Not a Brueghel, but—"

"Unfortunately not, I wish it were. Don't you remember? It was on the wall of the little salon at Mummy's. She gave it to me, and most of the other things, too," she added wistfully, indicating the ormolu clock on the mantelpiece and the Aubusson tapestry hanging on the far wall.

"She probably wanted to make sure you'd have them." He shook his head sadly. "So much had to go. I only wish she would have let me assist her more. But she wouldn't permit it." He raised his hands and sighed.

"Gosh, Giordano, how lapse of me, I never offered you a drink," India said, jumping off the sofa, not wanting him to become sad. "What would you like? A cup of coffee, or perhaps a glass of sherry?"

"I shouldn't, but I suppose—" He glanced at his watch and smiled. "It is a quarter to twelve, so why don't we indulge—as my dear Elspeth would have said—and have a little drop of sherry." He sighed. "I miss her so. She was…" He closed his eyes for a second then continued. "Of all the pains we humans are obliged to bear during the course of our existence, loss of our loved ones is the hardest of all."

"Yes, it is," India replied, quietly handing him the glass, and thinking not only of her mother, but of Jack and Molly's harrowing experience as well.

"Thank you, my dear." He took the glass and squeezed her hand. "I was very distressed that I was unable to attend the funeral. I so wanted to be with her to say a final adieu, but the doctor would not permit it." He shook his head sadly. "I talked to Elspeth the night before her—departure." He did not like the word *death*. "We were speaking of her return to Lausanne for the season. She wanted to be back before the Comtesse's annual Christmas ball, yet she sounded somewhat worried."

"Worried?" India sat up straighter. "Giordano, did she say anything to you?"

"No, no, merely that she had been feeling a slight malaise for the past few days. Nothing serious, you understand, just a little nausea, but otherwise she sounded fine. It was more the tone of her voice that had me concerned."

India hesitated, then decided to mention the letter she'd found at Dunbar.

"You know, Giordano, something strange happened when I was in Scotland for the funeral," India began, not quite knowing how to tell him.

"Yes?" His eyes became alert now. "Tell me."

"When I was in Mummy's bedroom, saying good-bye—" she gave him a little smile, and he nodded sympathetically "—I came across a note on her desk."

"Yes?"

"It was addressed to me, but it wasn't finished. It was as though she'd been called away in the middle of writing it. It was dated the day of her death, and perhaps written only moments before she had the attack."

"What is it about this note that concerns you so, my dear?" The Marchese leaned forward, posing his glass carefully on the table, his hand shaking slightly.

"If you give me a second I'll get it."

"Certainly." He nodded. "I would like to see it."

India slipped over to the small French writing desk in the corner of the room where she kept her personal correspondence, and pulled out the note. She handed it to the Marchese, who put on his glasses and began to read. India curled on the footstool next to him, watching attentively, anxious to see his reaction. Thoughts of Serena were suddenly ominous after this morning's shock.

"Why do you think she'd be worried about being over-

heard?'' she asked him anxiously. ''The only people I can
think of that might have been there were Serena and that
dreadful German boyfriend of hers, Maxi. And Kathleen
was with Great-Aunt Moira for the day.''

''Very strange,'' Giordano murmured, perusing the note
carefully. ''She said nothing to me of this. But you are
right, there is a definite feeling of concern in these words,
almost of fear. She obviously had something important to
impart to you for her to want you to go there at once.''
He lowered the letter. ''Do you have any suspicions about
Serena or this Maxi?'' he asked gravely.

''No, not really. Except I have just learned—that is, I
may have reason to believe—that Serena could have been
plotting to sell Dunbar behind my back,'' she said, swallowing hard. ''I think she and Maxi were making a dashed
nuisance of themselves. Serena had practically moved into
Dunbar, with him in tow. I do know Mummy wasn't happy
about that, but from there to suspecting anything, no.'' Or
not up until now, she realized, suddenly remembering the
documents upstairs and all their implications. Could this
all be linked in some horrible Machiavellian way?

''I should have gone to the funeral,'' Giordano said,
shaking his head once more. ''Perhaps we could have discovered something.''

''Of course you couldn't go. It would have been madness. Scotland's freezing in November. Mummy wouldn't
have wanted you to. She would have been miserable if
you'd taken ill on her account.''

''*Lo so, cara*, I know,'' he replied. But his mind, she
realized, was far away. ''Tell me, who is this Maxi,'' he
asked suddenly. ''Is he someone we know?''

''As a matter of fact, yes, he is. He's one of the Lowendorfs. He's the brother of Gunther von Lowendorf, the
financier.''

''Yes, of course.'' The Marchese nodded. ''I knew his

grandfather well. A most erudite man, professor of economics at the University of Heidelberg and the Sorbonne, and an eminent scholar of history. Gunther is very well reputed in his own field, too.''

"Well, this one isn't, I can assure you of that. I think his family's given up on him, and what he's doing with Serena or what she sees in him is a mystery to me.''

"Would you allow me to have a copy of this letter, India? Sometimes ideas come to one later.''

"Of course.''

Giordano seemed far away again, and India wondered if he was remembering Lady Elspeth as he'd so often seen her, sitting elegantly on the sofa, charming and gracious among chintz cushions, surrounded by her collection of silver-framed photographs of family and friends. She looked up, surprised to see him observing her closely, his old eyes reaching deep within her soul. She stared quickly down at her hands, hoping he hadn't perceived her agitation.

"Tell me, what is happening at Dunbar? Are you going to keep it? I imagine your sister is being difficult as usual. Elspeth put me *au fait* about the problems following your parents' marriage.'' He gave a wry smile. "Ah! The British, always so inflexible. In Italy a large fortune could obliviate a multitude of sins.''

"I'm afraid Dunbar will have to go.''

"I imagined as much.'' He nodded. "Do you have a prospective buyer or are you going to list it with an agent?''

"There may be a buyer.'' India was unable to hide her anxiety. "I just—'' She threw up her hands in a gesture of despair.

The Marchese reached over and took her hand, securing it between his quivering fingers. "India, your mother is watching over you, of that I am certain. I am having daily masses said for her. I know she would be so upset seeing you this way, *cara.* You must rise and go forward.'' There was strength in his querulous voice, and energy in the words that belied his frail body.

"Don't strain yourself, Giordano,'' India pleaded.

But he continued, as though sensing there was more to her distress. "I am an old man, India, I don't have much more time, and to tell you the truth, I don't want it. Life has changed. Every day I read the obituaries in the newspaper and someone else is gone." He shrugged. "Sometimes it's an old friend, at other times just a passing acquaintance. But each one brings reality home. My son Giacomo died ten years ago of cancer—it is not natural for the parent to bury the child—and now my beloved Elspeth is gone.''

"Don't, Giordano, please. You're telling me to get up and go on, but you must do the same. Think of all the places you love to travel to, the things you like to do.''

"Ah, child," he said benignly. "Seeing with these eyes is not important—'' he raised a fragile finger ''—it is the eyes of the soul that matter. You are right when you say we must go on, little one, but you must go forward differently than me. I am merely filling in time until the good Lord decides to put me in tomorrow's columns.'' He gave a frail chuckle. "And when that time comes, I want you to remember that I go with no regrets. You will learn, *bella,* that this life, which today seems so alive and vibrant to you, can become a heavy burden as time goes by. So take the time to stop and look about you, to see places and people with your inner eyes. Take whatever happiness God sends your way and grasp every moment with no regrets, for those will be your everlasting companions of the future should you not live your life now.''

Waves of energy and emotion passed from the old gentleman's hand to hers. He pointed to the ormolu timepiece flanked by mythical figurines on the marble mantelpiece.

"You see that clock? It ticks. Every day, every minute and every second, the hands go round and round, taking with them moments that will never return. Fill them with joy, with love. If your work gives you happiness, then work hard. If the right man enters your life, love him and cherish him without fear. Don't let foolish pride sway you from your destiny."

"But how can I know?" India wrenched her hand from his, rising abruptly from the stool, clenching her fists as she paced before the fire. "How will I ever know what is true and what isn't? How can I trust if at every turn I'm made to doubt?" she cried, no longer able to suppress the deep emotional battle raging within her.

He paused before replying. "The only true advice I can give you is to follow your own instincts."

"That's what I'm afraid of," she replied bitterly.

The Marchese looked piercingly into her eyes, then continued. "Things are not always as they appear. There are times when a conclusion seems obvious and absolute. But always remember to flip the coin and view the other side. If you are too blinded by hurt, then wait until you can think clearly. Some truths lie hidden until they are meant to be revealed, and until certain lessons have been learned. Life, *cara,* is nothing but a series of lessons, and most of them are imparted to us in ways we least expect."

India could not restrain her tears as she listened, cherishing his wisdom for a time when she might need it and he might no longer be there to remind her.

"Thank you, Giordano," she murmured.

"Do not thank me, *carina.* I can only share a little of what I have learned in these eighty-two years. So for what it is worth, take my advice and use it wisely. The lessons were hard won." He leaned back in the chair with a tired smile. "And now I must leave you," he said, taking a last sip of sherry and preparing to rise. All at once he seemed every bit his age. "My dear Dr. Kovats awaits me. It is thanks to her I am alive and well."

They walked back across the flagstoned hall to the front door, Giordano leaning heavily on India's arm. She whispered to Michelle, who was passing through, to make a photocopy of the letter, then turned to help the Marchese into his coat. They opened the front door and found Tino waiting, his shoulders hunched against the cold. He came forward solicitously, ready to take the Marchese's arm, careful not to let him slip on the icy cobblestone.

"*Ciao, cara mia,* I will see you soon," Giordano said, pinching her cheek as he had many years ago. "In the meantime I expect you to go to the hairdresser, buy a beautiful dress and get some life back into that pretty face."

"Thank you, Giordano."

He raised her hand to his lips, then India hugged him.

"Oh, the letter," she exclaimed, taking the copy from Michelle and handing it to him.

"Ah yes, the letter." He took it, folded it carefully and slipped it in the inside breast pocket of his coat.

India stood in the doorway and waved as the large Mercedes drove silently up the small incline, turned right onto the route de Vevey and disappeared.

Closing the door, she stared blindly at the empty hall, unable to stand it any longer. She simply had to know the final truth about Tenn Holdings. So she climbed back up the stairs to the loft.

"Well?" she asked, still holding on to a last lingering thread of hope.

"I'm sorry, Indy, but I'm afraid you were right. Michelle got on to Curaçao. It is the same firm as the one on your contract for the Palacio de Grès." Chloë handed her the fax. "I can't believe it. There has to be a mistake. Jack's just not like that."

"I got my friend at the bank to do an in-depth search," Michelle added quietly, handing her the fax regretfully. India read it twice, the last remnants of hope turning rapidly in to icy rage as it all sank in.

"The bastard," she exclaimed, anger and humiliation overwhelming her. "He must have decided he wanted to buy the estate after I was fool enough to show him the house. What an idiot I've been." She gave a hollow laugh. "He and Serena probably began hatching their plan on that drive back to Dalkirk—that's why Jack didn't make a fuss about leaving with her. It's so clear to me now. God, what a fool I've been." She paced the room, talking half to herself, half to Chloë and Michelle. "After all, I'd just made it abundantly clear there was *no way* I'd ever accept Dunbar being transformed into a hotel. He's certainly a fast mover. He must have thought it all out in the half hour after Serena returned," she exclaimed bitterly, throwing herself down among the cushions on the sleigh bed. "What a blind imbecile I've been. I should have at least sensed something. Think about it." She glanced at Chloë. "I've spent all this time, working, making love with him, taking care of his bloody problems and all the time—" She buried her face in her hands. "I can't believe I've let it happen again."

After a while she raised her eyes to Chloë's and sighed. "What hurts the most is how calculating he's been. Do you realize what lengths he's gone to to achieve his end? Even getting me involved in the Palacio de Grès, letting me become a part of his life."

"No. That's not true," Chloë replied staunchly. "I'm sure he wanted you to do the project, he couldn't have gotten anyone better. Indy, there must be some mistake. And everything that happened in Miami, that must be sincere,'' she said desperately. ''I wouldn't be surprised if Serena wasn't behind all this and has deceived him in some way, too.''

India gave an ironic laugh. ''Serena doesn't have this kind of ability. She can be nasty and scheming, but she's no rocket scientist. No,'' she said, shaking her head, ''I'm afraid this *coup de théâtre* can only be attributed to Jack Buchanan.''

She screwed the fax into a ball, crushing it as she wished she could her pain. She'd allowed him into her world, believing she could trust him, doing what she'd vowed she'd never do again. Christian should have been enough warning. But no, she'd gone back for more. At that moment India hated herself for allowing Jack to hurt her so.

And to top it all, her sexual inexperience had probably amused him. She raged, furious that his masculine ego was boosted by the knowledge that he could get her into that state—a perk that came with the task of getting his own way. Humiliation and anger warred with true grief, and when she heard her private line ring various times, she refused to pick up, sure that it was him. Chloë hovered round her, concerned, trying desperately to be of comfort, but it was useless.

''How could he have been so cruel, to have used me— and even poor little Molly?'' she asked. ''And to think I made myself conveniently available, running around him like a besotted idiot, all because he'd made me feel like I'd never felt before.''

''There's nothing wrong with that, Indy. It was about time you had a real experience with someone, don't you think?''

India couldn't reply. Tears choked her and she went to the window where she stared out at the rough waters of the lake, the brewing storm suiting her mood. He'd taught her pleasure, and allowed her to believe that his feelings for her were as deep as hers. It was agonizing to recognize that it been nothing more than a lie.

Then slowly her defense mechanisms took over, falling slowly into place like a heavy portcullis. To hell with Jack Buchanan. He had another think coming if he thought she was going to sit back and take this lying down. He wasn't the only one who could strategize.

She came back to the desk, her mind clear enough to begin planning. My God, she'd make him regret the day he was born.

"I know precisely what I'm going to do. First I need to get out a couple of letters, then I'll proceed to plan B."

"I don't like the way that sounds, Indy," Chloë said uneasily, glancing over at Michelle who indicated she was leaving them alone.

India didn't even notice the other woman's departure. She switched on the desk lamp as heavy black clouds darkened the low-beamed loft, her mind in another world. Pulling out a sheet of paper, she drafted a letter to Mr. Ramsey. After several corrections and rewrites she typed it out on the computer, printed it and inserted it in the fax machine.

Next she picked up the phone and dialed Hernan's apartment in Buenos Aires, methodically setting the pieces of her plan into place. Never had she felt so hurt or so determined. Christian's rejection was child's play compared to this. But then, Christian hadn't touched deep down within her as Jack had.

A cold, feral rage consumed her. Gone were the days of bowing her head and accepting the kicks lying down. She tugged savagely at the paper that had jammed in the fax machine. She wanted Jack writhing with the same pain she was experiencing, wanted him to feel the same deep, heartrending humiliation and agony she was feeling. And, God help her, she'd watch him grovel in the dirt at her feet and enjoy every second if it was the last thing she did.

Three days later India stood by, watching as Michelle spoke to Jack, nodding when the other woman cast a questioning grimace in her direction. She was perfect, India realized, grim satisfaction and torment sparring with one another. But she ignored them. He deserved every little bit of it, she assured herself.

She could imagine his anger and surprise, thinking she had left him for another man. Or would he merely be sorry that his master plan had been thwarted? A flash of doubt flickered, but she suppressed it, waiting for Michelle to finish the rehearsed conversation. No excuses, no going back. She knew what had to be done.

"Well? What did he say?" she asked anxiously as Michelle hung up.

"He said it wasn't possible. That you hadn't told him you were going skiing, and that Hernan was in Buenos Aires."

"Ha! That's where I've got him," she exclaimed with raw satisfaction. "Hernan *isn't* in Buenos Aires. He's skiing in Zermatt, just as you told him."

"He was furious, India," Michelle said, shaking her head doubtfully.

"I hope you know what you're doing, telling him this about you and Hernan Carvajal," Chloë added gloomily. "I hope you won't regret this. Maybe it's all a mistake, Indy, and Serena is to blame. I think you should at least *try* and find out, give the poor guy a chance."

"A chance my eye. Don't worry, I won't regret it," India murmured, trying to reassure herself. "And thanks, Michelle, you were perfect. I'm sure he believed every word."

"Yes," Michelle said woefully, "so am I."

"As for poor Hernan, I wouldn't like to be in his shoes if Jack gets a hold of him," Chloë commented.

"Hernan can take care of himself. And I wouldn't worry about the rest. I was an amusing pastime for Jack, conveniently part of a bigger plan. Now he thinks he can eliminate me and move on," India replied, laughing bitterly. "Jack Buchanan would never allow anything as insignificant as a woman to spoil a business relationship or deal."

"If you say so, but he sounded *furieux* to me." Michelle gave a Gallic shrug and returned to her computer. "What about Serena? Are you going to call her and at least try to find out as much as you can?" she called after India, who was ascending the stairs.

The red light was flashing on her phone when she reached her desk and she picked up. "Yes?"

"It's Serena," Michelle whispered. "I think you should try and find out as much as you can, Indy."

"You know I said I wouldn't take any calls from her."

"You have to find out what she knows," Michelle pleaded. *"Allez, courage."*

India flopped down in the chair. Michelle was right. It was time she discovered exactly what Serena's role in this whole sordid business was, and now was as good a time as any.

"Okay, I'll take the call. Sorry I bitched."

"Pas de problème. I'll pass her through." There was a short silence.

"India." Serena gave a sigh of relief, "I'm so glad you've finally taken my call. The most dreadful thing has happened." Her tone was dramatic.

"I gather Mr. Ramsey's told you I am not selling to Jack Buchanan now or in the future?" India answered dryly, flinging her jeans-clad legs up on the desk and crossing her ankles as Jack was prone to do, wondering how Serena planned to finagle her way out of this one.

"Yes, he did. Of course, it's all my fault. *Entirely* my fault. What a dreadful, horrible man. I shouldn't have trusted him an inch. I'm so sorry, India, so dreadfully sorry. If you only *knew*." A sigh followed. "And to think I've put you in this awful position. If I hadn't been so idiotic all of this could have been avoided." Her voice had become self-recriminating.

"Maybe I'm being dim-witted, Serena, but how could you avoid something of your own making? You told me a pack of lies the other day on the phone. You made up a phony story so that I'd agree to sell Dunbar, when all the while you were in cahoots with Buchanan. I must say, you have quite an imagination between the two of you."

"No, India, you don't understand, you've got it all wrong," Serena wailed.

"I don't think so," India snapped, irritated by this charade. "You and Jack have obviously worked things out very neatly between the two of you. You knew I didn't want to sell except perhaps to a family, and I'd made it very plain to him that first day he was at Dunbar that I would never allow the property to be turned into a hotel. I suppose you put your heads together and came up with this outrageous plan. I have to admit it was clever of him to get me involved in the Palacio de Grès, but it'll cost him a pretty penny. By the way, was that your idea or his?" She gave a harsh laugh. "I suppose the seduction ritual was planned, too. You obviously filled him in on all the details about Christian. What a good thing I read contracts thoroughly and have a good memory for names. Otherwise I would have been taken for a complete ride."

"No, no, please," Serena pleaded. "I know how awful everything must seem to you, India, but I did it out of desperation. I didn't want you to get hurt or anything like that. You simply don't understand. I'm down to my last groat. You know Dunbar has to go, you just don't want to recognize it. Jack promised me— He said the property was for his brother and their family, and I truly believed him.'' India heard her sniffling down the line and waited, wondering what else Serena had in store for her. ''He told me he'd be seeing you in Buenos Aires, that he'd *persuade* you that he'd— Oh gosh, it's too awful. How did I ever let this happen?''

''Whatever the reason, it's done. Now it's up to me to undo it.''

''But, India, we may never get another offer like this again.''

''He told you Chad wanted it?'' India mused.

''Yes. To live in and have as a small hotel, sort of more for houseguests,'' she added lamely. ''And he told me not to tell anyone, that it was a secret, and not to worry. He said you'd understand, and that his brother was using an offshore company to buy the property because of taxes.''

''So you knew he wanted to make Dunbar into a hotel and that we were seeing one another.''

There was a moment's hesitation. ''I did. To be honest, I was a wee bit jealous. I rather fancied him myself. After his brother was killed I thought the whole deal would fall through. I asked him what was going to happen now that his brother had died, and he said— Well, actually, that's when he insisted again that I not tell you anything. I—''

''Serena, you don't really expect me to believe this cock-and-bull story you're pitching? Of course you both planned the whole thing from the word go. You knew I'd never agree to sell if I thought Dunbar was going to be made into a hotel, and you were right. I won't. Not to him, anyway. The last person on this planet who'll get Dunbar is Jack Buchanan. I don't care if I have to give it away. I'd rather the place burned down around me than have him cross the threshold. And so you may tell him, with my compliments.''

"India, I swear it's not true. I did *sort* of know that there was a hotel in the offing, but I promise you, he told me his brother and wife wanted to live at Dunbar with their little girl. You *have* to believe me, India. He can be terribly convincing." The last at least was true, India admitted grimly. There was a short hesitation and she pricked up her ears. "But when he got me to sign the agreement to sell," Serena continued, "I told him you had to sign, too. He said it didn't matter, that it was a mere formality, and that we'd deal with your part later."

"You signed an agreement and it never crossed your mind to contact me?" India asked bitterly.

"To be honest, I was scared you'd screw up the sale. You see, you're not in my position. All I have now is my share of the property and that measly Hamilton trust, which barely gets me by." She wept down the line. "But it was all a lie," she wailed once more. "And now he wants to *enforce* the agreement. He says that if we don't sell to him it's fraud and misrepresentation. He's already taken out bank loans for the deal. I don't know what to do. I think we should just sell the place to him and be done with it."

"I'll bet you do." India got up in silent rage, not knowing whom to believe. Could Serena have been stupid enough—or cunning enough—to have signed an agreement that committed them to sell? She tapped a pen on her thigh. Of course she could. She probably signed it like a shot, hoping it would compromise them to such an extent they couldn't walk away from the deal. What a mess this whole thing had become.

"Do you have a copy of the agreement?" she asked.

"Yes, somewhere, I think." There was a loud sniff.

"Fax it over to me as soon as you can. I need to look at it."

"It won't be any use. He's determined to go ahead."

"Serena, the game's over. Send me the bloody agreement right now or I'll slap a lawsuit on both of you."

"He told Mr. Ramsey this morning he won't give up Dunbar."

"I don't care if he tells King Kong, just send me the damn thing. I'll have to talk to Mr. Ramsey. What a bloody mess you've made of everything, Serena. I hope you're satisfied with your own handiwork."

"I'm sorry." Serena's voice was low and anguished. "If only I hadn't gone against you. But I thought you wouldn't understand if I told you about the money."

"If you need money I'll send you some. Let me see what I can do about it. I'll phone Ramsey and get back to you."

"All right. And India, I'm terribly sorry, I never meant for things to turn out this way. I wanted to sell, but I didn't want to mess up your life—"

"We'll talk about that later. Just get me that document."

She hung up and took a deep breath, her heart pounding. What a manipulating, cold-blooded mercenary the man was. If it was true, that he was trying to enforce some written agreement that he and Serena had signed without her knowledge, then he was a darn sight worse than she'd first believed.

But there was no time to wallow in regrets. She knew now what she had to do. And there was no time to waste. The sooner she got on with it the better.

Serena lowered the receiver moodily and dropped her chin on her hands. "She says she won't sell to Jack. Now the fat's really in the fire."

"That's just talk," Maxi scoffed, looking at her speculatively. "The way things are set up she'll have to agree."

"Everything would be so simple if she weren't around," Serena sulked.

"Right. You've brought up a very good point."

Serena glanced at him. "Not really. We've screwed up and now she'll be doubly careful. Oh, Lord, it'll be too dreadful if we miss this sale. I have to think of a way to deal with her," she said, pursing her lips thoughtfully. "What were you thinking of, Maxi?"

"Some ideas come to mind," he replied vaguely. "When the time comes we'll talk about it."

"The whole thing's a damn nuisance," she said, dismissing the subject.

Maxi leaned against the doorjamb. Patience was the secret, and he had an abundance of it. He eyed Serena, weighing up just how far he could go. She was unbalanced, which meant he had to be careful or she'd blow everything. Better to take it slowly, he mused, restraining the little smile that spread to his lips. Better late than never.

11

Three whole days had passed and he hadn't heard a word from her, or been able to reach her. Then the fateful call with her secretary had followed.

It couldn't be true. She couldn't have betrayed him, not after what had transpired between them. And with Hernan of all people! It was unthinkable.

Jack got up, his mind in a frenzy, and stared for a long moment at a photograph of India and Molly that sparked off a plethora of emotions. There had to be some mistake. He turned away from the picture, trying desperately to come up with a logical reason for this all to have happened. But as he stared blindly out of his vast office windows, he was unable to find one, and unwilling to believe or accept what he had heard.

It had to be a lie, he repeated like a mantra, trying to diminish the unease, certain there must be a misunderstanding. Her secretary was probably mixed-up, and she'd gone skiing with a girlfriend. Yet the woman had sounded very sure of herself and there was the nagging question of why he had been unable to reach her. Worse was India's total silence.

A knock on the door made him jerk his head around,

glad to have something divert his attention from his worries.

"Come in."

Quince poked his head around the door, his face perplexed. "I don't understand this, Jack," he said, flourishing what appeared to be a fax.

"Understand what?" Jack moved back behind the desk and sat down, swinging back and forth restlessly.

"I just received this fax from Scotland. It's from Ramsey, the attorney for Dunbar." He looked across the desk, frowning. "He says they won't go through with the sale."

"What?" Jack sat up straight, his attention riveted.

"It's crazy. Listen to this. *Due to unforeseen circumstances*—this is the bit I don't understand—*one of the parties is not in agreement with the sale.* What parties? Am I missing something here? Didn't you tell me this Lady Serena was the sole owner of the property?"

"Let me see that." Jack reached out and took the fax Quince handed him, reading it carefully word for word. A sinking feeling akin to dread gripped him as the possible implication of the words sank in. Then he slammed the fax down on the desk and addressed Quince.

"Get Ramsey on the line." His voice was calm but his heart was racing. "Ask him exactly who the proprietors are, and why they don't want to sell. Tell him we have a written agreement signed by Lady Serena, and find out if it's enforceable."

"Right." Quince took back the fax.

"Just call from here."

"Okay." Quince glanced at Jack. "You okay?"

"I'm fine. Let's clear this up." He tried not to sound impatient, but the horror of what sprung to mind was overwhelming. Had Serena been lying to him? Was India also an owner of Dunbar? But no, that was impossible. India herself had made it obvious—on the few occasions the

subject had arisen—that it upset her deeply to talk about
Dunbar, that she didn't want to discuss it. It was under-
standable since she hadn't been included in an inheritance
she obviously cherished. Or was that merely his assump-
tion?

A chill ran down his spine and he rubbed a hand over
his eyes. For a moment he wondered if he was in the
middle of a gruesome nightmare from which he would
shortly wake up. He reached for the inlaid Burrell humidor
that stood on his desk and selected a cigar in an attempt
to hold his anxiety in check while he followed Quince's
phone conversation word for word.

"We fail to understand why you've retracted," Quince
was saying. "As you know, we have a signed agreement
from the seller."

Jack took a long time lighting the cigar, his nerves a
shambles.

"What do you mean *two* owners? We were led to believe by Lady Serena that she was the sole proprietor."
Another long silence followed while Quince shifted the
receiver to the other ear. "You mean, both sisters inherited
equally?"

Jack closed his eyes, Quince's voice a distant backdrop
for the commotion exploding in his head.

"But that was never made clear to us," he was saying.
"In fact, quite the opposite. My client has been grossly
misled. Lady Serena signed a document of her own accord
stating— What do you mean you were surprised, too? Oh,
I see. Well, that sure is a problem, Ramsey. I'll have to
call you back once I've discussed the situation with my
client. He's already taken certain steps in view of Lady
Serena's intent to sell."

Jack didn't even ask the question as Quince hung up.
He leaned silently forward and waited, clenching and un-

clenching his fist, already knowing but needing confirmation.

"We have a major problem," Quince stated. "It seems Serena's been leading everyone a merry dance. She told you she's the only proprietor to the property, right? Well, guess what? Her sister owns an equal share in it. Ramsey's very upset. It seems Serena lied to him and made him believe India was in agreement with the sale. Apparently Serena pretended that India had asked her to deal with any details concerning the sale. While she was away in Argentina, that is."

Jack sat in grim silence as the full impact hit home. Somehow India had found out he was buying Dunbar and believed he'd been trying to deceive her. Or worse. Perhaps she believed he'd connived with Serena. But surely she knew him better than that. She couldn't honestly believe he'd concealed his role in all this without good reason?

"What else did Ramsey say?" he asked bleakly.

"Well, that's where the story becomes even more weird." Quince shook his head uncomprehendingly. "It appears that India had agreed to the sale, but that *after* she received the contract, for some reason she retracted. Oh, and there's another thing. She said to tell the buyers they might as well withdraw their offer because she has no intention of selling the property to them, now or at any time in the future. This is crazy, Jack." Quince threw his arms up in despair. "What is going on? Didn't she know you wanted to buy Dunbar? Christ, you've spent enough time together. Surely you must have talked this over?"

"She thinks I was deceiving her." Jack's voice was as hollow as his heart. "I don't know how she found out, but this is bad, real bad." Jack was barely listening, speaking as though to himself.

"No kidding it's bad," Quince answered tartly. "We

committed on that loan yesterday, and we've signed a damn contract for the golf course worth—''

"I know exactly how much it's worth. You don't need to remind me," Jack snapped, aware that Quince had been telling him all along to wait until they'd closed before getting into any commitments. "But it's far worse than that."

"I don't see what could be worse than this mess," Quince mumbled, shaking his head.

Jack got up again and paced the room, in a world of his own. "She thinks I've been lying to her. That bitch Serena must've had it all planned. My God—'' he raked his fingers savagely through his hair ''—if only I'd talked to Indy, brought the whole thing out into the open instead of keeping it as a surprise."

Quince looked blank. "What surprise? I'm sorry, Jack, but you're not making any sense. Do you mean to tell me you never told India you were buying Dunbar?" he asked, amazed. "Why on earth not?"

"I thought she'd been cut out of the inheritance, and that was why she never talked about the place. Serena told me *she* was the sole owner, and everything I'd heard from other people seemed to confirm that. I had no reason to doubt her. Every time I tried to broach the subject with India, she clammed up, like it made her unhappy. That's when I got the idea."

"What idea?" Quince asked, his voice filled with foreboding.

"I thought once the deal was done, I'd offer her the restoration project—to keep her a part of Dunbar's future. After all, it's her heritage," he finished, deflated.

"Let me get this straight. You think India believes you set her up right from the start just to buy Dunbar?" Quince went suddenly serious.

Jack nodded bleakly. "That's what it looks like. She

hasn't taken my calls for two days, and an hour ago her secretary told me she'd gone on a skiing vacation with Hernan Carvajal of all people. Made it sound like they were off on a goddamn honeymoon,'' he added bitterly.

Quince let out a low whistle. "Damn. You really think Hernan would do a thing like that?"

"He was hot to trot where India's concerned." Jack stubbed out the cigar angrily. "The only reason he held off in Buenos Aires was because he knew which way the wind was blowing."

"Why don't you call his office, see if he's there? It might be a load of bull," Quince said speculatively. "If she's bitter at you because she believes you've been deceiving her about Dunbar, there's no saying what she might have made up to get back at you. Women can be the devil."

"You think so?" Jack grabbed at this last thread of hope and lifted the phone. He dialed Hernan's office, willing him to be there.

"No, Mr. Buchanan, he's away on a skiing trip in Switzerland,'' the secretary answered him brightly. "Would you like to leave him a message?"

"Yeah, you can tell him to—" But he stopped himself in time and slammed down the receiver.

"Well?"

"They're skiing."

"I see," Quince said uncomfortably. "She sure seemed in love with you. I mean, just think of all she's done for you, Jack. She can't be that fickle. She certainly didn't strike me that way at all. Quite the opposite, in fact." He cast Jack an anxious glance. "Surely she'd at least call you to find out the truth."

"I don't understand it either." Jack pressed his thumb to his temple, his head throbbing. "What happened between us wasn't something you just walk away from. I can't believe she'd do this, I— Jesus, Quince, I haven't felt anything like this since...well, since Lucy died," he finished quietly, the mere thought of India in another man's arms driving him crazy.

Then suddenly he smashed his fist down on the desk. "I won't have it," he swore explicitly. "I won't just stand by while that bastard takes her. She's mine, goddamn it."

"Nothing much you can do," Quince said sympathetically, picking up the fax and getting up. "We're not in the Middle Ages. You don't own her, Jack. She can go on vacation with whomever she chooses and there's not a damn thing you can say or do."

"To hell with that, she's—" He stopped, realizing suddenly how absurd he was being. "You're right. I can't do squat, can I?" He gave a harsh laugh. "I guess I'll just have to sit here while she—" But he couldn't bear the thought of Hernan touching her, caressing and then possessing her. He felt suddenly bitter at India for not trusting him enough to at least hear his version of the story.

He went back to the window and stared out into space. But India flashed before him, naked, arching for Hernan as she had for him, her eyes filled with that unadulterated pleasure he'd been fool enough to believe only he could give her.

He let off a sudden string of oaths, letting anger assuage his tattered pride and aching heart. Hadn't he known all along he should've walked? Yet he'd gone against his instincts, believing she trusted him and that together they'd forged a unique bond. What a joke. At the first signal of distress, she'd thrown herself into another man's arms without so much as a backward glance. He turned abruptly, smashing his fist again hard against the wall while Quince eyed him warily.

"I'm enforcing that goddamn agreement of Serena's, do you hear? I'm not giving up Dunbar. I'll do whatever it takes. She'll learn real fast how it is when I want something," he added with a bitter laugh. That India had not deemed him worthy of trust really hurt. The rest was only a matter of dignity.

As the next few days went by, Jack ached with a new-found anger that in some ways superseded his sense of loss. To make matters worse, she was everywhere, her image pursuing him with a vengeance. His first inclination was to remove the photos, wishing he could smash them, one by one, and eradicate her from his existence. But he knew how much they meant to Molly. Even the penthouse smelled of her, as though in her short stay she'd managed to impregnate it with her being. From the candles in the holders, to the scented potpourri she'd placed in heavy glass bowls, to the flowers which Rosa now changed every three days as India had instructed. Everything spelled her name.

At first Molly had babbled about India constantly. Then one evening he'd snapped and told her he didn't want to hear any more. He'd regretted it the second he'd spoken, watching, helpless and guilty, as the tears welled in Molly's eyes. And it had smarted when, at bedtime, she turned her face to the wall, refusing to kiss him good night.

Slowly his loneliness and sense of betrayal increased, and his anger grew. What right did she have to walk away as though everything between them had been an insignificant affair, so insignificant that it could be written off as inconsequential at the first brewing storm?

In his calmer moments he forced himself to take a step back and acknowledge the truth of the situation. He tried desperately to plan and make decisions, then realized bitterly that there were none to make. The decisions had been made for him and he had little say in the matter.

Unless he fought for what he now considered his, he

reflected, walking into the living room of the penthouse to wait for Quince.

He switched on the lamps and went to the bar. If she'd trusted him, confided in him, it would have been one thing. But she'd thrown herself into another man's arms at the drop of a hat.

Quince had sent off a number of letters and documents to the lawyers in Scotland, building up a paper trail. The next step was to file suit. Under the estate's present financial circumstances, if enough pressure were put on, they'd be forced to buckle under. He derived some grim satisfaction thinking about it.

He'd tried to avoid thinking about India, determined to overcome what he'd now convinced himself was nothing but a weakness. But he'd worn his temper thin. He lived permanently on edge, ready to fly off the handle at the slightest excuse. He glanced impatiently at the time, wishing Quince would get there. Now that he'd decided to go in for the kill, he was anxious to get on with it.

He turned to select a bottle of whiskey from the glass shelf then frowned, peering at the bottles behind the counter, realizing there was something amiss. Then a slow smile hovered around his mouth as he noticed that various bottles had been moved over to make room for some colorful vials with hand drawn labels. One said *wisky*, the other *shampain*. The third didn't have a label but contained an interesting violet concoction. Jack smiled despite himself, hearing the doorbell ringing in the distance, realizing Molly had been playing bar. As he headed for the front door a sudden image of his brother flashed before him, and with it his determination to win the battle increased.

Quince stood on the threshold dressed in white pants and a polo shirt, a red sweater loosely thrown over his shoulders.

"You're looking very dapper. New date?" Jack looked him over critically. "Want a drink?"

Quince laughed. "Nope, no date. Just dinner on a yacht that's in town. The *Andromeda*. Ever heard of her? She's docked at Bayside. An incredible piece of technology. Probably one of the most interesting sailboats I've ever seen. A hundred-and-twenty-footer. You should have a look at her, Jack."

"I've got enough on my mind right now."

He went behind the bar and Quince came and perched opposite on one of the high, leather-and-chrome stools.

"Anything new?" he asked, pouring Quince a bourbon.

"You mean from Scotland?"

"No, Outer Mongolia." Jack cast him a sarcastic glance.

"Sorree!" Quince raised a hand, laughing. He twirled the liquid in his glass before answering, a sure sign that something was afoot.

"Out with it, Quince."

"Seems India wants to file suit against you and Serena for conspiracy, and for attempting to defraud her of her property," he said slowly.

"What?" Jack slammed his glass down on the counter.

"Yeah. Apparently she'll go against you and Serena if she has to. Ramsey is very put out by the whole business." Quince threw him a speculative glance. "Says he thinks it's time an amicable agreement was reached, and frankly, if you want my humble opinion, I agree with him."

"What the hell are you talking about? Amicable agreement," Jack muttered angrily. "She hasn't a leg to stand on. The court—"

"The court will listen to Serena testify—in an edifying manner, I have no doubt from your description of her— that you threatened and blackmailed her into deceiving her own flesh and blood—"

"Good Lord, that's crazy. It's not true and it won't withstand a good defense attorney. I'll—"

"Jack," Quince interrupted him softly and looked him straight in the eye. "You have to let this go. It isn't worth it. If you want a hotel in Scotland, find someplace else, but cut bait, man, and let go of Dunbar. Believe me, it'll be better for you—in every sense," he added quietly.

"Let go? And let her and Serena get the better of me? Are you kidding? I'll fight this the whole way down the line. I don't give a damn what they say. I've always won my cases, and I'm not about to lose this one against that lying bitch and—"

"Get a hold of yourself, Jack. You're putting business and feelings in the same blender, and they're not a good mix," Quince commented dryly. "You've enough to take care of without this mess. There's the kid, and Chad's estate to deal with. You're obsessed with this whole affair and not giving enough attention to what needs to be attended to. Especially Molly."

"What do you mean?" Jack said huffily. "Of course I'm taking care of Molly. I'm just busy, that's all."

"Yeah? Well, maybe you'd better think about reallocating some of your time. You're not on your own anymore, partner. You've got responsibilities, real responsibilities that happen to involve a little girl who needs you more than anything else in the world right now. Don't let this mess blind you, Jack. I vote we call Ramsey on Monday and tell him we're dropping the whole matter."

"Most certainly not. I'll see it through to the end. And even if I did drop it, I'd want the money we put down on the golf course back," Jack said belligerently, knowing he sounded childish but unable to get India out of his mind. "Where is she anyway? Still on her honeymoon with Hernan, I'll bet." He gave a savage thrust at the nearest olive.

"As far as I'm aware," Quince said slowly, "she's at Dunbar."

"At Dunbar?" Jack laid his glass down in utter surprise. "How is that possible?"

"Well, that's what Ramsey said. Told me she was taking the reins until a suitable buyer could be found."

"Goddamn it, I *am* a suitable buyer," Jack raged.

"Not according to her. She wants someone who will live there, treat it as a home. Plus, she refuses to sell to you, so that's that."

"That's that my ass," Jack mumbled then downed the whiskey in gloomy silence.

"It isn't worth getting worked up over," Quince said quietly. "Just let it go."

"I can't," Jack replied obstinately. "I'll not rest until the deal's signed, sealed and delivered."

Quince swore under his breath. "Look, all that's going to happen is India will file suit and then everything'll be in a worse mess than it already is. At least now we can probably retrieve what we've already put in."

Jack left the bar abruptly, ignoring Quince's wise words. "Wants to play hardball, does she? Well, that's just fine by me. I just hope she's not out of her league."

"Do you think she'd really file?" Quince asked.

"I don't *think,* I *know,*" Jack replied, coming back and filling his glass with ice, clearly remembering India's determination whenever she'd decided to press a point she believed in. "We're going to have to put on all the pressure we can. We'll start by acquiring part of the debt. Do you have the file?" He became suddenly businesslike.

"Downstairs in the car. If you want I'll get it."

"Yeah. Let's take a look at who's holding the notes."

"Are you *sure* you want to go this route, Jack?" Quince rose reluctantly. "I don't like that look on your face one little bit."

Jack nodded grimly and downed another satisfying draft of whiskey. "If Miss India Moncrieff wants to bat, she's gonna find out just how hard I pitch. Get me those papers, Quince. I wonder how she'll like it when she has to cough up a few hundred thousand pounds or have me foreclose on the property. Maybe I won't seem like such a bad deal any longer!" he exclaimed with a humorless laugh.

"You're aware that there'll be no going back once it's implemented," Quince warned, shaking his head, clearly regretting the impulse that had prompted him to mention the latest developments.

"I'm perfectly aware of everything. Just bring the file up and let's get on with it."

"Okay, I'll get it." Quince made his way to the door with a sigh, leaving Jack to contemplate why India was in Scotland instead of skiing with Hernan.

Quince returned shortly with the papers and the next fifteen minutes were spent in deep concentration as the two men scanned each detail of the Dunbar file.

"Here." Quince showed him copies of the promissory notes. "They're all here if that's the route you want to go. I should think these could be acquired without too much difficulty. Especially the private loans."

"I'll think it over. You're probably right. We don't want to do anything too precipitate," he added gruffly, the fact that India was suddenly in Scotland still niggling in his mind.

Quince seemed surprised by the change in Jack's tone, but he shrugged and smiled. "It's your call, boss. I think you'd do right to think it over."

Jack sighed and got up. "We'll talk about it Monday. Now, go on and enjoy your dinner plans."

At the door Quince squeezed his shoulder, then hesitated.

"What is it?" Jack asked, suddenly alert.

"There's something else. I know it's rough, Jack, but Chad's stuff needs to be moved out of his office," he said uncomfortably. "We're going to need the space next week. I figured you'd want to go through everything yourself, so I haven't allowed anyone in there."

"I know." Jack nodded and sighed. "I've promised myself I'd do it, I just keep putting it off. I'll go in either later tonight or tomorrow. The office will be ready to vacate on Monday."

"If you need a hand just call me."

"I know. Thanks. But I have to face this on my own."

Quince nodded and the two men gripped hands silently, both knowing how hard it was going to be for Jack to go through Chad's effects.

A few hours later Jack glanced at his watch, unable to relax. There was nothing good on TV, the book he was trying to read bored him and it was too early for bed. He'd hardly slept the last few nights anyway. He walked into the den, realizing it was early and that he still had time to pop over to the office and begin clearing Chad's things.

He sat down at his desk, thinking of his brother, and opened the right-hand drawer, withdrawing a small velvet jewelry box and picking up the signet ring he'd gently slipped from his brother's hand before Chad was laid to rest. He hesitated for a moment before sliding it on his finger, deciding that he might as well go to the office and get on with the grim task before him. It was going to hurt no matter when he did it, and now was as good a time as any.

He grabbed a sweater and knocked on Rosa's door. "I'll be back in a while, Rosa, don't wait up."

"Sí, Señor Jack, está bien."

The evening was pleasant, the temperature in the low sixties, and he strolled down Brickell Avenue under a clear sky. Biscayne Bay shimmered under the full moon and the lights from the buildings downtown. He turned right at St. Jude's Church and walked along to the shore, gazing at the skyline of downtown Miami, its laser-lit reflection glistening in the dark water. Laughter reached him from across the water as a passing yacht headed toward the Rickenbacker Causeway, and a burst of fireworks from Bayside lit up the sky with a shower of sparkling colors. He quickened his pace, avoiding collision with a lady walking three large dogs, determined to get on with what had to be done.

When he reached the office building it was dead quiet. His footsteps echoed on the marble floors as he walked past the security guard and made his way to the elevator.

He entered the office and went straight to Chad's door. After a moment's hesitation he opened it, switching on the lights and gazing around him. Everything stood so hauntingly in place he almost expected to see his brother materialize behind the desk. Then all at once he shuddered as something strange streaked through him. He turned quickly, but there was no one. He relaxed a little, realizing it wasn't danger he was sensing but déjà vu, the same feeling he'd experienced at Dunbar, and once again on that memorable Sunday morning in San Telmo.

He shook his head, putting the feeling down to exhaustion and his imagination. With a sigh he went matter-of-factly to work, plowing through the piles of papers on Chad's desk. Mostly unfinished business, he realized sadly, placing each one methodically in its appropriate pile, not allowing his thoughts to stray to all that might have been.

But as he removed some documents from Chad's file cabinet, his eye caught the signet ring he'd slipped on his finger earlier and the memories flooded in. Although he was the eldest, their grandfather had left the ring to Chad, saying he was the only one in the family who cared about its history. Jack slipped the ring off curiously, twiddling it between his thumb and index finger, studying it closely.

He was about to slip it back on when the lamplight caught the engraved coat of arms. And suddenly he sat up straighter, his eyes narrowing. There was something oddly familiar about it. He stared at it closely, concentrating on the engraving, trying for the life of him to remember where he'd seen it before.

All at once excitement gripped him and he rose abruptly, as though some unseen force were propelling him toward the wall cabinets where Chad kept all his important documents. He opened the doors, seeing the shelves piled high with papers, old souvenirs and knickknacks scattered among files and large manila envelopes. Pain stabbed him as he gazed fondly at the objects, so many of which brought back poignant memories. But something urged him on. He put his feelings aside, driven by some mysterious inner urgency.

He took out a pile of papers before reaching for a tattered brown box that had Family Docs written on the side. Instinct told him this was the one. He dragged it out and sat down on the floor, gripped by a bizarre feeling of anticipation as he raised the lid.

The large box was filled with old relics—a small Venetian vase he remembered in his parents' living room, an old pocket watch that had belonged to his uncle and various thick manila envelopes. One in particular looked very ancient and worn. Jack reached for it instinctively and, for no reason he could fathom, his hands began to tremble.

Carefully he unfolded the ancient, crackling papers inside, so old the ink was brown and fading. He squinted, bringing them closer to the light in an attempt to decipher the contents.

Suddenly he recalled Chad's e-mail, a reminder that his brother had discovered something of obvious relevance to Dunbar.

Then, swallowing to ease the dryness that suddenly attacked his throat, he leaned against the wall and began to read with intense expectation.

12

The letter had been written from the Carolinas in January 1747. Although the fading brown script was difficult to decipher, the signature was clear enough: Mhairie Dunbar.

At the sight of the name Jack's pulse beat faster and he concentrated on the missive that appeared to be addressed to her son, Robert. From its tone he immediately recognized that the woman was dying. He paused for a moment, struck by the coincidence of the name.

Then suddenly his eye caught sight of the ring on his hand, and its coat of arms, and in a flash it all came back. As he'd been walking behind India along the corridor at Dunbar, he'd glanced up at the coat of arms carved above the bookcases. He felt certain now it was one and the same. Excitement gripped him as he set the letter aside, feverishly opening the other documents one by one.

The next was Mhairie's will, in which she'd left everything to her son, Robert Dunbar. Another was Robert's birth certificate, dated December 1746—shortly before the date of the previous letter—and the third was a marriage certificate, dated back to March 1746, validating the union of Mhairie Stewart to Sir Robert Dunbar of Dunbar. The marriage had taken place in Kranach—wherever that was.

Jack toyed nervously with the ancient documents. What connection could his family possibly have to Dunbar and its origins? He searched through the box to see if there was any other information, trying to recall the tales his grandfather used to tell on balmy summer evenings as he sat, swaying gently, in the rocker on the porch sipping iced tea. Jack had always smiled impatiently, too taken up with the present to bother about the past. But Chad had curled up at their grandfather's feet, avidly drinking in each word. All at once Jack wished he had listened more. Perhaps then he could have answered some of the questions that were hammering in his brain. Could he, by some curious twist of fate, be connected to Dunbar through blood ties?

He gazed around him, suddenly conscious of a number of details in Chad's office he'd never noticed before. The room was filled with relics of the past. There were old pictures and photographs, a needlepoint chair embroidered by a great-grandmother that had come from their home in Tennessee, and on the wall were his grandfather's ancient maps of Scotland, maps said to date back a few hundred years. And as he sat there on the floor, surrounded by the fragments of his younger brother's hopes and aspirations, he was overtaken by an overwhelming wave of sadness.

All at once he remembered Chad's words in their last phone call in Rio, the day before he'd died.

"You got my e-mail, right? When you get back there's something I've found you *have* to see, Jack. You're not gonna believe it," he'd said, laughing. "And if this doesn't teach you to be less pragmatic then nothing will. Dunbar came into your life for a reason."

"What is it?" Jack had asked.

"You'll see. It's stuff I've discovered about Dunbar but I need to confirm it first."

Chad's reaction when he'd first told him about Dunbar and the possibility of acquiring the property had been one of intense interest. His brother had been fascinated, smiling wryly when Jack told him the details of his meeting in the glen.

"You mean Dunbar as in *D-U-N-B-A-R?*" he'd asked, the deep furrow that sometimes appeared between his eyebrows deepening, in contrast with his boyish demeanor.

"That's right," Jack had replied, paying little attention.

He rose and returned the box to the shelf in the cupboard. Then he made photocopies of the documents before returning them to the envelope and crossing the hall to his office where he locked them in his safe. All at once he wanted to leave the office and get back out into the open— shades of the oak tree and San Telmo eerily disturbing.

He walked home driven with a new intensity. On reaching the apartment he glanced in on Molly who lay fast asleep, with Bart snoring at the foot of the bed, Jemima purring softly next to him. Then he poured himself a brandy before going into the den and switching on the sleek chrome lamp. He sat in his worn leather chair, the one relic he'd kept from his childhood days, experiencing a moment's hesitation. But the moment passed and he took a sip of brandy. Soon he grew accustomed to the flowery flowing characters, and before he knew it, he was immersed in another world.

An hour later he folded the letters carefully, eyes damp. The letters were deeply touching, the last message of a dying mother to her son. If the tale was true, it was unbelievable.

A nota bene at the end of one letter written in 1832 noted that Robert Dunbar, Mhairie's son, had been brought up by the Buchanan family and adopted their name.

Again the memory of the oak tree emerging from the misty shadows sprung vividly to mind. Had he perhaps been standing on the very spot Mhairie was referring to in her letter? He rose and went to his desk, then locked the documents carefully in the lower right-hand drawer. There was only one way to find out the truth. Monday he'd make a move. There were ways of tracing the authenticity of ancient documents. Instinctively he realized there was more to his connection to Dunbar than mere appreciation. He gazed at the drawer for a moment. If the instructions given in Mhairie Dunbar's letter were real, this could be an extraordinary set of circumstances.

But that was probably too far-fetched to be anything more than a legend.

Ten days later Jack stood under the huge branches of the burgeoning oak tree in the damp graying dawn, questioning his sanity. What, he wondered, could possibly have possessed him to come digging for long-lost treasure that probably didn't exist. Here he was, on other people's property at five in the morning, following directions dating two hundred and fifty years ago. It was the craziest thing he'd ever done, and he glanced around surreptitiously, making sure he was alone.

He'd slipped out from Dalkirk under the cover of darkness, crossed the field and the glen while everyone was asleep, and walked silently up the slope. The outline of the ancient oak was barely visible in the misty shadows, but intuitively he'd found it. Inhaling the raw damp air, he allowed instinct to guide him. And all at once he smiled, imagining India's expression if she could see him now, remembering her last reaction to his trespassing, and all that had occurred since. Then he concentrated on the task at hand, realizing that soon it would be daylight and people would be about.

Standing directly under the tree, his back to the trunk, he set the compass on his Breitling watch. When he found due west, he corrected his position and, feeling like a complete fool, walked the sixteen paces prescribed in Mhairie's letter. Then he brushed aside the damp grass, dead leaves and twigs, and marked the spot. Crouching anxiously, he opened up a collapsible spade, remembering the clerk at the camping store who had been curious as to why he needed the tool. What would he have said if Jack had told him he planned to dig for treasure in Scotland? The thought helped release some of the pent-up tension, and he began digging.

At first his hands trembled as he tooled the weighty dark soil and fragments of root, but then anticipation—either of success or embarrassing disappointment—got the upper hand. Soon his nails were filled with dirt as he loosened damp clumps of earth that the spade couldn't manage. He dug on feverishly, feeling more and more foolish with each passing moment.

After ten minutes he looked up. It was beginning to get light and as yet his efforts had yielded nothing. He shivered, the air around him suddenly chilly as the first glimpses of dawn pierced the misty shadows. It was probably nothing more than a fool's errand, he concluded, deciding that if he didn't find anything with a few more digs he'd give up, go back to Dalkirk and forget the whole thing.

It was then the spade hit something hard. Jack's pulse leaped and a shudder ran down his spine. He probed carefully, all feelings of foolishness vanishing as excitement gripped him. He paused, letting the enormity of it all sink in, knowing he was on the verge of a momentous discovery. Then, clearing the earth as best he could, he eased an ancient strongbox from the ground, surprised by its weight as he hauled it to the surface. A half-closed rusty bolt, rotted in parts, served as a lock, as though the person burying it had had little time to secure it in their haste to complete the task.

The wood was rotted in parts, but had suffered relatively

little erosion with the passage of time. Jack gazed in sheer awe at the small chest, placed here two hundred and fifty years before. Taking a handkerchief from his pocket he reverently brushed away the remains of dank earth that still clung to it, a thousand unanswered questions tormenting him. Slowly he worked on the rusty bolt. After some effort it gave way, as though loath to reveal the secrets it had guarded so securely for so long.

For a moment Jack hesitated. As with the diary, it was almost as though he were robbing his ancestors—if that was in fact who they were—of their right to privacy. But then, hadn't they also left this legacy to be discovered one day? Young Rob had apparently never returned, and by the look of things, neither had any of his descendants. Perhaps it had fallen upon him to discover the secrets harbored for so long. Perhaps some unseen force had driven him back here to reveal what, for centuries, had lain buried in the shadow of the ancient oak tree.

Not a leaf fluttered. Not a sound broke the silence. The morning mist hung in wisps, floating eerily around him, rising ghostlike from the frostbitten soil and damp leaves. He reached down and eased the lid. Suddenly there was a loud creak as it gave way, grinding noisily, sending the dust of two and a half centuries fluttering to the ground.

Jack sat back on his heels and gazed wordlessly at the cream-colored satin covering the inner contents. Except for some slight discoloration the fabric remained intact. Gingerly he removed the soft lining and looked inside.

A worn leather pouch lay to one side. Jack lifted it and its weight alone explained why the box had been so heavy. The jingle of coins made him loosen the strings, and he pulled out some gold pieces, staring fascinated at the still-crisp detailing of the coins. They were minted in 1715, the year of the first rebellion, he realized. During the past few days he had spent all his time gathering as much information about the period as he could.

He watched, fascinated, as the coins dribbled through his fingers, golden flecks sparkling under the faint silver threads of sun, the mist evaporating mysteriously, like a diaphanous figure disappearing into nowhere.

Jack looked about, then glanced anxiously at his watch, realizing he'd better hurry. Something at the bottom of the box suddenly caught his eye. Pouring the coins carefully back into the pouch, he retrieved a long sheaf of ancient parchment, similar to those documents already in his possession. There was also a small box. He opened it and gave a low whistle. Before him lay a signet ring identical to the one on his finger. Next to it was another exquisite silver ring of intricate design, inlaid with amethysts and diamonds, obviously meant to be worn by a woman. Slowly he removed the signet ring and compared the two. They were one and the same. His heart beat loudly as he slipped the ancient ring onto his other little finger. It fit perfectly, just as he'd known it would.

With great care he put everything back in the box, fearful the fragile papers might disintegrate. But they were amazingly intact for having spent two and a half centuries buried beneath the shadow of the ancient oak tree. For a moment he paused, aware all at once of the true significance of the passage of time.

Seasons had come and gone, children had played, lovers had kissed and quarreled under the heavy branches of the ancient oak and perhaps even duels had been fought at this very spot. Yet nothing had disturbed the missives lying intact below the surface, silently waiting to be discovered.

He set to work, replacing the clumps of damp earth and the tufts of grass. After the hole was filled he spread a splattering of leaves and broken branches, disguising the area where he'd been digging. Then, picking up the strongbox, he rose and gazed toward the house, mysterious and magical, just as he remembered it when he'd stood in this exact spot with India. He wondered if she lay asleep behind one of the windows whose panes gleamed with an elusive sparkle when the sun pierced the clouds.

For a moment he stood inhaling the potent Lowland air, listening to the first chirpings and rustlings of wind in the branches. All at once the intervening centuries vanished and he saw the land as it must have looked all those many years ago. The house would not have existed as it was today, but the rest would have been the same—the grass, the fields and, of course, the oak tree.

Jack closed his eyes and wondered at fate that had inadvertently brought him here. Or perhaps not so inadvertently, he reflected wryly. Then he heard whistling in the distance. He stood perfectly still, afraid someone might suddenly appear. But after listening intently he realized it must have been his imagination, and he headed quickly off toward the glen, his thoughts taken up with India. Perhaps the decision to retain Dunbar was more than just hurt pride and anger. How strange it was that two people who barely knew Dunbar, but whom fate had plunged into its midst, could feel such an intense connection to it.

He walked fast, entering the glen, slowing instinctively at the spot where India had fainted.

But it was time to go forward, not look back, to take action, and to shoulder whatever duties destiny had in store for him.

"It's perfectly ridiculous, of course," Mr. Ramsey stated, shaking his thinning gray head and shifting his spectacles. "Utterly pretentious. This *gentleman,* Mr. Buchanan, pretends to hold a claim to the property." He laughed disparagingly. "He says he can prove his line of sanguinity back to Rob Dunbar, who is thought to have died at Culloden, and claims to have documents in his possession to prove it.''

"What does this mean exactly?" India asked, trying to take it all in. She had been here for three weeks now, doing her best to learn the ropes, but ever since Mr. Ramsey had called to tell her about Jack's claim, she'd been able to think of little else.

"The Dunbar estate was entailed by your ancestor, William Dunbar, in 1302, shortly before his death. There are records to that effect. I have researched the family archives, and every one of his male descendants makes reference to William's will, except for Fergus Dunbar, who died in 1783. He makes no mention of the original will, nor do any of his descendants thereafter. Fergus's son David inherited, and the line came down to your uncle Thomas. It would have gone to your mother's younger brother, Lady Kathleen's father, had he not died three days before Sir Thomas. Thus, with no males left to inherit, the property passed to Lady Elspeth, the daughter of the eldest deceased male, and now to you.

"The will decrees that the entailed property must be handed down to the eldest male, thus securing the lineage and the land, and Mr. Buchanan claims that *he* is now the only surviving male heir descending from the original line originating from Rob Dunbar. He claims Rob's son was born to Mhairie Dunbar, his wife, in America. Rob Dunbar, as you know, was thought to have died in battle at Culloden Field without issue."

"But that's perfectly absurd. How can some silly American just come over here and try to steal our land?" Serena exclaimed, drumming her high-heeled boot on the carpet.

"I agree, Lady Serena, absurd is the correct term indeed, as we shall prove." He gave a supercilious smile.

"How?" India inquired, her curiosity piqued.

Mr. Ramsey gave a complacent nod. "The rule against

perpetuity does not allow for claims made twenty-one
years and a life in being after the death of the last fee
holder. This said, to be valid, the claim would need to have
been asserted within that period.''

"What does that mean? Do be clearer, Ramsey, please
don't ramble on with all that legal jargon," Serena said
impatiently, fidgeting on the edge of the sofa.

"It means that any claim should have been filed during
Fergus Dunbar's lifetime or twenty-one years thereafter.
That is the time span allotted for such a claim."

"Okay, so what you're telling us is that, even if Buchanan is some long-lost relation, it doesn't matter a hoot.
Is that it?"

"Correct, Lady Serena."

"So what have we got to worry about?"

"Absolutely nothing, Lady Serena. I'll have a meeting
with Mr. Buchanan's lawyers and the whole thing should
be settled in half an hour at the most. If he tries to take it
any further—which I doubt—the judge will send Mr. Buchanan and his far-fetched pretensions back to America."
He smiled, satisfied.

"I don't know." India eyed Mr. Ramsey doubtfully
from the opposite sofa. He seemed so pompous and sure
of himself. "Mr. Buchanan doesn't strike me as the kind
of man who would get involved in something like this
without first having done his research, and receiving good
legal advice," she said thoughtfully.

"Aye, you're right there," he conceded. "He's got a
fine firm of solicitors behind him, Miss India. Henderson,
Stewart and Mackay are one the oldest and most renowned
firms in Scotland, but I'm afraid even Henderson himself
will not be able to change the law for Mr. Buchanan," he
said, chuckling at his own joke.

"You see, India? He hasn't got a leg to stand on, pretentious pip-squeak, coming here and trying to take what's

ours instead of paying for it. It's just a way to get Dunbar on the cheap.''

"He was prepared to pay a very good price for it. In fact, according to Mr. Ramsey, he still is,'' India replied, uneasy.

"Which you wouldn't accept! If we'd just sold to him with no more ado, none of this would have happened,'' Serena said huffily.

"That's not the point, Serena. There must be some strong evidence for him to be making this claim.''

"So what if he *is* Rob's descendant? Who cares? Mr. Ramsey's just told us it doesn't matter a damn whether he is or not. He doesn't have any rights, and that's all we need to know.''

"That's correct, Lady Serena.''

India sat thinking as Serena nervously lit a cigarette.

"Do you realize that he may be related to us?'' she said, turning to Mr. Ramsey and Serena once more. "That he may be a distant cousin? Perhaps we should take that into consideration. After all, if he is a relation, it would hardly seem right not to— Well, I don't quite know how to put this, but if he's part of Dunbar, then he has certain rights,'' she finished lamely.

"What on earth are you talking about? Rights indeed! I'm afraid that just can't be helped. Undesirable relations have a habit of popping up like bad pennies,'' Serena snorted.

"Apparently so,'' India replied dryly.

"Oh, gosh, I didn't mean— Please don't take that personally, India. Now that we're getting over our differences, we can't let an outsider interfere.'' Serena cast her a quick, apologetic smile.

"Lady Serena is right.'' Mr. Ramsey nodded approvingly. "It would be most unsuitable for a *foreigner* to be given license. But there's no need to worry. The law will take care of him. Now, ladies, if you'll allow me, I'll be on my way. I'll keep you informed as to what is going on, but we should have this wrapped up before the week is out. Miss India, I hear you've been meeting with Mr. Mac-Innes. Is everything to your satisfaction? If I can help in any way, please tell me. I hear the tenants were pleased that you're taking the reins,'' he said with a polite smile.

"Well, only until we know whom the property is going to be sold to. Have you contacted Knight, Frank and Rutley, the estate agents, yet?"

"I'm afraid that until we've settled this matter with Mr. Buchanan, it would be unwise to proceed. Unfortunately there is still the matter of the signed agreement." Ramsey threw a meaningful glance at Serena, who went a dull red, then flicked her hair defiantly.

"You know Mr. Buchanan's offer is still open," he said, pausing at the door. "He's willing to pay the full price for the property, Miss India. I do think you should consider the matter seriously. You may not get better."

"I'm afraid it would be impossible to accept that particular offer," she replied firmly.

"What? Just because you've been to bed with him?" Serena laughed harshly.

India felt her cheeks turn bright red, and saw Mr. Ramsey's shocked expression. She accompanied him to the door, regaining her composure. "Thank you for your help, Mr. Ramsey. Now, you are *absolutely* certain there is no possibility of Mr. Buchanan winning his claim?"

"Miss India, it would be an aberration if anything but what I have told you here today were to transpire."

India closed the library door behind him, shrugged doubtfully and wandered over to the window, needing to cool off.

Gazing out over the east garden she saw new leaves sprouting and the grass covered in snowdrops. But her mind was elsewhere, remembering Jack as he'd aimed the 9 mm Beretta in Rio. Men like him didn't go into the fray without first carefully weighing the odds. Did he know something they didn't? She couldn't believe he would go ahead with this seemingly absurd claim without some assurance that he could prove it.

"A penny for your thoughts," Serena called blithely from the sofa where she'd thrown herself.

"I don't know. I think it odd that Jack should be making this claim. He doesn't strike me as the sort of man who does things unless he's very sure of what he's up to."

"Well, you should know, shouldn't you, darling? After all, I only did a quick survey—en passant so to speak—but you seem to have studied him pretty thoroughly."

"Serena, my relationship with Jack has nothing to do with this. Anyway, it's over," she finished coldly.

"Good. You should have listened to me when I first told you he was a cold fish," Serena said, satisfied. "But the claim's rot, India. He's just a frustrated American who wants to be part of a noble Scottish family. They can't help it. After all, they *have* no aristocracy, poor things, so I suppose they're all dying for titles." She giggled. "We'll probably find that *his* Rob Dunbar was a shepherd from Galshiels who happens to have the same name. For all we know, there may have been tons of Rob Dunbars—some of them may even be descended from one of William's bastards. But quite frankly, who cares?"

"Mmm," India conceded doubtfully.

Serena jumped up, a false girlish smile plastered over her face that did not match the hard look in her eyes. "Come on, let's have lunch. I want you to look at that silver I found in the cellar. You know so much about these things, darling," she added ingratiatingly.

India cringed inwardly. Serena was so transparent it was

pathetic. Her sudden reversal of behavior made India smile as she followed her sister to the dining room.

There was little point in speculating about the claim. They'd find out soon enough if it was real or not, and truly she was glad to be back at Dunbar, even if it was only for a short while.

What *had* come as a shock was learning Jack was at Dalkirk. It seemed she couldn't escape him. It was oddly disturbing to know he was so near, yet miles away in spirit, and she fought another inner battle with her torn emotions. But they didn't disappear, just as Jack's image never really left her thoughts.

The extraordinary matter of the claim was disturbing. If Jack was truly a cousin and heir, then his rights should be acknowledged. She couldn't allow her personal feelings toward him to blind her from being fair, or allow him to be alienated from his heritage as she'd been.

But that didn't mean she'd let him have his hotel. That was another matter altogether. The more involved she became with the running of the property, the more determined she was to keep Jack from achieving his dream. There would be no hotel, of that she was certain. They would just have to find a way of holding out until a suitable buyer could be found.

"It's very worrying," Serena exclaimed crossly, looking over at Maxi lounging in front of the television on the couch in her apartment. "The stupid girl even said that if he was a relation he should have a part of Dunbar. Maxi, we simply *must* do something. Things are getting out of hand. I can feel it." She brought over a glass of wine and handed it to him.

"Hmm." Maxi took the wine and sipped, continuing to watch the soccer game. "Maybe it's time to think in broader terms.'' He swung round. "You know, you could get the lot if you play your cards right.''

"What do you mean? I don't get you," Serena said, watching him attentively. Maxi was awfully clever. "You're up to something," Serena wagged her finger and went over to sit next to him on the sofa. Then she slipped her hand up his thigh. "What is it about you, darling, that makes you so alluring when you're planning something?" She giggled, feeling excitement rising just by looking at the gleam in his eyes. It thrilled her. He was going to make her rich, she could feel it. If anyone could deal with getting rid of obstacles, it was Maxi. With that happy thought she flicked her tongue over his lips and reached for his zipper.

Jack ducked his head and walked down the steps of the eighteenth-century building, striding along the gray-flagged pavement next to Quince, the wind hitting them head-on.

"How do you think the meeting went?" Jack asked, trying to make himself heard over a particularly strong gust. A lady on the opposite pavement struggled with her umbrella, and a man in a gray raincoat was having difficulty holding on to his dog's leash.

"Okay, I guess. Jeez, the weather in this place sucks. What about another hotel in the Caribbean instead of this?" Quince secured the golf umbrella he'd bought at St. Andrews in a firm grip.

"I don't mind it," Jack remarked. "We had our share of rain back in Tennessee, remember?"

"Yeah, but I'm not used to it anymore. And I'm wondering how long I'm gonna have to stand it. I'll take the sun any day," Quince shouted above the wind. "You know, I think you're crazy, Jack. Why don't you try and make things right with India? That's what all this is about, isn't it?"

Jack bristled, partly because it was true. "Whatever the reasons, I'm not giving up," he replied stubbornly, leaving Quince to shake his head. "What's the time?"

"Twelve-thirty. Where are we meeting Peter?"

"At the Café Royal."

"Good. I'm hungry and I have to make a couple of calls to the States. I'm damned if I'm gonna talk on my cell phone in this weather and on this godforsaken street." Quince trod along next to Jack in silence after that.

Lunch hour on Prince's Street was crowded. People bustled hither and thither in drab-colored mackintoshes and walking shoes, their heads bowed, oblivious to the weather. Jack glanced up toward the castle towering high above the Royal Mile. There was such a sense of history here. Even the tourist shops selling Edinburgh rock, oatcakes and tartan china could not spoil the feel of the place.

They turned up to St. Andrew's Square, then turned right into a small side street to reach the Café Royal. As soon as they entered they saw Peter Kinnaird.

"How did it go?" he asked.

"Great," Jack replied with more confidence than truth.

Quince raised an eyebrow and shook himself out of his raincoat.

"Well?" Peter turned to him, his friendly face questioning, his eyes alight with amusement.

"I think he's nuts," Quince answered, sitting down and eyeing the menu. "But knowing Jack, he'll probably get them to agree he's their long-lost relation. To what purpose, I still don't know—" he added, casting Jack a skeptical look. "Or, if it goes to court, he may even win the damn case. Ever since we were kids he's had a way of making things go the way he wants 'em to."

Jack shrugged and addressed the waiter, while Quince got up, a cell phone glued to his ear.

"He never stops." Jack grinned suddenly and began to relax.

"I don't know how you people live." Peter shook his head. "You don't even stop to eat. Can't it wait?" he asked quizzically.

"I guess not. We've important business to deal with back home, as you well know."

"True," Peter conceded. "Jakarta finally sent me the plans this morning."

"Sorry, but I have to leave, fellas." Quince clicked the phone shut.

"What about lunch?" Peter asked, astonished.

"I'll take a rain check, but thanks anyway." Quince grinned. "You stay. If I'm quick I can still catch the red-eye out of Heathrow and be in Miami in the morning," he said, pulling on his raincoat. "That Chicago deal's not working out, Jack. If it's okay with you, I'll take the car and go back to Pete's place to get my stuff. From there I'll hit the airport."

"Sorry you're leaving in such a rush," Peter said, rising and shaking Quince's hand. "We could've gone fishing on the weekend."

"Thanks—" Quince smiled '—but it'll have to wait for next time. Jack, I'll call you from Heathrow."

"You got it."

Quince left with his usual fast stride and Jack took out a pack of cigarettes, offering it to Peter.

"No, thanks. I've stopped. You should, too."

"I guess."

"I'm forty-six, time I did something for myself and the family."

"Yeah." Jack sipped his Macallan thoughtfully. "You have a great reason to stop. I would, too, if I were in your shoes."

"I'm sure you could find a hundred reasons if you tried."

"Like?"

"Molly for one, and Astra. Where would the company be without you?"

"Probably a hell of a lot better off!" Jack said with a cryptic laugh.

"Rot. You know perfectly well you *could* have a motive if you wanted one," Peter answered, staring into his glass, embarrassed.

"Hey. Why are you so worried about me all of a sudden?" Jack leaned back and watched his friend.

"I worry about my friends, old chap."

"Do I look as if I need worrying about?"

"Well, now that you mention it, yes. Di and I have become damned attached to you for some ungodly reason. Diana's got this motherly instinct, you know."

"Your wife is one hell of a nice lady."

"So's India."

Jack took a long drag. "Interesting you should mention that," he replied smoothly, feeling the same hurt anger that always rose to the fore when her name was mentioned. "I thought so, too—for a while. India is probably the loveliest woman I've ever known. But then I realized that she's a cheat and a liar, two things I abominate at any time, but doubly so in a woman. Bad mistake." He stubbed out the cigarette which had suddenly gone bitter in his mouth.

There was a short silence. "I don't mean to be nosy, but hasn't there been anyone else important in your life since your wife died?" Peter asked, picking up his knife and fork. It seemed to be a day for confidences.

"Nope. I guess I just turned off and put all my energy into my work."

"You certainly are success personified."

"You really think so?" Jack cast Peter a quizzical glance, then began eating.

"Aren't you happy with all you've achieved?"

"Yep. Though sometimes I wonder what it's all for. I used to think if anything happened to me, Chad would walk in my shoes and do a damn good job, but now— It all seems kind of pointless. Except for Molly, of course."

The two men ate in silence for a while and when they resumed the conversation it was on neutral ground.

After lunch they returned to Dalkirk. Jack noticed how the countryside was changing. Patches of white and purple were appearing on the hills. The air was milder and the sky clear, giving the feeling that spring was right around the corner.

As they entered the Dalkirk gates, Peter stopped for a word with Bob Mackintosh, his head keeper. Jack watched the dogs barking from the kennels, intrigued at the strong personal relationship Peter had established with all his staff and tenants, and the concern he showed for all the affairs on the estate. It was like going back to medieval times, to a period where the lord of the manor still took responsibility for other people's lives.

He walked into the hall and was met by the cheerful sound of girlish laughter and piano tunes drifting from the drawing room. He took off his raincoat, laying it on the hall chair, and headed for the half-open door. Just in time for tea, he reflected, amused at the regularity of these British traditions.

He pushed open the drawing room door then stopped, astounded, before quickly stepping back into the shadows. Leaning against the doorjamb he watched, caught up in a rush of emotions, wishing that everything were different and the scene could play out forever.

13

It was as though he'd walked into a picture book. India was at the piano singing nursery rhymes, Molly sitting starry-eyed next to her, while the little Kinnaird girls ran around the room playing musical chairs. Diana was curled into the corner of the sofa next to the fire, critically eyeing something she was sewing. Tea sat waiting on the table before her, ready to be served.

It was a beautiful scene. Jack's throat tightened as he contemplated the two women in his life, so right together.

Then reality felled him, pain crashing down as he realized how impossible it all was now. He waited a moment longer, loath to spoil the harmony he knew his presence would inflict. He was about to change his mind and retire unobserved when Diana lay down her sewing and saw him.

"Jack! What a nice surprise," she exclaimed. "I thought you weren't coming back until late tonight. Quince has already left. Mrs. MacC. was in a dreadful flurry because he hadn't had lunch." She glanced uneasily at India then smiled brightly. "Come in and have some tea."

The music had come to an abrupt end at the sound of his name, and Jack flinched at India's startled look. For an instant their eyes met and held. He could have sworn he read a myriad of emotions there, but just as quickly they disappeared, and Molly was running across the room to greet him. He hoisted her onto his hip and gave her a hug.

"Are you behaving yourself, pumpkin?"

"Yes." She gave him a huge hug and a kiss on his cheek that felt like a treasure. "Look who's here, Uncle Jack! It's Indy. Isn't that great?" She jumped down and tugged his hand, forcing him to follow her across the room.

India remained at the piano, her hands nervously crossed in her lap, dignified and remote, yet strangely vulnerable. The thought annoyed him. She had no business looking like that, making his heart leap in his chest. He tried to work up some anger but all he achieved instead was the desire to touch her, to take her in his arms and to hell with everything else. He approached, taking in every detail, from the gray-green of the cashmere sweater that matched her eyes, to the string of pearls around her throat. She fitted in here, looked so right. Finally he reached the piano, hiding his embarrassment by playing with Molly.

Diana jumped up. "Where's Peter?" she asked.

"He went to put the car in the garage. He'll be right in."

"We need extra cups," she said, fussing over the tray, then addressed her eldest daughter. "Caroline, dearest, run to the pantry, will you, and get some cups for Daddy and Uncle Jack."

India rose as Jack approached the piano. For a moment they stood only inches apart and he caught a whiff of the perfume he'd come to know so well. Then she stretched out her hand, her eyes distant, her fingers barely touching his.

"Hello. We weren't expecting you," she said tritely.

"I got back sooner than expected." He grasped her hand firmly in his, feeling the tension, not allowing it to escape. "It's good to see you. Please go on playing, it was beautiful." He searched her face for some sign, some indication of her feelings. All at once he felt as if he were dying of thirst and had been shown a bubbling spring from which he wasn't allowed to drink.

She smiled, a polite little gesture that didn't reach her eyes, and made an excuse. Jack writhed inwardly, annoyed with himself for his moment of weakness.

"India's going to be here for lots and lots of time. Can we stay a long time, too, Uncle Jack? That way we can do things together, and Indy's house isn't far away at all, and she says I can go over anytime and—" Molly was jumping up and down excitedly, obviously thrilled to see them together.

"Hey, calm down, chatterbox," he exclaimed, laughing. He crouched next to her, giving himself time to recover from the shock of feeling India's familiar touch, wondering if she'd felt the same. God, what he wouldn't give to know what was going on behind that proud, expressionless mask. He watched from the corner of his eye as she hastened to help Caroline secure a saucer that was about to fall.

"Ah! Glad to see you're all here. India, what a pleasure to see you, my dear. Looking wonderful as always I see." Peter walked into the room and gave India a peck on the cheek before joining his wife on the sofa. Jack caught the brief look that passed between them, one of those shared signals that people who are in perfect harmony and know the other better than themselves exchange. He felt envious, suddenly conscious of everything his own life lacked. Accepting the cup of tea absently, he went and stood by the fire.

"Thanks, Henny," he said with a grin to the Kinnairds' second daughter.

"You're welcome," she replied, and everybody laughed, for she sounded exactly like Molly.

"She's certainly got a flair for accents," India remarked,

avoiding Jack's gaze. "She'll probably be good at languages."

"Do you think so? I was never much good," Diana observed, spreading some strawberry jam on a scone for her husband. "Peter does better though. Your French is pretty decent, darling."

"Oh, I get by." Peter gave a deprecating laugh. "What about you, Jack, are you any good?"

"I'm still working on English," he replied, trying desperately to relax and not let India's presence get to him. After all, *she* was the one who'd walked out on *him*—and who'd cheated, dammit. That brought thoughts of Hernan to mind, and just thinking of the other man making love to her made him want to smash the cup into the fireplace. He restrained the impulse, drank some more tea and forced himself to carry on a civilized conversation. But inside, his blood boiled.

The tea seemed interminable. He wondered how long they would go on pouring cups and cutting endless slices of Dundee fruitcake.

Peter and Di were doing a great job at skirting any risky subjects, and the only thing remotely related to Dunbar was a remark by Peter concerning a fence that needed repairing, and how he'd have his factor talk to MacInnes in the morning.

Molly and the other children were playing Parcheesi, and Sam, Peter's Irish setter, lay next to India, where she kneaded him between the ears.

Jack wished he could turn back time, but it wasn't possible. It really was too late. Still, he decided, watching her out of the corner of his eye, he was damned if he'd go down without a fight.

India left her cake untouched and did her best to remain calm. When she'd raised her eyes and seen Jack standing in the doorway, she'd thought he must be an illusion. For one tiny instant she'd wanted to rush across the room, throw herself into his arms and feel the warmth and strength of him surrounding her once more.

But Molly had run toward him, jumping over the ottoman, and the spell had been broken. She wondered now when she could leave, realizing, to her discomfort, that she depended on Peter or Diana to get her home. Mr. MacInnes had dropped her off after they'd left the car at the local garage for an oil change.

"Indy, dear, why don't you stay for supper? Peter can give you a lift home afterward," Diana said hopefully.

"Thanks, but if you don't mind I'll see if old MacFee is available and leave now. I have so much correspondence to catch up on. What with one thing and another, I seem to be behind, and there are faxes that need to go out to Buenos Aires early tomorrow."

"I'm sure your employer will give you a break," Peter pitched in, grinning, and India sat speechless as he turned to Jack. "What do you say, India stays?"

"Sure, good idea." But the tone was noncommittal.

India rose firmly, determined to leave. "I'm sorry. I would love to stay but I really must go. Thanks anyway. No, Peter, don't bother," she said as he rose. "I'll get a taxi. I'm sure you've masses to do, and Di's making her new recipe for tarte tatin so she absolutely can't leave."

"I do wish you'd stay and try it," Diana insisted.

"If I eat any more I'll be fat as a pig soon," India replied dolefully. "All I seem to do here is eat all those delicious puddings and pies Mrs. Walker makes. I must have put on a few pounds since arriving, everything's getting tight."

"It suits you."

She whirled around nervously at the sound of Jack's voice. He was looking her up and down, taking his lazy time, stripping her of every piece of clothing, his eyes roaming possessively, letting her know he knew every little inch of her, from head to toe.

"I wasn't asking for an opinion," she said haughtily, feeling her face flush.

"It's free of charge." He flashed her a grin that made her wish she could slap his face. But the horror of Peter's next words obliterated all else.

"Jack, could you give India a lift home? I'd go, but I've got Mackintosh coming up at six, and Di's got this tart thing she's cooking."

"It'd be a pleasure," he replied, his eyes hooded, hiding the triumph.

India seethed, casting Peter a murderous look. Men, she reflected bitterly. It didn't matter what the circumstances, they hung together, thick as thieves.

There was nothing for it but to go gracefully, with as much dignity as she could muster.

Molly hugged her tight, and made her promise to return. India wished she could, for she missed the little girl desperately, but that would be out of the question now that Jack had returned.

They went to the garage and Jack pulled out a silver-gray Porsche that looked brand-new.

"I didn't know Peter was driving a Porsche these days," she remarked, knowing perfectly well he wasn't. "Or did you rent it?" she asked sweetly as he opened the door and she got in.

"I bought it," he replied, carefully closing her door.

The news hit her like a bolt. So he was planning a long stay. "Trying to impress the local yokels with your wealth and power?" she said sweetly as he got in and started the engine.

"Nope. Trying to get from A to B fast," he answered, pulling the car smoothly into the drive.

India realized crossly that he wasn't spoiling for a fight. She would have liked a good set-to with him. Instead she sat in rigid silence, wishing her pulse would stop racing and her heart stop aching.

A few minutes after they'd left the gates of the estate, she noticed they were going in the wrong direction. She glanced sideways at Jack, but his expression was inscrutable, and the dark didn't help.

"Are you aware that we're going the wrong way?" she said coldly.

"Uh-huh."

"What do you mean, uh-huh?" She turned angrily on him. "Take me straight home, Jack. I don't want to go anywhere with you." He didn't bother to respond. "This is most ungentlemanly of you," she threw at him as a last recourse.

"We need to talk," he answered grimly.

"No, we don't. I have nothing to say to you that can't be said through my lawyers. Not one damn word, do you hear?"

He drove on in silence, and India clenched her fists, tears of rage and frustration welling in her eyes. She knew she was losing her composure, her only safeguard, but at this point she didn't care.

"If you think I'm going to—"

"All I want is for you to have dinner with me for old time's sake. Is that so terrible?" he interrupted quietly. "Indy, we have to talk things over. There are too many misunderstandings in this whole darn mess—"

"As far as I'm concerned there's nothing to understand. And if you're thinking of a roll in the hay for *old time's sake,* you can forget that."

Jack pulled off the country road into a clearing and stopped the car abruptly. He sat for a moment in silence, then turned to her.

"Would you listen for just one minute to what I have to say?"

"I've had quite enough of your cajoling. I know you think you can wrap everyone—including the Kinnairds—round your little finger, but you can't fool me, Jack. I've had it with all your lies and pretense." She swallowed, hearing her voice crack.

"*My* lies? I never lied to you. *I* didn't give the impression I was ready to make a life with someone, then go skiing and partying with somebody else the minute his back was turned!"

"How dare you!" she exclaimed, outraged. Then too late she remembered the story she'd made up. But she'd heard the hurt pride in his voice and forced herself to regroup. "So that's it, is it? Your male ego has suffered a blow, has it? Well, let me tell you something. I enjoyed every minute of it. I had a wonderful time with Hernan. I'd go again tomorrow if I could and—"

Before she could get any further, he leaned over, pinning her hard and fast in his arms. "Perhaps I'd better refresh your memory before you go jaunting off again," he said, his voice husky, eyes flashing with suppressed anger. Then his mouth came down on hers, firm and possessive, reaching deep within her for some lost prize.

India resisted halfheartedly, the familiar touch of his lips leaving her weak. To her dismay she felt an ecstatic shaft of pleasure run from her throat downward in a never-ending trail, only to reach its shattering destination with pent-up longing. She moaned softly, limp in his arms as his hands moved swiftly below her sweater and his thumbs grazed her breasts. He whispered her name softly. Time stopped and she searched wildly for the feel of his hair, of his taut muscles, and the scent of his skin.

"We have to finish this," Jack whispered hoarsely, then lowered his head, pushing up her sweater and bra, his tongue flicking the swollen tips before taking her into his mouth, taunting and satisfying her as he had so often before. India tried to hold on to a thread of sanity. She knew she must stop him, but she couldn't. Sheer longing overtook her, and she gasped, unable to resist—and ashamed that she didn't want to.

The sudden flash of headlights made Jack sit up suddenly.

"Shit!"

India hastily pulled her top back down and straightened her hair, horrified at what she'd allowed to occur. The other vehicle stopped and someone got out. Then a flashlight hovered over the car, and she felt Jack slip his hand under the seat, poised for action.

A knock on the window made her jump.

"Are ye all right?" a friendly Scottish voice asked.

With a sigh of relief Jack opened the window.

"Good evening, Sergeant, we just stopped for a moment."

"Och, is that you, Mr. Buchanan?" The sergeant tipped his cap. "Is everything all right?" He looked closer, letting the beam of light fall on India. "Good evening, Miss Moncrieff, nice te' see ye. Are ye having engine trouble?"

"No, I'm just driving Miss Moncrieff back to Dunbar."

The sergeant smiled and nodded. Then he scratched his temple, puzzled. "But Dunbar's the other way, sir."

"I know. My mistake. I turned the wrong way leaving Dalkirk. Miss Moncrieff was just pointing that out to me. We stopped to turn around. I'm still not familiar with these parts."

An understanding grin covered the sergeant's ruddy cheeks, and he nodded. "Och aye, it's nae sae easy at first te' find yer way about. Is it true ye'll be making a hotel over at Dunbar House, sir?"

India bristled. So even the local community knew of his

project. The treacherous liar. By the looks of it, he'd already started lobbying.

By the time the sergeant departed and Jack closed the window, India was firmly in control, livid at herself for having succumbed to him.

"Whew! That was a close call," Jack remarked, revving up the engine, apparently unconscious of her change of mood. Good, she reflected savagely. Let him get her home, then he'd find out. She wasn't going to risk being stuck out here with him in the middle of nowhere any longer than necessary, and knowing Jack, he'd stretch it to the limit.

He leaned over and touched her cheek, then drove fast, back the way they'd come, past Dalkirk and on toward Dunbar. It was as though he couldn't get there fast enough. India sat in silence, letting her anger simmer, allowing him to think for a few foolish moments that she was going to give in.

They screeched up to the front door and Jack got out. But by the time he reached her side of the car India was walking to the front door.

"Let me lock the car," he said, glancing at her.

"What for?"

"Well, I—"

"If you're planning to come in you can forget it," she said icily. "You still don't have any rights to the place that I'm aware of. For all I know, those papers of yours may be phony. Perhaps Serena's right and you're just conjuring up a way of getting Dunbar on the cheap. As for letting you come in for any other purpose, why would I want to do that?" She stopped and took out her key, hoping her fingers wouldn't tremble too badly when she inserted it in the lock. "Hernan will be here in a few days," she continued, "and I don't think he'd like it if— Well, I'm sure you understand."

Even in the dim light of the lanterns, she could see him stiffen. Cold fury settled into his eyes and he took an angry step forward.

"Don't," she said, raising a hand and stepping back.

He stopped abruptly. "What are you playing at, India? What the hell's going on? You wanted me back there as much as I wanted you. Doesn't what happened between us mean anything to you? I'm ready to take you back, even after everything you've done."

What nerve the man had. How dare he imply he would graciously take her back, as if he was her owner and she owed him an apology.

"It was an unfortunate misjudgment on my part," she said coldly, praying her limbs would hold up until she got inside. She refused to give him the satisfaction of crumbling before him as she had once before.

"Don't give me a load of BS, India. I know you like I know myself."

"You *think* you know me," she threw at him, opening the door, "but you don't. If you believe for one minute I'll allow you to fill Dunbar with all your dreadful tourists, then think again. As for your magnanimous offer, you can keep it. Lately I've developed a taste for variety. The vacation with Hernan was fun, but there are other fish in the sea." She made a moue. "Actually, letting you kiss me back there was a good idea. It always helps to have an ample basis of comparison, doesn't it?" She cast him a last scathing glance, glad she'd hurt him as much as he'd hurt her. "Good night, Jack. I have nothing else to say to you, now or ever. If I were you, I'd take my silly claims and go back where you came from."

Then she rushed into the house and slammed the door behind her, leaning hard against it, chest heaving as the tears burst forth and poured down her cheeks. What had she done? What had induced her to carry on that silly lie about Hernan? What if she mucked up their business partnership? Slowly she slid down onto the cold stone floor, hugging her knees, burying her head there, trembling, wishing she could find it in her to hate him as much as she pretended to.

Minutes later she heard the angry rumble of the Porsche's engine, and the screech on the gravel, aware she'd just slammed the door on her heart's dearest desire. Pain ripped through her gut. Once before she'd thought her heart was broken, but the only thing battered had been her pride.

Now she knew the true meaning of a broken heart.

Jack sat simmering in the car. He'd started after her, then forced himself to stop. A surge of unmitigated fury rose in his throat and he wanted to throttle and kiss her all at the same time.

Abruptly he switched on the engine. "You're going to regret this, India, believe me," he muttered. There would be no more reprieves, no more excuses. He was taking no more prisoners. From now on it was out-and-out war.

He drove back to Dalkirk seething. How dare she? How dare she make a fool of him, playing with his feelings, and indirectly Molly's. He took a sharp turn, only realizing how fast he was going when another car flashed in the opposite direction. A few minutes later he pulled the car into the garage and walked into the house. In the hall he crossed Peter who was seeing Mr. Mackintosh out.

"Ah! You're back. Did India get home okay?" He closed the door and glanced at Jack. "Are you all right, old chap?" he asked, frowning as Jack tore off his jacket.

"No, I'm not fucking all right," he muttered.

Peter made a sign for him to lower his voice. "Di gets livid if we swear near the girls," he said with an apologetic laugh. "Come into the study and have a drink. You look as if you could use one."

Jack followed Peter into the study and threw himself into a large leather chair before the fire, gazing morosely into the flames while Peter poured two glasses of whiskey from the decanter.

"Damn her," Jack said suddenly, ramming his fist down on the arm of the chair. "How dare she?" He let off a string of oaths.

"India?" Peter asked, handing him a glass.

"No, Peter, Cinderella. Of course it's India, dammit. It's always India. What can you say of a woman who's in your arms one minute and telling you to forget it the next." He drank deeply.

"Uh—I thought perhaps you might bridge the rift." Peter sat in the opposite chair, rubbing hopefully at a stain on the arm of his old camel hair sweater.

"I can't believe she'd do this," Jack continued, oblivious. "I was ready to take her back, even after what she'd done, and what does she do? She shoves the whole thing in my face, like I'm some kind of moron who'll just stand there like an idiot while she sleeps around with someone else."

"Do you really believe that?" Peter asked doubtfully.

"Peter, do you live on another planet?" Unable to stay still, Jack got up and paced the room. "She and Hernan were at it the minute my back was turned. I wouldn't have thought that of him either, he seemed like a straight shooter. It just goes to show, doesn't it? You can't trust anyone," he said gloomily.

"Sorry to be nosy, but what exactly has been going on? I realize you're both arguing about the Dunbar issue, but I don't know all the details."

For a minute Jack hesitated, then he leaned against the mantelpiece and poured out all his woes. It was a relief to be able to tell someone, even if it made him look bad. But he just didn't care anymore.

Twenty minutes later he'd gotten some of it off his chest. "I'm filing suit first thing tomorrow. I want Dunbar. I have as much right to it as they do. It's like some quirk of destiny, Peter. Think about it." He stood with his back to the fire and began enumerating. "First you and I do business together, and we get along well. Then you invite me here and I love it. I meet India, I fall in— I have an affair with her. I find the papers, and it turns out that Jamie Kinnaird, your ancestor, was best friends with mine. How do you explain all that?"

Diana peeked her head around the door. "May I? I'd love a glass of sherry." She smiled knowingly at Jack. "Go on, I've been wondering when the bubble was going to burst," she said with an amused shake of her head.

Peter smiled ruefully and motioned for her to sit next to him. "It hasn't just burst, dear, now the fat's in the pan. We were talking about all the coincidences which seem to have brought Jack here. And he's right, it is amazing about Rob Dunbar and Jamie, my great-great... I can't remember exactly what anymore. Really a tremendous coincidence. I have to tell you, Jack, reading those letters and Mhairie's diary was a most moving experience."

"It was indeed," Diana corroborated. "I was weeping by the end. Poor Mhairie, I felt so sorry for her. And Rob, too, of course. But just imagining her all alone in a strange land, pregnant, and not knowing what had happened to her husband— Simply ghastly." She shuddered and laid a hand on Peter's. "Though I don't believe in coincidences, you know," she said, sitting on the arm of her husband's chair and accepting the sherry Jack had poured for her. "I've been certain all along that Rob has had a hand in all this."

"You mean some ghost is deciding our lives for us?

Come on, Di.'' Jack passed his fingers through his hair and laughed uneasily.

"Not exactly,'' she replied thoughtfully. "But some souls just don't rest until the worldly things that have been holding them back are sorted out.''

"You truly believe that?'' Jack suddenly remembered those strange sensations he'd felt.

"Diana believes in reincarnation and all that.'' Peter gave a skeptical smile and patted Diana's hand.

"Well, I wouldn't be too blasé about it if I were you,'' she replied, rounding on him. "I seem to remember very clearly you telling me that if you hadn't had that dream where Jamie told you about the problems up at the north farm, it would have caused quite a rumpus.''

Peter went a dull red. "Well, at the time I thought per- haps— But it could've just been my imagination.''

"Imagination my foot! You know perfectly well it was Jamie. We agreed about it at the time. Don't be embar- rassed just because Jack doesn't believe in spirits—yet,'' she added darkly.

"I never said I didn't believe,'' Jack answered slowly.

"It should be perfectly plain to both of you.'' Diana got up and looked them over, shaking her head. "Rob has been at work. He wants Dunbar back in the right hands. I don't know what that implies exactly, but I do believe that, in some way, both you and India are meant to be a part of it. Something's going to happen, something unexpected.'' She seemed suddenly far away, as though seeing far into the future.

"There's not much can happen, dear,'' Peter replied matter-of-factly. "When Jack goes to court the judge will rule either in their favor, or in his.''

"I know. Still, I can't explain. It's just a feeling.''

"You think I shouldn't file suit? Or just wait and see

what happens to the claim?" Jack asked. "Because I plan to go ahead tomorrow morning."

"Mmm. I know you are, but for all the wrong reasons," she said, looking him straight in the eye.

He glanced away, uncomfortable. "I'm filing because I have to," he mumbled.

"You're filing because you're as cross as a bear that India's not running around you like a bee with a honeypot," Diana declared.

"Now Di—"

"Don't now Di me, Peter Kinnaird! If we can't tell each other the truth when we need to hear it, then I don't know what friendship's about."

Peter cast Jack an apologetic glance.

"You're right, Di, but things have gotten out of hand. I can't draw back now."

"Men!" she exclaimed, casting them both a reproving look. "That wretched pride of yours is what gets in your way. I think you could sort this whole thing without taking it to court, or at least try. India's very reasonable, and Serena can be bought, we all know that."

"No." Jack answered stubbornly, a wall rising within him. "It's too late. We stepped over the line tonight, and there's no going back."

Diana sighed and raised her hands. "Then so be it. Let destiny sort it out. In the long run it always does. Now come along and let's have dinner, or Mrs. MacC. will be scolding." She kissed the top of her husband's head, then took Jack's arm. "Don't worry. Things have an odd way of sorting themselves out when you least expect it," she said, patting his hand in a motherly fashion. "It'll all look better in the morning, believe me."

14

But the days went by and nothing looked better.

Jack's mood was as bleak and dreary as the gray skies and heavy rain that poured down relentlessly, battering the few ambitious blooms that had recklessly dared poke their heads aboveground.

The girls were fidgety. Mrs. MacC. clucked around the kitchen shaking her head, muttering about the goings-on, and persistently relayed pieces of gossip to an overwrought Diana who had enough on her plate as it was.

The village was agog with the battle over Dunbar. Bets were being cast as to who would win the court case, and much discussion—some of it reaching back a few hundred years—provided nightly entertainment at the Hog and Hound. Some folks were in favor of Fergus's descendants, feeling that the passage of time had given them the right to be at Dunbar. But Mr. Hunter, the local butcher, who considered himself something of an historian, spoke for the majority when he defended Rob's descendant as being the true heir, foreigner or no foreigner. There had even been a journalist from America trying to glean information for a tabloid magazine, but—as Mrs. MacC. reported with a dark look and a sniff—she'd seen to it he was quickly sent about his business. Dunbar's destiny appeared to have become the focal point of interest for all and sundry.

Jack sighed, leaned his forehead on the windowpane and watched the trees on the far side of the lawn bravely withstanding the gale-force winds.

Diana was cross with all the gossip, and with him because Molly wasn't in school. She kept insisting that if he was going to stay for any length of time, something had to be done about the child's education. She was right, of course. He knew she also frowned upon his having filed suit. Not that she said much, but Jack could tell from the reproving glances she cast him from time to time. Peter didn't offer an opinion, and Jack felt oddly alone. Instead of Dunbar bringing him closer to his friends, it seemed to be alienating them.

He was glad his lawyer, Mr. Henderson, had been able to move fast. Quince kept him abreast of business back home, but Dunbar was the center of his focus right now. Would he achieve his objective? And what would he do if he did? Now he could better understand India's reluctance for the house to be transformed into a hotel, he reflected, blowing a misty pattern on the cold, damp glass. Somehow things looked a bit different when you thought of your own flesh and blood walking the land.

He watched the gardener, dressed in an oilskin cape and gumboots, cross Dalkirk's immaculate lawn, stooping to pick up an errant twig, unperturbed by the drenching weather.

Would Rob have approved of what he was doing? he wondered, a wry smile reaching his lips as he drew back from the window and moved toward the desk. Perhaps not, but times had changed and business was business.

At least the hearing tomorrow would finally set things in motion. But it was small compensation when compared with the frustration of knowing India was at Dunbar, only minutes away, apparently deeply entrenched in learning the ropes of how to run an estate, and determined to win the battle. He fiddled aimlessly with a silver paperweight, wondering if Hernan really planned to join her, his anger rising again. He knew it was childish, but if nothing else, filing suit had put a spoke in her wheel. She couldn't buy Serena out while the proceedings were taking place. That was one positive aspect, he reflected sullenly.

All he cared about now was putting enough pressure on her so she'd up and sell to him. At least Serena wasn't a problem. She'd sell like a shot. She knew his offer was superior to what she would get if she sold to her sister—or anyone else for that matter. He speculated, wondering if India could afford to buy her out. He wouldn't put it past her to try. Why couldn't she just admit she was licked and move on?

He glanced at his watch. That afternoon he was going to interview a possible tutor for Molly, a Miss Finlay. Molly was not happy with the arrangement, saying crossly that she wanted to go to a real school and not be stuck on her own. Jack sighed, realizing that he'd managed to put the backs up of all the females in the region, from India to Mrs. MacC. He didn't seem to be winning too many rounds lately.

He felt in his back pocket for his pack of cigarettes, only to realize he'd stopped smoking, too. Between them all—Diana, Molly, Peter and the girls—he hadn't stood a chance. Secretly he was rather proud of himself for not having lit up for two weeks, and surprised that it had been far easier than he would have imagined.

The phone rang and he waited for someone to pick up. When no one did, he moved over to the desk and answered.

"Dalkirk."

"Hello, could I speak to Jack Buchanan?"

Immediately he recognized the voice on the other end of the line, and bristled with suppressed rage. "Yeah, Hernan, it's me. What do you want?" he asked, his tone decidedly unfriendly.

"Hi, man, I've been looking for you all over. I can't find anyone," Hernan said cheerfully.

Jack controlled himself and answered coldly, "What do you want?"

There was a short hesitation. "Well, there are a couple of issues about the Palacio I need to discuss with you."

"Go ahead. By the way, how was your skiing vacation?" Jack asked sarcastically, his foot drumming against the side of the desk.

"Great. The skiing was wonderful, great powder snow, and the après-ski was even better." Hernan laughed wickedly.

"So I've heard."

"Yeah, well, you know how it is. I must be getting old. I used to love doing my hunting on the spot, that was half the fun, but lately I've preferred the in-house approach. What a body that girl has. You should see her ski. Believe me, she moves as well on the slopes as she does in bed. I had a hard time keeping up. It's tough going at it night and day."

Jack restrained himself, crushing the receiver savagely between his fingers. The bastard. How dare he? "What can I help you with?" he said icily.

"I guess the best thing is if I send you a fax. I wanted to say hi, too, though. We haven't spoken in a while."

"No."

"Well...I guess, I'll send the fax then. By the way, how's India?"

"I'm sure you can answer that better than me." Jack slammed the phone down. What damn nerve. And a good thing Hernan was a few thousand miles away or right now he and his "après-ski" engagement would be hanging from the nearest tree. A few seconds later the phone rang again, and he picked up, ready for battle.

"Jack?" Hernan's voice sounded confused.

"What the hell do you want?"

"What's wrong, Jack?"

"Wrong? I'll tell you what's wrong. You go behind my back, sleep with my girl, take her away on some goddamn skiing vacation and then come home to brag about it. I wish you were right here so we could have this out man to man."

There was a long silence while Jack breathed deeply, glad he'd had his say. But now business had to be dealt with, and he was going to have to talk to Hernan whether he liked it or not.

"Would you mind explaining yourself?" Hernan's tone had turned as arctic as the waters off Tierra del Fuego.

"Me explain? Ha! That's rich. You explain to me what you thought you were doing. I knew you were interested in her, you made that plain in Buenos Aires, but I also thought you knew how things were going down between us. What happened, Hernan? Did you have to prove you could beat me to the finish line?" he asked bitterly.

"Jack, I had no idea you were interested in Brigitte. She never said anything. I— In fact, the night I wanted you to go out with us, you said you'd take a rain check. I—"

"Brigitte? Who the hell is Brigitte?" he asked blankly. "Don't mess with me, Hernan. You know perfectly well I'm talking about India." He was nearly shouting, and he forced himself to calm down and lower his voice.

There was a long silence. "Jack, there's been some mistake. I haven't seen India since you both left Buenos Aires. I called her once from Zermatt, that's all. I don't understand what's going on."

Jack felt dizzy. His head began to spin and he sat down

in Peter's chair with a bang. "Don't mess with me, Hernan," he repeated, eyes closed.

"I assure you. The last I heard, India had gone to Scotland. Her secretary told me. Haven't you seen her there?"

"Are you telling me you weren't skiing with Indy?" Jack asked warily, listening for any betraying inflections in the other man's voice.

"Of course not, I just told you. I took Brigitte to Zermatt with me—you remember, the Swedish model who was shooting the Brazilian bikinis. The one with the great ass."

"Yes, of course I remember now, I—" Relief and embarrassment swept over him. "Gee, man, I'm sorry," Jack said, bewildered beyond belief. "There's been a misunderstanding. Forgive me, I'll have to talk to you later."

He hung up and gazed out the window across the windswept fields toward Dunbar.

She'd lied to him.

Anger was followed quickly by relief as ruefully he acknowledged he'd been taken for a ride. He laughed, feeling lighter than he had in days. She hadn't betrayed him after all. Finally he got up and headed to the door whistling *Dixie*—a sure sign things were on the mend.

Thursday dawned a drizzling Scottish spring day. India realized she'd dressed unsuitably for the occasion, the cream-colored suit and beige high-heeled shoes seeming out of place in the wet and windy weather. Never mind. She had a mackintosh with her, and a scarf to cover her head if things got really bad. Serena looked more appropriately clad in a tweed coat and skirt.

"I don't think I've dressed very appropriately," she remarked as they got into the car.

"Don't worry. You look fabulous as usual. The judge'll take one look at you and go barmy." During the last few days Serena had continued oozing charm, to what end India still couldn't fathom.

"Just wear your mac, dear, if it gets too wet," Kathleen agreed from the back seat.

They were to pick up Maxi at the flat on their way to court. India had no desire for him to be a part of the proceedings, but Serena had stayed the night at Dunbar to drive her into Edinburgh for the hearing, and—as Kathleen had rightly remarked—that made it difficult to be ungracious.

"I'm glad we're early," Serena remarked. "It may be difficult to park. Maxi can drop us off so we won't be late. Isn't this weather perfectly ghastly?" she exclaimed as the rain intensified, making it difficult to see three feet ahead.

"Mr. Ramsey's meeting us inside the courtroom," Kathleen said.

"Yes, it'll be easier. Are you worried, India?" Serena asked.

"A little. I don't know what Jack has up his sleeve."

"Not much by the looks of it. It's rather difficult to fudge up evidence after two hundred and fifty years." Serena gave a scathing laugh.

"I suppose so." But India was not so confident. She wondered uncomfortably what it would feel like to see Jack again after their disastrous parting the other evening. God knows she'd tried to blot him from her mind and think of him as the enemy. But every now and then a fleeting memory would slip through the screen she'd erected around herself. When these moments occurred, she tried to focus on anything and everything but Jack, and remember what a cold-blooded shark he was, trying to rob her of her heritage.

Maxi dropped them off in front of the courthouse, his behavior, like Serena's, so gracious and conciliatory that India began to wonder if she'd been dreaming. Kathleen smiled at her encouragingly and she took a deep breath to quell her jittery nerves, smoothed her suit and pulled her shoulders back as they made their way up the steps of the Court of Session. She walked regally into the courtroom, her head held high, her eyes looking neither right nor left. Serena followed quickly behind.

"Good morning, ladies." Mr. Ramsey rose to greet them, removing his spectacles. Next to him stood the barrister, Mr. Duncan. Introductions were made, then Mr. Ramsey pointed to the stiff wooden chairs behind the counsel's desk, inviting them to be seated. "This shouldn't take long," he assured them with a confident smile.

When India heard the other party enter she didn't look up. A frisson shot up her spine and she knew instinctively he was looking her way. But she kept her eyes firmly glued on the papers before her, trying desperately to concentrate.

It was about to begin.

For an instant she closed her eyes, wondering if Jack was nervous, too. Probably not, she reflected bitterly. All he cared about was his wretched hotel. Well, it was out of their control now. Dunbar's fate lay in the hands of the court.

Jack shook hands with his lawyers, exchanged a few words with McLaughlan, the barrister who would plead the case, and sat down. He could tell by her poker-straight posture that India was tense. He sat impatiently between Mr. Henderson and Mr. Mackay, the junior partner, and took a sidelong glance at her face. My God she was beautiful—regal and dignified. He had to give it to her, she had her act together. Then his stomach tensed as a wave of pride charged through him, and he basked in the knowledge that under all that outer poise was a woman who had trembled in his arms, unable to resist his touch.

Watching her he almost forgot what they were there for,

his mind so filled with yearning, memories and deep satisfaction. She hadn't betrayed him after all. Whether she liked it or not, she was his. Suddenly his mind became so set on thinking how he could right things between them, he barely noticed the entrance of the judge until a nudge from young Mr. Mackay brought him back to his present surroundings. He rose hastily. Dunbar seemed a distant second to all this. To tell the truth, it wasn't that important anymore.

The judge—middle-aged and portly in his white wig—entered briskly, his red robes flowing majestically behind him as he sat down behind the bench.

Once the court had settled, Mr. McLaughlan rose, his bespectacled countenance, wigged head and black robe a throwback to the ancestors who had preceded him in the legal profession. Time stood still and Jack felt as though he'd gone back a couple hundred years. This was very different from the various courtrooms he'd attended in the past. Here, computers were still part of a future era, and there were no microphones or cameras to be seen. Somehow it seemed far closer to what he imagined a courtroom should be.

"My Lord, we would like to introduce the following documents into evidence," Mr. McLaughlan said, carefully lifting the sealed cellophane bags containing the ancient documents from the file.

Jack's mind wandered again, for the process of introducing evidence was lengthy. He watched India out of the corner of his eye, but she never turned, never even acknowledged his existence. It was strange to realize they were distantly related to one another, even though the connection was slight. It still didn't change the fact that, as far as he was concerned, she was his. He longed to take the few steps across the aisle and wrap his arms around her, hold her close and fill his senses with the scent and taste of her. He shifted, reluctantly forcing his mind back to the proceedings at hand. Mr. McLaughlan was finally coming to the end of the introduction of evidence, and was ready to present his case.

"My Lord, the facts we have before us are simple. Robert Dunbar, rightful heir to the Dunbar estate, was cruelly murdered—not at Culloden by the Sassenach or Lowlanders as was presumed, but by the hand of his own kin." Mr. McLaughlan paused, letting the words sink in. "I ask Your Lordship's permission to read the court this letter, proved to have been written by Rob's own hand to his wife, Mhairie, whom he had sent to the Colonies—the Carolinas to be exact—barely a month before the tragic event that has affected the course of our history in ways unmentionable." He paused solemnly and raised the document for all to see.

"Granted."

"But My Lord, this is absurd…" Mr. Duncan rose from his seat, and Ramsey cleared his throat.

"I will hear the plaintiff's request."

"But My Lord," Mr. Duncan insisted, "what can the letter or the Battle of Culloden matter? *Res ipsa loquitur*—the facts speak for themselves."

"Do you contest the authenticity of the same?" the judge inquired, peering at Mr. Duncan, his eyes narrowed.

"Both, My Lord."

There was a murmur throughout the courtroom.

"Mr. McLaughlan, have you any proof as to the authenticity of these documents?" the judged inquired.

"We do, My Lord. After numerous tests and much research, Professor Mackintosh of the University of Edinburgh has confirmed the evidence to be authentic. The signature of Robert Dunbar corresponds to that found in the archives. This information has been verified by forensic specialists at the police department in Miami, Florida, the University of Edinburgh *and* Scotland Yard.'' He sniffed and cast a look in Mr. Duncan's direction. ''Professor Mackintosh is here today to testify if Your Lordship should so require.''

''Hmm. Mr. Duncan, do you wish to invoke your right to cross-examine the author of the report?'' Judge Mackenzie asked while viewing the pages presented to him by the bailiff.

Mr. Ramsey quickly shook his head and the barrister replied in the negative. ''No, My Lord. I will stipulate to acceptance of the author's findings into evidence. I do not want to expend the court's valuable time,'' he added dryly.

''My Lord, may we now read the text into evidence?'' Mr. McLaughlan cast his colleague a long-suffering look.

''I object.'' Mr. Duncan jumped up again, wig askew. ''Once more I must repeat, this is rubbish. What bearing can the scribblings of a two-hundred-and-fifty-year-old document have on the case before this court?''

''Mr. Duncan—'' Judge Mackenzie took off his glasses and wiped them meticulously with a large white handkerchief before slowly replacing them on the bridge of his beaked nose ''—if I am not mistaken, you have stipulated to the introduction of this evidence. Therefore, it is only logical that, unless the text is unintelligible, the same be read into evidence.''

Disgruntled, Mr. Duncan sat down next to Ramsey, and a hush fell over the packed courtroom, the nature of the case having attracted the press and the curious.

Mr. McLaughlan cleared his throat and moved to the center of the floor. When he spoke his voice was deep and sober. ''The missive I am about to read was written by Sir Robert Dunbar of Dunbar, to his wife Mhairie, in the year 1746, shortly after the defeat at Culloden.

"My beloved,

"The sun has set once more upon the Stuart reign, this time perhaps forever. The troops we were so certain would arrive from France never came, and the Prince has long since fled back across the water.

"So many died at Culloden as to break the heart of stronger men than I. We buried your father, Struan, and your brother, Douglas, in the clachan above Ballehoy House with our own hands. 'Twas a miracle we were able to get them home, but I could not leave them to weep with the souls who will haunt that bloody plain from this day forth.

"My dearest Mhairie, if you should ever read these words, understand that nothing is, or ever will be, the same. Scotland has changed forever. Those of us that remain do so as broken men, stripped of our weapons, reduced to herding cattle for the Sassenach and the traitors among us.

"My time is nigh, my sweet Mhairie. But I go in peace, at one with the Lord and with myself. My only regret is for you, my love, and the wee bairn you carry within you.

"Teach him the old ways, my Mhairie. Let him not forget that although the Dunbars who follow in my shoes may be traitors to the cause, his father was loyal to the true king of Scotland.

"If you are reading these words 'tis because you have followed my counsel and have come to the Dunbar oak as I instructed you. This land is our son's by birthright. May he be blessed to reclaim it for his own when all this is over and wiser men rule.

"I am weak, my beloved. I take with me the touch of your sweet lips, our love and the knowledge that we shall meet once more in Heaven. The blood I am shedding is the work of treachery, but I know within my heart that there are those who will one day return to right this wrong. Just as some day Scotland shall regain its own true sovereignty.

"Care well for our wee one, my Mhairie. I shall watch over you both from above.

"Your loving husband,
"Robert"

Mr. McLaughlan paused, assessing the effect his words were having on the hushed audience.

India raised a hand to her constricted throat. The scene was so vivid, so clear. Suddenly she envisaged the young couple, so in love, so full of longing, torn apart by terrible events over which they had no control. Naturally Rob would have stayed and fought for his sovereign, she reflected, taking a surreptitious glance at Jack, wondering how much of their ancestor he bore within him. He looked subdued and pensive, as though he too were far-off in the past.

Then Mr. McLaughlan's voice reminded them that the proceedings had by no means ended.

"The second missive is from Rob to his unborn son, My Lord."

"You have my full attention, Mr. McLaughlan. Please proceed."

Again there was a hush, as the crowd waited now in poignant expectation.

"My beloved son,

"I will never see your wee face, grubby with dirt from playing in the bracken, nor the proud swing of your kilt when you march off to battle. But I take you with me in my heart.

"My last hour is nigh. In a wee while the good Lord will call me, and I shall be on my way. Care for your dear mother, see that she never wants for anything.

"My last prayer is that one day, you or one of our kin may come to read these words, know the truth of what has transpired and reclaim this, your birthright.

"Keep the marriage certificate that is in your mother's possession. You are my one and only legitimate heir, and to you I bequeath my legacy.

"Be it known to my son that no lesion of battle causes my death, for I was one of the blessed few to escape Culloden with little hurt. 'Twas my cousin Fergus's dirk inflicted this treacherous wound upon me.

"I have entrusted my dear and faithful friend, Jamie Kinnaird of Dalkirk, who has proved his trust so oft, to bury these missives and the gold under the Dunbar oak. While it stands, a Dunbar will always walk this land. Such was the vow made by our ancestor William when he first acquired this ground.

"I go in peace, my son, sure in the knowledge that one day this treachery will be avenged, and you or one of our own will tread this land once more. My spirit will not rest until that day.

                                        "Your loving father,
                                                "Robert"

India held back the stinging tears. This was her family, her ancestors that were being discussed. Rob's woes brought home the horror of events she had skimmed through in history books, suddenly bringing them to light, their significance reaching down through the ages, touching her as though it were yesterday. If Mhairie hadn't gone to America, if— She turned her head slightly.

Jack's eyes met hers. Suddenly she knew he'd been sent by some force of God or destiny, to right a terrible wrong. Had Rob, through the strength of his spirit, pushed Jack to reclaim his birthright? She looked away, bewildered. His feelings for Scotland, his encounter and partnership with Peter Kinnaird—Jamie's descendant—all came to mind. But what of his plans to make Dunbar into a hotel?

An icy chill ran over her. Was he capable of using this tragic tale as a means to an end?

She turned hastily, seeing Mr. McLaughlan approach the bench.

"These documents, added to those already in your possession, are what substantiate this claim, My Lord." He handed Judge Mackenzie photocopies of the two letters. Silence filled the courtroom, and India's pulse beat so hard she wondered the judge himself couldn't hear it. The only sounds were noses being blown and the odd hushed murmur. The tremor in Mr. McLaughlan's voice, and the intensity with which he had read the letters, were not lost on the awestruck audience.

"Do you have any other testimony to proffer to this court?" the judge asked, clearing his throat and peering at the barrister.

"No, My Lord."

"Mr. Duncan, how would you like to address your case?" He turned toward India and her party.

Mr. Duncan rose and addressed the bench with a sympathetic smile. "My Lord, I am naturally touched—as I believe this whole court must be—at the sad words my venerable colleague has just read." He paused, allowing his words to register. "Still, we cannot—" he poised his index finger "—must not allow sentiment to deviate us from the true reason for this hearing. In fact, I am somewhat embarrassed that we are made to come here today to take up the precious time of this most honorable court, to defend what I am afraid can only be termed a baseless claim."

He cleared his throat. "The determination of title claims

to land in our realm is subject to the rule against perpetuity. Our evidence will show that this claim is pretentious and has no foundation. Simply stated, the petitioner's claim is barred by the law." He produced the Scottish rule of law. "My Lord, it is clearly stated that no living being can claim any land subsequent to twenty-one years and a life in being during possession of the fee. It is the year of our Lord 2000. The documents giving rise to the claim are dated 1746. If my arithmetic isn't failing me, it would appear that more than two hundred and fifty years have elapsed. Unless there is proof that Dunbar had a possessor in fee alive at the time of the letters, who died twenty-one years ago, the court has no alternative but to reject this claim outright." Mr. Duncan returned to his seat with a swish of his robes and a firm nod.

"Well put," India heard Mr. Ramsey whisper to his colleague.

"My Lord." Mr. McLaughlan rose once more. "My client's claim is firmly entrenched in notions of equity and fair play. We come to this court with clean hands. We merely wish to right a wrong perpetrated two hundred and fifty years ago. The evidence tendered will show Your Lordship, by a preponderance, that my client, Mr. Buchanan, is the rightful heir to the Dunbar estate." Once again, murmurs permeated the courtroom.

India watched as Judge Mackenzie pushed his glasses down his nose, his expression thoughtful. Would Jack be capable of going through all this effort for purely mercenary reasons? India wondered, clenching her hands together and biting her lip, her eyes drawn to him despite herself.

All at once she saw his gaze fall to her clenched hands, and she undid them, hastily folding them on her knee. But before she could drag her eyes from his, he raised his wrist swiftly to his lips, brushing them lightly over it in an all too familiar gesture. It was only a split second, but the heat rose hot and fiery to suffuse her face. The sudden image of Rio, his lips on her wrist and his eyes locked on hers as they'd made love, flashed before her. She lowered her head, her hair shrouding her face from view, and fought to regain her composure.

"There is no legal case or law that addresses the following facts, My Lord," Mr. McLaughlan was saying. "I could read you the letter Mhairie Stewart, Lady of Dunbar, left her son, but it would be a repetition of the information already set before the court. The only other fact contained there is the instruction from Rob to seek the documents, buried sixteen paces due west of the Dunbar oak, a feat performed personally by my client a month and a half ago.

"We request that Your Lordship hear the words calling from beyond the grave. Should not the wish and legal rights of a dying man be respected? A man who, may I remind the court, gave his blood for the rightful king of Scotland and returned home to his lands, only to be slaughtered by one of his own kin."

Mr. McLaughlan's voice was intense, his expression determined. "Rob Dunbar declared that his soul would not rest until this shameful wrong be righted. And it appears that destiny has played into his hands. Is it not uncanny that Mr. Buchanan—" he turned toward Jack "—through what would appear to be a series of strange coincidences, was brought into business and friendship with a man who sits in this very courtroom today, Sir Peter Kinnaird of Dalkirk? The very man, My Lord, whose ancestor, Jamie Kinnaird, befriended Rob Dunbar. And, moreover, that this ancestor, at his beloved friend's request, buried the very documents in evidence here in this court in a spot where they have lain for over two hundred and fifty years, waiting, My Lord, for justice to finally reign?"

Mr. McLaughlan addressed Judge Mackenzie eye to eye

now. "It behooves us, My Lord, to right this treacherous wrong. Rob Dunbar's spirit must be allowed to go in peace and no more roam the land in anguish and pain, seeking justice for his kin. As we said at the commencement of this case, we bid this court to do equity. The mere passage of time and man-made law cannot do away with the inalienable rights of ownership to land." He waived his hand disdainfully. "If this were to be allowed, any group of men could simply legislate away that, our most sacrosanct of rights.

"Therefore, we beseech Your Lordship to invoke his powers in equity, and honor the petitioner's claim to the title of the land."

Mr. McLaughlan ended with a dramatic flourish then retired to his seat behind the counsel's bench, mopping his brow. India watched as Jack turned and exchanged a long look with Peter. Her eyes filled again. That link had come down through the ages, the strength and loyalty of their ancestors' friendship bonding them like brothers. The whole thing seemed perfectly clear to her now.

Mr. Duncan rose again with a swish, his robe nearly catching the corner of the table.

"My Lord," he said with a laugh and a shake of his head, "I find it hard to believe that my esteemed colleague can in all good faith uphold this preposterous claim. There is little to be said, My Lord. I have only to add that any ruling other than one in favor of my clients would render two hundred and fifty years of established law a mockery."

Judge Mackenzie's expression was inscrutable. "We shall recess until Monday morning at ten o'clock, at which time I will render my verdict." With that, he rose and, with a stately nod, left the courtroom through a private door.

India's mind wandered as she thought of the oak tree.

A smile crept to her lips as she imagined Jack—probably swearing—digging for treasure at the crack of dawn. She sighed. Dunbar should be bringing them together, not tearing them apart, she realized sadly, slipping her damp hankie into her pocket and making her way into the aisle, Kathleen and Serena in her wake. Although she would not allow herself the indulgence of a single look in Jack's direction, she could not help overhearing the conversation as she passed the counsel's bench.

"Well, gentlemen, what will the verdict be?" she heard him say.

"It's very difficult to say, Mr. Buchanan. I have no notion how the judge will view the facts put forward here today. You were right about him though. He's a staunch Scottish Independent and a history fanatic."

"Much of the Mackenzie clan was massacred at Culloden, for whatever that's worth," another voice put in.

"Not much." She glanced at Mr. Henderson, who was shaking his head wryly. "Mackenzie will never allow personal feelings to interfere with his ruling."

"Well, I guess we'll just have to wait then." Jack got up. "Have a good weekend, gentlemen. I'll see you here on Monday." He walked to where Peter stood waiting for him near the door, then suddenly glanced in her direction.

But India raised her head high and continued walking.

After all she had heard today she could understand why he wanted Dunbar so badly. Of course, if it was all true, he had as much right to the estate as they did. What bothered her were his motives. Was his heritage really the reason he was fighting so hard? Was it because he, too, felt this indescribable bond with the land? Or was he merely using this emotional ploy as a means to an end. If that were the case, she would fight all the more to retain the property and see that it was preserved and cared for as it should be, she decided angrily, reaching the door and fol-

lowing Mr. Ramsey and Mr. Duncan out into the corridor.
He probably had no respect for the past, and his ancestor's
misfortunes—if ancestor he was—were like putty in his
hands, mere tools to be wielded at his convenience. But
Rob was her ancestor, too, and she would fulfill the obligations expected of her.

"That was quite a mouthful, Mr. Duncan," Serena said.
"What do you think, Ramsey? Do they stand a chance?"
she asked, waving her fingers languidly at Maxi, who
waited by the car at the bottom of the courthouse steps.

"Not to worry, Lady Serena. The arguments were well
put, of course—I would have expected no less from Mr.
McLaughlan—but the law is the law, and there is no getting round it."

"Are you sure? Don't you think the judge might be
swayed?" India asked, watching him closely, struck that
he might be more concerned than he let on.

"You never know, Miss India, but I don't believe so. It
would be amazing indeed, as I remarked before, if the
ruling were in favor of Mr. Buchanan." But she noticed
that the air of complete self-assurance was gone, replaced
by a more sober expression.

"Serena, we'd better get going," Maxi said.

"Yes, let's move. Come on, Kath, don't dawdle."

"You'd better put up the umbrella, Serena dear," Kathleen remarked. "It's beginning to drizzle. Mr. Ramsey,
Mr. Duncan, we'll see you here on Monday morning at
ten. Goodbye." They all shook hands.

Then India saw him. Jack was passing a hand over his
face as she'd seen him do so often, stopping at the mouth
as he was prone to when he was thinking. The familiar
gesture made her heart lurch. But she turned away. Peter
was close behind him. No doubt they were hatching their
beastly plans for the hotel, she reminded herself, walking
toward the car, furious at the thought of Rob's dying

wishes being used in this perfidious manner. If that were the case, it was revolting and he nothing more than a low, despicable son of a bitch who deserved to be hanged, drawn and quartered.

Yanking the car door open she got in and leaned back against the worn leather seat, turning away from the window as Serena's Volvo edged into the midday traffic. Let them hatch away, she reflected angrily, for all was not said and done. Monday they would all know how things stood.

"You look miffed," Serena remarked, glancing at her in the rearview mirror. "What's wrong?"

"Nothing. I'm fine. I just find it abhorrent that Jack would go to such lengths, dragging our ancestors through the mud, for the sake of monetary gain. Of course, if he really is our cousin, he does have rights, you know," she said thoughtfully, missing the quick exchange of looks between Serena and Maxi, and Kathleen's tiny smile, too caught up in her thoughts to pay attention.

"Well, it is rather clever of him, you have to admit," Serena conceded. "It won't get him anywhere, but I admire his gumption."

Maxi snickered in the back. "India, money's all that counts nowadays."

"Do you really believe that, Maxi? Because I don't. Some things are above it," she snapped.

"Aren't you getting a bit heated over this? It's not as if he's going to win the case."

"That's not the point. I can't believe anyone would go to such extremes and expense, play with people's emotions—" She stopped, aware she was betraying herself.

Serena turned in the front seat and glanced at her curiously. "I don't see why he's touched your emotions, unless you've still got the hots for him."

India looked away, angry at having opened herself up

like this in front of these two. "I'm just revolted at his callous behavior, that's all."

"Well, he's got about as fat a chance of winning this case as he does of winning the lottery. The whole thing's bloody idiotic, if you ask me. We'll win and that'll squash him once and for all. I can't wait to see that stupid face of his when the judge pronounces the verdict." Serena laughed stridently.

"Why don't you drop us off at the taxi rank, Serena," India suggested, suddenly tired and anxious to be on her way. "There's no point in you going all the way back to Dunbar when you'll be staying in town anyway."

"Oh no, darling, we don't mind taking you and Kathleen back, do we, Maxi? We wouldn't dream of letting you take a cab. We'll come back to Edinburgh after tea," Serena replied solicitously. She seemed determined to keep her sister happy at all cost.

India resigned herself to their company. Serena was so blatantly ingratiating, and as for Maxi, he was like a vulture circling a corpse.

It was a pity that the hearing had fallen on a Friday, thus obliging her to spend the entire weekend waiting. On the other hand, she could go on enjoying Dunbar and look through more of the effects. Chloë had phoned last night to say she'd be up sometime during the next week, which was a comforting thought. India felt suddenly lonely. Everyone was at Dalkirk, and that, of course, was the last place *she* planned to set foot.

She sighed, suddenly uneasy remembering Mr. Ramsey's look as he'd left the court. Surely there was no possibility of Jack winning the case. Or was there?

15

Instead of the quiet, relaxing weekend she had anticipated, India spent most of it in bed being violently sick.

Kathleen hovered, solicitous and kind, fussing over her like a mother hen, bringing her chicken broth and various herb teas.

"Darling, what can you possibly have eaten?" she asked for the fiftieth time, her face creased with worry. "It must have been that curry at the Indian restaurant," she repeated. "It's the only possibility." And India agreed wearily, not caring what the cause was as long as it would go away. Every time she got up, her head spun and her stomach lurched, and none of Mrs. Walker's or Kathleen's remedies seemed to help.

But on Monday morning she dragged her limp body out of bed, grimaced at the pale reflection staring at her from the Chippendale mirror and braced herself for the morning's events. By nine o'clock she was downstairs, drinking a cup of tea and nibbling on a piece of dry toast, ready to leave.

"Serena should be here any moment." Kathleen pulled back the breakfast-room curtain and peered out over the drive. "I hope this sudden gracious behavior of hers lasts," she added with pursed lips. "I wonder what she wants."

"Maybe she's doing penance for all the times she terrorized me when Mummy brought me to Dunbar," India said, making a feeble attempt at humor.

"That'll be the day. You beware of her. I don't know what she's up to, but knowing Serena, it's probably nothing good." Kathleen shook her head solemnly.

"Don't worry so much, Kath, Serena's not as bad as she seems."

"Mmm, we'll see. Anyway, we've more important things to think about. I shall be most interested to hear what the judge has to say, won't you? At this stage I would imagine Buchanan's bracing himself for a defeat," she stated, returning to the table and pouring another cup of tea.

"I don't know, and quite honestly, I feel so rotten this morning I'm past caring."

"You poor child. But don't worry, that will change," Kathleen replied with a fond smile. "Once you feel better, you'll be back in the saddle. I'm sorry not to be going with you, darling, but after all, the outcome is obvious, and I feel one of us should remain here, holding the fort so to speak. Mrs. Walker's wonderful, of course, but it's not the same as having family on the place. Besides, I need to inventory the laundry. Ah, that must be Serena now."

A screech of the old Volvo's brakes confirmed her words. Serena walked in punctually at 9:15, and India swallowed the bile in her throat, hoping her legs wouldn't wobble too dangerously as she walked to the car. She stepped carefully, thankful for the breath of fresh air, damp earth and morning mist.

"I'm sorry you're feeling so ghastly," Serena remarked, closing the car door. "You're not pregnant or anything, are you?"

"No." India laughed weakly, waving goodbye to Kathleen who stood firmly posted like a sentry on the front steps. "At least that's one thing I'm certain of, thank God."

"Well, you'd better be careful, it might be a virus."

"Perhaps, but I don't have a cold or any other symptoms. Maybe it was the curry the other day that didn't agree with me."

She gazed out over the rainy landscape, not barren any longer but lush and alive. Sheep grazed and a tractor drove slowly ahead of them as they approached the A-7.

"Doesn't this idiot see I'm behind him?" Serena exclaimed, honking her horn loudly. She received a cheerful, oblivious wave from the tweed-capped driver, and they drove on into town.

The courtroom was packed, the press and the curious agog to know the outcome of the case. But India sat in a daze, hoping it would be over quickly so that she could get back to Dunbar and rest. She'd told Kathleen she'd stopped caring what the final result was, but that was not strictly true. Just then another bout of nausea rose in her throat and she took a deep breath. She felt so awful she hadn't even bothered to see whether Jack was there or not. She closed her eyes, hoping the room would stop spinning, and waited for the proceedings to begin.

Judge Mackenzie walked briskly into the courtroom and sat behind the bench. After two minutes of sorting papers he began.

"On the one hand I have the claimant, who comes with a decisive and real argument to this court. On the other, the present owners, who are in no way to blame for acts perpetrated two hundred and fifty years ago." He paused, peering austerely at both parties.

Jack's eyes wandered to India. She looked pale, and all of a sudden he worried.

"To arrive at my decision I have had to go back into the annals of history and the legal system of this land. Also, I have taken into account the wishes of William Dunbar, who first entailed the property, and his descendant Robert, who suffered such a vile and treacherous death at the hands of his own kin." Judge Mackenzie drew himself up, his expression unyielding.

"Let us be reminded here today that, had the Jacobite rebellion succeeded, had traitors not looked to line their pockets rather than do right for their country, the lives of such loyal men as Robert Dunbar would not have been shed in vain. Scotland would be a very different land today, not subjugated to English rule and relegated to a secondary position up to this day. Such individuals as Fergus Dunbar are to be despised, for it was not honor or war that drove them to take treacherous action, but mere politics and cowardly greed.

"Irony has it that yesterday, the sixteenth of April, was a significant date in Scottish history. On Sunday, two hundred and fifty-four years ago, the most savage battle in our history was fought. One need only visit the unfortunate field at Culloden to know the truth of Rob Dunbar's words. Anguished souls still haunt the place until this day." There was a long silence as Judge Mackenzie paused and straightened his glasses. "It is a sad thing when a man forsakes his allegiance for the sake of wealth and his own kin for covetousness, allowing gain and profit to be his master, thus forsaking all honor and truth.

"Therefore it is my perception that all the parties before me today have rights." He ignored the murmur buzzing through the courtroom and continued. "And based upon these facts, I deem it only just and proper to rule in equity, dividing the property in three equal, indivisible parts."

Serena uttered a horrified gasp, and the judge glanced her way reprovingly. "If any of the parties desires to sell his or her share of the property, the other two owners shall have a first right of option. All expenses relating to the property will be equally divided among the parties."

"What?" Serena exclaimed, her cheeks livid as an amazed rumble of voices fluttered throughout.

Jack sat in total disbelief. Of all the outcomes, this was one that had never been considered.

Mr. Henderson seemed astonished but pleased, McLaughlan surprised, Ramsey flushed and angry. India sat, hands folded neatly in her lap, her face very drawn and pale. Too pale and thoughtful, he reflected, noting anxiously how thin she appeared. He would have given a great deal to know what she was thinking at that very moment, hoping suddenly this wasn't all too rough on her. Now they were co-owners. Any decisions would have to be made together. He turned and exchanged a glance with Peter, who smiled quizzically back, raising his bushy eyebrows.

"Perhaps not a wholly satisfactory outcome, Mr. Buchanan," Mr. Henderson remarked jovially, "but a positive one nonetheless. They'll appeal, of course. We must be prepared for that. But I've never seen one of Mackenzie's verdicts overruled. I'd be most surprised if it happened this time. Of course, that will take some time. In the meantime, if you wish to take possession of your share of the property, you may do so."

"I need to think about it, Henderson. This wasn't a possibility we'd envisaged."

"It has come as a total surprise to me. I'll be honest with you, I didn't expect it. But in all due consideration, it's a fair verdict," Mr. McLaughlan put in.

"I guess it is," Jack admitted.

They got up and headed toward the entrance of the

crowded courtroom. India was standing just two steps ahead of him. If he stretched his arm far enough he could reach her. They were so very close, yet worlds apart. He swallowed, that ever-present anger simmering once more. Why had she been so determined to throw away everything they'd shared? Then the doors flew open. Flashbulbs went off and reporters swooped down on them from all sides, avid for comments.

"How do you feel about the verdict, Mr. Buchanan? Will you be taking possession?"

"Lady Serena, can you get the Yank sent home? Or will he be moving in?"

But all he saw was India's bewildered expression as she tried to stave off the onslaught. In one quick movement he pushed forward, grabbed her by the shoulder and, slipping an arm firmly around her, steered his way determinedly through the crowd.

"No comment," he snapped at one reporter shoving a microphone at his mouth.

"Is it true there's a romance going on between you and Miss Moncrieff?"

Jack rushed her down the stairs, out of the building and down the stone steps. Light rain hit the pavement in a monotonous rhythm as he whisked her round the corner of the building, stopping only when he was certain they were alone and all was quiet. "Are you okay?" he asked, worried. She didn't looked good, and he held on to her arm, wondering where they could find some shelter.

"I'm fine, I'll be all right."

"What's wrong, Indy?" he asked softly, raising a hand to her cheek. "Has this whole thing been too much? Because if it has, I can—"

"Jack, please." She drew away. For a moment he thought she might faint, she seemed so gaunt. "I don't want to go on battling you. I've had enough. Just call

Ramsey and get the papers drawn up. I'm ready to settle with you and move on. I don't care anymore." Her voice cracked and tears welled in her eyes. "All I want from you is the promise you won't get rid of the staff or the tenants. That you'll take care of everybody, and that not one word of this gets out before I've left for Switzerland."

Jack halted, horrified by her air of utter defeat. "You can't give up like this, Indy, we'll come to an arrangement. We'll—" He was suddenly desperate.

"I can't be a part of Dunbar becoming a hotel. You know that. And I'm sick of fighting this. Just give me your word on everything, Jack, please."

He hesitated. This was truly the end. "Of course I promise, but before you decide, you have to listen to me—"

"No. I want to go home and forget this ever happened." She bent forward, leaning her hands on her thighs, and took a deep breath. Then she straightened her shoulders and gave him a sad smile. "I suppose all that's left is to wish you good luck." She held out her hand.

He took it automatically, raised it to his lips and held on to it tightly, not wanting to let go. She was slipping through his fingers and there was nothing he could do. Instead of uniting them, Dunbar was separating them, forever.

"Indy, don't do it," he pleaded. "We can handle this together, we can find an answer." He searched her eyes, hoping for some sign.

She shook her head. "It's no use, Jack. Let's admit it once and for all. You want one thing, I want another. You've achieved your objective. You've won this battle. Be happy with that and don't try to force the issue. It's too late."

"But—"

"Please." She raised a tired hand.

The words died on his lips. He didn't have the courage to go on arguing with her. Not now, not like this.

"Where's your car?" he asked quietly, his mind in turmoil.

"I came with Serena, she's somewhere about." She seemed listless, so unlike herself it frightened him. She let him take her arm, walking like an automaton. He'd never seen her defeated, as though all the strength had been punched out of her. And his heart wrenched in two as he saw Serena approach, frowning.

"India, we have to meet Mr. Ramsey at his office, immediately."

"She can't go like this," Jack protested.

"It's really nothing to do with you," Serena threw at him.

"It's all right, I'll go," India replied wearily. She turned to Jack. "Thanks." Suddenly she smiled, a weak little smile filled with regret. "Ramsey will be in touch with you, and I'll explain to Serena." Again she stretched out her hand, and this time it was final. "Goodbye, Jack."

"Goodbye."

He stood alone on the pavement, shattered, not noticing the rain or the strange looks of passersby as he watched her walk away with Serena toward the parking lot. This time he'd really lost her, he realized, devastated, knowing that nothing would ever heal the ache in his heart.

"The judge has used a most unusual avenue to arrive at his decision." Mr. Ramsey shifted the papers before him uneasily, his expression embarrassed.

"What the bloody hell do you mean, *unusual avenue*?" Serena barked furiously, scowling at Ramsey across the large mahogany desk.

"It's rather complicated, Lady Serena, but in short,

Judge Mackenzie has essentially thrown the law out the window and interjected his own opinion.''

"But that's impossible!"

"Unfortunately, it is possible. Our legal system allows a judge that kind of liberty. However, there is really no need to worry," he said on a cheerier note, "this ludicrous decision will be reversed on appeal."

"What do you mean? Does this charade have to continue? You mean the man now actually *owns* a part of Dunbar?"

"In a technical sense, yes. The verdict we heard pronounced today made Mr. Buchanan a co-owner to one-third of the property. Mind you, he can't just sell his interest, because the judge did say it was indivisible."

"What! Do you mean that if I want to sell I can't?"

"That's right, Lady Serena. Unless you have the consent of the other owners, you may not sell."

"This is preposterous! You told us that there was no possibility of anything like this happening."

"No, Lady Serena. I told Miss India when she asked me that it would be an *aberration* if such a thing were to occur."

"We should have taken another lawyer," Serena said decisively. "Don't you see, India?" She pointed a sharp, red-nailed finger at Mr. Ramsey. "It's his incompetence that has brought this on us. We must get other solicitors immediately. I can't believe you've allowed this to happen, Ramsey. You should be ashamed of yourself."

"It's not Mr. Ramsey's fault, Serena, he's not to blame. Judge Mackenzie arrived at his decision on his own."

"Then the legal system's wrong. Something has to be done. They can't just take what's mine and give it to some bloody American! How soon can we begin the appeal?"

Mr. Ramsey hesitated, glancing in India's direction. "That depends on Miss India. After all, she is the one financing this whole affair. As you know, the estate could not bear that expense." He pursed his lips.

"India, we have to start at once." Serena rose from her chair and bent toward her.

India felt dizzy and Serena leaning over her didn't improve matters. "I'm not going to appeal, Serena. I've had enough."

"What do you mean?" Serena's eyes glazed in horror. "What can you mean, not appeal? You must be utterly mad!"

"No, I'm just tired of the whole thing," India replied, exhaustion and depression enveloping her like a heavy cloak.

"I can't believe this. I won't just sit here and let you throw what's mine out the window! If you don't want it, then give me your share."

"That's not possible, Lady Serena," Mr. Ramsey said with marked satisfaction. "For that, all three owners would have to agree."

Serena cast him a look of loathing and prowled the room with her fists clenched. "When I think that I had everything under control—Jack, the bloody sale, nobody would have found out until it was too la—" She stopped suddenly and glanced, horrified, in India's direction.

At Serena's words, India raised her head, meeting her sister's eyes head-on. Then to her dismay she knew.

Jack had been the one telling the truth.

Desperately she held on to her composure as the truth hit home. Why only now, after she'd closed the book, had it been revealed to her? She hadn't believed him, hadn't given him a chance. As the horror of it all sank in, she knew she had to leave, get away from this place that had only brought unhappiness into her life. Nothing mattered anymore except getting away—from Serena, from Dunbar, from everything that reminded her of this whole mess.

She felt another sudden surge of nausea, unsure this time if it was physical or caused by this last, shattering revelation. Regret tugged at her relentlessly. How awful she'd been to him, how cruel, and she hadn't even stopped to give him the benefit of the doubt.

"Mr. Ramsey, I'm awfully sorry but I'm not feeling well. I need to talk to you about my decisions, but would you mind if we discussed this another time? I must get back to Dunbar." She rose, fighting the dizziness.

"Oh gosh! India, are you all right?" Serena came rushing across the room and took hold of her arm. "I'd better get her back to Dunbar, I'll drive her," she said to Mr. Ramsey, who was hovering, not knowing what to do. "Thank goodness we picked up Maxi. He's waiting downstairs in the car, India. We'll get you home."

"Thank you," she replied weakly, grateful even for Serena's support.

"I'm sorry to see you so poorly, Miss India. Perhaps a glass of water—"

"Don't worry, Ramsey, I'll take care of it." Serena brushed him aside peremptorily.

Slowly they made their way down the various flights in the ancient caged elevator, then out onto the street.

"Poor Indy's feeling awful, Maxi. We'd better get her home."

"Of course." He looked concerned. India found herself thanking them, glad she wasn't on her own, and sank into the back seat of the car, overwhelmed.

By the time they reached Dunbar it was midafternoon. She let Serena guide her to the sitting room, her mind detached from her body, and plopped onto the chintz sofa, grateful for the chance to rest.

"That's right, lie down, darling. I'll get you a cup of tea. You relax and I'll tell Kath we're back. Here, put your feet under these pillows and I'll cover you with the rug."

Serena made a to-do of tucking her in. "Maxi, come with me and make yourself useful in the kitchen. We'll be back in a jiffy," she said with a little smile. "Are you sure you'll be all right?"

"I'll be fine, don't worry. I'm sorry to put you to so much trouble, Serena. Thanks." India gave a weak smile, cursing herself for being so incapable of any action. She closed her eyes, glad to be alone. But all at once her throat tightened, and she turned her face into the cushions and sobbed, raging at her own lack of insight, torn between guilt and regret.

Another woman would have at least allowed him to explain, out of courtesy if nothing else, whereas all she'd done was lie to him abominably about Hernan, perhaps jeopardizing their friendship and business relationship forever. She sobbed wretchedly, knowing that there was no going back.

Serena grabbed Maxi by the arm and pushed him into the library. "She won't appeal and I'm going to lose the lot."

"But why won't she—"

"I don't know!" Serena stamped her foot. "Come on, let's get the tea. You go and keep her company. Actually, no. I need to go to the loo. You'd better go to the kitchen and ask Kathleen to get tea," she said, distracted.

Ten minutes later, Serena entered the sitting room holding a laden tray. "Here we are," she said cheerfully. "This should make you feel better." She cast a calculating glance at India, noticing her reddened eyes and wan expression. "Here, I'll pour. You'd better have lots of sugar, it'll help your energy level. Poor thing," she added, placing the cup at a convenient distance from her sister's hand. "You look awful, but the tea will perk you up. Isn't that what Mummy always used to say?"

India smiled wanly and Serena watched carefully as she sipped from the delicate Spode cup. "Now drink it all up and you'll feel much better. Maxi, some tea?"

"No, thanks, I'll stick to my Perrier." It took some time for India to finish the tea, but finally she got it down.

"Are you sure you'll be all right, Indy? I hate the thought of leaving you, but Maxi has to be at the airport at six. Do you mind? Kathleen's on her way."

"No, of course not," India answered.

She looked rotten, Serena reflected, positively green.

"We'll be on our way then. Do you need anything before we toddle along?" She patted the cushion behind India's head. "Ring me if you do, won't you?"

"Honestly, I'll be fine," India replied, waving a listless goodbye as they departed.

"Let's get out of here," Maxi said when they got outside. He hastened to the car. Serena jumped in the other side and slammed the door.

"I don't know what to do, Maxi," Serena said, worried. "If she doesn't—"

"Don't worry," he interrupted her curtly, his pale eyes glazed. "Trust me, I know what I'm doing."

16

Jack maintained a desultory flow of conversation with Peter on the road back to Dalkirk. He hadn't felt so depressed since the day he'd learned of his brother's death. But at least then *she'd* been there.

"Well? What happened?" Diana and Chloë came rushing into the hall expectantly. "I hope the judge told you to shove off, Jack." Chloë poked him in the arm, half playful, half serious.

"Really, Chloë, you never grow up," Diana exclaimed, frowning reprovingly. "You're as bad as the girls. Now, come on, Jack dear, don't keep us in suspense."

"The most surprising verdict," Peter said, shaking his head as he laid the car keys in an ashtray on the hall table. "Damned if I've ever heard the like."

"Come on, tell us," Chloë begged.

"We all got a piece of it. Dunbar has been divided in three," Jack said listlessly, shrugging off his coat, wanting to be alone, needing time to think——about India, Dunbar and the promises he'd made.

"What?" Chloë looked him over, cocking an eyebrow. "Well, aren't you pleased?" she exclaimed. "Wasn't that what you wanted? Poor Indy, now you'll be able to bait her from here to kingdom come. What a horrid man that judge must be.''

Jack looked straight through her, his mind adrift. ''It's all over now.''

''What on earth do you mean?'' Diana asked, exchanging a worried look with her husband.

Jack forced himself to act normally, wishing they'd leave him alone—with his thoughts, his memories, his sorrow.

''Tell us,'' Chloë prodded.

He passed a hand over his eyes and shook his head. ''I don't know what to think.''

Peter glanced at his wife, signaling for her and Chloë to disappear. ''Come on, old chap. I think we deserve a drink after all the goings-on.''

''Jack, don't forget that your friend's arriving this afternoon,'' Diana called as the ladies walked away.

''Westmoreland. I completely forgot.'' He glanced at his watch. ''Too late to put him off now. He'll be on his way already.''

He shrugged, following Peter into the library, and dropped heavily onto the worn leather sofa. Nothing made sense anymore. He didn't want another hotel—he wanted India. He took the tumbler from Peter absently, wondering what he could do to alter things. He threw back some whiskey, but it had a bitter taste, and he laid the glass down.

''Sorry I'm such bad company.'' He shot Peter a tight smile.

''Not at all. I'll leave you on your own. Don't get too down about all this. Things'll come about, you'll see. I'll pick up this chap at the airport later on. He seems very interested in coming on board if we do that hotel in Sydney.''

''He is. Thanks.'' Jack nodded distractedly and leaned

back, his mind miles away, realizing it had all been for nothing. Dunbar was a meaningless trophy without her. He felt more alone and lost than he would ever have believed possible, and for a long while he sat gazing into the fire, wallowing in a mire of regret.

Half an hour later Chloë popped her head through the door. "I'm off to see Indy, Jack." She hesitated. "Are you sure it's all over between you?"

"Yes. I guess it just wasn't meant to be."

"Hmm." She eyed him skeptically. "I've never seen you give up on anything. So much for true love," she remarked tartly.

"Oh, shut up, Chlo. Just go," he snapped, not in the mood for conversation, let alone argument. Chloë shrugged and closed the door behind her, leaving him to his somber thoughts and the crisp crackling of the logs.

"Hello." Chloë's voice echoed through the silent hall. Mrs. Walker had let her in through the kitchen and she'd made her way to the library in search of India. "Indy? Where are you?" she called as she headed to the sitting room.

No lights were on, yet the day was so bleak it was almost dark inside. Odd, she reflected, wondering if perhaps India was upstairs.

"Indy?" She popped her head round the sitting-room door just in case. Then a sound from the floor made her pause and she groped for the switch. "Goodness, Indy, is that you?" she exclaimed, gazing horrified at India lying doubled up on the floor, her face a whitish gray, her lips violet. Chloë rushed to where India lay and kneeled down, dragging her to the sofa, propping her head and shoulders against it, trying desperately to revive her.

"Indy, what is wrong with you?" she cried.

But she seemed unable to answer, her eyes closed and

her body limp. Beads of cold sweat appeared on her fore-head.

"Oh Lord," Chloë exclaimed, wiping India's brow anxiously. She got up, loath to leave her, but realizing she must get help immediately, and ran into the hall. "Mrs. Walker, Kathleen," she shouted desperately. "Please come, India's dreadfully ill."

At the sound of her voice, Mrs. Walker came bustling along the passage, rubbing her hands on the front of her apron, her plump face creased and concerned. "What is it, Miss Chloë? What in heaven's name has happened?"

"It's India," Chloë answered, distressed.

"Oh dear, what's wrong with her? She's not been too well the last few days."

They ran back as fast as they could. "Mrs. Walker, please call an ambulance, quick. We have to get her to the hospital."

Kathleen came hurrying down the stairs. "What on earth— India! Oh my goodness, what has happened? My poor child. I'll call an ambulance at once."

"A helicopter might be better," Mrs. Walker said, shaking her head. "Lady Serena mentioned before she left that Miss India wasna' feeling too good and to nae disturb her, but I never thought it was anything like this," she exclaimed.

Kathleen hurried to the hall telephone and dialed. "Oh, these wretched lines. It would be busy, wouldn't it? Chloë, keep reviving her while I try to get through," she called anxiously. After several tries she finally got a ring.

Twenty minutes later a helicopter landed in front of the house and the emergency team rushed in. In a matter of minutes India was on a stretcher, an IV in her arm, being hoisted into the helicopter.

"Will she be all right?" Chloë shouted to the young paramedic above the reverberation of the engine.

"I couldna' say. Something's very wrong. We need to get her to the E.R. at once."

Chloë held India's hand tightly, praying that all would be well, wondering what could possibly have affected her.

"I'll go with her," Kathleen said, agitated.

Chloë squeezed her shoulder. "No, let me. I only came to be with her anyway. I want to go. I have to."

"But I think I should—"

"Please, Kath, let me," Chloë begged. "Oh, and call Dalkirk. Talk to Peter so Di doesn't panic, and tell him what's going on. Thanks." She gave Kathleen a brief hug and waved to Mrs. Walker.

"Chloë, dear, I still think it would be better if I went," Kathleen insisted.

"Dinna' worry, Lady Kathleen," Mrs. Walker said, seeing the other woman's frustrated expression. "Miss Chloë will take good care of her. Dinna' fash yersel' to death now."

Kathleen watched as Chloë climbed into the helicopter, then turned to Mrs. Walker. "These young people are so volatile, you know. I would have preferred to make sure India was all right myself, but I'm sure you're right. Now I'd better go and make the call to Dalkirk." She bustled back into the house as the helicopter lights faded into the darkening horizon. She should have gone and made sure everything was dealt with properly. She shook her head. Too much was happening too quickly, what with the verdict and now India. She headed to the phone and sighed, realizing the only way was to plow ahead and hope for the best.

"Jack?" The sound of Peter's voice made him sit up and take stock of his surroundings. It was dark and he hadn't even noticed. Peter switched on a lamp. "Sorry to interrupt, old chap, but I've just had the oddest phone call.''

"Oh yeah?"

"To tell you the truth, I'm rather worried."

"What about?" Jack asked listlessly.

"The Marchese Ambrognelli's just called me from Edinburgh where he's staying at the Balmoral Hotel." Peter hesitated. "He called Dunbar to speak to India. Apparently he called there yesterday but was told by the housekeeper that she was ill."

"She's sick?" Jack sat up with a jerk. He'd known something wasn't right, and now all his misgivings were confirmed. "What's wrong with her? Where is she?"

"Calm down, old chap, everything's under control. Apparently Chloë's gone to hospital with her."

"The hospital?" Jack rose, horrified. "What do you mean, the hospital? Come on, let's go."

Peter laid a hand firmly on his arm. "No, Jack, I need you to listen." Something in Peter's voice made him focus.

"What's going on?" he asked, his senses alert now.

"As I said, the Marchese just called. He's an old and dear friend of the Dunbar family, an admirer of Lady El's actually. He's on his way here now. Apparently he has some information he wishes to impart to me, something he didn't want to tell me over the phone. He seemed very upset that India had taken ill." Peter glanced at Jack, frowning. "He seemed to think her illness might be linked in some way to what he wants to tell me." He shook his head. "I can't make head or tail of it, but I want you here. He should be arriving in about a quarter of an hour," he added, glancing at his watch. "I hope the trip won't be too much for him—he must be at least eighty-two, and I heard he took Lady El's death very badly."

"Marchese?" Jack said skeptically.

"Yes, old Venetian aristocracy—"

"What does all this have to do with Indy?"

"I haven't a clue," Peter replied grimly. "But something tells me it's not good. Let's see what we can make of it. Two brains'll work better than one. Oh, by the way, Westmoreland's plane lands at seven. As I said earlier, I'd go and pick him up, but I can't leave Ambrognelli on his own."

"Shit!" Jack exclaimed in frustration. "I want to go to India, for cryin' out loud."

"I don't mean to put a damper on you, old boy, but after everything that's happened, do you think you'd be a welcome addition?" Peter looked away, embarrassed.

He was probably right. She wouldn't want him there. Jack turned toward the fire, taking a minute to get a hold of himself.

Then the sound of wheels crunching gravel made them hasten into the hall and out onto the porch. Jack watched as an old gentleman alighted from an ancient Silver Cloud Rolls-Royce, helped by the chauffeur.

"Marchese, I'm awfully glad you could make it. Come in." Peter nodded to the chauffeur. "If you pop into the kitchen, I'm sure there's a kettle on the boil," he said, smiling.

"Thank you, sir." The chauffeur tipped his hat.

"Ah, dear boy—" the Marchese took Peter's hand and squeezed it firmly in his "—I'm glad I could come. A shocking business," he said, shaking his head. "A very shocking business."

"This is Jack Buchanan, my friend and partner from the United States."

The Marchese turned slowly and looked Jack over thoroughly. "So you're the young man who's been making my India so unhappy. I'll have a word with you later, young fellow. Now, both of you. This matter is most urgent." They entered the hall as Diana came to greet him.

"Giordano," she exclaimed as they embraced. "How wonderful to see you. What a surprise, I didn't know you were coming to Scotland."

There was a moment's hesitation and a look flashed among the three men.

"Ah, my dear, I'm afraid I should have warned you, it was remiss of me. Old age makes me forgetful of my manners," he said, holding her hand in his and smiling. "I was going to call tomorrow, but then a little business matter I thought Peter might be able to resolve came up, so I came over right away. I hope I'm not being a nuisance?"

"No, of course not." Diana smiled, glancing at Peter with questioning eyes, but too polite to say more. "Do come in, and, of course, you must stay for supper."

"Thank you, *cara*, that would be delightful." He raised her hand to his lips.

"We'll just pop into the library, Di."

"Of course. By the way, I've put Mr. Westmoreland in the green room. I wonder if Texans are fussy. I'm sure he's used to far more sophisticated accommodations."

"Don't you worry, Di, Lance is as easygoing as they come. We've known each other since the army, and believe me, there was no *green room* where we were!" Jack gave her a wink and a pat on the shoulder.

"Thanks, chaps." Peter sighed, relieved, as they entered the library and Jack closed the door. "I don't want to worry her unnecessarily. If she knows India's ill she'll have a fit. Giordano, do sit down. Can I get you a drink?"

The Marchese settled in a wing chair, crossing his legs elegantly, his hands clasped over the silver handle of his walking stick. He gazed for a moment into the fire, and Jack took the opportunity to look him over—dark gray silk suit, white starched shirt and burgundy silk tie. Although he was old, he didn't look frail. Maybe it was the keen glint in his eyes that made him seem so vibrant. Jack wondered what the Marchese knew about India and him, surprised at the older gentleman's previous remark.

"I'll take a drop of sherry as usual, Peter, thank you." The Marchese frowned, as though trying to decide where to begin. "To tell you this story correctly I need to go back to the time of my dear Elspeth's death," he began reluctantly.

Peter handed him the sherry. Jack wished he would skip the preliminaries and get to the point. He drummed his foot nervously as the older gentleman took a thoughtful sip, then flicked an imaginary speck of dust from his sleeve.

"The night before Elspeth died," he continued, "I talked to her on the telephone. She sounded fine, except for a little bout of nausea. But I wasn't overly worried. We older people are prone to minor ailments, so I merely counseled her to take a Fernet Branca after dinner—it's very good for the digestion, you know—and rest," he said, pausing for a sip. "It was only when India came back from Argentina—" he cast Jack a quick piercing glance "—and mentioned she'd discovered an unfinished note on her mother's desk that this whole business was brought to my attention."

Jack leaned forward attentively.

"India was worried, for the note was in Elspeth's writing and addressed to her. Strangely, she'd written that she was worried about speaking on the telephone, noting that she might be overheard, and begging India to come at once. But, alas," he said, sighing, "neither India nor I could fathom who she could have been referring to. The only people we knew to have been staying at the house were Serena, Maxi Von Lowendorf, the latter's boyfriend, and of course, Kathleen, her niece," he said, dismissing the last. "We discussed the matter. I knew of India's difficulties with her sister, for Elspeth had been worried about it for some time. Family relationships are sometimes complicated,'' he added, taking another sip. ''Nevertheless, something struck me as strange.''

''Go on.'' It had become obvious that this was no rambling old man, but a highly astute and intelligent individual.

''I asked India for a photocopy of the note. At the time I didn't want to worry her unnecessarily with my doubts, which might, after all, have resulted in nothing.'' He looked over at Jack and Peter, his gaze meeting theirs full on. ''It was then I began my own investigation. You see, I happen to have been acquainted with Maxi's family for many years. His grandfather and I were together in Paris many years ago, before the war, of course, and I remembered, somewhere in the recesses of my old mind, a little scandal that occurred some ten years ago. It concerned an aunt of this Maxi, who died under very odd circumstances.'' He stopped, his voice lowering a key. ''She was poisoned.''

''Poisoned?'' Jack glanced at Peter to see how he was receiving all this. It was a little too dramatic for his taste. An Italian marchese, Prussian family intrigues. He raised a quizzical eyebrow.

''Ah, I see you find it hard to believe,'' the Marchese said, noting Jack's skepticism. ''It is unfortunately true. The family hushed up the whole business, but I have it on the best authority that Maxi was a strong suspect, and that a large amount of money changed hands within the family so that no charges would be pressed. Since then he has been virtually banished. The family will have nothing to do with him, which is probably the reason he is trying to better his fortunes here,'' he added dryly, steepling his fingers over the handle of his walking stick. ''Gentlemen, I don't wish to alarm you, but I have reason to believe Maxi and Serena have not only poisoned my beloved Elspeth, but that they may very well be availing themselves of the same method to rid their path of India. The symptoms the housekeeper at Dunbar described were typical of arsenic poisoning.''

Jack was still skeptical. ''But why would Serena resort to murder? I'm buying India out, so Serena will get her share of Dunbar money. What would be the point? By the way, that's confidential,'' he added hastily, Peter's look of surprise reminding him he'd broken his promise.

''Serena is India's next of kin, is she not?''

''Yes.'' Peter nodded slowly, his eyes narrowing. ''I'm beginning to see what you're getting at. If Serena could rid herself of India before she sells to you, Jack, she'd not only inherit her portion of Dunbar, but India's, too. Not to mention that La Dolce Vita's been doing very well lately. Hasn't India just paid off her mortgage, Giordano?''

''India—thanks to her own efforts—is a well-to-do young woman. So was Maxi's aunt,'' the Marchese added grimly. ''Maxi thought he and his brother would inherit her fortune, for she had no children. The brother is beyond reproach, a fine young man, but the pattern here seems familiar. Maxi probably planned to rid himself of his brother as well. The long and the short of it is, he got nothing. She left the bulk of her estate to a foundation— something to do with the preservation of the Norwegian lemming, I believe. What *we* must realize is that we are dealing with two dangerous, unscrupulous individuals who will stop at very little to get what they want.''

Jack shuddered. It made sense. Even now India might be in danger. ''I wouldn't put anything past Serena, and what you say does make sense,'' he said slowly. ''But still, isn't it a little far-fetched?''

''Naturally we cannot rush to conclusions. The first steps are to have my poor Elspeth's body exhumed and get the doctor's results of India's blood tests. They should be ready shortly, at the latest tomorrow morning. When I called I insisted on haste.'' He shook his head sadly. "That it should have come to this is terrible, but justice must be done. If the results are the same, and traces of arsenic are found in both India's and Elspeth's blood, we can only assume the worst.'' The Marchese stopped, his eyes bright and determined. "Everything points in one direction and we must take immediate action. I will see Elspeth's death avenged if it is the last thing I do, and it is up to us to see no harm befalls India. She is our responsibility,'' he said, fixing his gaze on Jack.

Jack nodded, his mind in a panic. "Do you think she'll be safe at the hospital? They might try to get at her. We should hire bodyguards immediately.''

"That has been taken care of. I have already seen to it that two agents be posted outside her room around the clock. They will not be noticed, for they will be disguised as nurses, and will report directly to me.''

Jack was caught off guard. Who was this man who exerted this amount of clout so far away from his own backyard? It was impressive. He gave the Marchese an admiring smile. "You sure take care of business, sir. It's a relief to know she's safe,'' he added, suddenly feeling the wind taken out of his sails. "Are you sure there's nothing *I* can do?''

"Young man, you have another role to play in all of this. If things are as we believe they may be, there will be much to be dealt with, and I don't know about you—'' he shot them both a shrewd glance "—but in my experience I have found it is often better to deal with business—as you Americans like to put it—oneself, and not rely on the police for solutions.'' He rose slowly and approached the fire, laying a hand on Jack's tense arm. "There is no danger, no need to worry. She will be fine, and other matters can wait till later, *ecco?*" he said, wry smile lighting his wise eyes.

"I still think I should be with her."

"No no no," the Marchese exclaimed, shaking his head vigorously. "You must leave that poor child alone to recover. She has suffered enough at your hands already."

"But—"

"No buts. In this I must insist. You may run as many hotels as you like and fly all over the world like a maniac preparing yourself for a heart attack at forty—that is your personal choice. But in this matter, you will do as I say."

Jack hadn't been spoken to like this since he was a teenager, and he shut up, not knowing how to reply.

Peter gave him a sympathetic smile. "What are we going to do about Westmoreland?"

"Don't worry about Lance. He's the best you have on board in a situation such as this."

"Okay." Peter nodded, resigned. "It's up to you if you feel we should put him in the picture. He'll probably end up knowing anyway," he added gloomily.

"Okay. But what are we going to do about the other thing, uh—Lady Elspeth."

The Marchese turned to Peter. "You have influence with the local magistrate, I imagine?"

"I suppose I could pull a few strings. Why?"

"I don't imagine Serena will consent to this exhumation of her mother's body, and we cannot upset India in her present state. I would imagine the agreement of a family member would be required for such a proceeding to take place."

"Hmm. You're probably right," Peter said thoughtfully. "Perhaps I should phone Ian. He's a good chap, and as Lady El's nephew, he could probably sign any documents."

"Is he the guy I met at the cemetery?" Jack asked.

"That's right." Peter nodded.

"Good idea, Peter," the Marchese said. "In the meantime, we will go on as if nothing has happened. Not a word to anyone."

"We certainly don't want to worry the women," Peter observed. "Maybe we should let the doctor in on what we suspect."

"*Ecco,* don't worry, it's already taken care of."

"Is there anything you haven't taken care of?" Jack asked with a challenging glint in his eye. "And just to set the record straight, the score with India's even. She's not the only one hurting around here."

The older gentleman's face broke into a knowing smile. "It's very tough the first time, when things don't go exactly as we want them to with a woman, isn't it? I remember well." He smiled, reminiscing, his eyes filled with memories. "It was a long time ago, but believe me, I spent the next forty years thanking God I wasn't too proud to open my heart." He gave a wistful shake of the head. "Pride and youth are a dangerous combination. They should never be allowed to dictate one's actions. Remember that."

Jack glanced at Peter, mystified, and got a shrug in return. He stood up, then headed for the garage, his mind in a whirl.

It took him half an hour to reach Turnhouse airport and park. He forced himself to stop worrying about India and concentrated on finding Lance.

It wasn't difficult. Standing at the bar in the middle of the terminal was a tall straight back, the scuffed heels of a pair of Nakonas and a Stetson. Smiling to himself, Jack went over.

"Hi, Texas!"

The figure spun round. "Jack, good to see you. I'm mighty sorry about your brother," he added, thrusting his hand out. It was a firm silent handshake, the handshake of two men who knew the meaning of death and had saved each other's lives. "Drink?"

"Yeah." Jack nodded and smiled. "You know, you never change, man." He looked Lance over, the slim, wiry body, firm jaw and lazy gray eyes that always saw too much, exactly as he remembered them. He still had that telltale military stance. "By the way, we have a situation on our hands."

"Oh yeah?" The lazy eyes became immediately keen.

"I'll tell you on our way. We'd better get going."

They finished their drinks and soon were driving through the night. Twenty minutes later Jack had given Lance a quick and explicit breakdown of how things stood.

"So that's where it's at for now," he said, giving his friend a quick, sidelong glance. "No talking to the women, of course, and the less this Maxi and Serena know the better."

"Yep." Lance seemed to be thinking to himself. When they arrived at the house, Jack rolled into the garage.

"How are you packed?" he asked, retrieving the luggage from the back seat.

Lance's eyes narrowed, meeting Jack's across the Porsche's roof. "Smith & Wesson 9 mm," he said in a slow drawl. "I can pick up a Glock from the plane, too, if need be."

"Good. I'll see what Peter has."

"How'd you know I'd be coming to these parts packed?" Lance asked.

Jack gave him a knowing smile. "Old habits die hard."

Lance laughed and slapped his Stetson back on thick chestnut hair streaked by the hot Texan sun. "Not bad, Buchanan, not bad at all."

The two men entered the house by the side door, comparing notes on the qualities and defects of their planes.

As they passed the kitchen, Mrs. MacC. came bustling out. "Och, Mr. Jack, I'm glad te' see ye." She stopped in her tracks and looked Lance over critically.

"This is Lance Westmoreland, Mrs. MacC."

"Another American?"

"No, ma'am. Texan," he said, politely removing his hat.

"Hmm. Well, dinner'll be ready in a wee while. Ye'd better be gettin' along the two of ye."

"Wow." Lance cast Jack a questioning glance as they headed down the corridor.

"Don't worry. Peter, Diana and the family are great. You'll see."

As they entered the hall, Diana came down the stairs with a welcoming smile, while three little girls, dressed in their long nightgowns, peeked from between the spindles of the banister. Jack took one look at the scene and realized that things were going to be delayed. He bit back the annoyance and took the stairs two steps at a time. "Come on down, you rascals, and meet Uncle Lance." He hoisted Molly into his arms, her hair flowing down her back, her big blue eyes sparkling. His heart tightened at the thought of his other little girl, lying sick and alone in the hospital. But he stayed calm. The Marchese was right; he had another role to play.

Diana scolded Jack for having brought Lance in through the back door, and then the two other girls came tumbling down the stairs, asking him excited questions about his hat and Texas. Peter and the Marchese appeared from the library and joined the party.

"We need to get moving," Jack whispered to Lance after the introductions.

"Cute kid," he said, smiling at Molly and crouching to pick up her Pooh bear, which had fallen in the excitement.

"She's my brother's."

They made their excuses to Diana, anxious to get on, then went to the library and got down to business. It would be a long evening, for there was much to be discussed, but the plans would be laid, and tomorrow they would get started.

The next morning Jack banished India from his mind once more, and forced himself to focus. He'd squeezed as much information out of Chloë as he could without arousing her suspicions. She'd bought the doctor's story of food poisoning, and had not seemed to notice the two agents discreetly pacing the corridor outside India's room.

The men had decided to meet after breakfast while they waited for the Marchese and Ian to arrive, and Jack sat down, hoping Lance would find his way to the dining room.

"I hope Lance doesn't get lost," he commented, serving scrambled eggs and sausage onto his plate.

"Lance?" Chloë's head shot up.

"Yeah, Lance West—"

At that moment the door opened and Lance entered. Chloë went rigid in her seat and he stopped dead in his tracks.

"What on earth are you doing here?" she exclaimed, her face wreathed in smiles. "How did you know I was here?"

"He didn't, or he would have stayed home," Jack murmured.

"What a beastly thing to say!"

"Please don't start, you two," Diana said. "You both ought to know better."

"Lance is a friend of Jack's," Peter explained helpfully. "He's joining us in one of our business ventures."

"Oh." Chloë looked deflated, then a second later she

smiled, her old self again. "Never mind. What matters is you're here."

"You two know each other?" Diana asked, bewildered.

"Yes. Actually, Lance is my boss." Chloë returned to the table, blushing, while Lance smiled down at her.

"Ah, so you're the famous Texan," Jack interjected. "Good luck to you, pal. Have some breakfast. You'll need it. Don't tell me it's true you're buying a tabloid?"

Chloë cast him a dark look. "It's not a tabloid. You're so rude, Jack. No wonder India doesn't want any truck with you. I'm beginning to think she's quite right."

Jack turned to Chloë, who pretended to ignore him. "You make sure you behave, young lady. You're playing in the big leagues this time around," he whispered to her.

"Shut up. You could've told me he was coming," she hissed back.

"How was I meant to know he was your Texan?"

"You could have guessed," she replied haughtily, her voice rising.

"Will you both please stop it?" Diana exclaimed once more, exasperated. "Lance, I'm awfully sorry. You must excuse their behavior. Perhaps you can stop them quibbling all the time."

Jack grinned at Chloë. "Maybe he just can."

Lance ate his breakfast and watched the banter from across the table, obviously amused. Then, when they'd finished, the men rose and excused themselves.

"What's going on?" Chloë asked. "Why are they all in a huddle? Di, what are they up to?" she said, turning to her sister.

"I don't know, dear," Diana replied philosophically, casting Peter a questioning look as he reached the door. "But be patient, we'll find out."

I hope not, Jack reflected as he closed the dining-room door behind him and focused back on the matters at hand.

It was going to be hard to deal with this discreetly, especially if they were having major powwows behind closed doors.

"The girls are getting suspicious," he commented.

"I know, but I'll tell them we're all investing in a new hotel. In Italy, or Sardinia maybe. That would justify Giordano's presence, and Lance, well, I suppose you just got involved along the way. Amazing that you're Chloë's boss," he added.

"Sure is. Your sister-in-law's one heck of a girl. Her father's passed away, right?" Lance dangled a long, booted leg from the windowsill.

"Yes. My father-in-law died shortly after Di and I were married, I'm afraid."

"Then maybe I'll be paying you a visit one of these days," Lance said in his Texan drawl.

Jack's eyebrows flew up. So it was serious, after all? Who would have believed it, his old pal and Chloë. They would certainly make an interesting couple.

Peter was looking out of the window, clearly more worried about the Marchese and Ian's arrival than Lance's words. "I think that must be Ian and Giordano arriving now. By the way, chaps, the Marchese's moving in. It's too far for him to drive back and forth from Edinburgh, so you're going to have to give up your room and go upstairs, Jack. FHB, you know." Peter gave him an apologetic smile.

"Hey! Why me? Move Westy here out of his. And what in the world is FHB?"

"Oh, sorry. It means Family Hold Back. Di says you're as good as family, so you'll have to take the rough with the smooth."

Jack grumbled and the laughter that followed broke the heightened tension as Ian and the Marchese appeared.

"Any news?" Peter asked after they'd all said hello.

"Not good." Ian shook his head gravely. "The coroner says one of the girls has to sign." He looked worried. "Shocking business this, Peter. Very bad indeed."

The Marchese seemed thoughtful. "What about *una donazione,* a donation for the local police club, something of that nature."

"Sorry, but I don't think that'll fly, Giordano. They're pretty sticky about things like that around these parts," Peter replied ruefully.

"Hmm, a pity. It is most unfortunate, but I think we will have to resort to nonconventional methods to obtain the signature," the Marchese said.

"Such as?" Peter asked.

"Jack, have you had the documents prepared for the acquisition of Dunbar?"

"They're being drawn up." He didn't want to think about that.

"Call your lawyers, have them prepare the documents now. Both girls are willing to sell to you, *corretto?*"

"That's right," Jack replied tersely. He didn't need this reminder that all was over between him and India.

"*Va bene.* I think I would recommend a large quantity of documents, as many as they can furnish, all needing signatures. Prepare them for both girls, Serena must not be suspicious."

"Are you suggesting we get Serena to sign under false pretenses?" Ian asked.

"My dear boy—" the Marchese gave him an understanding smile "—think of it rather as a means to an end. I'm sure Jack will find a good excuse to get her to sign, After all, Serena may well have murdered your aunt, and, according to the doctor's reports that I received early this morning, may be responsible for your cousin India's illness, as well. It appears there are traces of arsenic in her blood." He allowed this to sink in.

"Good God," Ian muttered, and a hush came over the five men as they took in the news.

"Hell, I can't take this!" Jack slammed his fist on the nearest table. "I'm going out to get Serena and that son of a bitch right now."

"I'm in, partner." Lance gave him a nod from his perch on the window ledge.

"What do you say we go get 'em, guys?" Jack asked the room at large.

The Marchese threw up his hands in despair. "What impetuosity, *Dio mio*. Do not be so hasty, young fellow. *Ride meglio chi ride ultimo,* the one who laughs last laughs the best. Patience. You must learn to be calm, to wait, like the fox. Be astute, act in this as you would in the most complicated business deal. We have to observe Maxi's movements, catch him unawares, or he will flee."

"He's right, Jack, we can't rush in headfirst like bulls in a china shop, however tempting," Peter said ruefully. "I know it goes against the grain to get Serena to sign like this," he continued uneasily, glancing in Ian's direction, "but to be perfectly frank with you, I think Giordano's right. Everything points to her being involved. We simply have to know if Lady El was—uh—murdered," he finished quietly.

Jack saw the smoldering embers and fierce determination in the Marchese's eyes, realizing all at once that it didn't matter that he was old—his feelings were still as strong. He was preparing to avenge the death of the woman he'd loved. "Okay. I'll call Henderson now and see what they can do."

He left the room and went to the study to telephone Edinburgh, and Quince in the States.

Ten minutes later he returned. There was an expectant hush as he entered and the others all turned to him hopefully.

"Well?" Peter asked.

"I told them to drop everything and have the papers drawn up by twelve today. I called Serena and invited her to lunch. I told her I'm adding on a couple thousand pounds extra for all the trouble she's been put through," he added with a cynical bark. "I'll get her to sign once she's mellowed out with a couple of drinks. I'll tell her they're deviating the road."

"Good idea," Peter exclaimed. "I think we need to put surveillance on Maxi, though, don't you?"

"Definitely," Jack agreed.

"I will have an agent or two posted at Serena's residence. But they must be very discreet." The Marchese frowned. "This is no amateur we are dealing with, and if they have poisoned India, he must be worried that the results will show in the blood tests."

"You're right, Giordano. This demands the utmost secrecy. Well, are we all ready?"

It was finally decided that the Marchese would have the agents posted, and Jack would handle Serena. He realized that sitting with her, knowing her probable intentions for India, would demand his utmost self-control, and he wondered grimly how he would keep himself from throttling her. He'd pretend to celebrate their deal, get her to sign, and then— God help her when all this was over. Like the Marchese, he'd demand retribution for harm done to his woman. And he'd go the whole nine yards to get it.

17

India's head throbbed endlessly as slowly, one by one, the memories returned. The judge's ruling, her final decision to give up Dunbar and the dreadful moments spent writhing on the sitting-room floor. After that there was a blank. She opened her eyes and gazed down at the IV in her arm, then glanced around the sparse hospital room, wondering what could possibly have given her food poisoning.

Nothing had worked out in Scotland. Giving up Dunbar had hurt her more than she could ever have imagined, but the sooner she up and left the better. She wondered bleakly if Jack was having the papers drawn up, hoping they could get it over and done with quickly. The thought of facing him once more, knowing she'd judged him so unfairly, was excruciatingly painful. How she wished that she had picked up the phone that day at Chantemerle and given him a chance.

She plucked nervously at the sheet, bitterly conscious that everything was over between them, wishing there was some way she could repair the damage. But her reasoning mind intervened. *Stop dreaming,* she ordered herself. *You know he only wants Dunbar for his hotel. Anyway, why would he give you another chance, when you wouldn't even let him explain? At least he'd tried to be honest, while you countered with lie after lie.* Suddenly she recalled the urgency in his voice when he'd begged her to reconsider her decision.

She allowed herself one last indulgence—the memory of how bewildered he'd looked, standing in the middle of the pavement, rain sprinkling his face, his eyes filled with longing. She'd thought he wanted to say something more, and perhaps he had.

But now she needed to focus her energy on regaining her strength and getting back to Switzerland where she belonged. She buried her head in the pillow, determined to ignore the overwhelming depression that was hovering over her heart and soul.

There was a knock at the door. "Come in," she said weakly.

The door burst open. India winced and kept her eyes closed, presuming it was the nurse.

"Is it okay if I come in? Gosh, you look awful."

The sound of Serena's voice made her struggle to a sitting position.

"Hello. Serena, how exactly did I end up here?"

"Chloë found you on the floor of the sitting room ready to croak, so they brought you here by heli. Good thing, too. Apparently you were pretty much a goner. I hope you're feeling better," she said, looking India over doubtfully.

It was then she saw Jack standing in the doorway. Panic melted to confusion as she made a futile attempt to tidy her hair.

"Don't tire yourself, darling, we won't be long." Serena walked across the room, oozing concern. Then Jack slowly approached the bed.

"Let me help," he said, his strong arms supporting her while he pushed the pillows up behind her back. Her mind went blank. All she could think of was how good and familiar the scent of him was, and how she longed to stretch out her arms and bring him close.

"Thanks," she said, embarrassed, conscious of his hands, of his touch on her arm. Oh, how she'd longed for it, dreamed of it throughout those troubled dreams that had haunted her the last three nights as she lay recovering.

"I'm sorry we burst in on you like this," he said gruffly, standing back. "I—"

"That's fine," she replied quickly, determined to sound calm. "I suppose you've had the papers drawn up, and want to get on with the transfer of the property. Have you signed yet, Serena?" she asked with a pang. Of course, he'd want to make sure everything was signed and settled himself, rather than leave it to a third party.

"I signed them over lunch," Serena said blithely. She opened her bag and produced a check, which she waved in India's direction. "Best day of my life. I'm so glad you finally saw the light. I thought you'd never be persuaded to—"

"I'm glad you got things rolling so quickly," India interrupted hastily. "As soon as I can get up, I'll vacate my stuff from Dunbar and you can get on with your plans, Jack. The only thing I still feel strongly about is secrecy. Till I leave at least. I don't think I can handle much more emotional upheaval and I don't want to go through the trauma of goodbyes. Serena, you do understand that, don't you?"

"Of course, darling. Far be it from me to let the cat out of the bag."

"I'll see to it nobody knows anything about it. And as I promised you, everyone will be taken care of," Jack said softly.

"Good. As long as that point is well understood then we can go ahead. Where do we start? I'm sure you don't want to be dillydallying," she said breathlessly.

Jack hesitated an instant, then turned abruptly and opened the briefcase he'd been carrying. He pulled out a sheaf of papers and brought them over to her, his expression unreadable.

She watched him, handsome as usual, immaculate in a dark gray suit. She realized he was wearing the silk tie with the palm trees she'd bought him in Rio, wondering if he remembered. But as he turned toward the bed, she felt a sense of pending doom, for he looked more closed and cold than she had ever seen him. So much for some magical fairy wand making everything right. She fought the foolishness, determined to keep her end of the bargain, forcing herself to remember that Dunbar and the hotel were his true objectives, not her.

"Are you sure you're happy with this decision, India?" He addressed her, but his tone seemed stilted and stiff. "There's still time to retract. If you want to change your mind all you have to do is—"

"Of course this is what she wants. What a silly question." Serena gave a brittle, nervous laugh.

"Don't worry, Serena, I'll sign." India assured her, angry with herself for feeling sad, knowing he was merely reciting the words for form's sake, for he meant to have Dunbar whatever the cost. "I'm one hundred percent certain it's the best thing for all of us," she said firmly. "I think Rob probably wanted it this way, don't you? Could you give me something to lean on?" He handed her a clipboard. "Thanks, now let me see, there's quite a package here. Ramsey's been through them all?"

"Of course." Serena sounded anxious. India noticed how she fiddled impatiently with her belt buckle, her eyes fidgety, as though she couldn't wait to make sure the deal was signed and sealed. For a moment she toyed with the pen, watching as they stood in heightened anticipation. Let them suffer just a little. Then her eyes wandered over the first page, but the words swam before her eyes.

"I suppose this is it," she said, meeting Jack's inscrutable gaze full on before putting her signature to the various documents with a flourish she was far from feeling. At the bottom of the pile there was an envelope containing a check made out to her. It had finally come to this—Dunbar was nothing more now than a lump sum of money. "That's it," she said, handing him back the pen.

He took it, their fingers touching. "Indy, if there's anything you want from Dunbar, please just take it, okay?" He sounded terse.

She nodded, afraid that if she spoke, the tears hurtling to the surface would spring forth. She fixed her gaze doggedly on a nondescript etching on the wall, praying they would leave before she gave herself away.

"I guess we'd better go then," he said in an empty, expressionless voice. "I just wanted to—"

"Don't!" She snatched her hand away from his outstretched fingers. "Please, just go."

"Of course, darling. We won't bother you any longer, will we, Jack?" Serena purred, picking up her handbag. Jack turned abruptly, then closed the briefcase with a snap. He stood for a moment as though undecided, but finally he turned and nodded. "Goodbye then, and good luck."

"Goodbye," she whispered, barely able to get the words out.

"Toodle-oo," Serena said, waving from the door. "I'll be back to see you tomorrow."

India turned her face to the wall and waited for the click of the door that would close for good on the most important chapter of her life. When it came, she buried her face in her hands and hot tears poured down her cheeks.

This time it was over, forever.

The dreams would remain dreams, the hopes mere hopes. His whole attitude and stance had been that of a man dying to get things over and done with as quickly as possible. For him the meeting had been nothing more than a disagreeable but necessary episode. And now he was gone from her life. All of a sudden she wished she'd been looking nice, not pale and ill. Not that it mattered, but at least it would have given more dignity to this last encounter. She heaved a sigh, realizing sadly that all he would be in the future was a distant memory, a reminder that at least once in her life she had truly known love.

Jack walked down the corridor, livid.

Nothing had gone as planned. It had been a total mess, with Serena hovering over them and Indy obviously nervous and upset. Maybe he should have sent Serena to buy coffee or something. And worse, he wasn't able to show any emotions for fear Serena would suspect foul play. There had been a point there when he'd felt like slapping her vile murdering face, but he'd held himself in check, knowing India's life was at stake. He glanced back down the corridor before turning the corner, relieved to see the two agents in their hospital greens, hovering at her door.

"That went rather well, don't you think?" Serena pressed the button for the elevator. "I have to run to the bank now, I'm in rather a hurry, but thanks for lunch, Jack." She sent him a suggestive little smile. "Maybe I'll see you around now that you'll be spending more time in the area."

The elevator arrived and he mumbled a response, eyeing her with loathing. It had been too easy, he reflected cynically. The minute he'd dangled that check for the extra two thousand in front of her, and pitched her a patently phony story about the cemetery needing to be transferred because of road expansion, she'd signed happily. It had taken a supreme effort on his part to act normally during the luncheon, and when Serena had insisted on going to the hospital and getting India's papers signed, he'd made every excuse possible not to go. But rapidly he'd realized that either he went ahead or she'd suspect him of something.

He was frustrated, angry and miserable. This last meeting would have been the confirmation of all India's suspicions—that all he wanted was Dunbar.

They reached the lobby and stepped out of the elevator. "Goodbye, Jack. Give me a call sometime." Serena waved and walked quickly down the corridor.

He watched her go, eyes narrowed. He might have lost India but he could still protect her from Serena and her like. Turning on his heel, he strode to the parking lot, conscious of the weight of his briefcase, as though it carried a rock inside. In a way it did. In it was the cause of everything that had destroyed the most precious and unique relationship he'd believed he'd never find again.

But at least India was safe. Now that Serena had signed the authorization to have Lady Elspeth's body exhumed, it was essential to act quickly. They'd made arrangements for the coffin to be dug up tomorrow and he felt certain the toxicology results would prove positive. He drove fast, heading south on the A-7. He'd pass Dunbar, but he wouldn't stop. For though it was his now, there was no joy in it. The hotel had lost its appeal, and he wished he'd never dreamed of it in the first place.

Plus, there was urgent business to be dealt with, and Dunbar could wait. India didn't know it, but he'd made himself a vow to protect her, now and as long as he lived.

Perhaps this was all she'd allow him, but at least he'd make sure the woman he loved would come to no harm.

* * *

"What happened?" Maxi asked anxiously, hovering as Serena entered the flat. "Show me the check. Have you any news about when they'll let India out of the hospital?"

"Look, Maxi." Serena danced across the sitting room in her stocking soles and stopped suddenly under the dilapidated chandelier. Then she threw a wad of notes in the air, letting them shower over her, her eyes closed as she enjoyed the bliss of the moment.

"Are you mad?" he exclaimed in a thick guttural snarl, rising and grabbing the money as it floated to the threadbare carpet. "What do you think you're doing?"

She laughed at him. "There's plenty more where that came from, darling. Thank goodness it's all over." She scowled, suddenly remembering the one negative in all this. "The only thing that's unfair is I only got a third. After all, if we'd sold to Jack as I'd planned, I would have at least had my half."

"Do they have the results of the blood test yet? Did they say anything?" Maxi asked tersely, ignoring her comment.

"Nobody said a thing." She shrugged and sat down on the floor, making neat little piles of bank notes.

Maxi watched her, his eyes narrowed.

"What is it, Maxi? Why are you looking at me like that?" she whined, throwing a cushion at him playfully. "Come on, I want to celebrate. I'll get the champagne." She got up and went to the kitchen, taking two champagne flutes out of the cupboard. "Oh, by the way, I forgot to tell you. They're digging Mummy up. Have you ever heard of anything so nonsensical?"

"What?"

"I know, isn't it nuts? They're digging up all the graves. Something to do with the road. Damn messy, I should think. I had to sign some silly permission for them to do it. As if I cared. Let them dig away. Now, let's think where we're going on holiday, Maxi.''

"What are you talking about, Serena?"

"What I said. Monte Carlo, or perhaps the Caribbean. Jolly nice at this time of year, don't you think?'' She removed the bottle from the fridge. "Mmm, it's just the right temperature—''

"Will you listen to me, you stupid—''

Serena whirled around and faced him. "What on earth's the matter with you, Maxi? All I said is that the town councillors are expanding the bloody road and they're going to dig up all the graves. What's so terrible about that? Besides, I don't want to talk about it. I want to go on holiday.''

"Who told you that?'' he asked, his eyes never leaving hers.

"Oh, about the cemetery, you mean? Jack did, at lunch. He brought some paper with him to save somebody coming all the way—''

"*Ach, mein lieber Gott!* You're a complete idiot, Serena. Maybe they already have the results, maybe they already suspect something.'' He paced the kitchen.

"What on earth's the matter with you, Maxi? How should I know about India's wretched results? And who cares? Calm down for Christ's sake, you're always so paranoid.''

Maxi came over to the table. "Buchanan brought you the thing to sign, *ja?*''

"Yes, I already told you he did,'' she replied, exasperated with his boorish behavior. "Here, open this,'' she insisted, handing him the bottle. Maxi began opening it distractedly, and mumbled something under his breath.

"What *are* you rambling on about, Maxi? I think you're being utterly horrid. Just when I was enjoying myself,'' she said huffily, taking the glass and drinking the champagne in short gulps.

"What time is it?" Maxi asked her, drumming his fingers on the table.

"Oh, about five-thirty, I suppose. Why?"

"It's too late for you to phone the town council office and find out if what Buchanan told you was true. But you call first thing tomorrow morning, do you understand?" he said viciously.

"There's no need for you to be so bloody obnoxious," she exclaimed, thoroughly annoyed. She wasn't used to him acting like this, and wasn't sure she liked it. She took a long sip and smiled archly in an attempt to change the mood. "Come on, darling. Take a little swig. It's delicious."

But he ignored her and his glass stood untouched. "Is there any way you can think of to get India out of the hospital, Serena? After all, as her sister you could perhaps insist."

"Out? I suppose so, though I can't think why I'd bother. By the way, I deposited the rest of the money."

"Another mistake," he snarled.

"Why?" she asked with a sniff. "I don't want the money lying around here."

"We must remove her from the hospital at once."

"Oh, all right, if it keeps you happy," she answered indifferently while Maxi said nothing, his expression distant. Serena flopped onto the sofa and continued downing her champagne, her head filled with plans for the future. Life was going to be so pleasant now, she could feel it. A shiver of delight and anticipation ran through her, for at last things were falling into place. Which, she realized, was no less than she deserved.

"I think it's absurd they want to keep you here, India. Of course you want to get home." Serena cast a scathing look around the hospital room. "You get dressed and I'll go and deal with signing you out. Just think of all the hospital infections you're being exposed to.'' She gave a dramatic shudder.

India couldn't help but agree. The idea of leaving the hospital, getting her stuff from Dunbar and finally going home was foremost in her mind. ''You're right, Serena. There's no reason why I should stay stuck here, I feel perfectly all right. The doctors say they want to run more tests, but I don't see any point when they've already established the food poisoning. It seems a waste of time and I want to get moving. By the way, Serena, you do understand how important it is to me that you don't mention our deal with Jack to anyone before I leave, don't you?''

''Of course, darling. I told you yesterday not to worry. The last thing I want is a bunch of yokels hopping about in panic. And Kathleen and Mrs. Walker blubbering in hysterics,'' she added, raising her eyebrows disdainfully.

India had to be satisfied with that. ''Let's get going then.''

''Absolutely. All they want to do by keeping you here is to charge you for more days. Robbery, that's what it is. I'll go. You be ready in fifteen minutes, and Maxi and I will drive you back to Dunbar.''

''Thanks, it's jolly decent of you,'' India replied, watching Serena leave the room. Perhaps she really had changed After all, she had no ax to grind now that Jack owned Dunbar. Maybe they were finally burying the past and something positive would have come out of all this mess, she reflected, getting out of bed and heading for the bathroom. She took a quick shower, dressed and then packed the few things Serena had brought her.

Already she felt better. The thought of being out of there in a matter of minutes cheered her up. She opened the door and smiled at the two male nurses who seemed to be permanently at her beck and call. The attention in the hospital was quite impressive.

"Goodbye. Thank you so much for all your kind attention. Do say thank you to Mary, the night nurse, for me, won't you?" She was surprised at the look of consternation that passed between the two men. "Is something wrong?" she asked.

"I don't think you should be leaving like this, Miss Moncrieff. I don't think Dr. Macgregor will be very pleased," the taller of them said lamely.

"Oh, rubbish, I feel fit as a fiddle." She laughed. "Don't worry, I'm in good hands. That was my sister you saw just now. She and her boyfriend are driving me home, so there's no need for any concern. I'll be fine." She gave them a firm smile of dismissal and picked up her bag.

Serena came rushing down the hallway waving a slip of paper enthusiastically. "What a fuss. Such a boring lot of old fogies! But don't worry, it's all dealt with." She smiled brightly. "Let's go. I'll carry that for you, don't strain yourself."

India noticed the two nurses exchange another worried look, and then one hastily disappeared. What could be troubling them? she wondered. But she forgot as soon as they reached the lobby and went out into the fresh spring air. Ah, how good it felt to be outside again, away from that smell of disinfectant that characterized hospitals everywhere.

"Hello, India." Maxi came forward and took the bag from Serena. "I'm so glad to see you're feeling better." He gave her one of his sallow smiles and formal little bows. Maybe she had misjudged them both, India reflected, trying to be as positive as she could. But she was still unable to shake off the uneasiness that reigned whenever they were around. Perhaps it was Maxi and not Serena, but something didn't feel right.

As they drove, her thoughts drifted back to Jack and all she was about to leave behind, so preoccupied she didn't even notice the scenery. She felt a pang of intense regret as they drove up the drive, but she tried desperately to persuade herself that it was better this way, knowing she had to disconnect.

As they reached the house, Mrs. Walker came bursting out of the kitchen. "Miss India." Her face beamed as she hurried over, drying her hands on her apron before hugging her. "Och, I'm sae pleased te' see ye, dearie. You come in and sit yersel' doon, ye dinna' want te' be getting tired. Lady Kathleen's been keeping me abreast of how ye are. Here she is now."

"Darling," Kathleen exclaimed, hurrying toward them, her tweed skirt dipping badly at the back. "Finally you're here." They embraced.

"It's good to be out of the hospital, Kath. I've missed you and Mrs. Walker."

The two women bustled around her solicitously, Kathleen insisting on taking her arm and guiding her down the corridor to the sitting room.

"I'm fine, Kath, I'm not an invalid," she protested.

"Ye canna' be too careful after something like this," Mrs. Walker said, shaking her head and obliging India to sit down in an armchair before the fire. "I'll get this lit right away. It's spring, but there's still a nip in the air, and we dinna' want ye catching cold, now, do we?"

Serena and Maxi entered the room. "I'll get you some tea, India, that should do you good. No, don't worry, Mrs. Walker, you deal with the fire, Maxi and I can take care of it."

"Thank you, Lady Serena," the housekeeper replied grudgingly as they left the room. "I shouldna' be saying this, Miss India, it's not ma' place, I know, but that man, he's nae good. I canna' understand what Lady S. sees in him." She shook her head and lit the match. "It's a crying shame, the likes of him around here. I'll always believe that what precipitated yer mother's death was that critter hangin' around, and the two of them wheedlin' away at her." She bent down and lit the fire.

"What do you mean?" India asked, leaning forward.

"Och, nothing. I'm probably just getting too old, but I still dinna' like him—or her," she added dourly.

India gazed around the room, forlorn now that she'd packed most of the photographs and her mother's lovely cushions. It looked bare. She wondered if Jack would find the same peace and comfort here as she had. But for all she knew, he might turn her favorite room into the hotel accounting office.

"Anybody home?"

Her thoughts were interrupted by Peter Kinnaird's cheerful face popping around the door.

"Hello, Peter, what are you doing here?" she asked with a surprised smile.

"I have a surprise for you, look who's here."

The Marchese came forward, beaming. "My dearest India, how wonderful to see you, *cara*." He came over to the couch and they embraced. "You look well, a little pale perhaps, but on the mend," he said, studying her carefully. "Are you feeling all right?"

"I'm fine, Giordano. But what on earth are you doing here in Scotland?"

"It's a long story, my dear." The Marchese patted her hand gently.

"Well, it's wonderful to have you here. How long are you staying?"

"I'm not quite certain, a few more days, I believe. Tell me, *cara*, are you sure you are feeling well?"

"Absolutely." She gave him a fond smile, touched by his obvious concern.

Kathleen came in with a large tray, passing Peter in the doorway. She stopped abruptly. "Hello, Peter," she said not too graciously. "What are you doing here?"

"I brought the Marchese to see India. He's in Scotland on a visit. We didn't want to take him near the hospital for fear he might pick something up," he said in a low voice.

Kathleen glanced at Maxi, who'd entered the room behind her, then after a moment's hesitation she turned to address the room. "I don't think we'll need this any longer. Probably everyone would prefer a drink. After all, it's almost twelve." She laid the tray on the hall table and turned to reenter the sitting room. "What can I get you, Peter?"

"I'll have a whiskey, thanks."

"Marchese," Kathleen gushed, coming over to them with her hand extended and a fixed smile on her lips. "How wonderful to see you, welcome to Dunbar," she said in a proprietary voice. "It's been an age, hasn't it? Serena, come over and say hello."

The Marchese took Kathleen's hand and bowed slightly over it. But India was surprised to note how cold his eyes became when he turned to Serena. She didn't think she'd ever seen that icy chill below his urbane front.

"I see *you* are in good health," he remarked dryly. It was normal not to like Serena, India acknowledged, but she was taken aback at such hostility coming from him.

"Oh, I'm in cracking form," Serena answered, oblivious.

"Can I get you a drink, Marchese?" Kathleen asked graciously.

"Why not? Such long absence should be celebrated. A glass of Tío Pepe will be perfect, thank you." Once more he inclined his head, and Kathleen went to get the drinks, while Serena wafted off in the opposite direction.

India watched how Maxi's eyes flitted nervously back and forth from Peter to Giordano. He seemed uncomfortable, and there was an odd tension in the room.

"Your grandfather and I were at the Sorbonne together, many years ago. He was a most cultivated and interesting man, highly respected in his field. I wonder, do you take after him?" the Marchese asked Maxi, who suddenly had the look of a hunted rabbit, his skin color sallower than usual. Giordano accepted the glass from Kathleen with a gracious inclination of the head.

Peter came over and sat down next to India, and although he carried on a polite conversation, she felt he was distracted.

"Oh goodness, I didn't expect to see you lot here!" Serena exclaimed, glancing toward the door. "This is turning into a house party. Maybe we should all have some champagne!"

India raised her eyes and saw Jack, her cousin Ian, and another man, who, from the description she'd had of him from Diana, could only be the Texan they had staying at Dalkirk. What on earth were they all doing here? She must have shown some surprise for Peter smiled and leaned toward her.

"Jack brought Ian and Lance over. They're interested in the plans Jack has for the property. Let me introduce you." Peter got up and beckoned to Lance, who came over and gave India a firm handshake and an appraising look. She returned it, liking what she saw.

Jack stayed in the doorway. She knew he was staring at her from across the room and purposely avoided his gaze, her pulse beating faster.

"What a surprise!" Serena exclaimed once more. "Do come in. Jack, what about a drink? Sit down," she added, smiling graciously at Lance. "Are you another American tycoon? We seem to be getting them in droves lately,'' she said archly, extending her long bony hand to him.

At that moment Jack and India made eye contact. For an instant they were united by a common bond of amused understanding. Serena was acting up again and India suddenly felt like laughing. But it didn't diminish the tension in the air. It was disturbing, Maxi looking paler by the minute, everyone else standing on edge, as though expecting something to happen.

"Peter, is everything all right?" she asked in a low voice. "Everyone seems rather tense, don't you think?"

"Really? I hadn't noticed."

But he too seemed somewhat uneasy, and she wasn't reassured. She glanced at Jack, wondering whether he would take those few steps across the room toward her, or if he would continue as he was, at a safe distance.

It was then she turned toward the door and saw Maxi talking to Kathleen before furtively leaving the room.

18

Kathleen was enjoying herself, entertaining the unexpected guests and acting graciously as the lady of the house. She rubbed an imaginary speck of tarnish from a newly polished photo frame and let out a long sigh of contentment, realizing this was just the beginning. Once everything had been suitably dealt with and Dunbar finally belonged to her, she would see to it that things were run as they ought to be—as Daddy would have expected.

For a moment she gazed out of the window and over the lawn, admiring the daffodils, remembering those childhood visits with her widowed father, the long walks through the gardens and the glen, when he would expand upon Dunbar's history and his own plans after Uncle Thomas died and he inherited the property. Even at that early age she had seen herself as mistress of Dunbar, knowing that, as her father's only child, one day those duties would be hers. And now, after so many years, her long-cherished dream of restoring Dunbar to its former glory was on the brink of becoming a reality.

She turned her back on the window and glanced across the room. Noticing India standing by the fire with that old Italian, her elation diminished. If it weren't for Chloë's untimely interference *that* issue would have been taken care of, she reflected sourly. A few more minutes and India would have been out of the running for good. And to crown everything, Chloë had insisted on accompanying India to the hospital, robbing her of another ideal opportunity to finish the job. It was rotten luck, and that Chloë a meddlesome little so-and-so.

She took stock of the room—Serena smiled archly at Jack Buchanan and the other American, while Peter Kinnaird talked to Maxi. Her eyes wandered thoughtfully back to Jack, but she didn't anticipate much difficulty from him. He was obviously potty about India and once *she* was safely out of the way he would leave, of that she had no doubt. This last thought cheered her considerably. After all, India, Jack and the rest of them were nothing but bothersome obstacles in the bigger scheme of things. Again she felt raw determination seep through her. Nothing could be allowed to come between her and Dunbar. She had been groomed for the role, and fate—which had taken a misguided turn—was about to be set aright.

Then she caught sight of Maxi, his face an odd yellowish green, and an idea that had been burgeoning for some time in the back of her fertile brain suddenly blossomed. After all, now was as good a time as any to get him out of the picture. He'd served his purpose and was becoming a dreadful nuisance, nagging, always insisting on phone calls from the street instead of the house, and complicating her life no end. Added to that, she was obliged to keep up the silly pretense of having succumbed to his charm. Ha! She gave an inner chuckle. As if she didn't know exactly what he was up to. But thank God that would very soon be over. In a matter of hours, or perhaps minutes, if her newborn plan went right, the first part of her mission might very well be completed.

Coming back to earth she recalled her immediate duties,

mingling once more with her guests, throwing Lance a
gracious smile while offering the Marchese another sherry
and murmuring graciously to India *en passant.*

It was then she realized Maxi was making some sort of
signal with his eyebrows, and she sidled over to where he
stood sandwiched tightly between Jack and Peter, heavy
beads of sweat forming on his puckered forehead. These
telltale signs made her pay closer attention. Time was closing in on them and this was the moment to act. This was
the very chance she needed, she realized gleefully. Jack
and Peter didn't look at all friendly and she sucked in her
cheeks, hiding her triumph before joining them with a
bright smile.

"Have you everything you need? Jack, you look as if
you could be topped up." She turned swiftly. "Maxi, dear,
I wonder if you would be awfully kind and run to the
kitchen for another bottle of Glenfiddich. I should have
thought of it earlier."

"With pleasure," he murmured, escaping hastily.

Then Kathleen stopped and listened. "Is that *another*
car I hear? I can't think who else could possibly be coming
here today, can you?" she asked innocently, catching the
strange look that passed between Jack and Peter. Her body
tingled with repressed excitement for, at last, after all the
years of patient planning and praying, she knew her moment of triumph was nigh. But this was no time to be
counting her chickens before they were hatched, she admonished herself briskly, waiting a few more interminable
seconds before remarking casually, "Serena, do you suppose Maxi's looking in the wrong cupboard? I'd better go
and look for it myself. Do feel at home," she added before
leaving with a gracious nod as she'd so often seen the
queen give and had taken many hours to perfect in front
of her bedroom mirror.

Crossing the library, she hastened her step, hurtling

along the corridor and down the back stairs, wondering anxiously if she'd make it before Maxi. At last she reached the cloakroom and pushed open the door, peering out into the courtyard. Making sure no one was about, she rushed to where Serena's old Volvo stood parked. She lifted the hood dexterously and scrutinized the engine. Her eyes narrowed and she knew exactly what to do. In two deft movements the job was done. Lowering the hood, she hastened back indoors with a sigh of relief.

Seconds later she heard footsteps hurrying down the back stairs and held her breath as Maxi rushed toward the side door, eyes wild, his pale face sweating profusely.

"What on earth's the matter, Maxi dear?" she inquired, stepping out from among the shadows of the cloakroom.

He gave a startled shriek. "They know. They have made an autopsy. They must have found out everything," he croaked, his eyes shifting furtively, like a trapped rabbit. "That car we heard, that was the police arriving. Where are the car keys? Give them to me," he cried, panicked.

"Here. But why are you so worried?" she asked, taking them off a hook next to the door.

He grabbed the keys with a snarl and shook a finger at her. "I don't know why you're so calm, but don't be too sure of yourself," he shouted, his accent thicker in his rage and fear. "If I get taken in I'll tell them everything, you hear me? Everything! And they'll be after you, too," he added, a hideous glint lighting up his eyes.

"Oh, Maxi, how can you say such dreadful things? Run. Go. Don't worry about me, I'll stave them off," Kathleen answered in a concerned tone while pushing him toward the door. He gave her a last suspicious glance, then mumbled something in German before tearing out of the door, his tweed jacket open and his tie askew.

Once again Kathleen slipped back among the shadows of capes and mackintoshes, pulling her mauve cardigan closely around her shoulders, waiting patiently by the narrow window, hoping—no, praying—she could kill two birds with one stone.

Serena looked at her watch and fidgeted, bored with having to chat. She glanced at the door but there was no sign of Maxi. Or the champagne, or whiskey, or whatever else it was Kath had told him to bring. There wasn't any sign of Kathleen, either. Then she remembered her cousin saying she'd go look for the bottle herself. It was odd she and Maxi were taking so long, though. She looked at Jack and Peter, noticing how serious they appeared. Then she heard the front-door bell. All at once she was gripped by a peculiar sensation, and, excusing herself to Lance and Jack with a seductive smile, she left the drawing room and headed quickly toward the kitchen, meditating crossly upon the injustice of having to share any of the proceeds of Dunbar. The sight of Jack and India together in the drawing room was a sharp reminder of the unfairness of her plight.

"Maxi," she called when she got close to the kitchen. But there was no answer. She frowned. "Kath? Are you there? Did you find the bottle? Perhaps Mrs. Walker put it somewhere else," she remarked, walking into the kitchen, irritated when she found it empty. Then she glanced impatiently out of the window and gave a sudden gasp at the sight of Maxi next to the Volvo, obviously agitated, dropping the keys on the cobblestones and then jumping into the car as though fleeing something. She rushed out of the kitchen and down the stairs, not wanting to be left behind. Plus, it was *her* car. He had no damn business driving off in a tizzy without asking. What bloody cheek!

Kathleen's hands twitched as she fingered the pearls at her throat. A present from Aunt El, she remembered cynically. A gift to a poor relation for which she had to be eternally grateful. To think the old bitch had only left her a couple of miserable worthless brooches, and enough money to feed a cat.

As so often before, she found herself lamenting those three drastic days that had changed her destiny. If only Daddy had hung on seventy-two more miserable hours, *she* would have inherited Dunbar, and *they* would have had to kowtow to her. But enough of that. By taking destiny into her own hands she would finally obtain what some warped twist of fate had denied her.

She hoped Serena had heard her remark as she'd left the drawing room, for there was still no sign of her. Surely she would wonder where Maxi had gone and look for him? She glanced anxiously out of the window, relieved that the old Volvo needed time for the engine to warm up.

Kathleen's nerves were on edge. Where could the wretched girl be? It would be too unjust if after all this trouble her plans were thwarted again.

But at last she heard footsteps echoing from afar and Serena's high-pitched voice calling in the distance. Then she watched and waited in breathless apprehension as her cousin came tearing through the cloakroom, hair flying, nearly falling on the bottom step before racing through the door and dashing toward the now-moving vehicle. Kathleen clasped her hands tightly, heart pounding as Serena grabbed the car door, pulled it open and flung herself in beside Maxi.

As the vehicle picked up speed, Kathleen stood behind the net curtain and smiled. "Bon voyage," she whispered, raising her hand and waving as the car disappeared around the corner. Closing her eyes, she relaxed, jumping to the next phase of her plan, allowing it to take shape although it was still vague.

All at once she remembered her ancestor Fergus. He, too, had been faced with a similar plight. She felt the tug of the past reaching out to her and wondered all at once if he was guiding her from beyond the grave. Suddenly she remembered his dirk, that deadly dagger with its jewel-encrusted hilt lying sharp and lethal on the velvet bed of a small glass-topped cabinet, exhibited amongst many other family treasures. A smile touched her lips and she left the cloakroom with a newfound sense of power. She was on a mission, a mission directed by powers reaching out from the past.

When she reached the landing, she straightened her old tweed skirt and resumed her previous composure, then made her way sedately down the passage and back to the drawing room, where her guests would naturally be expecting her.

"Hey!" Serena shouted petulantly. "What do you think you're doing grabbing my car without asking? You were leaving without me!"

"Get in and shut up." Maxi leaned forward, gripping the steering wheel frantically, and screeched down the drive. "Is there any other way out of here but the main drive?"

"Yes, but it's blocked. Why are you in such a hurry to leave? I thought we were staying for dinner," Serena shrieked as the car picked up speed.

Maxi ignored her, pressing his foot down hard on the accelerator, his eyes glued to the rearview mirror.

She twisted her head around. "Maxi, those are police cars back there. Why are they following us?" she cried, desperately trying to fasten her seat belt. "Don't go so fast, you're insane!"

"*Ach, lieber Gott!* Don't you see, you *dummkopf?*" He glared at her sideways, viciously. "They know everything.

They saw the body and the results of India's blood test. I tell you, they know. *Scheise!*'' he exclaimed, looking in the mirror again. "They're on to us."

The car swerved at the end of the drive and out onto the narrow country road at one hundred and twenty miles an hour.

"What are you talking about?" Serena screamed, fear and desperation gripping her as she tried to make sense of his words. "Slow down, for Christ's sake, you'll get us killed."

But he paid no attention, taking the corner on two wheels. Serena glanced back through the rear window, terrified, seeing various cars on their tail and wishing desperately that Maxi would slow down, yet knowing something dreadful had occurred.

"Maxi, what have you done?" she whimpered, hanging on for dear life. Then the truth suddenly dawned on her. "Oh my God," she cried, gazing at him in terrified horror. "India, Mummy. That's why you were so worried about the graves that day, wasn't it? There wasn't any road being widened at all and Jack knew. Oh my God! It was you. *You* killed Mummy and you were trying to kill India, too. They probably think I—"

In that last dreadful moment before the car swerved off the road and smashed into the tree, Serena let go a horrific scream, a last desperate plea of agony and remorse.

Then only darkness prevailed.

As soon as he saw the car crushed against the tree, Jack drew off the road and slammed on the brakes, skidding to a halt as mud splattered the Porsche. "I'll go take a look," he said grimly, unfastening the seat belt and jumping out.

Lance got out the other side and nodded. "I'll keep you covered."

The accident looked bad but Jack approached cautiously, careful not to slip on the wet soggy ground. The Volvo had obviously hit the tree head-on for there was little left of the hood, squashed like an accordion against the heavy tree trunk. It was doubtful anyone could have survived the impact. He could hear the other cars stopping behind him, realizing Peter, Ian and the police must have arrived close on their heels.

Soon he was close enough to see two inanimate bodies lying covered in blood, mud and shards of glass. Serena had been thrown through the windshield, and leaves and a branch had fallen on her, while Maxi was slumped in the driver's seat, his head lolling against his chest at an odd angle.

Jack went immediately to the passenger door, trying desperately to open it, anxious to see if they were still alive. But it was jammed, and he pulled harder, trying to dislodge it. Finally he wrenched the door open and reached for Serena's drooping arm, his hands grazed by the splinters of shattered windshield covering her as he desperately felt for her pulse. But there was no response. Not even a weak throb. Gently he drew her mangled body back through the broken windshield, glass falling like a shower of crystals, swallowing hard as her mane of blond hair, covered in blood, fell back to reveal her gashed, torn face.

At that moment, Peter, Ian and the others reached him. The police rushed to the other side of the smashed vehicle, trying to ascertain if Maxi was still alive.

"She's gone," Jack said quietly, laying Serena's body back gently in the remains of the tattered seat.

"Good Lord," Ian exclaimed, white with shock. "This is unbelievable, simply dreadful."

"A shocking business," Peter agreed gravely, casting a sad glance to where Serena lay like a broken doll. For a moment the four men stood in silence.

Then Lance voiced a tough yet pragmatic opinion. "It's

a terrible thing to happen to anyone but at least that's taken care of business, and India won't be in any more danger, thank God.''

''Yeah.'' Jack agreed, looking away. ''Still, I would rather have seen justice done.''

''Perhaps it's better this way,'' Peter said thoughtfully. ''If Serena had been tried for murder, it would have been ghastly for everyone. Maybe it's a blessing in disguise.''

''I still find it hard to believe Serena would be capable of such a heinous act,'' Ian said, shaking his head miserably, unable to withdraw his horror-struck gaze from Serena's lifeless form. ''She used to be quite a pleasant little thing as a child, you know. Really quite sweet,'' he murmured absently.

Peter took his arm and drew him away. ''We'd better leave and let the police do their job, old chap,'' he said quietly, guiding him back to the road.

''Yes, of course,'' Ian mumbled, obviously still in shock. ''I just can't imagine why she'd *do* something so dreadful. My God, to think of poor Aunt El—not to mention India.''

When they reached the cars, Jack asked the question that was preying on all their minds. ''Who's going to tell India?''

''Why don't you?'' Ian asked.

Jack shook his head and walked to the Porsche. ''No, but someone has to. Peter, maybe you'd better go.''

''Are you sure? Don't you think you should be the one to tell her, all things considered?''

Their eyes locked for an instant and Jack hesitated before replying. ''No, you go.''

''All right.'' Peter sighed.

Jack stopped for a minute before getting into the car, wondering if he should be the one to break the news to her, if only to let her know how much he cared. But he changed his mind and got into the Porsche. It was too late and there was no point in prolonging the agony that seeing her again would bring. He jerked the key in the ignition, waved to Peter and drove off with Lance to Dalkirk. He was depressed, sick of the endless trail of deaths that seemed to follow him everywhere. His only relief was the knowledge that India was finally out of danger, and he needn't worry anymore.

On seeing the men exchange quick tense glances, then leave the room without a word, India had risen, agitated. "Giordano, what on earth is going on?"

He laid a soothing hand on her arm. "I will explain everything, *cara*, but first we will sit down next to the fire. Perhaps another glass of sherry," he suggested.

"Allow me." Kathleen came hurrying forward to relieve him of his glass, then moved toward the silver tray of decanters. India perched nervously on the arm of the sofa, waiting impatiently while Giordano settled opposite.

"What was that all about?" she asked, waving toward the door. "Why did they all leave in such a flurry?"

"They did seem in rather a rush," Kathleen agreed, frowning while handing her a glass of sherry that she didn't want. "It was almost as though something wasn't quite right. Didn't you think Maxi looked rather pale, India dear?"

"Now that you mention it, yes, he did. And Serena left the room like a scalded cat. Then those police officers arrived and everyone went rushing out of here as though the place was on fire!" she exclaimed, throwing up her hands and almost spilling her drink. That was all she needed. Being in the same room as Jack for over half an hour had left her tense and anxious. And now, to crown everything, there seemed to be some other problem going on that she wasn't privy to.

She glanced at Giordano, knowing there was no use hurrying him. He'd tell her in his own time. With a pang she recalled Jack's expression as he'd rushed out of the door earlier. He wore the same look he'd had that terrible night in Rio. Instinctively she knew something was very wrong.

The Marchese crossed his tapered fingers thoughtfully over his knee and sighed. "I am afraid that what I am about to disclose is no pleasant matter, *cara*. In fact, it may cause you much pain. But alas, the truth must be revealed and the culprits brought to justice."

"What do you mean?" India leaned forward, now seriously worried.

"It was the letter. You remember the letter you gave me in Lausanne, India?"

"Of course I remember."

"It was the letter that made me put two and two together. That and Mrs. Walker's detailed description of your symptoms," he said with a shake of his head. "I called Dunbar from Switzerland, and after what she told me I caught the next plane out."

"I'm sorry, Giordano, but you're talking in riddles."

He sighed, putting his glass down carefully on the small lacquer table before looking at her sadly. "The terrible truth, *cara mia,* is that Serena and Maxi von Lowendorf poisoned your mother and were attempting to do the same to you."

"Excuse me?" India exclaimed.

"Oh surely not, Marchese. Poor Aunt El, it's too dreadful!" Kathleen gave a horrified gasp.

"I am afraid so, my dear," he replied sympathetically, leaning toward her as she sat, face puckered, hands clasped in her lap, her expression one of appalled disbelief.

India was digesting Giordano's words. Her mother murdered, and she herself barely escaping a similar fate at the hands of her own sister? It couldn't be true, it was too far-fetched. Serena was not a pleasant person, but from there to accusing her of murder— There had to be a mistake. "Are you perfectly sure, Giordano?" she asked doubtfully.

"I'm afraid we have every proof, my dear. Your so-called food poisoning was nothing other than arsenic." He stopped, letting the words sink in.

"Arsenic?" Kathleen parroted.

"Giordano, you can't be serious," India cried, jumping up from the sofa and pacing the room. "I know Serena's impossible, but to believe she'd be capable of murder— I'm sorry—" she shook her head "—but that's an awfully long stretch."

"Not so amazing, I'm afraid, since Maxi killed his aunt in exactly the same manner a few years ago. The family hushed up the scandal, of course, but when you gave me Elspeth's letter, a little bell went off in the back of my old brain. It didn't take long for me to have some private research done, and after my subsequent talk with Mrs. Walker, I knew sadly that my suspicions were amply founded." He rose stiffly, removed an envelope from his breast pocket and handed it to her.

She took it hesitantly, then opened the envelope and withdrew the contents. It was an autopsy analysis. She raised her eyes to Giordano's in appalled dismay as her mother's name leaped from the page. She read the date, startled to find it had been performed only yesterday. "You allowed them to do this to Mummy?"

He nodded, his face gray and furrowed with sorrow. "It was inevitable, I'm afraid. We had to have the body exhumed to get the proof we needed. You see, your blood test contained arsenic, and we had to know if there was some in poor Elspeth's body, too." He sat down again, leaning heavily on his walking stick as he did so, exhausted by the effort.

"But this is simply dreadful," Kathleen cried, her eyes

filling. "Poor Aunt El. Oh, and you, too, poor dear," she exclaimed, turning to India. "It's too awful. And to think we allowed that dreadful creature into the house as a guest." She pressed a hankie to her lips and shook her head vehemently.

"But why didn't the doctor say anything to me?" India asked, bewildered, glancing now at the second page where the results of her own blood test were listed. They left her in no doubt as to the truth of the Marchese's words. "I was never shown any of this in the hospital. In fact, the results showed that it *was* food poisoning."

"We didn't want you to panic, *cara,* or do anything foolish. It was too dangerous and you were very unwell," he responded quietly.

"How could Serena have done this? No wonder she was so frightened. I should have realized something wasn't right, I should've been more observant and come sooner, I—" She paced the floor once more, the test results still dangling in her hand.

"Nobody is to blame except those who murdered her," he answered bitterly. "And they shall be brought to justice. It was a tragedy that neither you nor anybody else could have avoided."

"How could you possibly be held at fault, India, dear?" Kathleen asked as she sat on the edge of the sofa, her eyes welling with unshed tears. "If anyone's to blame, I am. I never should have gone up to Great-Aunt Moira's that day and left her alone with them." She hid her face in the handkerchief.

"India, there is another thing I must tell you, something else that was discovered. Apparently Elspeth had a slight heart condition that none of us knew about." For an instant his eyes fell on Kathleen, but then he smiled sadly. "It was so like her not to worry anyone with her health. I'm afraid the poisoning merely precipitated her death."

"That doesn't make it any better, Giordano."

"I know. But we must resign ourselves. There is nothing else we can do," he said softly.

She nodded reluctantly. "I still find it hard to believe Serena was capable of it. She must be mad, but Maxi's not. He obviously put her up to it, because frankly, I don't think Serena has the brainpower to concoct something as sophisticated as this," she ended bitterly, still wanting to doubt Serena's involvement and wondering if her half sister would be charged with murder. Perhaps they could get her off on a plea of insanity, for it was clear that she was not in her right mind. As for Maxi—she ground her teeth—that was another matter. She clenched her fist angrily. He *was* a murderer. He'd killed her mother, tried to kill *her* and pushed Serena over the brink.

Kathleen got up and, murmuring something about Mrs. Walker, slipped quietly from the room.

India massaged her throbbing head, feeling dizzy. She leaned against the mantelpiece, trying to connect all the pieces, realizing that something didn't make sense. Why, now that they'd sold the property to Jack, would Serena bother to take the risk of killing her? After all, she'd made enough money from the sale of Dunbar to keep her in the style she enjoyed for the rest of her life.

"Where are Maxi and Serena?" She'd forgotten about the immediate situation, her mind so taken up with the horrific news. "And what about Jack and the others? What have they got to do with all this?"

"A lot." Giordano sighed before giving her a tired little smile. "Jack has been *splendido*. Also Peter and the other American, Lance. As for those two rogues, Maxi and Serena, I believe they fled when they heard the police cars approaching. That is why the boys rushed out in that precipitate manner."

"You mean they're actually chasing them?" India exclaimed, suddenly realizing Jack might be in danger.

"I believe so. I hope that by this time they have already apprehended those dastardly villains and have them safely under lock and key. It would not do to have them on the run," he remarked dryly.

"But this is ghastly!" She ran her hand through her hair as visions of Jack lying dead with a bullet through him flashed before her. She turned quickly to Giordano. "What about Jack? What if something happens to him?" she asked, suddenly panicked.

"*Calma, carina.* Jack knows how to take care of himself—" Giordano gave her a wry smile "—and I think he would know how to take care of you, too, if you'd allow him," he remarked, watching her closely.

India shook her head and walked across the room to the window. "That's all over now, I'm afraid," she said, looking out into the gray afternoon but seeing only him. "It was my fault. I wouldn't listen when he tried to explain about Dunbar. I never even gave him a chance. And afterward, well, afterward I made up a lot of lies and suddenly it was too late." She turned and came closer to the fire, hugging herself tightly, wishing she could rid herself of her fear for Jack and the terrible pain and sense of loss that all this tragedy had caused. *Please, dear God, let him be all right,* she prayed silently.

The Marchese gave a soft chuckle. "It is never too late, *cara mia.* Where there is love there is always room for forgiveness and new beginnings."

India stared at the dying embers shifting in the grate, wishing Giordano's words were true. But he hadn't been present at the hospital, hadn't seen Jack's stony expression as she'd signed the documents, or the stiff formal manner in which he'd left. And it would be foolish to forget the true reason he wanted Dunbar.

"It still doesn't change the fact that what he really wanted was his hotel, Giordano. He still does. Even though he didn't connive with Serena, he wanted it all the same. I've tried to convince myself otherwise, but deep down I think business is all that really matters to Jack."

"Do you?" The Marchese raised a sardonic eyebrow. "Do you really believe that a man who is putting his life on the line to protect you and do justice for you at this very moment thinks only of business?" He rose, straightening himself stiffly, then leaned on his cane and came over to where she stood. Putting his finger under her chin he looked at her severely. "You are a bright, intelligent girl, India, but you are also as stubborn as a Sicilian mule. That man cares for you. Don't be too blind or too proud to see it for what it is. Remember what I told you back in Lausanne?" He lowered his hand and placed it over his heart with a deep smile. "You must learn to see with the eyes of the soul."

India was about to answer when the door opened. Her heart stopped when she saw Peter.

"Awfully sorry to interrupt," he said, hesitating for a moment before joining them before the fire. He shoved his hands in the pockets of his corduroys, seemingly engrossed by the faded geometric pattern of the Turkish rug.

"Tell us everything, Peter. Is everyone all right? What happened? I mean, did they catch Maxi and— Oh, it's too awful to think of Serena as a criminal, isn't it? I'm sure that man must have put her up to it," India said, appealing to him desperately.

"Actually, I've some rather rotten news, I'm afraid." He coughed, embarrassed.

"Not Jack," she whispered hoarsely, closing her eyes in silent prayer. "Please, tell me it's not Jack."

"Good Lord, no! Jack's fine. He's probably back at Dalkirk by now.'' Peter gave a nervous laugh as India's head spun, dizzy with relief. ''Actually it's Serena.''

''Did they catch them?''

''Well, it's a bit more serious than that, I'm afraid. There's been an accident. They were driving awfully fast, you see.'' He glanced at her and hesitated once more. ''They must have taken the bend at a terrible speed because the car had obviously lost control. I'm afraid she and Maxi were killed outright when they crashed into a tree,'' he finished quietly.

India gazed at him in horrified silence, Jack's safety forgotten as the shock of her sister's death hit home. She closed her eyes as regret and a yearning nostalgia that things might have been different engulfed her.

''You had better tell us all about it, Peter,'' Giordano insisted, seating himself back in the wing chair.

After fifteen minutes and a full account of the events, India felt deeply saddened, yet accepting of Serena's death. She hoped her sister would now find the peace that had eluded her in life.

''Thanks for coming here and telling us, Peter,'' she said finally. ''You're a brick.''

''That's what I'm here for,'' he replied gruffly, giving her arm a squeeze. India reached up and kissed his cheek gratefully. ''I suppose I'd better be getting back,'' He glanced at his watch. ''Di must be getting worried. Marchese, will you be coming with me or would you rather stay? And what about you, Indy? Why don't you come back to Dalkirk and join us for dinner? You shouldn't stay here on your own.''

For a moment she hesitated, then thought better of it. There was no point. It would merely place her and Jack in another awkward situation. ''Thanks, Peter, but I'd better stay. The police may want to talk to me. And I suppose I'd better talk to the minister and make arrangements for

Serena's burial," she said quietly. "I'll leave for Switzerland directly after it's over." Then she raised her eyes, perplexed. "Why do you think they did it, Peter? If I'd gone on refusing to sell to Jack I could understand the motive, but now that's all been settled I don't understand why they would bother. Unless she wanted to inherit my share as well. That's the only possible reason."

Peter looked surprised. "I didn't realize you'd sold to Jack."

"I asked both Jack and Serena not to mention the sale to anyone before I'd left for Switzerland."

"I see." His thick sandy eyebrows joined in a frown. "It is odd about Serena, now that you mention it. I knew she was greedy, but I wouldn't have imagined she'd go to such drastic lengths. After all, Dunbar was no paltry sum. Probably more than even *she* could have spent in a lifetime. It's not in character with her behavior at all." He shook his head sadly. "I hate to say this, Indy, but it's probably a blessing they went this way."

"Perhaps." She hesitated then decided to say it anyway. "Peter, please thank Jack for all he's done." She looked away, embarrassed.

"Of course. But why don't you come and thank him yourself?"

She shook her head firmly. "No, Peter. We've said all we had to say to one another, but thanks anyway."

"It's your call." He shrugged helplessly and turned to the Marchese who was looking sternly at India.

"You are being most foolish, *cara*," he said. "I hope you will not live to regret it. Anyway, you should not remain here on your own. Come with us."

"Don't worry, Marchese, I'll be here." Kathleen, who had slipped back into the room unobserved, smiled reassuringly. "What a dreadful business," she said, turning to Peter. "So awful to think that poor Aunt El was murdered in cold blood. Serena must have been demented,'' she added with a deep sigh.

Peter frowned for an instant, then nodded regretfully. "I suppose we'd better be off."

"E, non che niente da fare." Giordano threw his free hand up in despair and gave India a disapproving shake of his head before allowing her to embrace him. She slipped her arm through his to assist the slow descent of the porch steps to the front door.

Then Kathleen and India stood on the front steps, waving as the car drove off. The sky had darkened subtly and approaching thunder could be heard in the distance.

"I think we're in for some bad weather," Kathleen remarked as they linked arms and walked back up to the hall.

"So much has happened, Kath," India said gazing at the drum table, remembering her mother. "So many dreadful things. But in all this I've been blessed to have you next to me." She gave her cousin a warm hug.

"You poor dear," Kathleen murmured, her face a mask of sympathy and understanding. "You must be exhausted. But I do think we should tell Mrs. Walker right away, don't you? I'd hate her to learn the news of Serena's death through the bush telegraph. She'd be dreadfully hurt. It's going to be an awful shock for her as it is."

India agreed, and as they headed toward the kitchen, she felt deeply grateful that, in all this chaos, there was at least one person left she could truly trust.

That evening Jack dressed for dinner in a somber mood. He felt like hell. He'd lost the woman he loved and acquired a property he now didn't want. In fact, looking at it objectively, he'd pretty much screwed up his life. He opened the chest of drawers and took out the first sweater in the pile, pulling it on aimlessly, his mind filled with

Dunbar. All his grandiose plans had evaporated so mysteriously, like the early morning mist up on the moors. Gone was the vision he'd harbored of a perfect getaway with tastefully decorated rooms filled with finely selected antiques, where guests chatted over silver pots of afternoon tea, while a discreet, impeccably trained staff catered to their every whim and fancy.

Now he envisaged another Dunbar, a tad less shabby, with more of _her_ touches, _her_ scent, _her_ flavor. If he closed his eyes he could almost reach out and touch the image. And there was laughter—her laughter and Molly's.

He pulled himself up sharp and dragged his fingers through his hair in frustration. The truth was, it was too damn late.

A bolt of lightning ripped across the sky, followed by a shattering blast that left the old-fashioned windows shaking in their casements. It was a grim night—and it reflected his feelings perfectly.

His thoughts strayed back to India, wondering what she might be doing at this very moment. Peter had told him she'd taken the news of Serena's death sadly but philosophically. At least she wasn't alone since her cousin— who seemed almost overprotective at times—would be there.

By the time he reached the dining room his mood had deteriorated another couple of notches, and Chloë's cheerful greeting didn't improve matters.

"Gosh, you look simply ghastly, Yank," she said, looking him over critically as he walked in.

Jack mumbled a grouchy hello, gave her a sour look and went to the Georgian sideboard, decked with silver and Royal Doulton dishes, to ply himself with truite à l'amandine and baby potatoes.

"Are you in one of your moods?" she asked between mouthfuls, her knife wobbling precariously. "It serves you jolly well right. You deserve to feel rotten after everything you've done to poor Indy. It's all your fault. If you hadn't wanted Dunbar in the first place, none of this would have happened."

"Chloë, leave poor Jack alone and stop interfering. He can't help being a Dunbar descendant any more than India can," Diana murmured reprovingly.

Jack bit back the response that hovered on the tip of his tongue and sat down, casting a forbidding look in Chloë's direction.

Lance grinned at her and made the time-out sign.

"Oh, all right, be like that." Chloë shrugged and gave an umbraged sniff. "If you can't take a joke, far be it from me—"

"Chloë!" Diana exclaimed and frowned at her, then turned to her guests. "Jack, dear, will you be going to Serena's funeral?"

"I don't know. Maybe, maybe not. I haven't really thought about it."

"You see? He can't even make up his mind about something as simple as that."

There was a simultaneous "Shut up, Chloë," from the table at large and finally she subsided, taking refuge in the creamed spinach.

Peter picked up the bottle of wine he'd been examining. "Interesting bottle, this. I have to say that I'm partial to a good Montrachet. I hope you'll enjoy it, Jack."

"Perhaps it would be nice if you *served* it, dear, before everyone finishes their fish," Diana hinted patiently.

"Yes, yes, of course." Peter gave a sheepish grin and fixed the corkscrew into position.

"Indy'll be glad to get home and leave this dreadful mess behind her," Chloë observed with a woeful sigh, not about to let Jack off the hook. "Of course, there really isn't much for her to stay for now that you've stolen Dunbar from her, is there?" she added sweetly.

"I did *not* steal Dunbar from her," Jack snapped, irritated in spite of himself. "I paid a very fair price for her share," realizing as soon as he'd spoken that he'd messed up.

"Well, excuse me! I'm sorry if I've offended your sensibilities. So you did get her to sell to you, after all. What about Serena? I suppose she wanted the lot!"

"I've no idea," he mumbled, angry that she'd got him to betray his promise to India.

"I suppose you were meant to keep it quiet," Chloë added astutely as Jack's temper rose with his color.

"You know, this woman needs taking in hand. Some poor idiot should marry her and give us all a break," he commented through gritted teeth, casting a glance at Lance.

"Sticks and stones may break my bones, but words will never hurt me," Chloë quoted blithely, raising her pert nose in a dignified fashion, then smiling mischievously at Lance who sat across from her, obviously enthralled.

Peter finished his rounds with the wine bottle, and dinner proceeded with no further interruptions. The Georgian dinning table was attractively laid with white lace tablemats, the family sterling and two handsome candelabras flanked by colorful wild flowers tastefully arranged in a faience soup tureen. But the candlesticks only served as a reminder of San Telmo. Jack looked away, wondering if there would ever be any reprieve from having his memory and his heart jolted. Life had presented him with a unique opportunity to recapture happiness and he'd blown it.

The Marchese was taking a benign view of the banter and, smiling congenially, he raised his glass. "I would like to make a small toast," he said. "To justice, and to the triumph of Good over Evil. *In sumo,* let us drink to all that ends well."

Murmurs of *Hear! Hear!* followed, then they drank in silence, each reminded in their own way of the events of the day.

The strident ring of the old telephone in the hall broke the momentary silence.

"Oh gosh, I think Mrs. MacC. is still in the kitchen. Darling, can you get it?" Diana appealed to Peter.

"Of course," he replied, laying down his napkin and excusing himself.

The Marchese continued to chat with Diana, while Chloë smiled seductively at Lance. The two seemed to be getting on like a house on fire, Jack thought, smiling despite himself for the first time that day. Texas was definitely on Chloë's agenda.

The door opened and Peter returned, his step hurried, his face pale. "That was the constable."

Jack's eyebrows shot up. "What's wrong?" he asked, pushing his chair back automatically and rising.

"It wasn't an accident," Peter said in a thin voice. "Serena's car was tampered with." He exchanged a distressed look with the other men. "Someone fiddled with the steering so that the car would go out of control at a certain speed. That means—"

"Someone wanted them out of the way," Lance supplied.

Jack felt unsteady. He gripped the back of the dining chair, his head spinning. "Who?" he asked. "Who could possibly want them dead. It doesn't make any sense—"

"Oh, but it does."

They all turned as Diana spoke, her face ashen as her eyes met her husband's.

"Oh my God," he whispered, horrified. "I should have realized, should have thought of this before."

"We all should have," Diana replied anguished. "Think about it. Kathleen's always portraying herself as the mistress of Dunbar. Perhaps missing out on the inheritance by so little has been eating her up all these years and none of us ever knew. Oh good Lord!" she cried jumping up. "India's alone in the house with her. Something has to be done at once!"

"I'm going to Dunbar." Jack hastened to the door. "Peter, you get the police, and meet me there as soon as you can. Di, if I can't get in do you know where there's a spare key?"

"Mrs. Walker leaves the key to the side door in a flower pot on the left of the back door entrance," she whispered hoarsely. "Do be careful, Jack. I'll get your jacket." He nodded absently, reaching the door but not hearing the latter part of the sentence; his only thought was to reach India in time.

Lance had risen and was pulling something out of the small of his back. "Better take this," he said, handing Jack the Smith & Wesson he'd had on him since earlier that afternoon. "Sure you don't want company?"

Jack shook his head. "Thanks, but I'll handle it. This is my call." He slipped the gun into the pocket of the shooting jacket that Diana was handing him.

"Be careful driving, won't you?" Chloë called after him as he departed hastily, leaving Peter and Lance to get the police while Diana, Chloë and the Marchese stood silent and helpless, with nothing left to do but hope and pray.

"My, what a dreich night." Mrs. Walker sighed, shaking her head woefully as she peeled four large potatoes for the Scotch broth simmering on the stove. "To think of poor Lady Serena murderin' her ain mother and now lying cold in the morgue herself. My, oh my. Ma' poor nerves canna' take much more," she said sniffing loudly.

"I know, Mrs. Walker. This whole dreadful episode has been so trying on all of us. Imagine, Serena actually plotting to kill poor Aunt El with that dreadful man," Kathleen sympathized, counting the napkins she was folding. "Mrs. Walker, there are still three missing," she exclaimed frowning. "I don't know what happens to napkins—they're like socks, always a couple lost."

"Aye, but never heed Lady Kathleen, they'll turn up sooner or later. Poor Miss India," she continued, raising her eyes and shaking her gray head once more. "She told me earlier that she's leaving straight after the funeral." She heaved a gusty sigh. "I suppose she's right to go, poor wee lassie. What is there for her to stay fer now that the American gentleman's bought us out? I just canna' imagine Dunbar as a hotel, can ye?" She attacked the last potato. "But I'm awf'y relieved we're all going to be able to stay. Miss India said he gave her his word as a gentleman," she added, throwing the potato peels into the sink.

"What *are* you talking about, Mrs. Walker?" Kathleen asked blankly.

"Ye mean she hasna' told ye?" Mrs. Walker asked, surprised. "She told me this afternoon that the only reason she'd sold her share to him and allowed Lady Serena to do the same was because he'd agreed to keep the staff and the tenants on. Such a sweet, thoughtful lass that she is."

Kathleen sat erect, the last napkin lying half-folded before her. "She's said nothing of this to me."

Mrs. Walker shrugged and began chopping the carrots. "Och well, ye canna' expect her to remember everything wi' all she's got on her mind, poor lass. She was probably going to tell ye later this evening. Poor Lady Serena. Such a troubled girl she was, and madness in the family of course, as ye yersel' pointed out, Lady Kathleen. All the same, I still canna' believe it." She sighed and gazed at the carrots. "And that dreadful critter putting her up to it, nae doubt. To think we had a murderer under our very noses and we didna' ken.'' Mrs. Walker gave another disapproving sniff and pursed her lips.

"Yes. Simply awful,'' Kathleen murmured absently, her thoughts miles away as she registered the horrifying truth—Dunbar, sold by those two traitors to a stranger.

She stared down at the napkins in disbelief. All the months and years of careful planning shattered in a single sentence. To come so close, to be within a hairsbreadth, to have executed the first part of her plan to perfection that very afternoon only to have it all smashed to smithereens. It was unbearable. She closed her eyes for a second, trying desperately to keep a grip on herself. She must hold on, must see it through. There had to be a way. Fate could not be so unjust as to deny her the one dream she had coveted for as long as she could remember.

She steadied herself, then got up. "I'd better make sure all the windows are closed, and lock up for the night. This weather is dreadful.'' She shuddered as another clap of thunder burst overhead and the wind rattled the windows.

"Och, that was a bad one!'' Mrs. Walker exclaimed, peering through the window as more lightning zigzagged across the sky in a mad frenzy. "Dinner'll be ready in just a wee while.''

"Don't worry about that tonight, Mrs. Walker. We'll just take the trolley into the sitting room. You finish off here and then go and put your feet up for the evening. You must be worn-out after all the strain. India and I can fend for ourselves.'' Kathleen smiled kindly.

"Och, thank ye, Lady Kathleen. I canna' deny that ma' legs are fairly achin'. A wee rest'll do them nae harm, what with tomorrow an' all.''

"Exactly. You get a good rest, Mrs. Walker. Goodnight. I'll pop along and see how India's doing, poor child, and put these in the laundry on my way.'' Kathleen picked up

he pile of folded napkins and headed for the door, her
mind filled once more with the image of her ancestor Fergus. If anyone had wanted Dunbar as much as she did, it
was he. Fergus, she knew, would have understood. And
like him, she would override any obstacles to reach her
goal.

Jack drove blindly, scarcely able to see beyond the
fogged-up windshield. Lightning ripped through the dark
gloomy night and thunder roared ferociously overhead,
like the fierce, unrelenting wrath of an avenging god. All
he could do was follow the road instinctively, fear for India
and his determination guiding him where his vision failed.

What should have taken fifteen minutes took him close
on thirty. Then, to his relief, he was able to distinguish the
gates of Dunbar through the downpour. He went up the
drive, increasing speed slightly.

The house stood in eerie darkness, the only light coming
from the periodic flashes of lightning and his headlamps.
Instinctively he switched them off and headed quietly
through the back, past the unused stables into the courtyard. He turned the engine off abruptly, then pulled his
jacket over his head. In a few quick strides he reached the
back door. It was locked. He bent down, groping in the
flowerpot for the key. Finally he found it and slipped inside
the cloakroom.

He stopped and listened, removing the gun cautiously
from his pocket, making his way swiftly up the back stairs,
every instinct alert. There was no sound except for the
storm growing more distant. But the tension was there,
sharp and pungent like the cutting edge of a well-
sharpened blade. He sensed danger nearing as he mounted
the stairs, stopping only when the ancient wood creaked
too loudly. Slowly he continued, reaching the corridor that
he knew led to the library. Holding the gun high, his back

to the bookshelves, he eased down the passage, stopping
every few seconds to listen and feel, trying to distinguish
something that could help or guide him. When he finally
reached the library he peered carefully round the door
deliberately focusing his vision on the furniture outlined
by the glow of the dying embers in the grate.

The room stood empty. Nothing stirred but the ghostly
shadows prancing playfully back and forth from the windows to the bookshelves. Stealthily he moved toward the
door that led into the hall, stopping dead in his tracks when
he heard Kathleen's voice close by, trying to ascertain
which direction her voice was coming from. Then in tense
agony he waited—waited till the moment was right.

19

When a burst of lightning plunged the house into darkness, India left her room, meeting Kathleen on the landing. Together they crept gingerly down the stairs to search for candles. The next thing India knew, her back was to the wall, the sharp icy point of a blade pricking the skin of her throat.

Kathleen's hate-filled voice ranted above the storm.

"None of you ever stopped to think about how *I* felt when I lost Dunbar. Nobody even cared," Kathleen hissed, pressing the blade closer, making India shrink as far back as she could.

"All those years of 'Kathleen dearest, would you mind awfully fetching my hankie?' and 'Oh dear, there's a dreadful draft, do close that door, would you, Kathleen dearest?'" She gave a strident laugh, like a wild hyena. "As though I was a lapdog, willing to fetch and carry for measly treats and a pat on the head instead of receiving my rightful due. None of you cared that you'd robbed me of what should have been mine," she cried, her glinting eyes filled with hate, rage and bitterness.

"Dunbar was my father's right—*my* right. And because of three miserable days, I was denied." She gave a hysterical laugh and withdrew the dagger slightly. "But you're all fools, and you've played into my hands, each and every one of you. Even that imbecile Maxi. Did you really think it was Serena he wanted? Ha, not him. He planned to do the lot of us in and get everything, everything, do you hear me? He would have killed Serena, then married me if I allowed him, then killed me, too. After all, things could have gone badly for him if I'd been around to tell the tale. Or perhaps he thought of doing it the other way around, killing me off and then her." She laughed heartily. "What a fool. I can't tell you how amusing it was watching him try to seduce me, so full of himself, certain I was a randy old maid, desperate for sex. I led him on, of course, let him believe he was succeeding. It was his idea to eliminate your mother, poisoning her little by little, when I mentioned her heart condition that she didn't know I was aware of," she added almost casually.

"It was brilliant, letting that weak, tender heart of hers slow down, until one day it simply went. Pop! Just like that. And at such a convenient moment. I wasn't even here." She moved back, giggling like a silly schoolgirl. "It was a merciful death—more than she deserved, actually, now that I come to think of it. Of course, I knew I'd have Serena and that gigolo to deal with, but that wasn't difficult, not with that old Volvo she drove around in."

India trembled. It could all end right here. Horror and chagrin battled with the underlying will to survive, forcing her to calm her raging wits and summon up enough strength to keep her mind clear. It was her only weapon. Kathleen hovered over her, a dark mass distorted by shadows and lightning, her eyes glazed and gleaming like those of a stalking panther.

"You feel this?" India flinched as the blade nicked her throat and a tiny trickle of blood trailed down her neck. "Do you know to whom this dagger belonged, India? Do you? Of course you don't.'' Kathleen laughed wildly. ''Well, I'll tell you. I'll let you in on a little secret. It belonged to Fergus Dunbar, the one who had the good sense to kill his cousin Rob and take what he knew should be his. This dirk has power. It shaped Dunbar's destiny once and will do so again tonight. Your blood and Rob Dunbar's will mingle on it, and finally Dunbar will be mine.''

India prayed for an escape, a diversion, a split second of opportunity to turn the tables. But the risk of having her throat slit was all too real, with Kathleen looming over her like an evil, distorted gargoyle. Suddenly she wished Jack were there. But that, of course, was impossible. All she could do was pray for a miracle. Then she heard the ancient hall clock, ticking monotonously as it had for centuries, and she concentrated on the sound, trying to extract herself mentally from the murderous blade and Kathleen's demented presence. Her determination to escape increased at each tick. With it came strength, as though some supreme force were urging her to survive, refusing to let her fall victim to the evil madness that had killed her mother and sister. Her blood was not about to mingle with that of Rob Dunbar's. Enough had been shed already. It was time to change the course of history, to purge Dunbar, freeing it once and for all from its past treachery.

All at once she remembered the little boy in the portrait on the stairs, realizing it must be Rob Dunbar—and Jack's spitting image. She shuddered, excitement overcoming her fear, knowing instinctively that Rob's presence was around her, and that somehow he would help.

Jack realized India must have been pushed against the wall next to the door for he could hear Kathleen's shallow, hysterical breathing.

''But you,'' he heard her snarl, ''my sweet little do-gooder India. You turned up like a bad penny." He shuddered, anxiety increasing at the sound of her harsh, brittle laugh. Her voice was no longer hysterical but frighteningly casual in its tone.

"At first I thought it was a joke when Ramsey read the will. I couldn't believe it," she continued conversationally. "I always thought Aunt El would leave Dunbar to Serena. I realized that I'd have to rid myself of her. But the mere thought of Aunt El letting *you* get your hands on the estate was the last straw."

"You did something to the car, didn't you?"

"Damn right I did," Kathleen's voice held a tinge of pride. "Spent half my girlhood putting engines together with my father, then taking them apart. Serena's car was child's play," she scoffed. "And now I'm two down and you're all that's left between me and Dunbar."

"No, you're not. Serena and I sold Dunbar to Jack Buchanan. *He's* the owner now. Even if you get rid of me, you still won't have Dunbar."

Jack held his breath, a distant clap of thunder muffling India's faint voice. But it was enough to tell him she was trying desperately to fight. He ached to rush to her, to burst open the door and put an end to her agony, but the moment wasn't right. So he waited, hand on the doorknob, and listened.

"You're lying, lying to save your worthless skin. He's in love with you, that's the only reason he wants Dunbar. Once you're gone, he'll go away and Dunbar will be mine. I'll own your share and Serena's." Kathleen's voice had taken on a manic edge.

Silently Jack twisted the brass doorknob. The moment was now. Now, before it was too late.

"It's not a lie," he said loudly, stepping into the hall while keeping her covered.

Kathleen whirled around, her crazed stare visible in the

flash of lightning that illuminated the hall and allowed him
a glimpse of the short, lethal-looking object glinting in her
raised hand. Then there was darkness, followed by a roar
of earsplitting thunder overhead, as though the storm, having distanced itself, was now returning with a vengeance.
He barely heard India's warning scream as Kathleen
lunged toward him, the dagger aimed straight at his heart.

What happened after that was a blur. Before he could
fire the shot, he felt himself pulled roughly to the right by
some strange, unidentified force, and the gun shaken from
his grasp. Then he heard a thud, followed by a groan, and
all he could see was the outline of Kathleen's form crumpled on the carpet at his feet.

For a moment he stood glued to the spot in shocked
amazement, certain someone had intervened, dragged his
weapon from him and pushed him out of harm's way. Instinctively he searched the darkness, conscious of a presence, but all he could distinguish was India, motionless
against the wall. He wanted to go straight to her, but once
more training forced him to bend down and slowly turn
the body. Kathleen's eyes were wide and her mouth gaped
open. The lethal dagger was embedded deep in her heart,
the jeweled hilt glinting outlandishly on her chest like an
ornate brooch.

Then he and India moved toward each other, arms outstretched, and all else was forgotten.

It was so natural to allow his arms to encircle her, to
nuzzle her head against his hard shoulder, allowing the
tension to ease, his warmth and strength more comforting
than any words. They stood embraced, the communing of
two yearning souls who had searched too long for one
another.

Nothing mattered anymore. Kathleen, Dunbar and the
horrors of the day all faded as she inhaled his familiar

scent, feeling the slight roughness of his chin gently grazing her cheek before their lips finally met. They kissed softly, cherishing each touch, knowing nothing more could keep them apart.

"I'm never letting you go," Jack murmured into her hair. "Every time I turn my head something happens to you. I can't believe she almost killed you."

"She was mad," India whispered. "She believed the dagger that killed her was the same one that killed Rob. I know you'll probably think I'm crazy, darling, but I could have sworn I felt his presence here tonight."

Jack held her away from him and stared into her eyes. "I never would have believed I'd say this, Indy, but someone pushed me out of her way and made me drop my gun. Otherwise I would have killed her myself. But there's nobody here." He gave a quick glance around the dark hall.

"Oh, darling." India closed her eyes and threw herself back into his arms. The windows rattled and the storm still beat down on them, but it was quieter now, as though it too had come to the end of its cycle. "Thank God it's all over," she whispered, caressing his cheek, and Jack lowered his mouth passionately on hers, claiming it for his own.

Then the sound of approaching sirens reached them above the howl of the gale.

He raised his head reluctantly. "That must be Peter and the cops," he said as a flash of bright orange lit up the stucco wall. "We'd better tell them it was an accident. How else can it be explained?"

"I think it was," India whispered, wanting to stay in his arms. "I believe she tripped on the ragged edge of the carpet. Serena mentioned it before Mummy's funeral. She'd fallen and hurt her leg. But it was so strange, Jack, as though someone was orchestrating it all—"

"I know. I felt it, too."

All at once the lights burst on and their eyes met, and Jack saw the trickle of blood.

"My God." He raised his fingers gently, then hugged her close, as loath to let her out of his arms as she was to leave them.

But loud banging at the front door brought reality home and he dropped a kiss on her forehead. "Don't move," he ordered. Then, turning on his heel, he descended the porch steps to let the party in. And she smiled, knowing he'd never change, nor did she want him to.

Peter and the Marchese stood on the front step, flanked by four policemen.

"Is she safe?" the old gentleman asked querulously, grabbing Jack's arm. He seemed to have aged in the past hours.

"She's fine," Jack reassured him. "But Kathleen is dead. She fell on a dagger. I think she must have tripped on the carpet in the dark and landed straight on it," he added, giving Giordano's arm a warning squeeze as he helped him inside the porch.

"*Non è possibile,*" he cried, reacting immediately for the benefit of the sergeant standing just behind. "Such a delightful woman, *che tragedia, Dio mio.*"

"Och, my. What a terrible set of circumstances. And ye thought there was a burglary, Sir Peter. Well, well. What a terrible to-do." The burly sergeant followed the Marchese and Jack through the door. "I dinna' like to bother ye, Mr. Buchanan, but would you and Miss Moncrieff mind answering a few questions?" A red-haired man in his early fifties, he clearly took his duties seriously, although his tone was apologetic and his eyes friendly. Puffing up his chest, he strode forward and, taking the lead, mounted the steps followed by the others. "Good evening, Miss Moncrieff. Mighty sorry I am to be here," he said with another shake of the head.

"Good evening, Sergeant Macintyre," she replied, pale but composed. "I'm afraid we've another calamity on our hands."

Macintyre surveyed the scene and then called over his shoulder. "Call the station in Dalkeith. Dinna' move the body, Ferguson," he said disapprovingly as a younger sandy-haired officer crouched next to it.

"I was merely observing a wee piece of paper attached to yon skean," he answered with a sniff, pointing to the tag on the weapon.

"Ay, but nae gud'll come from yer fiddlin' with it, so dinna' be pokin' yer fingers where they dinna' belong. That's fer Detective Morrison to do."

"A' wasna' going to—"

"That's enough, Ferguson. Miss Moncrieff, I'm awf'y sorry you've had another frightful experience. Still, I'm going to have to bother ye a wee bit more." He took out his notebook, removed a pencil from his breast pocket and gave the lead a determined lick. "Perhaps ye could explain how the events took place."

India was holding Giordano's arm tightly now. "Of course, Officer, but perhaps it would be more comfortable if we sat in the library," she suggested, casting a last glance at Kathleen's body before Sergeant Ferguson covered it with a blanket. She swallowed, squeezing Giordano's arm tight as they entered the library, unable to erase the image of the affable, kind woman she'd come to know and love, so different from the demented creature of moments earlier.

"Nasty things, carpets," the sergeant remarked, looking at the ragged edge where Kathleen had tripped to her death.

India raised her eyes to Jack's, a silent acknowledgment passing between them.

"Let us proceed, Sergeant," the Marchese said, recouping some of his customary flourish and leading the way into the library. "I'm sure we could all use a drink."

"Of course." India came out of her daydream, realizing that her hands were shaking from belated shock. "Jack, would you mind?"

"Sure thing."

"Well, that's awf'y kind, I'm sure," Sergeant Macintyre replied, rubbing his hands and casting a look of superiority toward Sergeant Ferguson standing uncomfortably in the doorway. Jack poked the dying fire and set another log on it before heading to the Boule desk and the decanters, intently focused on how best to handle the situation.

"Whiskey, Officer?" he asked with his most charming smile. "We all deserve one on a night like this."

"I dinna' usually indulge while on the job. I'm not officially on duty tonight though."

"Great, then you don't have a problem," Jack replied, handing him a heavy cut-crystal tumbler amply filled with single malt, straight up.

"A drop of whiskey never did anyone any harm," Peter added encouragingly before accepting his glass.

"Well, I canna' refuse a wee dram on such a dreich night," Macintyre agreed appreciatively, seating himself on the sofa opposite India and the Marchese. Jack handed them each a sherry, then perched next to India on the arm of the sofa, discreetly placing his hand on her shoulder.

Sergeant Macintyre took a satisfying sip before clearing his throat and opening the notebook once more. "Miss Moncrieff, perhaps you'd like to tell me exactly what events led up to the accident."

Jack gave her shoulder a squeeze then intervened. "Damned nasty business," he said, shaking his head and rising to stand in front of the fireplace, subtly detracting the sergeant's attention from India. "In some ways I feel doubly responsible, since a while back Kathleen had promised me she would pick out some of the more interesting weapons from the Dunbar collection for me to see. Just the other day she told me there was one in particular I would find fascinating."

"That's right," India added. "She said you would find the dagger fascinating since it was in some way connected to your ancestor, Rob Dunbar. That was why she'd brought it downstairs, for when you next came over."

"Oh? Was there something special about it? Are you a collector?" the sergeant inquired.

"Yes, as a matter of fact I am. Unfortunately I didn't get the opportunity of seeing this one properly. After I arrived here, and we'd ascertained that there were no intruders, Kathleen was about to show me the dagger when she heard a noise that frightened her. Then the lights went out and the accident happened," he finished soberly, exchanging quick glances with India and a surprised Peter, while Macintyre wrote painstakingly in his notebook. He gave a knowing nod.

"When she heard the first noise and called you at Dalkirk, Sir Peter, she would have naturally picked the dagger up."

"Ahem. Quite so," Peter murmured. Jack was thankful the sergeant spent more time writing than studying the people in the room. Peter was a very bad liar. "Was there any sign of a break-in when you arrived, Mr. Buchanan?" he continued, oblivious.

"None at all. We believed there might have been a burglary when Peter got the phone call from Kathleen. It was just after they'd called from the station about Serena's car."

"Perhaps you'd like to tell me more, Miss Moncrieff?"

To Jack's discomfort Macintyre turned to India, but she seemed composed, picking up where he'd left off. He relaxed and listened, ready to intervene if necessary.

"I was in my room when I heard Kathleen calling me. She sounded worried, almost distraught, as though she was afraid of something. I came hurrying down. By that time Jack—I mean, Mr. Buchanan—had arrived and they were talking. Kathleen was about to show him the weapon when the lights suddenly went out—" she paused for a moment "—and then this dreadful tragedy occurred. My sister tripped and hurt herself on that same bit of carpet a few months ago. We should have had it repaired immediately," she ended, gazing sadly at her hands folded in her lap.

"My, my, a tragic loss indeed. Lady Kathleen'll be sorely missed in the village. She did a beautiful job playing the organ at the kirk on Sundays."

"As you say, Officer, a very sad loss. Perhaps you should have the house checked to see if there is any sign of intruders. Poor Lady Kathleen, such an admirable woman," the Marchese murmured, shaking his white head gravely.

"Dinna' worry, sir, ma' men are all about the place as we speak. There's nae one'll get away. Still, it's been an awf'y strange day." Macintyre scratched his brow, the whiskey, the warmth and the exalted company all taking their effect. "Are there any other details you'd like to add, Miss Moncrieff?"

"No, I don't think there's anything else. Poor Kathleen," she said with a sad smile. "She was so loved. Perhaps we can bury her with Mummy and Serena. I think they would have liked that. As for Serena's car, I think that can be explained," she added, a sudden gleam in her eyes making Jack nearly choke on his whiskey. "Maxi fancied himself something of a mechanic and Serena was complaining the day before yesterday about the car. Perhaps he tried to repair it, unsuccessfully.''

"You're quite right, my love." Giordano patted her hand. "The Lowendorfs all had a mechanical streak. Maxi's great-grandfather, whom I once had the privilege of meeting, was a pioneer in automobiles at the beginning of the century. He built the engine of his own machine. Quite impressive." He sighed and smiled sadly. "Apparently his talent was not inherited by his great-grandson. Count von Lowendorf must be turning in his grave at the thought of his descendant proving to be an incompetent mechanical imbecile. Most unfortunate," he added with convincing concern. "Now, if you will excuse us, Sergeant, I think this child should be allowed to rest. The events of the last few days have been most traumatic for her, as I am sure you understand.''

"Of course." Sergeant Macintyre rose, picking up his cap; the second tumbler of whiskey that Jack had discreetly slipped his way sending a warm glow through him. "I'll be on my way. Anything else can be dealt with in the morning. Detective Morrison may be here in a wee while, but dinna' worry. I'll give him the report. Good night.''

Jack showed him out while peppering him with pertinent questions about upcoming police fund-raisers, assuring the officer of his generous support. Then he returned to the library and closed the door behind him.

"Very well handled, young man. Let sleeping dogs lie. The least said the quickest mended.''

"Hmm, it goes against the grain, but you're probably right," Peter agreed somewhat doubtfully. "If this got out on top of the poisoning business, there'd be hell to pay around here for years to come. Not good for business or anything else," he added. "But perhaps you'd like to tell us what really did happen?''

"I'll brief you later." Jack nodded toward India. "This

kid has had a long day. She deserves a rest. But you're right about business," he added thoughtfully.

India looked up. "Perhaps it could be made into an attraction," she murmured faintly, a sardonic gleam lurking in her eyes. "Think of the number of interested guests you might draw in. I can just see the brochure—'Visit sight of double murder in Scottish castle. Special effects upon request. Treachery packages available.'"

"Madonna mia." The Marchese cast his eyes to heaven then turned to India. "Don't quarrel with Jack, please. Let us have some peace after all this chaos. I think you should come over to Dalkirk, *cara.* You will not want to sleep here alone tonight."

Before she could reply, another knock on the door interrupted them.

"Oh no, not someone else," India moaned.

"Must be Detective Morrison. Just keep your facts in order," Jack reminded them before opening the door. "Come on in." He smiled cordially at the two men waiting on the threshold and stood aside patiently as the detective—a portly man in a navy mac and tammy—and his thin, weather-beaten assistant entered the room.

"Ah, Detective Morrison, I presume." The Marchese raised his silver-knobbed cane and indicated the sofa. "Please. Come in and sit down."

"Good evening. I'm awf'y sorry to be bothering you sae late at night. The sergeant gave me a brief report and it seems a pretty clear-cut case. You're aware of whom the weapon belonged to, I suppose?"

"No, whose was it?" Jack asked, looking suitably intrigued.

The detective paused, making sure he'd captured the audience's attention. "It belonged to Fergus Dunbar," he said with strong momentum.

"You mean Fergus whom we now know killed Rob Dunbar?" India asked, awe oozing out of every word.

"Aye, one and the same. This may seem far-fetched, but I couldna' help wondering— I followed the case fairly closely, ye understand. There seem to have been such a number of strange circumstances attached to it, such as yer meeting with Sir Peter, Mr. Buchanan, then the discovery of yer family's link to Dunbar and— Och, well, I shouldna' mean to be fantasizing, but—" His eyes took on a faraway look then he shook his head and smiled. "It must be the weather. A night like this'll even have an old dog like me imagining things. Poor Lady Kathleen. My condolences, Miss Moncrieff, and fer yer sister as well. We'll be leaving ye to rest."

"Thank you." India smiled, her face soft and mystical in the lamplight. "Let's hope that this sad accident will bring an end to all the tragedy that's happened over the centuries at Dunbar. And that Mr. Buchanan will have peace and quiet for his guests," she added, looking away.

"Indeed." The detective turned to Jack who'd been watching India through narrowed eyes. "I wish you luck with the hotel, sir. We werna' sure the council would agree, but 'twill be good business for the village, though a shame the family'll nae be here any longer. Well, it's the way of the world today I suppose." After that he said good-night and left, followed by his silent companion.

In the hall Mrs. Walker was dabbing her eyes while sniffing loudly into a large hankie provided by Peter, who was soothing her patiently.

"Te' think poor Lady Elspeth mentioned the carpet needed repairing not two days before she died," she said with a heavy sigh. "She wanted to get a wee man from Glasgow—he was from one of those places ye hear about on the seven o'clock news, Persia I think it was—who repaired Oriental carpets. She was going te' phone him hersel'— Och, and te' think poor Lady Kathleen came to her death on the very same spot. A' dinna' ken where this'll all end.'' Mrs. Walker broke down again and India went to her.

Peter nudged Jack. ''I'd better get Giordano home. He must be exhausted. I presume you'll be remaining?''

''You presume right.'' Jack threw him a grin.

Peter cleared his throat. ''We'll leave you to it then. She still doesn't seem too happy about the idea of the hotel though. Good night, old chap, and good luck. Give us a call. The Kinnairds are always ready to rally if you need us, you know.'' He winked.

''I'm afraid this is something not even two hundred and fifty years of friendship can solve,'' Jack answered with a rueful smile.

''I don't know,'' Peter muttered. ''After the last few days, I'll believe anything.''

India went back into the library and lay down on the sofa, knowing Jack would return in a few minutes once the others had left. She snuggled into a corner, heavy clouds lifted from her, as though Kathleen's strange death had brought final closure to Dunbar's treacherous past. She sighed, reaching down to pick up a cushion that had fallen to the floor. He would come, that she knew. She had seen the look in his eyes, heard his words and felt the soft touch of his lips on hers.

But what of his belief that she'd betrayed him with his partner, and his determination to make Dunbar into a hotel?

She blinked back the bitter tears that lurked in her eyes, wishing things could be simple between them. She loved him enough to want the best for him and for them both, and the best was not a woman who allowed insecurity and pride to blind her from the truth. Neither could they pretend to themselves that Dunbar wasn't an issue on which they stood poles apart.

India reached over and turned off the Chinese lamps, sinking back into the cushions and the shadows. She gazed into the flames, her heart full of wistful hope, knowing what she had to do.

Now it was up to fate to decide.

Jack snapped his fingers at Angus. "Come on, old buddy. Let's see what we can do to straighten this mess out." The dog rose and followed him lazily across the hall toward the library. He stopped for a minute and leaned against the doorjamb, watching the woman he loved, her profile outlined in the gentle light of the dying embers. Then he moved quickly toward her, closing the distance between them.

Closing it, he hoped, forever.

The moment couldn't be avoided any longer, but neither could she deny her own feelings as he stood before her, tall and rugged, his eyes demanding yet loving.

"We have to talk, Jack," she said, rising from the sofa and bracing herself.

But he drew her into his arms, holding her fast and tight. Oh, it felt good. Too good. And Hernan, Dunbar and the hotel project all faded as she melted into his embrace, his lips skimming her skin, his hands moving over her with the assertive confidence of possessive recognition. Was it wrong to crave one solid thing in this whole crazed world? No! But she had to let him know the truth, whatever the cost.

Gently she drew away, just enough to look into his eyes. It was hard, but she wasn't going to be a coward.

"We have to talk, Jack. There are things I have to tell you." She looked him straight in the eye.

"Couldn't they wait for later?" he asked with a rueful smile.

"No." She shook her head, determined to get it over with.

"Okay." He gave a resigned shrug and drew her down onto the sofa. "But this time you're going to listen to *me* first."

She was about to protest, then seeing the gleam in his eyes realized it was fruitless. "All right," she murmured.

Jack cocked a suspicious eyebrow. "Just like that? No protests, no Jack-I-have-to's?" He eyed her skeptically and she let out a half laugh, half sigh. The time had come; there was no use postponing it. She slipped from his hold and rose, going around the room lighting the candles, determined to be calm when she spoke. When she'd finished she sat down on the floor in front of the fire and pulled over a silk throw she'd left lying on the cushions.

Then she looked up at him and smiled, ready.

"You're not leaving."

"What do you mean I'm not leaving?" She sat like an Indian goddess, the wine and gold of both the silk throw and her hair glinting in the soft glow of the firelight and flickering candles, making him want to shut up, forget everything and make love to her.

"I don't want you to leave here, Indy. There's no need. You see, I've thought this all out. Your place is right here. You belong here." He leaned forward wondering why, when it came to her, he found it so hard to express himself? Damn, he could talk his way around anything or anybody—except India. His beautiful, beloved India, with her soft skin, her firm mouth, her proud shoulders and generous heart. A heart he wanted so desperately to own, and was determined to have.

"No, it isn't. Not any longer. Dunbar's yours now. I've moved on. Don't feel you owe me anything, Jack. You don't. It all happened for a reason. Plus, there's something else besides Dunbar. Something I need to tell you.''

He rose and prowled the library, unable to stay still, running his fingers through his thick dark hair. He finally stopped in front of her.

"I love you, Indy. Love you more than anything in this world. I may be a presumptuous son of a bitch, but I think you love me—"

"Jack, I—"

"No." He raised his hand like a vigilant traffic cop. "It's my turn. Every time I've let you have your say, I've ended up alone and miserable. I know this is all my fault, that I should have told you I was buying Dunbar. Then none of this mess would have happened. It was stupid wanting to surprise you and keep you a part of your heritage, but that's all over now. It's done with. We can look toward the future together.''

"What do you mean you wanted to surprise me?"

"It was dumb, I know. That day in San Telmo you looked so sad and I felt badly that you hadn't inherited Dunbar with Serena, as she'd led me to believe. Then, every time I tried to broach the subject of Dunbar to you in Buenos Aires, you clammed up. I assumed you were upset that you'd been cut out of the will. It was then that I came up with the idea of giving you the restoration project once I'd closed on the property. To keep you a part of Dunbar's future, so to speak. You'll probably think I was being a chauvinist," he said with a rueful smile. "Indy, I want you. I love you, and I don't want to lose you ever again." He moved closer, looking down at her, knowing she was everything he'd ever dared hope for and more. Then he leaned down and lifted her into his arms. "I want to marry you, Indy, make you my wife and have a home together with Molly. Have a bunch of our own kids, too,'' he added, grinning. ''I think you'd look beautiful pregnant.''

''Preg—''

''I haven't finished.'' He plowed on. ''You know as well as I do we're meant for one another, that all this happened for a reason. I'm no mystic, and I'm not even going to begin trying to explain what happened here tonight or what Rob's been up to. But he wants us here together, of that I am sure. In your heart of hearts you know it, too.'' He paused and held her at arm's length. ''I know now I was wrong seeing Dunbar only as a hotel, not seeing what you saw. I realize now you were giving up what you've always longed for—roots. A real home that you know is truly part of you, where you belong. That's what I want for us, Indy. Here at Dunbar. I won't have it any other way.''

''You mean you'd give up the hotel?'' she asked, amazed.

''To hell with the hotel. There will be no hotel. I'm darned if I'm having my wife and kids living above the store.'' He laughed, happy, as he gazed into her eyes. ''Dunbar's for you, for them, for us, Indy. You were right all along, and thank God you stuck to your guns.'' He gave a low chuckle, hugging her close, realizing with a wave of relief that he'd finally admitted to himself what he really wanted out of life.

''I can't believe you're saying this.'' She drew back, gazing at him, eyes bright with love and unshed tears. ''Are you really telling me you'd give up the hotel for me?''

''That's right.''

''But what about the cost of keeping up Dunbar? The debt on the property's tremendous. It wouldn't be practical to—''

''Are you arguing with me?''

"Yes. No. I don't quite know," She laughed, shaking her head. "It's like a dream. I never thought you'd understand, that it would never mean the same to you as to me, yet here you are making this preposterous yet wonderful proposition—"

"Not a proposition, a proposal. Is it preposterous to want to marry the woman I love? To make you my wife? To live with you in the home that has belonged to our ancestors since time immemorial, to allow our children to be a part of their heritage? Don't you think we owe 'em that? Indy, if everything that's come down between us is anything to judge by, I'd say we'll have a pretty good life together. And I'm not just referring to sex," he added as an afterthought, suddenly afraid she might misinterpret him. He glanced impatiently at a guttering candle, then back at her. "Indy, will you answer me for Christ's sake?" He raised her fingers to his lips, kissing them gently. "Will you marry me?"

"But I can't, Jack." She withdrew her hands, suddenly tense. "You don't understand. I've lied to you, I've—"

"Honey, I don't care—"

"Jack, please." She wrenched away from him. "You have to listen to me. I lied about Hernan. I never had an affair with him, I was so upset I never even let you explain about Dunbar, never even gave you a chance. I've been so thoughtless. When I think that you and Hernan could have broken your partnership, that I didn't stop to allow you to tell me your side of the story... You deserve someone who doesn't allow herself to be blinded by pride and jealousy."

Jack let out a low chuckle and tilted her chin up. "Do you think I'd be here if I didn't know that nonsense about you and Hernan was merely your way of defending yourself? Don't you think I'm capable of understanding how raw you still were about your marriage when all this came down?"

"You knew? All this time? You could've told me. To

think I was worried out of my mind, and all this while—''

Jack pulled her to him and closed his mouth on hers, kissing her long and hard, not allowing her to finish. Then he whispered, ''I'm never letting you go.''

The storm had subsided, the night strangely silent now except for Angus who'd resumed his usual snoring by the dying fire.

Gently Jack began kissing her eyebrows, her cheeks, her lips. Softly one moment, relentless and demanding the next, his hands roaming until they reached her taut breasts, fire catching hold, its flames leaping hot, reaching deep within to melt down the barriers of pride and reason, leaving only passion as together they sank to the floor, the musky scent of jasmine and patchouli spiraling from the candles.

Suddenly they were tearing at each other's clothes, unable to hold back any longer. Mouth to mouth, skin to skin, their hands discovered the other once again with a new depth of passion hitherto unknown, yet hauntingly familiar.

India arched, all reason and logic forgotten as shadows danced against his bronzed skin. His eyes gleamed, full of such fierce ardor it took her breath away. She rose to his touch, arched when his fingers grazed her breasts, ready like a blank page for him to write the tale of passion and desire that his eyes, hands and body so clearly wanted to tell. Then she closed her eyes and lay helpless and happy in his arms.

And for the first time, India recognized the true meaning of fulfillment, knowing she wanted him inside her being and her soul, now and forever.

She didn't feel the threadbare carpet or the hardness of the floor under her, only the delicious feel of him as he lay on top of her.

How she'd longed for this. And now that she had it, she wanted to savor each moment, each touch of her lips, each shimmer of candlelight outlining his taut muscles and gleaming damp skin.

He shifted, but she pulled him back. "Don't. Not yet. Stay a little while."

"I'm too heavy," he mumbled, kissing her ear. Then he raised himself on his elbows, eyes gleaming, satisfied and possessive. "I'm not going anywhere."

"Good," she whispered, kissing his chest, enjoying that look of passion and determination, that hint of masculine triumph.

"Are you sure you're ready to give it all up, Jack? The hotel, everything you'd planned?" She needed to be doubly sure.

"I won't be giving anything up, Indy. If you'll have me, I'll be achieving all I want out of life—having you and our family, here, in our true home."

"But what about business. You'll be sacrificing—"

"Nothing. Indy, why don't you stop questioning the reasons behind everything and just accept that I love you? Don't you understand, my darling? I'll be sacrificing nothing. The only sacrifice would be if I were fool enough to walk away from the one woman who means everything to me."

India smiled, her heart full. There was such longing, such true love written in his eyes. "Giordano was right," she whispered.

"Probably. He is about most things. Did he tell you to marry me?" He grinned down at her devilishly.

"No, but he hinted." She smiled at him through her long lashes, then brushed his hair back from his brow. "Jack, do you feel what I do here? That everything else seems unimportant, like running around the world from one project to another, from one deal to the next? It all seemed so worthwhile before, but somehow here at Dunbar there's just—peace.''

He nodded, rolling off her, lying next to her and leaning his chin on his elbow. "I know exactly what you mean. This is true peace. Not the kind of peace you get when you split for a long weekend or on a vacation. This is real. It comes from somewhere deep inside. Darn it, Indy, I'm no good at explaining these things. Can't you just give me an answer before I burst?'' He kneeled, pulling her up until they faced each other amidst the sparkle of embers, rumpled silk and guttering candles. Then gently he took her face between his hands and waited.

It was the most important answer of her life, yet she had no doubt or hesitation, merely joy, and the desire to prolong this enchanted moment for as long as possible, engraving it in her soul forever.

"I want to hear you say it,'' he whispered.

And she did.

20

◌◦◦◦◦◦◦◦◦◦

"Where's Uncle Jack?" Molly inquired between mouthfuls of bacon and egg, feeding Felix who waited hopefully under the dining-room table.

"I haven't seen him this morning," Diana replied vaguely.

"Jack? He spent the night—" Peter lowered the magazine he'd been glancing through, stopping short when he met his wife's horrified gaze. "Ah, yes, quite so. I believe Jack went out early to deal with some business at Dunbar," he amended hastily.

"He's over at Indy's place? That's great." Molly turned to Chloë, who sat sipping coffee thoughtfully. "Aunt Chloë, don't you think it would be a great idea if Uncle Jack married Indy?" She tilted her head, her expression pensive. "Indy's all on her own, and Uncle Jack's all on his own. They used to like each other quite a bit, you know," she added in a conversational manner. "Maybe we could go find them."

Chloë looked doubtful, then smiled wickedly. "Excellent idea," she replied, glancing at Lance tucking into a large Scottish breakfast that belied his tall slim figure. She sighed and spent an envious moment wondering why some people could eat huge amounts of food without putting on weight, while others, like herself, were reduced to having only large cups of strong black coffee. But her mind was more taken up with the goings-on at Dunbar, her curiosity rampant, longing to see whether India and Jack had finally worked things out.

"All right, Molly. I'll drive you over. Anyone else want to come?" she asked the table at large.

"Darling, I don't think this is a good idea," Diana murmured. "It's really none of our business." She cast her sister a meaningful look.

"Why on earth not? Don't be such a wet blanket, Di. Surely they can't be doing it—"

"Chloë, that's quite sufficient!" Diana turned bright red and Lance looked up, grinning.

"I'll take a ride with you to Dunbar. Any bets on?" he asked, eyes gleaming."

"One hundred says it's a no."

"Done. Pounds or dollars?"

"Dollars," Chloë replied quickly, calculating the exchange rate if she lost. "Any more takers?"

"Really, Chloë, this is *most* unladylike behavior." Diana glanced at Molly, thankful the child was busy feeding the dog, apparently oblivious to the conversation.

"I'll call Jack and tell him you're on your way." Peter started getting up but Chloë stopped him.

"Oh no you don't, Peter Kinnaird. I'll never speak to you again if you warn him. Come on, be a sport."

"I don't know where you've come by this meddling streak, Chloë," Diana exclaimed, shaking her head. "To be gallivanting about the countryside with Molly—"

"And Lance," Chloë added helpfully.

"Oh, I give up." Diana threw up her hands. "I wash my hands of the lot of you. Peter, you'll just have to deal with it. I have far too much to do as it is." With that, she rose and left the dining room.

Peter sighed. "I suppose it would be useless to try and dissuade you?"

"Utterly." Chloë grinned.

"Thought so." He nodded, returning to the latest issue of *Horse & Hound* that had arrived that morning.

"Come on, you two." Chloë got up. "By the way, I accept cash," she said sweetly as Lance held the door for her and Molly.

"Great." He gave her a wide grin, then followed them out the door.

Jack stood under the oak tree, one arm encircling India, the other plunged in the pocket of his shooting jacket. Together they gazed over the Dunbar lands that stretched for as far as the eye could see, taking silent pleasure in the sight and in each other. The lawn smelled of freshly cut grass, and the branches of the ancient oak tree hung heavy with burgeoning leaves and newly built nests.

"It's truly ours now," Jack murmured into her hair.

"Mmm-hmm," she answered, content just to lean against his shoulder and enjoy the moment.

"Hey, what's this?" Jack pulled something out of his pocket and opened his palm.

"It's my pendant," India exclaimed, taking it. "I've been looking for it ever since the day you shot me."

"Missed you," he corrected.

"It must have been in your pocket all this time."

"Waiting for the right time to be returned to its owner," he supplied, grinning.

India looked at him quizzically. "Stop trying to give everything a mystical spin, Jack Buchanan. Just because Rob is your great-great whatever it is, doesn't give you *total* creative license."

"Maybe not, sweetheart, but it can be mighty handy at times, don't you think?" he asked wickedly, spinning her around. "As in soft cushions, rich silk throws and love in the library?"

"Jack, really—"

He kissed her hard before she could continue, his hands beneath her sweater before she had a chance to do anything but sigh and give in.

But the sound of running feet and panting breath made them raise their heads. India hastily adjusted her sweater, surprised to see Molly racing toward them across the lawn.

The little girl stopped in front of them, catching her breath.

"How'd you get here, pumpkin?" Jack asked, smiling at her.

But Molly ignored the question. "Have you asked her, Uncle Jack?"

"Excuse me?"

Molly looked at him and pursed her lips, obviously questioning his sanity. Then she took matters into her own hands and turned her huge blue eyes to India. "Indy, will you marry us? Please say yes. I know Uncle Jack can be silly, but between us we can handle him," she assured, screwing up her face expectantly.

India looked at her doubtfully. "Are you sure? I don't want to be landed with him and then not be able to get out of it. After all, marriage is a serious thing."

"I promise, Indy," Molly assured her seriously. "He's not as bad as he seems when you get to know him better. In fact, he's really pretty cool," she added with an encouraging smile calculated to diffuse any doubts.

Then Jack's eyes met India's, full of love and laughter, over the cascade of blond curls.

"Well, will you have us?" he asked with a lopsided grin.

"Hmm." She frowned, debating the matter. Suddenly she felt a little hand tugging at her sweater, and seeing Molly was truly concerned, she laughed and ruffled her hair tenderly. "Of course I'll marry you both. I can't think of anything I'd love more in the world."

"Really?" Molly squeaked, jumping up and flinging her arms around India's neck. "We can work on Uncle Jack, we can—"

"Hey, do I get any say here or have you decided everything between the two of you?" Jack asked in mock anger. "Am I really that bad?"

"Don't worry, darling, we can bear with you the way you are."

"Thanks. You're both mighty generous," he answered, shaking his head and laughing.

"Uncle Jack says we're going to live here at Dunbar, and I can go to school with Caroline and Henny. Isn't that great?"

"Oh, you did, did you?" India raised her eyebrows at Jack. "You must have been very sure of yourself. How did you know I'd agree?"

"I'll explain that to you later. In the library. Right now we've got company." He waved at Chloë and Lance, who had sat down on a bench close to the house.

"Do you think there's any future for those two?" he asked, slipping an arm around India once more.

Molly skipped ahead, running to meet Angus. Jack and India followed slowly across the lawn, content, all business meetings forgotten, not in a hurry for anything or anyone any longer.

The morning was cloudy, and it looked as if there might be rain later in the day. But all at once, a radiant burst of sunshine broke open the heavens. Together they came to a halt, gazing in awe at Dunbar. The house stood gloriously enveloped in a magical halo of light, as if all their ancestors, from William down to Lady Elspeth, were bestowing their approval and giving them their blessing.

"It feels as if they're here, doesn't it?" India murmured.

"Maybe they are." Jack looked down at her, caressing her with his eyes. Then he felt again in his pocket. "Close your eyes," he said, taking her left hand in his. And when she did he slipped the ancient diamond and amethyst ring, destined for his great-great-grandmother Mhairie—onto her third finger, where it slipped perfectly into place.

India gazed down, entranced. "It's perfectly beautiful, Jack. Thank you." She raised her lips to kiss him tenderly.

"Don't thank me, thank Rob. It was in the strongbox under the oak tree, waiting for you. There's something else I want you to have. Here," he said, handing her the deed. "I promised you Dunbar and now it's yours, forever."

"Oh, Jack, darling, not mine, *ours*."

"Hopefully one day it will be our son's but for now I want you to know you're really home. After all, when he's born," he added thoughtfully, "the wound will finally be healed, and Dunbar'll be whole again."

"How do you know it won't be a girl?" she said, laughing at his male arrogance, her eyes wandering to where Molly was skipping up to Lance and Chloë. "We haven't talked much about that, have we?"

"I figure it's not something that needs much talking about. I'd rather get on with it."

"Jack!" But he swooped her into his arms before she could protest further, before being interrupted by wolf whistles coming from the bench. They pulled apart and headed to greet Lance and Chloë.

"Well!" Chloë exclaimed. "Do I conclude you two reached a happy ending? Damn, I've lost my bet. Of course, I'm thrilled for you both," she added, embracing India.

"I, too, take cash." Lance grinned at her.

"I'll bet Jack tipped you off. If you've cheated, Lance—" Chloë gave him a dark look.

"Not a word, I swear. Scout's honor."

"Oh, all right," Chloë gave in, scowling.

"Don't be a sore loser. Tell you what, I'll bet you ten grand we'll be married within a year."

"Ha! You're on. At least that's one bet I can't lose," Chloë exclaimed, laughing hard.

"Westmoreland," Jack pleaded, "do me a favor. Go finish your conversation in the sunken garden or in the grotto or, I dunno—but find somewhere else."

"You got it." Lance grinned, linking arms with Chloë.

Molly had run up the steps and opened the glass door to the oak room. Jack and India followed, hand in hand. But as they entered, Molly raised her hand, frowning.

"Do you hear that?" she asked, stopping suddenly to listen.

"Hear what, Molly?" Jack glanced at her.

"Can't you hear it? Indy, you hear it, don't you? There's music. Somebody's whistling."

They remained totally quiet and listened.

"You're right, it's 'Charlie Is My Darling,' an old Scottish ballad."

"And that's a horse galloping!" Molly exclaimed, turning toward them expectantly. "Who could be riding a horse, Uncle Jack?"

In reverent silence they listened as the cantering hooves and whistling faded gently away.

Then Jack and India exchanged a long, understanding smile. "I guess Rob figured he could move on, and that we'd take care of business," he said softly, taking her in his arms.

"And William's vow will be kept after all," she whispered, feeling a warm rush of happiness. At last, despite all the odds, they'd completed their journey home.

One small spark ignites the entire city of
Chicago, but amid the chaos, a case of mistaken
identity leads to an unexpected new love....

Susan Wiggs

On this historic night, Kathleen O'Leary
finds herself enjoying a lovely masquerade. She
has caught the eye of Dylan Francis Kennedy. The
night feels alive with magic...and ripe with promise.

Then fire sweeps through Chicago, cornering the young
lovers with no hope of rescue. Impulsively, they marry.
Incredibly, they survive. And now Kathleen must tell
Chicago's most eligible bachelor that he has married
a fraud.

But the joke's on her. For this gentleman is no
gentleman. While Kathleen had hoped to win Dylan's
love, he had planned only to break her heart and steal
her fortune. Now the real sparks are about to fly.

THE MISTRESS

"In poetic prose, Wiggs evocatively captures the
Old South and creates an intense, believable
relationship between the lovers."
—*Publishers Weekly* on *The Horsemaster's Daughter*

On sale October 2000
wherever paperbacks are sold!

MIRA®

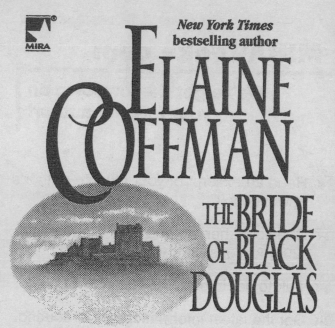

MIRA®

New York Times
bestselling author

ELAINE COFFMAN

THE BRIDE OF BLACK DOUGLAS

Lady Meleri Weatherby is desperate to escape marriage to her cruel fiancé, and Robert Douglas must find a wife or risk losing his ancestral home and noble name.

Set against the dramatic backdrop of 1785 Scotland, this is an unforgettable romance about a marriage that starts off to defy fate and that just might end in love....

"Coffman's writing is deft, capable and evocative."
—*Publishers Weekly*

On sale November 2000 wherever paperbacks are sold!

New York Times **Bestselling Author**

PENNY JORDAN

POWER PLAY

Eleven years had passed, but the terror of that night was something Pepper Minesse would never forget. Four men had taken from her something sacred. Now she was determined that each should lose what he most prized.

Fury fueled her success. The files she held on each would destroy them. For three men, her death is the only solution. Only one man, who hides a truth more devastating than Pepper's own, is capable of defusing the time bomb she has set ticking....

"Women everywhere will find pieces of themselves in Jordan's characters."
—*Publishers Weekly*

Available the first week of November 2000 wherever paperbacks are sold!

*From seduction in the royal sheikhdom to
high adventure in the hot Arabian desert comes a
breathtaking love story by international bestselling author*

DIANA PALMER

LORD OF THE DESERT

Gretchen Brannon was completely out of her element when she aligned herself with Sheikh Philippe Sabon, the formidable ruler of Qawi. They came from different worlds, but he made her aware of her own courage. She, in turn, aroused his sleeping senses like no other woman could.

But now that Gretchen's heart belongs to the Lord of the Desert, she's become the target for vengeance by the sheikh's most diabolical enemy. In a final showdown that will pit good against evil, can love and destiny triumph...?

**"The dialogue is charming, the characters likable
and the sex sizzling..."
—*Publishers Weekly* on *Once in Paris***

On sale October 2000 wherever paperbacks are sold!

MDP617

SHARON SALA

All that stands between a
killer and a secret...
is one shattered woman...

China Brown is a young woman whose luck ran out long before
she found herself in the wrong place at the wrong time...long
before she was shot in cold blood after witnessing a murder. Now
she's alive, but barely. She's lost the only thing that ever mattered to
her: her baby. Ben English is the tough-as-nails cop assigned to the
murder. Drawn to this lovely, fragile woman, he must convince her
to help him find a killer. And as the murderer closes in, China must
place her trust in one man, because her life and heart depend on it.

"Spellbinding narrative...Sala lives up to her
reputation in this well-crafted thriller."
—*Publishers Weekly* on *Remember Me*

*Available mid-November 2000
wherever paperbacks are sold!*

Butterfly